Harlow's Castle

JENNIFER FERRANNO

The Reading Glass Books
1-888-420-3050
www.readingglassbooks.com
fulfillment@readingglassbooks.com

Also by Jennifer Ferranno

Dakota Pass
ISBN 0-595-12893-9

The Senator's Wife
ISBN 0-595-17041-2

Antonio's Woman
ISBN 0-595-20707-3

The S-2 Project
ISBN 0-595-31326-4

Questions
ISBN 978-1-5246-8543-0

Jennifer may be contacted at:
jferranno@aol.com

Dedication

I would like to dedicate this novel to all of the 80s hair bands who brought me such joy during a trying time in my life. Their music, the concerts I attended, the bands I worked with, and the musicians I partied with gave me the basic knowledge for the story you are about to read.

At the top of my thank you list is my awesome son Christopher Horton. An extraordinary artist, Christopher designed the cover for this book. He is a great person who makes me very proud, every day. If you want to see more of his art, go to: *www.facebook.com/Gobblynking* He makes every day of my life interesting.

Next, I want to give a shout-out and a thank you to my favorite authors who have inspired me to keep writing, even when I was just staring at a blank computer screen. Brad Thor tops the list because he is the absolute best in the field and a wonderful person. I had the pleasure of meeting him twice and he is an all-around great guy. David Baldacci, next on my list, has a great sense of humor when he is giving his talks. I am happy to learn I don't have to be serious all the time. Reading the J. D. Robb books taught me to understand that a bedroom scene didn't need to be sleazy to be powerful.

Thanks to Bonnie Pinkston for reading and rereading this manuscript and offering constructive criticism.

To any aspiring authors out there, never give up. Your first draft will be terrible and that's okay. It's where you start. Don't get bogged down with perfection at the beginning. Get the story on the page. Then tweak it until it's the best you can make it.

Thank you to my readers. Without you, this would be just another story. My goal is to keep you entertained. I hope I have succeeded in that goal.

Love and thanks
Jennifer

Chapter One

Page Harlow crossed the room with the grace of a panther, his blue eyes twinkling with mischief. At the window he turned, running long fingers through his shoulder-length flaxen blonde hair, working hard to conceal the smirk that twitched at the corner of his lips. "You have lost your frigging mind," he stated, addressing the older man who sat in the chair. His manager, mentor, and friend; the present object of Page's intense gaze.

"Page, it's a grand idea," Tommy said, hoping to convince the superstar of the merits of the newest promotional gimmick. *A promotional gimmick already in full swing.* If at midnight Page refused to sign off on the idea, thousands of dollars would have been wasted on the campaign.

"A grand idea? A stranger spending ten days at my home?" Page shoved his hair away from his face, only to have it drop back in the same position. "Who came up with this idiot idea?"

"Actually, I did. And it's not just any stranger, it's a fan. You know, those glorious people who have made you a multi-millionaire? Fans?" Tommy took a deep breath and silently counted to ten, then took another breath. Arguing with Page Harlow only made him more stubborn. He fished an antacid from his pocket.

Page crossed the spacious room to the bar and poured a liberal amount of bourbon into a glass. "A fan. A stranger. Same thing. You want me to turn the keys to the castle over to this person? What if shit happens?" He looked at Tommy, wide-eyed. It was what he referred to as his 'surprised' look.

Tommy shifted uncomfortably in the overstuffed chair. "What sort of shit?"

Page leaned against the bar and fixed his most serious look on his manager. "The top of my list would be bodily harm in my sleep. Second on the list would be the theft of my possessions. Third, but not last or least, would be an accusation of me doing something for which I would be arrested. And the list goes on." He held up each finger in turn.

"When did you become so down on your fans?" Tommy asked.

"I am not down on my fans. But, I like them in their place, Tom. At the concert with security between them and me. Lots of security, Tom. I don't know how to break it to you pal, but not all my fans are the law-abiding types. Some of them are downright criminal or crazy. Thank you, but I really do not want them in my home."

"You're too young to be paranoid," Tommy said with a sigh. This meeting was going downhill fast.

"I'm too smart not to be," Page replied. "Besides, you of all people should want to protect your investment. I don't have time to be distracted. I need to focus on the details of the tour. And…" he ran his fingers dramatically through his hair… "I need my rest."

"It's good publicity. Shows that you want to be close to your fans. With the tour in the works and the CD's release a mere two months away, you need to get your name back in the news. Good publicity. This is good, Page."

"Rock Star feeds fan to Piranhas. Grand publicity. Rock Star accused of assault on house guest." Page refilled his glass.

"Can't you find anything positive this morning? Did you stub your toe before breakfast? Did Anna burn your toast? What?" Tommy argued, shifting in the chair again. Well, nobody ever said managing a rock star would be easy. Lucrative yes; easy, never. "Look; the legal staff wrote an agreement the winner has to sign. The small print on the entry form allowed us to do a background check. I mean, granted nothing is foolproof Page, but we covered all the bases. For God's sake, we wouldn't turn just anyone loose in your home. Give us some damn credit. If the background check doesn't pass we pull another name from the hat."

Page sighed. "What are the contest rules?" He had no intention of revealing that he had been aware of the contest for weeks. It was more fun to watch the poor guy fidget in his seat.

Tommy hid the grin. If Page was asking questions, then he was at least considering it. "Must be 21. Must agree to background check. Must be able to travel within the given time frame. If, after forty-eight hours either party wishes to sever the castle visit, a hotel of the contestant's choosing will be paid for, as well as reasonable expenses."

"So, if I don't feel comfortable I can ship the fan off to the Hilton?"

"Yes."

Page downed his drink, crossed the room to the coffee table, and picked up the legal paperwork, pretending to study it. "When do we pick the lucky lad or lady?"

"Friday. Look, if it's a guy take him barhopping or to a soccer game. Just pal around with him. That's not too much to ask, is it?"

"And if the winner is female? Then what? I don't see a 'keep your hands off the merchandise' clause." Page arched a blond eyebrow.

"When have you ever turned down attention from a female fan?" Tommy teased.

"When she has green teeth and body odor? When she hasn't taken a bath in a week? Tommy, I like to pick my own grapes, if you get my drift. I have a weakness for tall, willowy blondes with boobs. Of course, redheads or brunettes with boobs will do." He frowned and dropped the paperwork to the table, shaking his head. "Actually, to be quite honest with you, I'd like to spend time with a woman who has a brain. You know; one who can string a complete sentence together and not butcher the English language? She could even be flat-chested with straight hair. She could be short. Even dumpy. Too bad we can't make the fan take a test, like an exam to become a Rhodes Scholar."

Tommy laughed. "In your dreams, Page. If women with brains listened to the racket you call music, they would never enter a contest to spend time in your house." Tommy handed Page his pen. "Sign this.

Says you read and agree to the contest rules. Word to the wise. The last tall, willowy blonde you had anything to do with cost you millions. Take some good old-fashioned precautions, will you?"

"My bank account can't survive another paternity suit," Page groaned.

"DNA proved you were the guilty party. Eric's your son. I'm surprised with all your hotel room activities, you only have one child."

"I believed Sasha loved me. Stupid on my part, but that's why I quit taking precautions. If she had loved me, she would have married me. Then we could have raised Eric the way children are supposed to be raised. With a set of parents. Till death do us part? We could have had another child or two. I don't want Eric to go through what I did growing up. I don't want him to wonder if his father hates him, the way I wondered. No child should have to go through that."

"Eric will know who his father is. Your attorneys will damn well see to that. If you ever did get married, you could probably fight for custody."

"Sasha's a good mother. I wouldn't take that away from her. But, I do intend to know my son."

"Well, he's only six. By the time he's old enough to be in school full-time, you should be able to curb your tours back and spend a good deal of quality time with him."

Page crossed the room again to stare out the picture window, shoving his hands in the pockets of his jeans. "I really thought she loved me. I mean, I was good to her. I was even faithful. When she told me she was pregnant, I was overjoyed." He shrugged. "It went downhill from there. I would give anything to meet a woman like your wife. Janet adores you."

"Unfortunately, women like Janet don't date musicians with your reputation. And they would never, ever enter a contest. You could get a mail-order bride from one of those teeny third-world countries."

"I want a wife, not a possession. I want a woman who can hold her own in a conversation. One who plays chess and likes opera. One who appreciates the value of a dollar." Page grinned. "Of course, if she had a great body and were hot in bed, it would be good too."

"You're hopeless." Tommy rolled his eyes.

"I hope the winner is a guy. We can hit every dive in Paris, get drunk, and be obnoxious. Play guitar in the middle of the night. Watch football and fake wrestling."

"It'll be a good contest. It'll show that you enjoy spending time with your fans. That you aren't the demigod egomaniac that the press claims you are."

Page chuckled. "Trying to upgrade my bad boy image, Tommy?"

"Heaven forbid! Your image is everything."

Page sighed, signed the paperwork and Tommy put it in his briefcase.

Chapter Two

Rebecca Morrison closed the legal reference manual and pressed her fingertips to the bridge of her nose. She glanced at the wall clock and groaned. Past quitting time and she still wasn't finished with the Harper Research for her boss. Well, the legal brief didn't need to be filed until next Monday, so she still had a few days. Days like this made her wish she had chosen a different career path. Real Estate or Accounting or something less demanding. She stood, her green eyes catching her reflection in the smoked glass window. Her red hair was pulled back in a professional knot at the nape of her neck. Smoothing her suit jacket and brushing a piece of lint from her emerald blouse, she replaced the book on the shelf, scooped up her notes, and headed down the carpeted hallway to her office. Her bosses had already left for the day, and the offices were all dark except for hers. She smiled. Being single had turned her into a workaholic. In three years she would be thirty. Never had a serious boyfriend and heading over the hill. She chuckled as she dropped the notes on her desk. Her assistant, Gina Demarco glanced up from the laptop, her head moving in tune with whatever noise came from the earphones. Gina could type up to ninety words a minute while listening to heavy metal music. Her spiked hairdo was naturally jet black, and her long blood-red nails did not hinder her efficiency in the least. Rebecca sat in her chair and put the notes in order.

Gina clicked off the music and dropped the headphones on the desk. "I'm going to go home and jump out the window," she said with a dramatic sigh.

"Break up with the boyfriend of the week?"

"No. It's almost six, and I did not yet get a notification that I won. Of course, that could be the time zones between here and Europe. What time is it in Europe?"

"Won?" Rebecca grinned. "You entered another contest?" Gina entered every contest there was to enter. She had won the candy bar for a year contest among others. "Almost midnight, Saturday. Six hours difference, I think."

"This, Ree is the contest to end all contests."

"I think they call that the lotto, don't they?" Rebecca teased.

"This is the Ten Days at Harlow's Castle contest."

"Harlow's Castle?"

"Page Harlow. He's a musician. He owns a castle. One lucky fan gets to spend ten days as his guest."

Rebecca shook her head. "Those types of contests are rigged, Gee. Think about it. A musician wouldn't allow a stranger to reside under his roof for ten days. Think of the legal liabilities involved."

Gina frowned. "Were you always a wet blanket, Morrison? Did you murder butterflies as a child?"

"Butterflies are adult worms."

"Good grief." Gina rolled her eyes and did her Charlie Brown imitation. "Look," she produced a magazine from her desk drawer and handed it to Rebecca.

Rebecca stared at the cover picture of a man, wearing skin-tight pants and knee-high boots. His hair fell across bare shoulders in a cascade of blonde. "Looks like a hair color ad."

"That is Page Harlow. Isn't he something?"

"Something? He's definitely something. The question would be what? He looks gay. Eye makeup and earrings would be a clue to that."

"He's not gay."

"And what would be your source for that information?" Rebecca teased.

"He has a child and ex-mistress, and he has been linked romantically with bunches of actresses and models."

"So he's not careful enough to take precautions, leading to a woman becoming pregnant. He's unfaithful and probably carrying a zillion germs. And that is not proof he isn't gay. Not entirely anyway."

"I read that he really loved her."

"He probably uses that as a line."

"But it's every woman's dream."

"Nightmare in tight pants if you ask me," Rebecca chuckled.

"The contest is ten days as his guest. At his castle. A real authentic German Castle."

"Castles are old and drafty. They have bugs, dirt, and outdated plumbing. Now a real prize would be at a mansion in Palm Beach. Or the Grand Cayman Islands."

"Ten days in Europe, free of charge."

"Would be a grand contest except for one minor inconvenience."

"What?"

Rebecca tossed the magazine back onto Gina's desk and laughed. "Him."

"Ree, he's the reason for the contest. Every woman in the free world is entering this contest."

"Not quite every woman," Rebecca said. "I didn't enter."

"Actually, yes you did. By proxy."

"What? Did you enter me? Why? What were you thinking?"

Gina laughed and opened the magazine to the center. "I was thinking…. The second prize is a complete state-of-the-art sound system. I've seen yours, and it came over on the Mayflower. And you would be grateful enough to give me the complete set of Harlow's CDs and his DVD which is part of that prize. The third prize is a five-foot big-screen TV and unlimited movies for a year. Since you never date and have no social life I figured you would enjoy the movies at least."

"And what about the first-place prize?"

Gina held up the centerfold photo of Page Harlow, standing at the front of a castle. "Thought you said it was rigged. Therefore, you need not worry about it. And if it isn't rigged, you get to enjoy a free trip to Europe. You said you wanted to go there. You have a vacation coming. I'll even water your plants."

Rebecca rolled her eyes. "If you think for one minute I would spend ten minutes alone with that creature, much less ten days and nights… you have a serious mental deficiency. And I don't have any plants."

"It's a contest. I doubt that he would do anything that would result in a lawsuit. I mean, as you said, think of the legal liabilities. As a matter of fact, he probably won't even shake your hand. A sexual harassment lawsuit wouldn't be good. I mean how would it look for his image?"

"This is a moot point and a goofball conversation. As I said, the contest is rigged. In this day and age, he would be insane to allow a total stranger access to his home."

"Don't you ever date?"

"I haven't found anyone who interests me."

"What type are you looking for?"

"Someone who can carry on an intelligent conversation enjoys classical music, and maybe opera. Someone who's interested in me as a person and not just a sex object." Rebecca shrugged. "I don't think I will find my Mr. Right anytime soon."

"Mr. Right is an imaginary creature. Someone's mom invented him to keep her daughter in line. Settle for Mr. So-So."

"Sorry, I am not one to settle for so-so. I would rather live alone."

"What fun is that?"

"I don't have to impress anyone when I wake up looking like death eating a cookie. I can wear my ratty-looking faded terry cloth robe all weekend. I eat whenever I get hungry and sleep when I get sleepy. The remote control is all mine, and I can drape my lingerie all over the bathroom with not one worry."

Gina frowned. "Gotta hand it to you. It almost sounds good. But you don't have anyone to hold you or kiss your hurts."

"Ah, but I don't have anyone who will be the cause of hurt either. Do you know what the divorce rate is these days?"

"I bet wherever you went as a child, it rained and ruined everybody's fun. I will just hold on to the fantasy that I might win this contest, get to his castle and he will fall madly in love with me."

Rebecca put several file folders in her briefcase and zipped it shut. "Whatever gets you through the night, Gee. I'm going to spend the night with the Carson Case files. My fantasy is that the bosses give me a large raise and a promotion. Or sponsor me for a scholarship to Harvard."

"With your looks, I don't understand why you aren't a model," Gina said. "I mean if I had your peaches and cream skin tone, that perfect hair, and your measurements, I'd be Playboy of the Month. Do you know what kind of money models make?"

"There is such a thing as too much money. You wouldn't know who your true friends were. You would never know if your friends like you for you, your money, or your career. I would be miserable."

"I'll bet you could have easily been Miss USA or Miss Universe."

"My Aunt Darla was in the Miss America contest."

"And that didn't pique your interest?"

"Lord no," Rebecca shook her head. "I just wanted peace and quiet. I wanted a 4.0 average. I wanted a scholarship to Harvard. But I like the research too."

Rebecca and Gina walked to the garage, waved goodbye, and agreed to meet for coffee before work on Monday.

Chapter Three

Page sat at his desk, nursing a drink as he flipped through the paperwork Tommy brought over. He glanced over where Tommy sat in the chair, flipping the remote for the TV. "Who dreamed up this phony report," Page asked softly.

"That's as real as it gets, Page."

"Rebecca Morrison? You expect me to believe that a twenty-seven-year-old member of the legal profession, with a notable New York Law Firm, entered a contest to spend ten days with a rock star?"

"That's what the report says." Tommy shrugged his wide shoulders

"Same job, same home, a degree from a university. Single. This is a joke, I know. Maybe the guys in the legal department thought it would get my heartbeat up." Page laughed and finished his drink. "Tell them they better have done a real investigation on this woman. If she turns out to be a crazy lady, I will hurt someone."

"This is what they gave me. I agree it sounds as if something is off-center. Maybe she's a closet groupie."

"Maybe. If she works for a reputable firm, I think it would be a safe bet to assume she doesn't have body order or green teeth. Might be chubby, but I can deal with that for two weeks. Or she's rail thin with those coke-bottle glasses."

"Well, at least you don't have to worry about her stealing the silver or stabbing you in your sleep. Appears to be stable."

"Can't be totally stable," Page laughed. "She entered this insane contest you thought up. What time is it in New York?"

"Ten a.m. on Saturday morning."

Page reached for the phone. "Let's see if she answers her phone."

Rebecca jotted notes on the papers on her desk and sighed. Here it was Saturday morning, and she was up working out the details of the law case, a half-eaten bagel next to her laptop. Heaving a sigh, she went into the kitchen and poured herself another cup of coffee. A smile crossed her lips. When she moved to New York, away from her small town in Indiana, her parents worried she would end up involved with a wild crowd. Be out all night, drinking and raising hell. In the last conversation she'd had with her mom, she had been told that it wasn't healthy to work all the time and not to have a social life. Her parents were concerned about never being grandparents. They reminded her they had been putting money aside for a really lovely wedding, should she meet someone special. She frowned. How in the hell could she meet anyone who shared her sense of values? Her dates in college never called her after they discovered she did not sleep around. The only guys who hung around with her were guys who couldn't get a date, and they all treated her like their sister. There was Kelly Norman, another paralegal she met for drinks a few times. He had a partner, Jerry, who was a doctor across town. Sometimes the three of them went to the movies or out to dinner. There was something to be said for that, but she didn't get invited to parties or dances as someone's date. She turned as the phone rang and reached for the receiver.

"Hello." She frowned. Not many people called her on a Saturday. From an unknown number. Probably a sales call.

"Is this Rebecca Morrison?"

"Yes." She shifted in her chair and sipped the coffee. Nice voice. Yep. A sales call.

"Rebecca, this is Page Harlow."

"Who?"

"Page Harlow. You entered a contest…" his voice trailed away, and he frowned at Tommy.

"Haha. Tell Gina she isn't funny and I didn't fall for the joke."

"I don't know anyone named Gina, and if you have caller ID, you'll notice this call is from Germany. I'm holding a piece of paper with your name and this phone number on it." Page stared at the phone, then back over at Tommy.

Rebecca took a deep breath. The contest! "Mr. Harlow, I'm afraid there has been a slight error."

"Error? What type of error?"

"Well, you see, I personally did not enter your contest. My secretary entered my name."

"Well, nevertheless Miss Morrison, yours was the winning entry."

"I'm afraid that's impossible. I mean I don't know you. I can't just go off to another part of the world with a total stranger. And legally, I didn't enter."

"I've had my rabies shots. I don't beat women, and I can be quite charming. It isn't as if I am Jack the Ripper."

"I told Gina this contest was rigged. I mean what person in this day and age would have a stranger stay with them for ten days? Mr. Harlow, think of the liabilities."

"I had that same discussion with my manager. There was a cursory background investigation done. You have no criminal record."

"That's an invasion of my privacy."

"Not really. It's all public record. You of all people should know that." Page took a long sip of his drink, sat the glass down, and leaned back in his chair. Tommy had stopped playing with the remote and was looking at Page with a questioning stare, following the conversation.

"But, Mr. Harlow, I don't know you. However, my secretary showed me your picture, and quite frankly…"

Page laughed. "Are you saying you had no idea who I was?"

"Not until yesterday evening. And I can tell you, you aren't anywhere near my type. Therefore, as much as I am happy to have won, perhaps I could change places with the person who came in second?"

"So? You probably aren't anywhere near my type either. I tend to be attracted to the traffic-stopping drop-dead babes with hair color from a bottle and the brains of a gnat. But you won, and you are entitled to ten days in Europe as my guest. If we decide we cannot stand each other, you are more than welcome to spend the remainder of your trip at the hotel of your choice. At my expense. And no, you may not trade places with the runner-up." He chuckled and shrugged his shoulders at Tommy's puzzled expression.

"Why?"

"Why what?"

"From what Gina tells me you could have any woman on planet earth. Almost any woman that is. Why this contest?"

Page laughed. "I have an idiot for a manager. He thought it would be a great idea. A publicity thing. Get to meet one of my adoring fans and all that. I promise you I wasn't at all thrilled. I prefer to choose my own dates, but he pointed out that lots of guys entered so they could hang out with me for ten days. You know, play guitar, and get drunk… that sort of stuff. The background check was to make sure the fan wasn't going to slit my throat or rob my castle. But, after talking to you, it might be different to hang out with someone who isn't a fan. Someone who will treat me as a person. It will definitely be a unique experience for me. You don't happen to play chess do you?"

"Actually, I was a member of the chess club in college. I haven't played in a very long time though."

"Great. Nobody around here plays, and if they do, they always let me win. Not much fun in that. Can you get ten days off? I mean, this is an all-expense paid vacation for ten days. You don't need so much as a nickel of your own money. Well if you want to do massive amounts of shopping for Paris originals, you might want to bring a credit card or two. But, for food, lodging, and sightseeing, you won't spend a penny. The flight is first class."

Rebecca thought about the caseload at the office, then frowned. In five years she had never taken any time off. "I have vacation time I haven't used. When would I be coming? If I agree, that is."

"Next Friday. If that presents a problem, we can change it. Do you have a passport? I realize it isn't a lot of notice but frankly, we weren't expecting the winner to have a serious career."

"I do have a passport. I had planned a vacation, but it fell through. You know, this is totally out of character for me. I would never have entered this type of contest. I tend to play it safe in life."

"What's the fun in that?" Page asked with a chuckle. "You only live once, and you aren't going to get out of it alive. Might as well have some memories for your golden years. Adventures to tell the grandkids?"

"For there to be grandkids, there would have to be kids, which means a husband. Dating hasn't been high on my 'to do' list."

"Plan to stay single?"

"I'll take that time when it comes. I guess I am still waiting for Mr. Right. You know, the perfect man… madly in love…." Rebecca laughed. "With my workload at the office, it will be a long wait."

"That type of love sneaks up on you. You don't go looking for it. It hits you like a damn two-by-four across the forehead. I know. I've been there. And if it turns bad, you want to jump off a bridge, or push the other person off the damn bridge."

"I don't know if I want to take those kinds of chances. I want the happy ever after, Cinderella love."

"Sometimes Cinderella's love ends up like Romeo and Juliet."

"I guess that's why I'm not dating. I don't take chances."

"Rebecca, you take chances every day. You wake up and take a chance you don't choke on your breakfast or slip in the shower. You take a chance when you get in your car."

"But those are necessary. Dating isn't."

"Well, at least you won't have anything to worry about for the ten days you're here. I vow to be on my best and most gentlemanly behavior."

"That's all I could ask for, I guess."

Page laughed. "However, if you find yourself overwhelmed by my charm and want to get crazy, I would try to oblige you."

"Don't hold your breath."

"Can I call you tomorrow? I'm sure you weren't just sitting by the phone doing nothing."

"Actually I was working on a legal brief."

"Good grief. Are you a workaholic?"

"Most of the time. This would be my first vacation since I started with the firm. Well, not counting time off when my father fell ill."

"I promise you'll enjoy yourself."

"Thanks."

"Goodnight, Rebecca."

"Goodnight Mr. Harlow."

"One other thing…" Page said quickly.

"Yes?"

"My father was Mr. Harlow. I'm just Page." He chuckled. "In reality, my father was Lord Harlow, so there is no *Mister Harlow*."

"Goodnight, Just Page." Rebecca laughed.

"Goodnight Rebecca. I'll call you tomorrow."

Rebecca hung up the phone, poured her cold coffee down the sink, and opened a bottle of wine. What in the hell was she getting into? Europe for ten days with a stranger. Well, Gina was right. There was no way he would get out of line. The legal liabilities were extensive. And since he lived in Europe, he would be an excellent tour guide. She grinned as she sipped her wine. All expenses paid. Europe. She would enjoy herself, she decided. Maybe it was time for her to come out of her shell. She could go shopping. In Paris. After all, she could pick up some beautiful outfits for the office. She groaned. There she was, thinking about work. She could find some great casual clothes. Maybe it was time the caterpillar turned into a butterfly. Perhaps she had spent enough time in a shell. Perhaps she was losing her mind, she thought to herself. Well, he had said he would put her up in a hotel of her choice, so she could stay in Paris and check out all the art stuff. She could rent a car and tour the countryside. Sure, it would be fun. There was no doubt that after one day Harlow would be thrilled to ship her off to a hotel. From what she guessed, he would not be happy with a woman who didn't fall at his feet or into his bed.

Chapter Four

By midnight, Rebecca had researched the life and loves of Page Eric Harlow. He had an extensive arrest record but no convictions. He had been linked to actresses, models, and a princess and appeared to be an egomaniac in the press, but Rebecca guessed it was an act because he didn't seem that way on the phone. He was born in Norway where he lived until his mother died when he was twelve, then uprooted to England where his father, Lord Harlow, placed him in a private boy's school. That's when his behavior pattern turned toward the risqué, and he went from one school to the next. Expelled four times. At sixteen, he left England and went to live in Germany with his grandfather, and at the death of his father, he inherited a small fortune, an estate in England, and the German castle. Gifted with an ability for music and languages, he spoke French, German, Spanish, and Italian as well as Norwegian and English. His musical talents included guitar, drums, piano, flute, and bass. At twenty-one, he hooked up with Tommy Madison, who became his manager, and Harlow's Black Angels were created. His first CD shot to the top of the charts, and he shot to stardom. The band sold out arenas across the globe, touring non-stop for nine months. They took a break long enough to record the second album and were off and running again.

Rebecca continued to research, digging as deep as she would her research for work. Page dated model Sasha Weeks for six months before she became pregnant. His statement in the press was that he was ecstatic and looking forward to the birth of his child. He stated that he and Ms. Weeks would be wed in a quiet ceremony soon. Sasha Weeks, however, told the media there was no way she was giving up her career to change diapers or ruin her nails washing pots and pans.

They broke up, and she sued for millions of dollars, the home in Spain, and living expenses. Plus more monthly child support than Rebecca made in six months.

Rebecca frowned. Page had down a downward spiral of self-destruction for almost a year, then seemed to snap out of it. He returned to the spotlight by making another CD and going on a tour of fifteen countries. His fans were thrilled to have him back, making all of his shows complete sell-outs. His CD rocketed to number one on the charts. Rebecca's heart ached for the hurt he must have felt when Sasha left him. No wonder he was a playboy. Well, she would undoubtedly be a change of pace from the type of woman he was used to. She had never had a serious relationship. There was a close call in college and some backseat groping in high school. For Rebecca, sex would come after the marriage ceremony, and when she explained this to an overeager date, there was never a second date. It seemed men wanted to conquer her without commitment. Men saw her ample curves, and red hair and thought she would be easy. She tried glasses, hoping to disguise her flawless facial features but they never hid her emerald green eyes. Baggy sweatshirts didn't do much to conceal her full breasts. However, as her attitude toward men chilled, the dates stopped. By the time she graduated from the small New York University, she had the reputation of an untouchable ice maiden. Well, at least with Harlow she wouldn't have that worry. He had been specific about the type of women he was attracted to, and she definitely wasn't it. The thought caused her to smile. *"Brains of a gnat,"* she said to herself.

Rebecca turned off her computer and laughed out loud when she thought about Gina's reaction. Of course, she couldn't mention the contest when she asked for her vacation. She could say she won a trip. Not a lie. No need to expound on that. The same went for telling her parents. They would never accept that she was a guest of a man in Europe. That would seem like a big sin in their eyes. Rebecca undressed for bed and frowned. She was twenty-seven years old and still worried about what mom and dad thought or didn't think she was doing. If they didn't trust her judgment by now, there was nothing to do that would change it. Lying in bed, she sighed. Maybe Harlow was the catalyst she needed to fix the rut she had gotten into. Someone once said a rut was a grave with the ends removed. Damn. Gina had been right. She was a wet blanket. Where would she be in ten years? Pushing forty with nothing to show for it? No one? Not that Page Harlow was the great white hope for her future, but maybe in Europe, she could learn how to relax and enjoy life instead of being so uptight.

Chapter Five

Page hung up the phone and turned to Tommy. "Well, I don't know what to think. She seems too damn good to be real. Oh, granted, she's probably as plain as a piece of dry toast. My guess is she's the typical law firm library type. Heavy glasses and a bad haircut. Or a hairdo pulled up into one of those old maid-type twists on top of her head. But hey, she says she plays chess, so that is at least common ground. She's totally anti-romance and down on men. I guess she was probably the ugly duckling in school and built up a defense by saying she wasn't interested. Doesn't matter. I will be on my best behavior. I'll treat her like a sister or something. Maybe like a sister of a friend." He glanced up as his housekeeper entered the room. "Anna, just the person I need to talk to. We have a guest coming. The contest winner."

The older woman ran her hand through her ash-blond hair and set the dust cloth down on the bar. "Really?" She'd been told that Page's manager was running a contest and that a stranger would be staying and even though Page wasn't enthusiastic about it, he was going along with it.

Page shrugged, "A young woman from New York. Rebecca Morrison. She isn't the type of woman I usually have around, but I'm sure she is very nice. She's sort of a plain Jane type and works for a law firm. Plays Chess. I'll try to find out more about her likes and dislikes. Would you make sure the guest room is done up elegantly?"

"Of course. I can put on the peach satin sheets and that lovely matching spread."

"I'll leave that to you. I just want her to feel welcome and enjoy the stay. We'll probably do a lot of sightseeing because I'm sure she'll want to visit the major tourist spots. Paris, Rome, Venice, and possibly Madrid. Make sure we have a good variety of food and snacks. You know better than I do what to do about houseguests. I don't know why I think you need my input." Page laughed. "Like I told Tommy, I'll treat her like the sister I never had."

"If you talk to her again, you might ask her what her interests are," Tommy suggested. "Find out where she wants to go, what she wants to see. Ask her what food she likes. Take some of the guesswork out of the visit."

"Good idea. I want to make sure she enjoys herself. I mean, she almost refused to come. I wouldn't want her to wish she hadn't."

"Who knows? This might change your outlook on women. Get you away from that bubble-headed bleach-blonde type." Anna crossed her arms in front of her, wondering what type of woman would enter a contest of this sort, and then almost back out.

"It'll be nice to actually be able to carry on an intelligent conversation. And play chess." Page smiled at her. "I can't remember the last time I played chess."

Tommy winked at Anna. "Maybe he'll find out he can have a woman as a friend instead of just a bed partner."

"I hope he will enjoy himself around her because he won't have to put on that horrid act. That bad boy image. It's a fake you know." The older woman winked at them.

"Anna, don't let out our big secret," Page teased.

The next morning Page sat in the kitchen, staring out at the pouring rain. "I hope this isn't an omen."

Anna poured his coffee and smiled at him. "Best to rain now and have nice weather for your guest. Even in a castle this size the two of you would get cabin fever stuck here for the whole time."

"You have a point. I'll call her later. Ask her what food she likes and what she would like to do. I told her I would call her. I'm betting that most men don't ever call her back after a first date. I'm guessing all her friends have set her up with a bunch of blind dates. You know how uncomfortable that can be. And even this contest wasn't her own doing. Someone else entered her name. Probably as a prank."

"That's how I met Hans. My best friend couldn't go out unless she found a date for her visiting cousin. She had to beg and bribe me with Swiss chocolate cake."

"But you were pretty." Page grinned. "Grandpapa showed me pictures."

"You don't know that Miss Morrison isn't pretty."

"I've never seen any woman who worked in a law library who was remotely pretty."

"Well, the old adage is that beauty is skin deep. I'm sure she's a charming person inside."

Page grinned. "I'm sure you're right. And being plain will probably help me behave myself too."

"You aren't that shallow. This is me you're talking to Page Harlow, not some reporter. If you really like someone, you wouldn't care if she had two chins."

"Anna, you know me too damn well." he laughed.

Page spent the rest of the day in the studio he had made in the basement. With the CD completed, he didn't have anything pressing, so he played aimlessly on the keyboard. When he returned to the upper level, it had stopped raining but was grey and overcast. He picked up the phone and dialed New York.

Rebecca picked up on the third ring. "Hi again," he said.

"Mr. Harlow. Hello."

"Thought you agreed to call me Page," he chastised.

"Occupational habit, I suppose. Hello, Page."

"After I hung up yesterday it occurred to me that I should ask you what you thought you might like to do in Europe for ten days. There are, of course, all of the normal tourist things to do, but I was wondering if you had anything special in mind."

"I'm afraid my tastes and yours are probably worlds apart."

"But this is your vacation, Rebecca."

"Do you think I could see the Louvre? It's been a dream of mine since I was a little girl."

"Absolutely. I haven't been there in about two years. The whole tour takes hours, but it's well worth it. And Paris is chock full of other art galleries if you'd be interested. I know most of them. Just promise me you won't be on a diet while you are here. You haven't lived until you've eaten European pastry. Not to mention tasting Anna's cooking."

"Who's Anna?"

"My housekeeper. She's like a grandmother to me. Her husband Hans cares for the outside, and she cares for the inside of the castle."

"I always imagined castles to be dirty and cold."

"I only live in a part of the castle. I have a sound and recording studio downstairs as well as a fitness center. Lots of bedrooms on the second and third levels. The fourth, fifth, and top-level aren't used. Hell, most of the castle isn't used. The living areas are well-kept. Anna is a German version of Good Housekeeping and Betty Crocker. Which brings me to food. Any favorites?"

"I like almost anything. I don't much care for Brussel sprouts."

"Okay. At least you aren't asking for alfalfa or bean sprouts."

"Yuk. Rabbit food. Mr. Harlow, I have never been on a diet in my life. I certainly don't intend to be on one in Europe. Could you arrange a ticket for an opera? Any opera would do."

"Not a problem." He chuckled, "and it's still… Page."

"I'll leave anything else I get to see up to you, Page. I'm sure you know your way around Europe much better than any tour book map. It'll be nice to see things that aren't in the guidebooks."

"Fair enough. You'll need one day to acclimate yourself to the horrid six-hour time change. You'll fly from New York to Paris, and my pilot will fly you from Paris to Munich and drive you here."

"You know my secretary may jump out a window when I break this to her. She was so hoping to win."

"We'll remember to get her souvenirs from everywhere."

"I think you were the souvenir she really wanted."

"Story of my life," he sighed.

"You would probably have more fun with her, you know. I'm not nearly the social butterfly she is."

"I have a phone book filled with the social butterfly types Rebecca. But you know what? Not one of them has ever asked to attend an opera. Nor do they know a rook from a knight. I think I might enjoy the change of pace. I only hope you enjoy it here as well."

"I'm afraid you will find me dull and boring. I don't date, I'm not promiscuous. I don't get drunk or do drugs. I am a very old-fashioned girl."

"Something to be said for that."

Rebecca laughed. "My secretary calls me a wet blanket."

"Somehow, I doubt you're all that bad. You must have one or two bad habits. Most everybody does."

"I have the habit of being dull. Part and parcel of my career choice, I suppose. I spend a lot of my days with legal research. Not much for a conversation topic at parties. Of course, I don't get invited to parties, so it doesn't matter."

"Are you happy?"

"I beg your pardon?"

"Are you happy? With your life? Your choices." he asked.

"I'm content."

"Would you change anything if you could?"

Rebecca laughed. "I would have been born male. I would have gone to Harvard Law School."

"You don't like being female?"

"I don't like being treated differently because I'm female. Equality of the sexes isn't big in New York."

"So if I hold your chair or open your car door, do you intend to kick me?" he laughed.

"No. I'm not referring to that type of treatment. I'm talking about being talked to as if I can't comprehend anything complex. I'm talking about being talked to as if I am a moron. And I would probably fall over in a dead faint if a man opened a car door in this day and age."

"Well Rebecca, I do open car doors and hold chairs. My mother would haunt me from beyond the grave if I lost my manners. Not to mention the head of Gantley's school for young men. He would like to think he beat some manners into me."

"You must try awfully hard to maintain that bad boy image."

"In my career, that image is everything. There is no such creature as a gentleman hard rock musician. It would be the kiss of death."

"I see."

"Well hey, I'll put together a list of things to do around here. You can pick out what appeals to you. As for food, I'll let Anna shop the way she always does. Your paperwork and airline tickets will arrive tomorrow or the next day. It's warm weather here, but the nights can be chilly. Pack light. Paris is a shopping bonanza. Oh, by the way.... My new video will debut on the music channel tonight at ten. If you feel like watching."

"Okay. I guess I can sit through three minutes of hard rock."

"I'll call you later in the week to make sure you haven't wimped out on me."

"My word is my bond, Page. My parents taught me that at a very early age."

"Good. I'm not going to ask you what you look like. I think I'd rather be surprised. Besides, it sounds so sexist."

Rebecca laughed. "From the research I've done on you, you try hard to be sexist. More image?"

"Unfortunately. The metamorphosis takes place when I step off the tour bus or step in front of a microphone. I get drunk, act out, and act up. It's fun to a point not to have to obey those rules of society that's expected of civilized people."

"Don't you ever get tired of it?"

"Yes. But it pays well. Sort of like clown makeup. Clowns don't look like that except when they have an audience. Well, hey, I have a million things to do, and I'm sure you do too. I'll call you later."

"Okay. Goodbye." Rebecca hung up and slipped a DVD into her recorder, setting it for the music channel. She set the timer from nine till midnight, in case the times here were different. Maybe Gina would like to come over and watch it. She grinned. Gina would have a fit when she got the news. Rebecca reached for the phone.

"Hello," Gina said picking her phone up on the first ring.

"Hey, it's me. You doing anything this evening?"

"Eating leftover pizza. Why? What's up?"

"I have information that the new Page Harlow video debuts at ten tonight. Thought you might want to come over and watch it with me."

"Wait… wait… wait… Are you watching Harlow? Who told you it would be on?"

"He did. When he called to invite me to Europe."

"Yeah right. Thought you said the contest was rigged."

"I was wrong. Stranger things have been known to happen."

"Are you saying you won the contest?"

"I won the contest."

"And you agreed to go?"

"I agreed to go."

"To stay at the castle? With Page Harlow? For ten days?"

"It's your fault for entering my name. You coming over or not?"

"I'm coming over."

Gina arrived at seven that evening, bringing a bottle of wine and a bag of potato chips. "I can't believe this. It calls for a celebration! What's he like on the phone? Oh, my God, I would have been speechless."

"He seems very nice. Asked what I would like to see, and where I would like to visit. He asked if I had any favorite food. Stuff like that."

"I am in shock!"

"I was too. It took me a minute to realize who he was. I thought you had put someone up to call me as a prank. Then I tried to talk him into letting me change places with the second-place winner. But he promised to be on his best behavior. Of course, for him, I don't think that's all that wonderful. I'm guessing we will hate each other after a day and he will happily ship me off to a hotel. I can't see him gritting his teeth and asking me to stay."

"Maybe he will fall head over heels in love with you."

"About the time orchids start growing at the North Pole. I am not his type. He won't want a woman in his home who won't sleep with him. If I know anything at all from what I have researched it is he's a sex maniac."

Gina began laughing. "You researched Page Harlow? Did your computer melt?"

"Damn near. His lifestyle borders on pornography. All sorts of legal woes stemming from his overabundant sex drive. He doesn't cope well with rejection. Therefore he and I will not get along. Besides, I can't picture him dragging along while I visit the Louvre and attend the opera."

"Opera? You want to go to an opera?"

"It's my vacation, remember. So yes, I asked him if he could get me a ticket."

"And he agreed?"

Rebecca opened the wine and poured them each a glass. "Just because he agreed to get a ticket doesn't mean he will get two tickets." She shrugged. "But on the bright side, he does play chess."

"Chess?"

"He asked me if I played chess."

Gina rolled her eyes and groaned. "Good grief."

They both turned their attention to the TV when the woman began talking about Page Harlow's upcoming tour. She announced there would be an interview with him after the commercial break.

Rebecca refilled the wine glasses and brought the bottle to sit on the end table.

Page Harlow appeared on the screen. Gina sighed with delight as he strutted across the soundstage, where they were rehearsing. He wore tight jeans, suede moccasins, and a blue tank top. His hair was held back with a blue scarf. He answered questions about the new CD and the tour. He introduced the other members of the band and recited a long list of cities he would be invading. He winked at the camera. "My Norse ancestors were very good at invading foreign lands. I hope to make them envious." The interview was over, and the video came on. When it was over Rebecca shook her head. "Borderline porn. That's all it was. Porn put to music."

"I hate to break this to you…" Gina giggled. "Most red-blooded women over twelve would be panting with desire after seeing that."

"Or panting because they are trying not to throw up," Rebecca teased.

"You're hopeless. Totally hopeless."

"Miss Ice Maiden, USA. Yep, that's me. And the wet blanket award goes to… Rebecca Morrison." Rebecca lifted her wine glass in a mock salute, and Gina burst into a fit of giggles.

"Poor Page. Ten days of opera and chess. Geeze…"

"And ten nights sleeping alone." Rebecca shrugged. "Actually, he will be free to share those nights with anyone he chooses. He will send me to a hotel in Paris and resume life as he knows it. I have no intention of cramping his style."

"Let me play devil's advocate. What is there's chemistry between you? I mean what if, in this case, opposites attract?"

"Not this much opposite," Rebecca shook her head. "Oil and water."

"It could happen."

"In your world maybe. Not in mine. Harlow isn't going to want anything to do with me. Oh, he might try just to see how far he can get. But once I convince him that I have no intention of sleeping with him, he'll be glad to ship me off to a hotel."

"What if you find yourself attracted to him?"

"Never happen. Page Harlow's not the type of man I would want to be attracted to."

"You have to admit he's quite handsome."

"He wears makeup. His hair is as long as mine."

"Nice body, though," Gina commented.

"Okay. Yes, he has a nice body."

"Lots of muscle but not too much."

"Agreed."

"Nice blue eyes. Great smile," Gina continued.

"Dimples. He does have sexy dimples. Okay okay… he's quite handsome. Be more so without the makeup."

"So, are you saying if he tried, you wouldn't even kiss him? Just a kiss?"

"I wouldn't because that would be leading him on. A kiss would make him try for the next step."

"Well, at least you aren't totally dead. You admitted he's sexy. That's a start."

"Want to go shopping with me after work one evening? My whole wardrobe consists of career clothes. This is a vacation. I could use three or four new outfits."

"Three or four? For a ten-day trip?"

"I plan to shop in Paris. I mean what's the point of going to Europe if you don't shop?"

"I see your point." Gina nodded.

"You may have to help me shop. I'm hopeless when it comes to shopping for anything other than office apparel. I don't want to get off the plane looking like his legal counsel."

"Well, I could suggest short skirts, tight tee shirts… body-hugging jeans…" Gina grinned.

"Don't make me hurt you."

"I already see a change in you. You are usually so serious."

"That's because I am usually at work and we have a serious profession. People who sue other people don't make for lighthearted conversation."

"Well, I guess I'll see you for coffee in the morning."

Gina left, and on impulse, Rebecca replayed the video. Well, admittedly, he was a very sensual male. At the end of the video, there was a parting shot of him releasing the black towel draped around his hips. The camera followed it as it dropped to the carpeting and there was a sound of him laughing and the female model in the video sighed. Rebecca groaned, turned off the TV, and went to bed.

Chapter Six

Monday morning Rebecca requested her vacation, explaining she won a free trip to Europe if she could travel within the specified time frame. Mr. Jenkins leaned back in his leather chair and removed his glasses. His brown eyes held hers in a moment of silence before he nodded. "Send us a postcard from Paris or somewhere," he chuckled. "I never won anything free in my life, much less a trip. Unless you count being in the service as free travel." A slight smile displayed dimples which gave him a boyish look. A look that had been underestimated more than once by the opposing counsel in court.

"Join the service and see the world?" Rebecca asked with a grin. Of the three partners, Steve Jenkins was the easiest to talk to. She wondered if he would be surprised she was spending ten days in the company of a musician and decided, probably not.

"Go to faraway lands, see the sights, and meet people who want to kill you."

"Weren't you an attorney?"

"JAG lawyer. I think my parents were hoping I would go into politics. By the time I retired, I was sick of politics and even sicker of politicians. Well, back to the problems at hand. Before you go join the jet set, what's the status of your caseload?"

"Two pending at the moment. Gina has two more. Hers aren't due for trial for another six weeks or so. We're in good shape."

"Great." He smiled at her as his phone rang and Rebecca left his office.

"He okay your vacation?" Gina asked as Rebecca entered the room and crossed to her desk.

"Asked me to send postcards. Gina, I hope you know how important it is that we keep Mr. Harlow a secret. I don't want the office to know the details."

"Rebecca this isn't the dark ages. You're permitted to have a boyfriend. Or two. Three even."

"I know, but it could escalate into a variety of problems when I return. So far I've been above reproach in all my actions with this firm. I want it to stay that way."

Gina grinned. "You think that if someone here thought you were spending ten days with Harlow they might think you were available to them?"

"It crossed my mind, yes."

"Okay. No mention of your hot date," Gina said, breaking into a fit of giggles.

"I should be angry at you for putting me in this predicament to start with," Rebecca said, then chuckled despite trying to be serious. "Look, let's plan on leaving here right at five. It's still daylight so we can walk to the stores and catch a cab back for our cars."

"Page is already becoming a bad influence on you," Gina teased. "I've never known you to cut out of the office on time."

"He didn't exactly give me a ton of time to get ready for a vacation, and I need to pick up a few things."

"Hate to break this to you Ree, but most women have a closet full of clothes to wear places other than work. I mean I have an entire walk-in closet for going out type stuff."

"I don't have any because I don't go out anywhere."

"And whose fault is that, may I ask?" Gina teased.

"I hate going out alone." Rebecca fingered the papers on her desk. "Besides, it's not safe at night. Alone."

"I can't believe no one in this firm has ever asked you out."

"I work here. It isn't a good idea to date co-workers. And I have gone out with Kelly and Jerry. That's always fun, but they have their own lives."

"Well, don't you ever do anything besides work? You can meet guys anywhere. At lunch, grocery shopping, at the convenience store." Gina shrugged her shoulders. "You could go out with me sometime. I know lots of people."

"I wouldn't fit in with your crowd Gina. Your music would give me a migraine. Your friends would never speak to you again if you showed up with me in tow."

"Well, shopping is fun. If you're not in a hurry, we can grab dinner someplace."

"Sure. Mr. Harlow said it was nice weather but a little chilly at night. I'm thinking of nice dresses, maybe slacks and a sweater for the evening. Oh, and I need a gown."

"A gown?" Gina asked, arching a dark brow.

"For the opera. It's traditional to wear a full formal to the opera."

"Got a price range in mind? I mean gowns in the city aren't cheap."

"If it is what I want, it will be worth it. Now, let's finish up the rest of this Morrow Trial, so we can leave on time." Rebecca handed Gina a file folder, and they both returned to the workload.

At five, they hurried into the streets of New York. Since the law firm was centrally located, it only took a few minutes to walk to the several stores a few blocks away. Gina had Rebecca laughing as she jokingly picked out a red leather miniskirt and black bustier. Rebecca pulled a long plain dress off the rack and held it up. "I think my grandma used to have one of these." In the upbeat department, they agreed she should buy clothes in style and color. One dress stood out, and Rebecca fingered the soft material. When she tried it on, she shook her head, but Gina nodded approval. "It's like a second layer of skin" Rebecca protested, looking at her reflection. The dress had a scoop neck, and it clung to each curve. *Curves she had tried to hide for years.* She sighed and nodded.

"The yellow offsets your hair color. It really looks great." Gina commented.

They continued their shopping by adding a pair of gray slacks made of soft cotton with a deep rust sweater. Two knee-length skirts and silk blouses were added at another store. Heading toward the corner deli, they passed a small shop fit snuggly between two larger stores. In the window was an emerald gown. Rebecca gasped and grabbed Gina's arm. "I need to try that on." They entered the shop, and a small bell rang in the back. A short chubby woman with gray hair entered the room from behind an open archway. "What size is that gown in the window?" Rebecca asked.

"It's a seven. I'll get it for you." The woman opened the glass door gathered the gown in her arms and pointed toward the back. "Dressing room is this way, Miss."

Rebecca stepped out minutes later and turned around for Gina. "It's perfect. Oh, Gina don't you think so?" It fell in layers of silk and lace, subtly hiding a thigh-high split up the side. There were tiny pearls sewn in at the neckline and at the sleeves.

"Only you could find a full-length gown in this city without even trying. I have to try on ten dresses just for a simple date. Yes, it's perfect. You just need shoes and jewelry, and you are all set Cinderella."

The sales lady nodded. "It's as if it was made for you, dear. Odd too, because it's been reduced three times. Seems no one wants something quite so elegant and formal these days. I have several pairs of shoes on a rack on the back wall." Rebecca was delighted to find a pair of heels in the same green and topped off the purchases with faux pearl earrings, a ring, and a necklace.

Over coffee, they examined each item again. "Lingerie," Gina said matter-of-factly.

"What about it?"

"You cannot have all new clothes and wear plain underwear."

"Why not? Mine don't have holes in them."

"Ree…You need new clothes from the skin out. Lace. Maybe a Wonderbra…" she laughed. "Never mind. You don't need that much lift."

"No one is going to see my underwear," Rebecca stated in a whisper.

Gina winked. "You cannot be certain of that, Cinderella. Your prince awaits you in Germany. It's a damn castle for cripes sake."

"The prince is a toad, and he will not, I repeat… not see my underwear."

"Humor me, Cinderella. I'll bet you are wearing plain and very drab stuff under your oh-so-professional lawyer clothes. That sweater deserves to have a lift, so it looks like the designer meant for it to look. Now isn't the time to revert to being a wet blanket on me."

"Okay. But no Wonderbra!"

"You act as if cleavage is a bad thing," Gina laughed.

"No sense advertising wares that are not available. Not even to the Toad Prince of Germany."

"Maybe so, but at least you should want to look great. After all, heads turn where ever he goes so at least look as if you belong on his arm."

"See, this is why I stay at home. Too much work to get all dressed up for a guy."

"You always look good at work," Gina said.

"They pay me to come to work, so they expect me to look good."

"Free trip to Europe should count for something."

Rebecca sighed. "Okay. New stuff."

It was almost nine by the time they returned to the parking garage at work. Rebecca drove to her brownstone and carried the packages inside. She made a list of things she still needed. Toiletries, a bottle of cologne, and maybe a new pair of tennis shoes to go with her slacks. Or at least flats comfortable enough to walk the streets of Paris. She called her mom to share her excitement.

"I'm taking my vacation," she said after the initial hellos and idle chat, mostly about her father's health.

"Are you coming home?" her mom asked. "Your dad hasn't been feeling too well, and we would both like to see you."

"Actually, I won a trip. It's ten days, all expenses paid."

"Oh honey, those free things are always a gimmick. You have to buy something."

"No, this is a free trip."

"One of those expensive resorts? You should come home, so you don't have to spend all that money."

"I'm leaving for Europe on Friday for ten days. I'll be staying in Germany."

"Europe? Oh dear, what if something happens? I mean those countries aren't very safe these days. Why, anything could happen. No, young lady, I won't hear of it. You are much too innocent to be cavorting all over those countries."

Rebecca glanced at the gown lying across her bed, then over to her old terry cloth robe draped over a chair. "All the arrangements have been made. I'll be just fine."

"No, you won't be just fine! You'll get taken advantage of and end up in some sort of trouble. The men are unscrupulous. They'll drug you. They'll get you drunk or something. Why can't you be sensible for once and just come home?"

Rebecca counted to ten. "I was hoping you would be happy for me. I am getting the trip I have always dreamed of and not paying a fortune to go. I am going to the Louvre and a real opera. Things I've wanted to do since I was a little girl."

"How can I be happy for you when you are throwing your life away? I don't know why you insist on staying in that awful city anyway. It isn't as if you couldn't find a job here in town."

"I like my career. I have a home here. I don't want to come back to a small town and get a job. Or a husband either, so don't start on that. I called so you won't worry if you try to call and I don't answer. Not sure how the cell phone service is over there. I'll be gone for ten days or so." Rebecca said goodbye and hung up the phone, dropping into the chair near her bed. No wonder she was a wet blanket. Her mother had raised her that way. She stared at her image in the full-length mirror, then called Gina. "I need your help. It's time for a change. Do you have some outfits I could borrow? I've decided I need a new look. Not sexy, but eye-catching. If I'm going to be stared at I might as well at least look damn good to the person staring."

"Yeah, I have a couple of miniskirts and a black mini-dress. What brought this on?"

"I realized that the wet blanket attitude was taught to me by my mother and I am rebelling. She demanded I cancel Europe and come home for my vacation because I was too innocent. She thinks I'm too stupid to come in out of the damn rain. Men will drug me or get me drunk. Yada, yada, etcetera, and blah, blah."

"Well, it's time for a crash course in being sexy, then. Why don't I toss some things in the car and come to your place after work tomorrow?"

"Okay." Rebecca agreed. Hanging up the phone, she ran her bath water and eased into the bubbles. *What was waiting for her in Germany? A man with a reputation. A man who looked like he was carved from the image of a Norse God. A man whose voice made her feel warm and at the same time, dangerous.* As she was drying off, the phone rang. Maybe it was her mom calling back. Or Gina with another idea. "It's your dime," she said with a laugh.

"Yes, it is." Page agreed. "Busy? You sound breathless."

"I just stepped out of the tub and darted for the phone."

"Are you dripping water on your carpet?" he teased.

"Nope. I am dripping on my tile kitchen."

"So, are you coming? On Friday?"

"Yes. I had my vacation approved and went shopping with my friend, Gina. She agreed it wouldn't do for me to get off the plane looking like your legal counsel."

"Shopping is good. I hope you saved some of that shopper's energy for Paris and Rome."

"I did."

"Did you watch my video?"

"Yes. Gina came over, and we split a bottle of wine and a bag of chips."

"And? Did you like it?"

"Well, you have to understand it isn't exactly my type of music."

"I don't play it around the house," he laughed. "And for the record, I don't dress like that either. I'm really a jeans and tee shirt type of guy. I called to tell you I got us tickets to see an opera in Vienna. I thought we could be tourists and look at all the music stuff while we're there."

"Really? You're going with me to the opera?"

Page laughed. "Does that surprise you? I'm not at all like my image in the videos."

"Oh good because that image is too sultry for me."

"I do own a tux for the occasion."

"I found the most perfect gown. It was even on sale. Also found pearl jewelry to match. Not real pearls, but they're pretty."

"Sales are always a good thing. I'm used to women who don't bother to even look at a price tag, much less look for a sale."

"I am the queen of bargain shopping," Rebecca laughed.

"So what else did you buy?"

"Gina tried to con me into a red leather mini skirt and a most outrageous top. Looks like a bra with sequins."

Page chuckled. "She sounds like a wild child."

"She is. But she's so good at her job it doesn't matter."

"Well, I can't fault her taste in clothes. Bra with sequins sounds great."

"I would look ridiculous in it. Or look like I was standing on a street corner."

Page frowned. If she were overweight or flat-chested, she would look bad, but it wasn't up to him to comment. "I want you to be comfortable here so don't let anybody pressure you. Wear whatever you want. I just plan on making sure you enjoy your stay. Hell, wear blue jeans. All women of all sizes look good in jeans."

"Good idea. I did get some slacks, skirts, and dresses. You know, I can't remember ever talking to a guy about buying clothes." She laughed. "Of course, usually my conversations with men are along the lines of what a judge has decreed he pays for whatever he is being sued for."

"I hope you have a bunch of new experiences while you're here. I'll FedEx your ticket in the morning."

"Okay."

"I'll say goodnight and let you go dry off. It's after three in the morning here, so it's my bedtime as well,"

Rebecca looked down at the puddle on the tile and laughed. "Good idea. Goodnight Page." Hanging up the receiver, she sat in the kitchen, aware of being content for the first time in many years. Page Harlow would definitely be a life-changing catalyst. Whether or not that was a good thing or a bad thing remained to be seen.

Page sat in his huge living room gazing at the landscape, visible from the picture window, reflected from the light of the moon hanging over the distant mountains. He liked the sound of her voice. Her laugh. Oh sure, she was probably plain as dry toast, but at least she wasn't an idiot. He wouldn't have to be the bad boy he pretended to be. He could be himself, and she would probably be just fine with that.

Chapter Seven

Page called each night during the week, and they talked easily as if they had been friends for years. Rebecca was less worried about the two of them getting along as she uncovered his real personality. He had only loved two women in his life. One was his mother, and he was devastated when she died. The other was Sasha Weeks, the mother of his son, Eric. Gina came by after work and Rebecca found herself laughing as she tried on some of Gina's more outlandish party clothes, settling on two mini-skirts which would probably never make it out of the suitcase. Rebecca had to reluctantly admit, they looked great on her, showing off her long, well-toned legs.

Gina drove her to the airport, where they dealt with Rebecca's sudden streak of nervousness by sitting in one of the airport lounges until it was time to go through the TSA checkpoint. Rebecca finally boarded the plane and located her seat in first class. She text-messaged Gina *'here goes nothing',* added a smiley face then turned off her phone. Despite her case of nerves, once she was airborne, she relaxed and eventually dropped off to sleep.

It was morning when they landed in Paris, and Rebecca remained in her seat until everyone else had passed her to exit the plane. As she followed the passengers into the airport, it occurred to her she had no further instructions. Wide-eyed she glanced around her. Hopefully, there was someone here to meet her. Maybe Page? An announcement stated passengers could be greeted after they passed through customs, so Rebecca headed in that direction. Well, at least she was in Europe. Even if everything went south, she was in Paris, and she could make do.

Finally, after Rebecca finished getting her passport stamped and had her one piece of luggage, she looked for an indication someone was waiting for her and noticed a man in a sports coat and tan slacks holding a sign with her name on it. Breathing a sigh of relief, she walked over to him and introduced herself.

The man exhaled as if he had been holding his breath. "I'm Tommy Madison of Madison Management. Welcome to Europe."

Rebecca took the man's extended hand and gripped it firmly. "Thank you."

Tommy tossed the sign in a trash can, and ran his fingers through his greying brown hair, trying not to stare at the woman. Page had convinced himself the winner was plain, probably with thick glasses, looking like a school teacher or accountant. He sure as hell wouldn't be ready for a traffic-stopping redhead. Tommy led her to a waiting car and escorted her to the area where the private jets were kept. "Page is very anxious to meet you. I understand the two of you have spoken several times on the phone." *There was an understatement,* Tommy thought. Page had called her every night during the week and talked about her as if they were old friends.

"Yes." She grinned at the man. "He doesn't seem as bad as his reputation."

"He's well-behaved when he's at home. Anna would box his ears if he acted out." He shook hands with a man in a pilot's uniform, then turned to smile at Rebecca. "This is Greg Jarvis, Page's pilot. He'll fly you to Germany and drive you to the castle. It's been a pleasure to meet you, Miss Morrison. I hope you enjoy your stay with us." Tommy handed Greg her luggage, shook her hand, and chuckled to himself to his car, then dialed Page's number on his cell phone.

Page answered on the first ring. "Well, your houseguest arrived," Tommy said, trying for a subdued tone.

"What does she look like?"

"Female. Two eyes, two ears, one nose, one mouth, not deformed, not fat."

"That's not much of a description, Tommy."

"She's… ah… well… hard to describe. No green teeth and she smells nice."

"Try." Page gritted his teeth and glared at the phone. It shouldn't matter. He loved the sound of her voice, the way she laughed. She was smart, witty, friendly, and ethical. So what did it matter what she looked like? Why did he care?

Tommy sighed. "Okay, how's this? She's a traffic-stopping redhead with the greenest eyes I have ever seen and could be Playboy of the Year material. Happy now?"

"You aren't going to tell me are you?" Page asked.

"I never could describe women, Page. I'm a married man, remember?" Tommy teased.

"Well, I'll be nice to her no matter what she looks like. She's very nice on the phone."

"I know. It'll be fine Page, honest." Tommy disconnected the call and laughed aloud. He watched as the doors closed on the jet.

Greg offered her his most charming smile. "So, you're the contest winner…."

"Only by default, Mr. Jarvis."

"What?"

"My assistant, Gina, entered my name. I had never heard of Mr. Harlow before that day."

Greg grinned. "Page must be doing something right. You're saying you had no idea?" he let the question hang.

"Not a clue."

"Well, this should prove to be an interesting ten days." He carried her luggage up the steps. "Would you like to sit up front or in the passenger area?" he asked motioning her to follow, watching her expression as she gazed around the luxurious interior. Since this was Page's home away from home, he had spared no expense in the furnishings. "Would you care for something to drink before we take off?"

"I don't drink much, Mr. Jarvis. A glass of cola would be nice, and yes, I'd love to sit up front."

Greg hid the grin as he went to the built-in bar and retrieved two bottles of Coke. Page had talked to him about the contest winner, confiding that the woman was probably plain with thick glasses. He had gone on to guess that she had been an ugly duckling in school, due to the fact she didn't date and was a workaholic. Greg assured him that the woman could have two noses and three ears and he would make her feel at ease on the flight. He lifted his plastic bottle in a toast. "Well, Miss Morrison here's to the next ten days of your life."

"Thanks. I'm really excited. I always wanted to come to Europe, and I had the money saved, but Dad had a stroke, and I took unpaid leave for three months, so goodbye vacation." She followed him to the cockpit and sat in the seat to his right. "Mr. Harlow offered to take me to the Louvre and an opera. I think it is terribly nice of him to put himself out like this for a stranger."

Greg spoke to the control tower, then they were airborne, and he watched her visibly relax in her seat. "So you like opera? Page does too, but you won't find that tidbit of information in his interviews." He laughed.

"I'm guessing there are a lot of tidbits he doesn't share with the press. I get the feeling he's not the man his fans and the press portray him to be."

"It's a Jekyll and Hyde thing with him. When he's on tour, he goes out of his way to create controversy and havoc. It's like a two-year-old acting out or something. But his fans expect it, and the media darlings live for his next face-off with the law." Greg grinned at her. "I've been his pilot and friend since the beginning. It's been one hell of a roller coaster ride. He and I attended private school together when we were teens."

"I researched all I could, and I have no doubt that's the truth. At first, I didn't want to come. I mean, technically I hadn't entered so legally Page could have picked someone else."

"Page doesn't always do what is expected." Greg shook his head and chuckled softly. "The word, 'technically' isn't in his vocabulary."

"I gathered that much. I always had a preconceived idea that castles were old, dirty, and drafty. I can't imagine anyone actually still living in one."

Greg laughed. "Anna would keel over in a dead faint if there was so much as a single dust bunny found in the living quarters. She worked for Page's grandfather, and sort of came with the castle. Wonderful German lady. Sturdy grandmother type and the one person who can keep Page in line. You'll like Anna."

"I thought Page got the castle from his father."

"Only legally. The old man was up in years and deeded it to his only son on the condition it be passed along to Page on his eighteenth birthday and Page lived at the castle anyway, so it was a natural thing to do. Page's father was a total jerk, but even he wouldn't defy the old man."

"Do you live in Germany? It must be difficult when he's on tour."

"I have a house near the Munich airport because I'm always on call. When we hit the tour trail, we stay in five-star hotels. Not a bad way to live for nine months. Great food, nice beds, maid service."

"I assume you aren't married."

Greg laughed. "The only person in our entourage who is married is Tommy. His wife is great. She says she looks forward to getting him out from under her feet."

They both lapsed into a comfortable silence as the jet cruised toward Germany. It wasn't a long flight and Rebecca watched as the German countryside came into view. The plane touched the runway and rolled to a stop. Greg gathered her luggage and escorted her to a midnight blue Mercedes Sedan.

Chapter Eight

Anna and Hans watched as the car approached. Page had taken off on Thunder, his ebony stallion saying it might be less intimidating to Miss Morrison if he were not the first person she met. He promised to be back in time for dinner after his guest had time to rest and refresh. Anna confided to her husband she thought Page was nervous about meeting the lady. Having a woman in the house who wasn't interested in him would be a unique experience for everyone. Care had been taken decorating the guest room with peach satin sheets and a matching silk comforter. There was a selection of easy-listening and classical CDs next to the state-of-the-art sound system.

Greg waved at them, then opened the passenger door causing Anna to inhale sharply when Miss Morrison stepped from the car. The woman was a beauty. Page would be shocked, considering he had psyched himself up to believe the worst. Anna met the young woman and enveloped her in a quick hug. "Welcome to Harlow's Castle. I'm Anna, Page Harlow's housekeeper. Let's get you settled in, shall we?"

Rebecca glanced around, then followed the woman through the double doors into the foyer. The room was as huge as she imagined a castle room would be, but it was spotless and homey with highly polished wood and slate grey stone. A tall, thin man took her luggage from Greg and carried it up the spiral winding stairway, and Anna ushered her toward the brightly lit kitchen nook. "Page said he would be back in time for dinner. He felt you might like to have a few moments to relax before the two of you met. He's very considerate like that. My husband, Hans, is taking your things to your guest room. I thought you might like a snack or beverage. I know airplane food is simply horrid. I've made some sausage croissants, and Page mentioned you drank coffee."

"That was very considerate. A croissant would hit the spot. It's nice to know there is another woman in the house," Rebecca said with a smile. Greg was right. Anna was the epitome of a German grandmother, straight out of a children's fairy tale.

Anna produced a plate of several croissants and a cup of coffee for Rebecca and poured a cup of tea for herself. She asked about the flight over, and Rebecca found herself relaxing in this woman's company. After the snack, Anna led Rebecca up the stairs to the guest room and pointed out the large bath area with the sunken tub and the huge walk-in closet. Then Rebecca found herself alone. The room was designed with a feminine touch. Off-white walls and pale blue carpeting. The windows were tall, letting in the sunlight. The bath was all inlaid gold and white marble with a wall of mirrors, causing Rebecca to frown at her unkempt appearance. She smiled when she saw the stack of music, choosing a CD of golden oldies. As Billy Idol sang of a white wedding, she washed her face, brushed her hair, touched up her make-up, and then changed into a knee-length green plaid skirt with a green silk top. Restless and not tired in the least, she left the room and returned to the kitchen. "Would it be okay if I stepped outside for a walk?"

Anna smiled. "Of course. There's a lovely garden area off to the side. Just follow the path to your left."

Rebecca stepped out into the sunlight, smiling as she took the path. The garden was beautiful. There was a small fountain with benches and a table, surrounded by flowers and shrubbery. She followed the trail and came to a barn. A man stood in a stable stall, brushing a black horse and speaking to the animal in soft German. Rebecca smiled as he turned and noticed her approach. He wore jeans and high boots, a gray body-hugging shirt, and a baseball cap. His eyes were hidden behind a pair of aviator sunglasses as he watched her.

"Hello," she said, stopping at the entrance to the barn.

"Hello. Are you lost? This is private property."

Rebecca stood still. "Page? Mr. Harlow?" The voice was the same one she'd heard on the phone for the past week.

"Rebecca? I would hug you, but I'm afraid I'm a bit dirty." He stared at her in disbelief. "Tommy called to tell me you were on the plane. I'm sorry I lost all track of time. I take it you met Anna and Hans? Are you settled in?"

"Yes, to all of the above. Changed my entire concept of castles."

"Looking at you changed my entire concept of legal researchers. You're definitely not what I was expecting." There was an understatement, he thought. She was so beautiful words couldn't describe her. "I'm sorry… that sounded seriously sexist, didn't it?"

She shrugged. "What were you expecting?"

He chewed on his lower lip for a moment, then grinned. "I always thought legal people were dull and drab. Plain. Thick glasses? Hell, I don't know. At least that's been my experience, and I've had a lot of experience with legal people."

"I am dull and drab with this awful red hair. Lucky for me, I didn't end up with a ton of freckles." She shoved a lock of red from her face, tucking it behind her ear.

Page was trying not to stare. *Did she really consider herself drab?* "I'm a terrible host. I just need to finish brushing Thunder, and I'll walk you back to the house or give you the garden tour."

"I passed a bench on the path. I'll just go sit there and get out of your way."

"Okay, wonderful. Give me about fifteen minutes." He didn't take his eyes off her until she disappeared around the curve in the walkway. She'd made herself out to be a loner, but he couldn't believe a woman as beautiful as she was didn't have a full calendar of dates. Probably lawyers and doctors. People who played chess and went to operas in New York. Okay, so they had somewhat different lifestyles. She was probably used to being romanced. Not really his style, but he could manage. The thought caused him to smile, and he wondered if her kisses would be tender or frantic. Hopefully, he'd find out soon enough.

Rebecca sat on the bench and smoothed her skirt nervously, crossing and uncrossing her legs at the ankles. Her heart pounded in her chest, and it wasn't from exertion. Photos and videos didn't do the man justice. My God, he was a work of art in human form. It had taken all her willpower not to stare at him from his boots to his cap. She closed her eyes, willing his image to go away but it lingered, a hot sensation in her stomach. Hard not to notice his smooth skin and full lips. "Take deep breaths, Ree. You will not succumb to him. No. You did not travel to Europe to experience sex, you came to see the sights. Be on guard." *Sex… the man oozed sex and desire. Not much left to her imagination as she'd soaked up the way his jeans clung to his thighs.* Opening her eyes, she focused her gaze on the garden. Roses of all colors seemed to be everywhere. Detecting movement, she watched as he came up the path toward her. He had removed the cap and the glasses, so his hair fell wildly around his face and across his broad shoulders while his body moved with the grace and power of a large cat. A very untamed, wild, cat. Forcing herself to look away, she pretended to study the roses as he sat down beside her. When he fixed her with a gaze the color of the summer sky, she couldn't help but notice his long golden lashes, which matched hair of silk. *Dear God, help me.*

"Sorry, I still smell like a horse. I thought you'd arrive and want to rest in your room after you unpacked. Otherwise, I'd have been showered and dressed for our formal introduction. Welcome to my home, Becca."

"I guess I was too nervous to rest. Visiting Europe has always been my dream." She caught herself nervously twisting her fingers and forced herself to sit still.

"I'm happy to make your dreams come true, Rebecca." He held her gaze until she broke eye contact. "You have eyes the color of emeralds. I guess you've been told that before."

"No, can't say that I have."

"Then the men in New York are blind." He grinned at her, displaying dimples on both cheeks.

"I spend five days a week in an office filled with attorneys, reading through law books, writing legal briefs. The only men I go anywhere with, outside of the office, are Kelly who's a paralegal, and Jerry, who's a doctor."

"So you only date those two?"

Rebecca chuckled. "No. Those two are an item, and they let me hang out with them sometimes. Dinner, movies, occasional drinks."

"Oh. Why don't you date? Tell me if I'm too nosey, but I can't imagine men not asking you out. I would think you'd have a full social calendar."

Rebecca realized she needed to answer him, to set the record straight about her attitude toward men in general. "Truth is, I don't date because I choose not to. Men tend to believe that paying for dinner or a movie makes you their property, to manhandle and they hate being turned away without the expected kiss or an invite to spend the night. I am saving myself for my wedding. Now, I know that might seem terribly old-fashioned, but that's the way it is. I was raised in a very strict home with high expectations." *Never mind what a playboy footing the bill for ten days in Europe might expect. Oh God, had she made a mistake coming here?*

"At twenty-seven you're waiting for your wedding night to have…" his voice trailed off.

"Yes. So, you see, that's why I think you would want to ship me off to the Hilton."

He surprised her by laughing and burying his face in his hands. Finally, he looked at her and shook his head. "No."

"No?" She stared at him as if he had just confessed he was from Mars. "No?"

"No. I will not ship you off to the Hilton because you won't share my bed. I told you over the phone, I have a book filled with women who would. To be honest Rebecca, I have never had a woman just as a friend, one who likes to converse and play chess. One who can just sit with me on this bench not giving a damn that I look like crap and smell like horse shit and sweat. Unless you choose the Hilton, I would like for us to spend this time together. As a matter of fact, I solemnly vow to you that unless you specifically request it, I won't even attempt to seduce you."

"Unless I specifically…" It was her turn to laugh. "You think you're all that, don't you?"

"I never said I wouldn't hope. I only said you would have to make the first move. I'm not made of stone. Deal?"

"Deal," Rebecca said, wondering if she was strong enough to keep her own promise. Just sitting next to him caused her to feel dizzy with an emotion she didn't want to acknowledge. It would be up to her to make sure the deal was kept.

"Come on. Let's go back to the house. I need a shower," he said, offering her his hand.

Chapter Nine

Page kissed Anna on the cheek. "Look who I found wandering around the castle grounds. We should lock her up in the dungeon as a spy. Can't be too careful these days."

Anna smacked Page with a dishrag. "Off with you! Don't come back to my kitchen until you smell human."

Page winked at Rebecca. "See how horribly I'm treated in my own home? Fine. I'm just going to go soak my head." He took the stairs two at a time, disappearing out of sight, and the sound of his laughter faded as a door slammed on the second floor.

Anna poured Rebecca a cup of coffee, fixed herself one, and sat at the table shaking her head and smiling. "He's a hellion sometimes. Normally he showers and changes clothes in the barn before he comes inside. When he goes on the road, he hires a stable boy to tend the horses and barn. There's a small cottage attached for living quarters."

"I only saw one huge black horse."

"Thunder is his favorite, but there are two more. Do you ride?"

"Never tried to. I'd probably fall off."

"Nothing to it. If you wanted to try, Page could put you on Jenny. She's the smallest and as gentle as they come. He wouldn't let you get hurt."

Page entered the room, dressed in a light blue body-hugging polo shirt and stone-washed jeans, his damp hair draped across his shoulders. "Did I interrupt a serious discussion?"

"We were discussing your horses. Miss Morrison has never ridden one. I told her you could saddle Jenny for her if she wanted to give it a try," Anna said, handing Page a bottle of Lowenbrau from the refrigerator. "Miss Morrison, would you care for a German beer instead of coffee?" Anna asked.

"Sure. That would be great. Please, call me Rebecca."

"Very well, Rebecca." Anna handed her a bottle. "Now, both of you get out of my kitchen, so I can start dinner. Page can give you a tour of the rooms. I'll let you know when the food is ready. Now go."

Page laughed and nodded toward the great room. "We've been evicted. Come on. Can't have you getting lost, now can I?" He guided her through the area she saw when she arrived, into a room with floor-to-ceiling bookcases. A white grand piano sat to one side, offset by a wall of plate glass. A sofa and two chairs faced a massive fireplace with a flat-screen TV above it. Thick forest green carpet covered the floor, accented by several oriental rugs.

"Wow. If I lived here, I'd never leave this room. Look at the view!" Rebecca stood at the window, looking at a lake in the distance, the mountains farther away. A pathway of stone went from the garden area toward the lake.

Page was enjoying the view standing near him. Did she have any idea how ravishing she was? The sheer look of innocence surrounded her like a halo. He fought the overpowering desire to pull her into his arms and kiss her until neither of them could breathe. "There's more to see," he said softly, reaching for her hand.

The next room was his office. One wall was covered in photographs and news articles while another held his framed platinum albums and various awards. The desk was light wood, the walls a canary yellow. There was a file cabinet, computer, and large monitor. There was one photo in a gold frame, of a small boy sitting on Page's lap. "Is that your son, Eric?" she asked.

"Yes. Taken here on his second birthday. Sasha was on a photo shoot, so I was lucky enough to have him for an entire week."

"Does she give you a hard time with visitation?"

"No. After all the papers were signed, and the dust settled, we managed to be civil for Eric's sake. She's a good mother or tries to be. She has a nanny who dotes on Eric. It wasn't Eric she had an issue with, it was me. She didn't want to be married, and I put my foot down. I can be an ass at times, but I wanted a wife and a family. I wanted her to live here and cut back on her workload and I would cut back on my tours. Sasha hated this castle and most of the surrounding country."

"Any hope of getting back together?" Rebecca asked.

"None. I discovered she was dating me more because of the publicity than any true feelings. We made a stunning couple, and it was good for her career." He shrugged, "It didn't hurt mine either; well not until I fell in love like a total fool."

"Glad you worked yourself out of your blue funk. I read where you did a downward spiral for a while."

"I'd like to say I learned from my past. It would take one hell of a woman to get through the wall." He shoved his hands in the pockets of his jeans, to keep from running his hands through her hair. It was difficult not to imagine the fiery curls spread across his black satin pillow. *Damn.*

"Love 'em and leave 'em. I read that too. You have quite the playboy reputation."

"I often wonder if there's someone out there for me. Maybe not right now, but later in life." He perched on the edge of his desk.

"I've wondered that myself Page. I decided I'll take each day as it comes. I believe coming here was a big step toward allowing myself to venture outside the lines. My mother expected me to cancel Europe because I was too innocent and would be taken advantage of by some man. She wants me to come home, get a job, and a husband, and give her grandbabies. It's what women were created for, so she says. She even has a list of her choices for her son-in-law." Her gaze slid over Page's physique, and her mouth went dry. *How did he get those jeans on, she wondered.* Their eyes met for a second, and she quickly turned to look at the photos on the wall.

"That's a bit harsh," Page chuckled. "Sounds like the Dark Ages. Or… a Jim Jones cult."

"I have a career I enjoy, a home to call mine and I'm okay with that. I don't need to depend on a man for anything. She just doesn't get it."

"It's your life Rebecca, not hers. Do what makes you happy. Like is too short to conform to what others want."

Rebecca sipped her beer. "I'll drink to that."

"Ready to see my dungeon?"

"Sure."

Chapter Ten

As he led her into the elevator, she laughed out loud. "I know this did not come with the original castle. I can't believe you had an elevator installed."

"I can tell you installing it was a bitch. Of course, so were the rest of the renovations I had done. All the wiring for the computer, the flat screen, and here…" he motioned as the doors opened, "This is my studio. Speakers, microphones, soundproofing, drums, keyboard, recording equipment. The works. My fitness center is also down here. Weights, treadmill, torture machines, steam room, dry sauna, and a Jacuzzi which seats six although it's usually just me. I value my privacy, so this area is usually off-limits. Everything you see required a lot of rewiring and plumbing. And, there's a full bathroom and a bar."

"Huge open spaces," she commented following him from each piece of equipment to the next. He opened a set of sliding doors to enter the fitness area. "And here I thought all those muscles were natural," she teased.

"Oh, the lady noticed my muscles," he said with a grin.

"Hard to miss on your video. Plus there was that centerfold Gina showed me. I definitely noticed." *She was indeed aware of them now; much more than she should.*

"Well. You weren't what I expected. Wait, I already said that. See? You have me repeating myself already." He crossed to the bar and fixed himself a bourbon on the rocks. Rebecca was still sipping on her beer.

"Dare I ask exactly what you expected? I mean other than a plain Jane type."

"Yeah, I guessed you would be plain, with glasses and hair pulled back into a bun or piled on top of your head. Honestly, I thought the reason you didn't date was that you were drab and dull. Maybe chubby or rail thin. I didn't know what to expect, so I didn't concentrate on your appearance. I liked your voice. Your intelligence, your humor, and your common sense. I liked that you had ethics. In the crowd I run with, I don't see much of that."

"Well, I wasn't sure what to expect either. I knew about your reputation. I didn't want to come, truth be told. But I called my mother and when she forbade me to come to Europe something just snapped. It finally hit me that I got my ice-maiden attitude from her. The fact I always played it safe. Other than the day I announced I was leaving my small hometown and moving to New York to attend college, I never rebelled in my life. This trip is the Godzilla of rebellion for me." She looked into his eyes and slowly exhaled. "You… are the Godzilla of rebellion for me, Page Harlow."

"But you will still want your white wedding, picket fence, and a puppy. A husband who comes home each night. "

"Yes, I do. I hold wedding vows very high. I don't want to be a statistic. Divorced. Single mother."

"I really want the same. Unfortunately in my world, with my lifestyle, I don't see it in my future. Hell. I barely see the same female twice. Most of them don't see me as a person. I'm an object, someone they can have for a few hours at most." He laughed, but it sounded forced. "And yes, I really do have a black book and a rating system. Great sex on a scale of one to ten and all that."

Rebecca perched on the bar stool. "Don't you ever get tired of it?"

"Oh hell yes. But that's the image that makes me millions. I'm not blowing my money, so at some point, I'll be able to fade away into the sunset. Maybe do a reunion tour when I'm sixty-five. The rest of the band have decent savings and stocks because we aren't stupid enough to think this roller-coaster will last."

Rebecca nodded. "Sometimes, late at night, I wonder if what I want is even attainable in today's society, and if it is, will I be happy even if I get it? Yes, I want the marriage, the house in the suburbs, two cars, two kids, and a picket fence so to speak, but another part of me still wants the challenge of a career. I'm terribly independent which might present a challenge. What would be the point of getting a law degree and not use it? And if I was married and working, would I still end up divorced?"

Page discarded her empty beer bottle and leaned on the bar next to her, shoving his hair away from his face. "I don't think life comes with guarantees, Becca. I really loved Sasha. I stopped sleeping around and gave her a ring, which she was delighted with. When she said she was pregnant, it never occurred to me she wouldn't want to get married. I never asked her to give up her career. At first, I thought it was hormones or whatever happens to women when they get pregnant. But while I was planning a wedding, she was talking to an attorney. With her, it was all about image and money. In the end, I gave her everything she asked for without a fight." His cell phone beeped, and he fished it out of his pocket, glanced at the text, and then put it away. "Anna says dinner will be ready in about ten minutes."

"Dinner. My body doesn't know if it's time to eat or to sleep. I don't wear a watch except at the office, so I don't know what time it's even supposed to be." She laughed. "However, I'm on vacation, so I don't care what time it is at the moment."

"Well, when your system decides it's time to sleep, then you go to sleep. No alarms so whenever you wake up, we'll take it from there. Fair enough?" He guided her back to the elevator and toward the dining room.

Dinner started with a salad and warm fresh baked bread and continued with cooked chicken, carrots, onions, celery, and potatoes, served in a clay pot called a Romertopf. Anna explained how the clay pot sealed in all the natural juices and flavor eliminating the need for oil or seasoning. The woman beamed with pride when Rebecca expressed delight at the taste of everything she ate. After Anna placed the German chocolate cake on the sideboard, she nodded to Page. "If you don't need me for a while, I'm going to go have dinner with Hans now. I'll be back to clear the table later, so just leave it when you're done."

"Take your time," Page said softly. Anna smiled at both of them and hurried away, happy to see Page enjoying himself again. She hurried away, toward her part of the castle. "They've been married forty-something years and still have a great relationship. It gives me hope for humanity because I can see the way they look at each other, even after all these years."

"Same with my parents. Well, not forty years but still together."

"I never really saw my father much. My mother was his mistress. His wife, Lady Harlow was in England, and refused to relocate to Norway for the two years he was there. He didn't divorce her even though he claimed he loved my mother. Lords and Ladies don't divorce, even when there are lovers and other children. Oh, don't get me wrong, we were very well cared for. When his wife died suddenly, I thought he would come for us, but he didn't. However, he arrived when my mother took ill and promised her he would care for me as far as education and such. When she died, he sent for me and promptly dropped me into a private school." Page waved his hand as if to dismiss the memory. "Ah, but my grandfather Harlow was a very colorful character. I came here to spend a summer and couldn't get enough. He was everything my father wasn't. Wicked sense of humor, and loved his horses and his home. We would ride like the wind, full gallop across the fields, and hunt quail. Or swim in the lake. He allowed me to climb trees and get dirty. I finally came to live here after I was expelled from four different schools. Gramps offered, and Daddy dear couldn't unload me fast enough. I miss him a lot. He would have liked you. Of course, he would have probably pinched you on the butt too." Page laughed as he cut into the cake.

Chapter Eleven

After dinner, they returned to the library and stood in front of the picture window, gazing at the setting sun, as it dropped behind the mountains in the distance. She looked up at him after a few minutes of silence. "Is it hard to leave here when you go on tour?"

"Yes and no," he answered softly. "I really do love it here. I enjoy my private time and being alone, not having to answer to anyone. But, on the flip side, I love the energy and the excitement of performing. To walk onto a stage like Madison Square Gardens and hear the crowd react… it's a definite head rush."

"How many people go with you from place to place?"

"Well, there's the four of us, plus Tommy and Greg. Each of the guys has a personal assistant to help with their equipment. We usually have ten semis with things like our lights and soundboard, plus a million miles of cables and cords. We have five members of the sound team, three more for special effects. Four for wardrobe. Anywhere from twenty to thirty roadies who do anything and everything to set up the stage and break it down. Ten personal security people go with us, plus we hire local police. Our merchandising team takes care of the tee shirts, photos, and all the goodies people buy."

"That's some serious payroll."

"Tommy handles almost everything. He has his own staff. I have a personal assistant who is on call if I'm awake. Her name is Ashley. I can tell you she's worth her weight in gold."

"Doesn't she get jealous of your harems?"

Page laughed out loud. "Ashley is an employee. Not a girlfriend. Never has been. She's more like a sister to me and the band. She keeps us organized. I have no idea how mind you, only that she does. You'll like her."

"When would I have an opportunity to meet her?"

"Well, unless after ten days you decide you never want to see me again, my tour kicks off in three months in Madison Square Gardens. I would hope you would come. I know someone who can get you backstage." He winked at her, causing her to burst out laughing.

"Well, I'll have to check my calendar. I might be busy, you know, reading War and Peace or something. It might be the night I need to bathe my pet goldfish." It was her turn to grin mischievously at him and wink.

"Well, I suppose a clean goldfish would be really important. For now, though, I think you might want to go to bed." He chuckled when she arched a brow. "Alone, most likely. Whenever you wake up, we'll start planning our European invasion. The opera tickets are for three nights from now, so we'll have to plan around that. And you mentioned the Louvre. Any place else on your must-see list?"

"Monte Carlo. I don't know why. Maybe because I probably shouldn't want to go where there's gambling but remember, I'm rebelling."

"Okay. I love Monte Carlo. I will do my very best to assist in your rebellion. Oh, before I forget, at some point, we will need to sit down for an interview."

"Why?"

"The media is always interested in my life, God only knows why. This contest was a hit. I'm guessing you had no clue it was the talk of at least three magazines. Hype from my manager to get me back in the spotlight before the tour. Unless you want them to use their vivid imaginations as to how we are spending ten days, you might want to make an appearance to set the record straight. Totally up to you."

"And where is this chat supposed to take place? When?"

"Where ever and whenever you choose, Rebecca. I'd suggest somewhere around day five or six."

"Add that to the long list of things I've never done before, I guess." She shrugged. "For right now, I guess I am a bit sleepy."

Page took her hand and led her up the stairway to her room. "You know I want to kiss you goodnight," he said softly. "I won't, but I want to."

She stood there, gazing up at him. "Why not?"

"Why not… what?"

"Why wouldn't you kiss me goodnight?"

"I don't want you to feel uncomfortable. Or to think I am trying to take advantage of your jet lag. There's a six-hour time difference."

"I wouldn't think that."

He traced her lips with the tip of his finger, then slowly lowered his mouth to hers. When her fingers caressed the back of his neck, he pressed harder and wrapped her in his arms. Releasing her mouth, he smiled down at her. "Another item for your list of rebellion?"

"Hmmm. You have a very sensual mouth Page Harlow."

"So do you, Rebecca Morrison. So do you. Now, take your sexy body out of my sight so we can both get some sleep. Whenever you wake up, come find me."

"Okay. Goodnight Page." She opened the door to her room, closed it, and exhaled. "Good God," she sighed, crossing the thick carpeting to the bathroom. Well, she didn't look any different because she had been kissed by the Playboy rock star, she mused with a grin. He certainly had a great mouth, even though he hadn't kissed her the way she had expected. She washed her face and undressed for bed, easing between the soft satin sheets. What had she expected? A hard possessive kiss to be sure, filled with desire and passion. Instead, he had held back. Well, that's what she wanted, wasn't it?

Page stood in the hallway staring at the closed door, then turned slowly and walked back downstairs. *Damn.* "Be careful what you wish for because you just might get it," he said aloud as he stepped outside into the garden. Here was a woman who was not only beautiful head to toe but intelligent, witty, and unspoiled. A woman who seemed to like him for himself instead of his status or his money. What in the hell was he supposed to do now? She was everything he had ever wanted, and he couldn't have her. She wanted a white wedding, a husband who was home at night, a home in the suburbs, a fenced yard, kids, and a puppy. He would go stark crazy living like that. Nine to five. Was there a compromise? He returned to his office and powered up his computer.

An hour later he turned off the computer and poured himself a bourbon over ice. Give or take with stocks and properties, he guessed he was worth a little under a billion dollars. After the tour, he would be worth more. Royalties would continue whether he worked or not. There was always the option to manage other singers. He could write music for others. That could be a compromise if need be. Not precisely a nine-to-five office job but he wouldn't be living on a bus or in hotels for nine months. He sighed and downed his drink, then headed for the kitchen.

Anna was just finishing up the dishes. "Page Harlow, if you've come to make a mess, I'll box your ears," she said with a grin. "You look as though you might want a piece of cake."

"That would be nice. I also want some advice."

Anna cut him a slice and then cut one for herself, placing both of them on paper plates. "Does this have to do with our guest?"

"I think I might want to marry her."

"What would be your reasoning? Not saying you shouldn't. I mean, from what I've seen she is well-mannered. Intelligent. Ladylike, to be sure."

"Maybe because she isn't what I am used to. She doesn't even care who I am or what I am. Had no clue who I was. She's intelligent.

Charming. Can hold a real conversation, with real words. Loves opera and plays chess."

"Well, there is all that in her favor. But Page, she has a career a continent away. Parents. Friends. I don't believe she would accept a marriage proposal at this point. Besides, you never really know a person at first meeting. Finish out the ten days first and then see how you feel. More importantly, you need to see how she feels about you after ten days."

Page laughed. "Yeah, there is that. She may want to feed me to the wolves after a week. I know her idea of marriage is a home, a husband who is home at night, kids, and a puppy. I just ran all my financials, and it isn't as if I need to go on any more tours after this one. So, I could be home, wherever the hell home would be." He shrugged and finished his cake. "I guess we'll just wait and see how it goes. Thanks, Anna." He put his plate in the trash, kissed the woman on her forehead, and headed for his bedroom. It was still early, compared to his usual bedtime, but he planned on riding Thunder for a few minutes before she was up. *Love at first sight? Was that even possible or was it because she represented something he had convinced himself was unattainable?*

Chapter Twelve

Rebecca woke up and lay perfectly still beneath the satin sheets, taking in her surroundings. Lots of windows, letting in natural sunlight, but there were also heavy drapes on each side to block out the light if a person wanted to sleep late. The furniture looked like a set from a fairy tale, maybe Cinderella. The only thing missing was the canopy over the bed. The thought caused her to chuckle. Where was Prince Charming? Still asleep or out on his horse? Hell, what time was it anyway? What did he have on the agenda for the day? Where to go? What to see? They had a tour to plan. Vienna, Monte Carlo, and Paris. No telling where else.

Thinking about him brought back the confusion she felt last night as he walked away from her. The kiss was not what she had expected from someone with his reputation. It had been so gentle she wondered if he thought she would shatter like glass. His explanation made sense. The six-hour time difference was brutal to her system, and she had dropped off into a dead sleep the minute her head hit the pillows.

She eased out of bed, and into the bath area, taking a quick shower. Choosing a pair of tan slacks and a matching clingy knit sweater, she pulled her hair back at the nape of her neck and headed down the stairs.

Anna wasn't in the kitchen, but there was a pot of coffee on the warmer, next to an empty cup and two muffins. She poured her coffee, put one muffin on a napkin, and headed outside toward the garden and the stable.

Page was scooping feed into a large container for the horses, his back to her. She took a few minutes to enjoy looking at him. It occurred to her she couldn't remember ever actually admiring the male anatomy before. How many other things would she add to her list of experiences? More kisses? The comfort of his arms around her? What if Gina was right? What would happen if opposites did attract? Especially now, knowing they did have things in common such as opera and chess. Classical music. Weren't those all the qualities she listed when thinking about the perfect Mr. Right?

Page caught movement from the corner of his eye and turned, surprised to find her leaning in the doorway, nibbling a muffin, holding a cup of coffee. "Good morning. I thought you'd still be asleep since it's around three am in New York."

"Just woke up."

"Want a riding lesson? I can saddle Jenny. We don't have to go far. I'd love to show you the property. Maybe ride to the lake?"

"Sure, why not? Add it to the things I never did before."

Rebecca watched as he stroked a smaller, tan horse, then gently saddled it, all the while whispering as if reassuring her she was safe. He repeated the process with a more massive horse, lighter than Jenny. "This is Dante, Jenny's brother. Jenny could never keep up with Thunder, plus Thunder just returned from his run." Page entered a room off the side, and Rebecca followed, surprised to find herself in what seemed to be a small cottage. He chose several beers, and a pack of crackers and scooped up some carrots tossing it all in a canvas bag. "Snacks. Picnic at short notice," he grinned.

Mounting Jenny wasn't as difficult as she had envisioned and they headed out at a slow pace. Rebecca tried to imitate his posture and finally found a comfortable position. Page instructed her to guide Jenny with the reins. She watched him, fascinated by his poise and command of the animal. As if they were one. "Page, how much of this is your land?"

He tilted his head and pointed toward the distant mountains. "I own the lake and the foothills beyond, but not the biggest of the three mountains. Not sure as far as acreage goes but suffice to say it's a lot of property."

"Looks like the setting for the sound of music."

"That's Austria. You can see it the day after tomorrow. Rivers, lakes, gardens. Beautiful country. I will not take you to the concentration camps or the prisons. I know it is history, but it was an ugly time in humanity."

Rebecca nodded. "Yes, it was."

They arrived on the other side of the lake and Page helped her dismount, circling her waist in his hands as she wrapped her arms around his shoulders. Somehow, being in his arms seemed comforting, and she just stood still, gazing into his blue eyes. Slowly, she parted her lips, her fingers curling in his windswept hair. It was an offer he accepted, lowering his mouth to hers, feeling the warmth of her breath as if she was holding it, and waiting for his decision. Kiss followed kiss as he pulled her into his embrace. He nuzzled her throat and an earlobe, pleased when she followed suit as if allowing herself to experiment with new emotions. At long last, she stepped back, and he released her, although she still gazed at him.

"Page… I'm not sure what just happened."

He arched a brow and offered a slight grin, "Regrets?"

"Not even a small one. This brings to mind conversations I had with Gina. She wanted to play devil's advocate. What if opposites attract? I assured her it wasn't remotely possible…"

"Opposites as in you and me?"

"Our lifestyles." She chewed her bottom lip. "Wow. I don't even know where I planned on going with this train of thought. You confuse me, Page Harlow."

He guided her to sit on the grass while he retrieved the bag of snacks. Dante and Jenny had walked to the water to drink, and he opened each of them a beer and a pack of crackers. "You've come to realize I am not the criminal pervert the press makes me out to be. Hopefully, you are realizing I am well-bred, a man of my word, and honorable. So, that being the case, Becca, we aren't so opposite after all. I had a similar discussion with Tommy. I told him I wanted to meet a woman who could string a sentence together, one who appreciated opera and chess. I wanted to have a relationship, not a one-night stand, with someone like Janet, Tommy's wife. And, here we are. Now remains the question as to what do we do about it?"

"Somewhat of an unexpected dilemma, isn't it?"

"Well, let's take it a day at a time, shall we?" Page said, sipping his beer. "Although I do need to make a confession."

"Okay."

"After you went to bed, I had another piece of cake with Anna. I told her I thought I might want to marry you." He held up his hand as she opened her mouth. "She suggested we at least give it a few days, in case we decided we hated each other. And she reminded me, that you had a career, a home, friends, and family a continent away. And I have a nine-month tour commitment. You want a husband, house, kids, puppy…"

Rebecca grinned at him. "What? You don't like puppies?"

His head jerked up, his mouth opened and closed several times, and then he dropped on his back in the grass, laughing hysterically. Her laughter joined his, finally subsiding into fits of giggles. Page wiped tears from his cheeks, still chuckling. "That caught me off guard."

"Sorry. It just popped out without warning. I've always been so serious and straight-laced. This trip is definitely a terrible influence on me, Page Harlow. Doing things I've never done, saying things I've never said, thinking things I shouldn't think…" She lifted her gaze to his as she leaned onto one elbow and added, "Wanting things I shouldn't want…"

"Serious territory, Becca. Anything in particular?"

"I'm twenty-seven, Page and I have never been kissed the way it is described in books and movies. When I listened to Gina describe her dates, deep inside I wondered if there was something wrong that I've not even had the inkling to feel that way. Now I realize it's the way I was raised. Everything is sinful and evil. Touching, kissing, wanting… it's been drilled into my head that nice girls don't do those things. Then, last night, when I went to bed, it occurred to me there was nothing wrong with what I felt. What was wrong was how I was raised."

Page moved closer, laying side by side. He casually caressed her hip, trailing his hand down her outer thigh to her knee and back to her waist, tracing the seam of her slacks. "I will not take advantage of our friendship." When she nodded, he trailed his fingertips upward, caressing the soft knit material, returning to the hem of the sweater.

Her lips parted, and she inched toward him. A surge of excitement shot through her at his touch. Like a hungry baby bird, she hunted his mouth, her hands curled in the silkiness of his hair. This kiss was nothing like the chaste one from last night. This one took control, and possession, demanding her submission. When his tongue eased between her lips, they opened eagerly, imitating his moves. Her breath came in gasps, and her heart pounded against her ribs. He inched her sweater upward, exposing her creamy skin and silk bra. When he lifted his lips from hers, she whimpered at the loss, only to exhale in surprise when his mouth pressed against her ribcage. He teased her with feathery kisses then stopped, his gaze returning to her lips. "That… Becca… is how you are supposed to react to a man's attention if you care for him. Nothing evil or wrong about it, was there?"

Rebecca took a long swallow of her beer, her eyes never leaving his. "Oh, my God."

"What did you feel?"

"It was beyond anything I could have imagined. Beyond anything Gina described."

"So much for evil, sinful, and wrong, I guess. That is the way two people should respond when there are feelings. Not just sex. Emotion. That's where the difference lies. Any two people can have sex. It could be considered a full-contact sport. You don't even have to have anything in common other than lust. Trust me, I'm an expert on that subject. It's what my bad-boy reputation is based on. Oh, don't get me wrong, I'm not one to complain." He grinned at her playfully. "But late at night, after the party is over, I end up alone, wishing for what I can't have."

"Which is what?"

"A woman who likes me for me. Someone who shares the same likes and dislikes. Opera. Chess. Classical music. Enjoying each other's companionship. Someone like you." He stood up and reached for her hand. "We should get back to the house and start our tour plans before I drop to one knee and propose."

Unsure of what to say, whether he was teasing or not, she allowed him to help her mount Jenny, and they made the return trip in silence, her mind racing in a thousand directions.

At the stable, Page showed her the proper way to brush Jenny and helped her reward the horse with the carrots. After both animals were cared for, they walked hand in hand back to the house. "We both need a shower," Page said softly, "so I'll meet you back in the library when you're finished."

"Okay."

"Then we can decide on our destinations, what to see."

"Sounds like a plan," she agreed.

In her room, Rebecca peeled away her clothes, laughing as she picked grass from her sweater. After a quick shower, she chose a pair of snug-fitting black slacks and a red cotton tee shirt.

Page was sitting at the piano, dressed in jeans and a tee shirt with his own picture on it, from the last tour. "I had a thought," he stated as his fingers trailed across the keys. "After lunch, are you up for a drive into Munich? It's the closest town to here. Lots to see. We could tour Nymphenburg Palace and have a nice dinner. The view of the palace is breathtaking. Flowers, water, walking paths. Food, beer, more beer, large zoo. Let's not forget Hard Rock Café. Did I mention beer?" He stopped playing, resting his hands on the keys.

"Sounds like a perfect start." Rebecca considered sitting next to him at the piano but decided on the overstuffed sofa by the window instead.

"Okay. I originally thought of us sightseeing by train this week. But, even though it's a great way to get from place to place, I'm leaning toward just driving. That way we can go at our own pace and can come back here between sights, so not as much packing and unpacking clothes. Plus there is always the possibility of someone seeing us going into a hotel and your pristine reputation would be flushed down the toilet. Once a photo hits the news, trust me, there is no way to undo it and the more you deny it, the guiltier you seem. By car, we can stop if we see something of interest or want a sandwich, a souvenir, or a stroll through a park. The final reason is less chance of me being followed by fans and photographers. On a train, it would take one person to notice, and mayhem follows. Trust me that is not for the faint of heart." He got up and crossed to a bookshelf. "Tour guide."

"I'm open to suggestions, Page."

He brought the book over to the sofa, dropping down next to her, opening the book to the center. "Venice is about five hours from here. Back here for the night and then out the door to Vienna which is about a four-hour drive, give or take. Pack your gown and my tux. We can see the sights, have food, and more sights, and then rent a room to change into our nice stuff. Enjoy the opera and a stroll through the streets, back to the room to change back into normal clothes. Then, maybe a break for a day, here. Game of chess?"

"Wow. I see you've given this some thought."

"Yep. Although anything is open to change. Driving makes it flexible. Continuing the tour would be the drive to Monte Carlo which takes about seven hours, then we would need to stay over and head to Paris. Otherwise, you'll miss out on a lot of the art tours in Paris. And who knows how long you might want to shop? Plus, it's a good place for the interview. Then we return here, and Greg can fly us to Norway if you'd like to see my childhood home. Then back here until your flight to New York. Option number two would be to get Greg to fly us from here to Monte Carlo, then to Paris, then to Norway. I can rent a car at the airport near Monte Carlo for the day. We'll figure it out." He curled a strand of her hair around his finger and grinned at her. "You can always call your boss and ask for an extra week's vacation."

"That would go over like a ton of bricks," she chuckled.

"I can always hope," he said with a dramatic sigh.

Page flipped through the thick book on places to see in Europe, touching on bits of history as he went. Castles everywhere seemed to be a favorite tour specialty. River cruises came in second. She glanced up at him, contented to be sitting on the sofa, close enough to touch, yet knowing he wouldn't. *Unless she asked for it.* The thought came from nowhere, startling her into almost gasping aloud. Saved by Anna leaning in the doorway announcing lunch, she breathed deep and followed Page into the kitchen, where sandwiches, cheeses, and fruit sat on the small table.

Page retrieved each of them a beer and smiled at Anna. "You get the night off to spend hanging out with Hans. I'm taking Becca to Munich for the evening."

"That sounds lovely. Rebecca, make sure you wear comfortable shoes. Lots of walking, if you plan on seeing the sights. Take lots of pictures. The palace is stunning, especially at sunset."

"I'm so excited. New York is going to be so boring after all this." Rebecca said.

"I'm sure you will have plenty of happy memories to take back to New York," Anna nodded.

Chapter Thirteen

Rebecca decided to wear the yellow dress Gina had talked her into for the evening in Munich. She brushed her hair until it cascaded around her shoulders in waves, added a light floral scent, and after studying her reflection in the full-length mirror picked up her small handbag and headed downstairs.

Page exhaled as he watched her take each step. She looked like a princess going to her first ball. He offered her a playful grin. "Wow. Love the look. If you dress like this at work, you can probably get a judge to just agree to whatever you're asking for. I still can't grasp that you don't date. Lucky me."

"Lucky you? Why?" she asked as she followed him out the front doors, where a midnight blue Mercedes convertible sat in the drive.

"Because I hate competition. I know it's selfish of me, but I don't want to think about you with anyone else."

"Is that a new pickup line?" she laughed.

He turned and gazed into her eyes, a slight arch to his blonde brow. "No. My pick-up lines are usually short and mostly profane. When I'm not on tour, I'm not looking to pick up anyone. I keep to myself and my music." He opened the car door for her and chuckled as she slid in. "Nice legs, babe. Is that better?"

She waited until he had settled in, fastened his seat belt, and started the car before she punched him in the arm. "Toad," she teased. The move caught him off guard causing him to laugh out loud.

They rode in silence until he eased the car onto the main road. Traffic was light, and the sun was bright in the blue sky. He glanced over at her as she took in the scenery. "You do know if you kiss a toad he becomes a handsome prince, don't you?"

Rebecca arched a brow. "Says who?" she teased.

"Why… says the toad of course."

"Oh, silly me. The Toad. Of course."

"Or," he teased, "the lady becomes a girl frog, and she and the toad live happily ever after under a large mushroom. Or wherever toads live."

When she stopped laughing, she shook her head. "You are a piece of work, Page Harlow; toad prince of Germany." When he reached for her hand, she submitted and her breath caught in her throat as he curled his fingers through hers. It seemed too good to be real, and as Rebecca watched the breathtaking scenery, it occurred to her this had been the happiest she had felt in many years. Here was a man who could have almost any woman with a nod of his head, yet he was taking her to dinner, holding her hand, and being a total gentleman. *Exactly what she would expect from Mr. Right.*

He glanced at her, curious as to what thoughts were running through her mind. "I think we should just park the car in town and wander through the streets like tourists. Grab a beer and pretzel or pastry and just take in the sights. We can spend as much time as we want walking through the English Garden, touring the palace, and then hitting the Chinese Tower for dinner. Maybe do some shopping?"

"Wait," she said with a confused look. "English Garden and Chinese Tower? Really?"

"Cross my heart."

"If you say so," she said shaking her head.

"Munich is a fascinating city. The English Gardens are huge. Well, you have to take into consideration that the palace we're visiting is a half mile from one end to the other, built over several hundred years. Each Bavarian king added his own touch and even smaller palaces and buildings. Plus if you want to do some serious shopping they have a monster of a shopping area."

"I always pictured Germany as quaint little towns with stone houses." Rebecca watched the countryside speed by, looking over at Page every few minutes.

"We have a good share of those between one city and the next." Page glanced over at her as he drove. Traffic was light, and he was eager to watch her expression when she got her first look at the palace. "Sometimes it takes a visitor to make us locals remember the beauty of the city we take for granted. I'm glad I can show you the sights."

"You're a much better tour guide than I would have gotten if I'd booked a tour with a group. It's going to be wonderful to see the places I've only dreamt about."

"Munich is sort of a city built around a town, in a way. The old part remains what you would expect. Cobblestone streets, no vehicle traffic in areas, lots of outdoor cafes and fountains. Around it is the newer areas. There are lots of gardens for the public, pretty much everywhere. We could spend days just in Munich and still not see everything. I'd like to take you to the palace first so we can stroll through in no rush. Then we can decide where to eat. Again, you can choose from quaint and local cafes to upscale restaurants."

"I'm still trying to envision a building a half-mile long. Did the King or whoever actually live there?"

Page shrugged. "Off and on. It was originally supposed to be their summer home. I think it just evolved from that. Now, of course, it's a museum. A reminder of who we were, so to speak. I use the term 'we' loosely because I have very little German blood in me, to my knowledge. My mother was fully Norwegian, and my father was English. My Grandfather was English, but my step-grandmother was German. He fell in love with the country and never returned to England after my father became an adult. Even though I have property in England, I don't consider it home." He turned his attention to the roadway as he left the main road and maneuvered the car through a residential area. "I'm taking the scenic route so you can see the small cottages and cobblestone walkways."

Chapter Fourteen

After driving around the smaller streets, pointing out the different types of houses, Page finally turned into the entrance road to the palace. "Welcome to Nymphenburg Palace," he said as he turned the corner and it came into view.

"Holy crap! Oh my God, Page, it's huge." She dug into her small handbag and retrieved her cell phone. Page stopped the car so she could get several clear pictures of the entire palace.

"It still takes my breath away, and I've seen it a lot. Wait until you see the inside. And the gardens. And the swans. Oh, let's not forget the hundreds of paintings." He smiled enjoying the look of amazement on her face, then drove closer, finding a parking space not too far from the main entrance. Opening her car door, he offered her his hand. "Keep your cell phone ready for lots of pictures. When we get home, you can download them to the computer and print them out if you want to. You might want to send some to Gina. You know, to let her know you aren't being held as my sex slave chained in the dungeon."

"Ha! Gina would want to know why not."

"Excellent question, if I do say so. Glad you brought it up." He chuckled as he led her toward the walkway, near the lake with white swans. Taking her phone, he motioned for her to sit by the lake and he took several shots. A woman approached them, speaking to him in German. He nodded, handed her the phone, and went to sit next to Rebecca, slipping his arm around her shoulder. "She offered to take a photo of me with my wife. Who was I to refuse?"

Rebecca looked up at him, surprised at the comment, but before she could speak, Page covered her mouth with his own as the woman took several pictures. They stood up, and she returned the phone, exchanged a few words, and hurried off to catch up with her friends. "What did she say?" Rebecca asked.

"She wished us a happy marriage, said you were quite lovely and we would make beautiful children together." He grinned playfully at her.

"Right. Married to the Toad prince of Germany. I don't think so, hotshot."

He laughed as he pulled her against him as they walked toward the entrance. "Begging the lady's pardon, but I am not a prince. Technically, I'm an English Lord."

"Good grief," she teased, rolling her eyes.

"I realize as a little girl you probably dreamed of being a princess. A ladyship is the best I can do, I'm afraid."

"Do you have fevers with these fits?" she asked, trying hard not to laugh.

He paid the entrance fee, and they walked through the doors into the palace. "Shall we just wander from room to room and I'll fill you in on the highlights, or do you want to tag along with the group of tourists who entered ahead of us?"

She was aware his arm was curled comfortably around her waist, and a bit surprised she didn't mind a bit. "I think I'd rather just wander, just the two of us. Is it really a half mile long?"

"It's sort of broken up into sections, and there are a lot of trails outside leading to other sights, ponds, statues, and such. Lots of benches to rest." Page guided her into the enormous room, pleased when he heard her catch her breath, her gaze trying to take in everything at once. She took pictures of as much of it as possible.

"Paintings. God, they loved their artwork and just look at the decorations. Page, did people really live here? I mean, I thought I was familiar with German castles and palaces, but it didn't even come close…" Her voice trailed off as she looked up at the painting covering the ceiling, still capturing the art on her phone.

Each room seemed more elaborate than the last. Page stopped and pointed toward the painting on the ceiling. "Zimmerman was the painter. He laid flat on his back for over ten months to do this one. Which is bad enough as it is, but he was in his seventies. By the way, most of these are older than America. And they have never been touched up."

"How is that even possible?" Rebecca asked, unable to turn away from the artwork.

"Don't know." He guided her through more rooms, stopping to admire more art, and finally entering a room with portraits of women. "This was King Ludwig's collection. If he saw a beautiful woman, he had her portrait painted. Thirty-six of the most beautiful women in the world. All nationalities. He was quite the ladies' man, I've heard."

"Must be an ancestor of yours," she teased.

"Not that I'm aware of, but who knows? Shall we stroll outside in the gardens?"

Rebecca walked beside him as they left the palace and headed down a pathway. The tour group was ahead of them, also enjoying the scenery. Page led her to a bench, where they sat looking out, over the grass and perfectly designed flower gardens. She leaned against him, neither of them saying anything. She took several more shots of different sections, then turned the phone and quickly took a picture of them together. One shot led to several more as he made faces, and finally caught her just as she snapped the tab, kissing her on the cheek. Laughing, she put the phone down. "You're a lunatic."

"Thought I was a toad. Make up your mind woman," he teased.

"Should I send these to Gina? You do know she's going to grill me worse than a prosecutor on a murder case don't you?"

"I'm not getting in the middle of that call, Lady Harlow. I'll just sit here… on my toadstool." He shrugged his shoulders and covered his eyes with his hands. "Nope. Not going there."

They sat for a few more minutes, Page watching as she sent the pictures along with a text message to Gina. When she was finished, he stood up and reached for her hand. "The tourist bunch should be finished looking at Amalienburg, so we can browse through it leisurely. Then, unless you want to continue exploring old buildings and gardens, we can head downtown."

"Lead the way, my Lord," Rebecca started to curtsey but ended up laughing too hard. She heard the tour group as they continued walking on the pathway. Page was correct in assuming they were leaving the building, stepping further away.

This building was much smaller, and they covered the three rooms in just a few minutes. Rebecca stood in the middle of the main room, looking in awe at all the gleaming silver and glass. "How in the hell did they get all this to stay in such good shape?"

Page arched a brow and shook his head. "I'm guessing it's treated with something, but no idea what."

Rebecca followed him back up the path, aware that for the first time, for as long as she could remember, she felt utterly worry-free and comfortable. Glancing over at Page, she had to wonder if he was part of the reason. If he was, why? She'd spent her life avoiding anything remotely romantic, yet here she was. The interlude at the lake was still lingering in her thoughts. The ecstasy she felt as he kissed her. *The desire she felt for more.* A slight shudder ran through her as she remembered the pleasure of his caress. He glanced down at her, easing his arm around her waist, pulling her close. "Chilly, Becca? There's a slight breeze, isn't there?"

"A little, I guess," she agreed. No way was she about to confess her thoughts.

"Hungry?"

"I will be soon, I suppose."

They strolled back through the gardens and stopped to take more pictures of the lake and the swans, before continuing to the car. Just as they reached the car, a young girl ran up to them. "Excuse me for asking… are you Page Harlow?"

Rebecca watched as Page turned on his rock star image, beginning with his smile and a wink. "Guilty as charged. And you would be…?"

"Helen. Helen Morris. I'm from the States. Kansas. I have all your CDs. I can't believe I am this close to you." The girl ran her fingers nervously through her straw-colored hair. "My friends are going to turn green when I tell them I met you in person." She hesitated as if thinking about what else to say. "Could I take your picture?"

"Absolutely my love. Here's a better idea though…" Page handed Rebecca the girl's phone. "How about we ask my ladylove to take a picture of both of us? Becca, would you please?"

"Certainly," Rebecca said with a smile, realizing that this probably happened everywhere Page appeared. Page slipped his arm around Helen's shoulder, curling his fingers in her hair. In the second picture, he embraced the girl, and in the third picture, he cupped her chin with his hand and lowered his mouth lightly to hers. When he released her, she stood still, her fingers touching her lips, wide-eyed.

Page was silent for a moment before handing Helen her phone back. Finally, he asked, "Are you planning on attending the concert?"

"In Kansas City? Oh yes. Wouldn't miss it. When does the CD come out?"

Page arched a brow and remotely opened the trunk of the Mercedes. "Your copy comes out… now." He retrieved a CD from a box, along with a Sharpie and a piece of paper. Rebecca watched as he signed the CD cover 'To Helen with love, Page.' He wrote something on the piece of paper and handed the two items to the girl who still stood with her mouth open. "Here's the CD. Your advance personal copy. This paper will save you the cost of the concert ticket. Made out to you. Good for you and a friend as my guests in Kansas City. Come in through the VIP entrance. I'll see you there."

Helen looked at the CD and the pass as if they were winning lotto tickets. Then she looked over at Rebecca. "I guess you're used to all this. Does it bother you? I mean when he kisses his fans? Not that I'm complaining one bit…" her voice trailed off.

"Part and parcel to being involved with someone famous. No, it doesn't bother me. Page loves his fans."

"So, are you, like, his steady girlfriend?"

Rebecca was about to answer when Page interrupted. "If you can keep a secret Helen, Rebecca is going to marry me after the tour. Well, she hasn't said yes yet," he shrugged, "but she hasn't said no either. I am holding on to the hope she will succumb to my charms and profess her undying love to me soon."

"You are the luckiest woman on the planet. Thanks for the CD and the pass and oh my God the pictures. I need to go before my parents think I got lost."

"See you in Kansas City," Page said as she hurried away, clutching her gifts against her. Page closed the trunk, opened Rebecca's car door then slid behind the wheel before heaving a sigh. "Wonder how many more we'll deal with before the end of the night."

Rebecca laughed. "Oh stop. You love the attention, and you know you do. Where would you be if nobody cared who you were? I thought she was sweet."

"Well, at least I have all my body parts intact, no claw marks from fingernails, no torn clothing." He chuckled as he eased out of the parking area. "Now I'm hungry, and I want a beer. Or two or three."

Chapter Fifteen

Page found a place to park near the English Gardens and took Rebecca's hand as they strolled casually along the walkway. "We can walk, ride in a carriage, or rent a boat," he said casually.

"How big is this park?"

"Over nine hundred acres. The beer garden is ahead of us. Not a long walk really, but there are acres of grass, trails, and of course, the river. Germans love their outdoor spaces. Depends on how much of this you want to explore. My thought was to have something to eat, then take you downtown to the city square or one of our many museums."

"I took Anna's advice and wore comfortable shoes, so I'm okay with walking." She glanced up at him. "What kind of museums?"

Page grinned at her. "Rembrandt, Raphael, Van Gogh and Cezanne. We also have a modern art museum with some nice Warhol. There are car museums and science museums, but I'm guessing you're more interested in art."

"I love art. Sometimes, on my day off I go to the New York Museum. I just wander through each room over and over."

"Well then, let's get some food and head toward the museums, shall we?"

They walked toward the sound of people gathered in the outside beer garden. Everyone seemed to be talking at once. Rebecca took a deep breath as Page guided her through the crowd to the actual building. It was a sight to behold, towering high above the people sitting all around at tables. Rebecca retrieved her cell phone from her handbag and took several pictures. "Page, this is… I don't know… there are no words to describe it."

"The restaurant is over there. Sadly, we can't go into the tower because it isn't safe. But we can look at it while we eat." He guided her through the crowds, to a pretty building with a terrace, where more people gathered. They chose a table facing the tower and the massive crowds. When Rebecca looked at the menu, she arched a brow and sighed. Page chuckled. "Do you trust me to order for you?"

"German food. I want to try real authentic German food."

Page ordered for both of them in rapid German and was rewarded with a smile from their server, who immediately presented them with two massive steins of dark beer. "You want German food, you get German food. Bratwurst, potatoes, and dark beer."

Then the food arrived, and Rebecca shook her head. "If I ate like this every day I'd be two hundred pounds."

"One reason I have a workout room at home."

"Page," Rebecca needed to ask him something but wasn't sure how to phrase the question. Straightforward would be best, she decided and took a sip of the beer. "When we were at the palace, you told that young girl we were getting married. Why would you say that?"

Page sat down his beer stein and stared at her. "Seems that I did mention it to you. You didn't run shrieking away so I would take that as a positive sign. Of course, you didn't jump up and down and throw yourself into my arms either."

"How is that thought even possible? You're a die-hard playboy. Women fall at your feet. You have a world tour coming. Where would you fit a wife into that equation? Especially me. Besides the fact I'm female, I am nowhere near your type."

"And tell me, my love, what would be the type of woman for me to marry?"

"Who says you have to marry anyone? Why would you even want to? Would you want a wife who tolerates your backstage antics with whomever you chose for the night? That's not a marriage."

"If I took a wife, I wouldn't be having any antics backstage or anywhere else. Contrary to what you read, I do have some ethics. If I got married, it would be a lifetime commitment to one woman. One exceptional woman."

Rebecca took a moment to chew her bratwurst. "We only met yesterday. This whole idea is insane. Or do you think that by mentioning marriage, I'll go ahead and sleep with you?"

"That never crossed my mind. Trust me, Rebecca, if I were determined to get you into bed, I wouldn't have to lie about what I wanted to get you there. I certainly wouldn't suggest marriage. I can't explain it. You are everything I have ever wanted. But, sadly, you're probably right. Obviously, I'm not what you're looking for in a husband, so let's just chalk up my comments as bullshit and enjoy the rest of the day."

After they finished their meal, he escorted her back through the crowds, back to the path. Silently, he reached for her hand as they strolled away from the tower in the opposite direction of the car. "Page, are you angry?"

"Do I seem angry?" he asked.

"Somewhat."

"No, Becca, I'm not angry. Well, at least not with you. I shouldn't have mentioned marriage to you or little Helen. Even though Anna can confirm I mentioned it to her. I should have listened to her advice, and I didn't."

"What was her advice?" she asked, stopping to look up at him.

"She suggested I wait awhile because we didn't know each other well enough yet. I'm not the patient type, and I'm not known for my ability to follow advice. So there you have it. When I was a child, my mother told me to go after my dreams and not to let anything stop me. Plus I never believed in love at first sight before and I'm guessing you certainly don't."

"And… you think after one day, you want to spend the rest of your life with me?"

"That's exactly what I want. Obviously, it isn't what I'll get now is it?"

Rebecca started to say something but stopped herself. What was there to say? How could she even begin to admit she found him desirable, both physically and mentally? *But, love at first sight? Did that even exist?* Boldly, she stepped closer to him until they were touching. Her hands circled his waist, caressing his back and then easing into his hair. "You keep me off balance," she whispered, her lips brushing across his throat. "I can't think. I can't be objective. It's all happening so fast. Oh my God, Page, this is so crazy."

He pulled her against him and took control of her mouth. He felt her stiffen for a moment, then she was returning his kiss, allowing him to plunder her, teasing her with his tongue at first, then possessing her, urging her to follow his lead. His hands explored her back, across her hips, and back up to caress her face as he broke the kiss. They both stood still, breathless, gazing at each other. "Damn, woman…." He murmured.

"I have officially lost my mind," she said, then chuckled. "And for the first time in my entire life, I don't seem to care."

He leaned down and kissed her forehead. "Is that progress?"

"Somewhat. Maybe." She shrugged, chewing nervously on her bottom lip. "I'm worried because I've never allowed myself to react before. My whole life, growing up was a laundry list of 'thou shalt nots.' Kissing was frowned upon. Sex was a dirty word, never to be spoken. I never questioned it. Even when I left home and moved to New York, those 'rules' stuck. And now…. I am beginning to see they were rules made by someone to keep me in line."

"I'm sure your parents had the best of intentions."

"I suppose they did."

"Come on, let's go stare at some ancient paintings, shall we?" He took her hand and headed toward the car. He sat in the driver's seat, silently looking at her. When she met his gaze, her lips parted, and she leaned forward. He kissed her lightly, first on the lips, then on her left cheek. "Becca. You are wonderful. Now, let me concentrate on driving."

"You're pretty damn awesome yourself. For a toad."

The spell between them was broken, and he laughed, shaking his head. It only took fifteen minutes of driving before they were parking again. He led her toward an old building. "The museums are close to each other. First is the old museum. Old, old paintings. Shouldn't take long to see them all. Then we cross the street to the newer museum and see more old paintings."

"Do you come here often?"

"I used to come more often. But after a while, it's a bit boring coming alone." He escorted her inside the enormous building, and they walked from room to room. Page told her a bit about the paintings as they walked, still hand in hand. It was as quiet as a library, Page speaking in whispers as they went.

Almost an hour later, they left the museum and crossed the street, walking around the more modern building to the entrance. The woman in the front lobby area greeted him by name, and they exchanged a quick conversation in German. Page turned to Rebecca. "I lost track of time. They close in about thirty minutes. We can see some of the more famous pieces though. And I doubt Greta will toss me out."

"Okay. Pick some," Rebecca said quickly.

He spoke to Greta again, and she guided them through several rooms before stopping. Then she turned, smiled at Rebecca, and walked away. Page waited until she was gone before leading Rebecca to the closest one. "I thought you would like Van Gogh and Monet at least. If you want to see the rest of the paintings, we can always return another day."

"Sure, if we have time, that would be great."

"Of course, we still have the galleries in Paris. You might be overloaded with visions of old art by the time we leave the Louvre."

They walked in silence as Rebecca studied each painting as if trying to memorize them, one by one. Finally, they returned to the central area, and Page stopped to speak to Greta. He walked over to Rebecca and smiled. "Give Greta your phone so she can take some pictures of us if you want." Without waiting for her response, Page retrieved the phone which was exposed in the handbag, and handed it to the tall blonde woman. The first picture caught Rebecca by surprise as Page scooped her up into his arms. His kiss was intense, and Rebecca felt the heat of desire. Without a second thought, she boldly returned his kiss, matching his intensity with her own. After several deep kisses, Rebecca pulled away slightly. Just an inch, but Page took the hint and slowly released her and took the phone back.

Outside on the steps, Rebecca took a minute to look at the photos. "The only thing missing from these would be a bed in the background."

Page arched a brow. "I could arrange that if you ever want me to."

"I don't think so. No, not happening. Nope. Not a chance."

"Okay. Just be aware, it's an open offer," he said softly, touching her chin with his index finger.

"Duly noted, toad."

"It's still early. Up for some shopping, then maybe a drink or two? We have a Hard Rock Café here."

"I need postcards. I promised my boss I'd send a postcard from Europe."

"Right. Postcards. Let's go shopping." As they walked toward the car Page laughed. "Becca, you are definitely one of a kind. I say 'shopping' and the best you can do is 'postcards'? Not jewelry, clothes, trinkets, makeup, perfume… postcards. God, I love you."

As he opened her car door, she looked up at him and grinned. "I wouldn't object to any of the aforementioned items being purchased on my behalf if someone so chose to do so. And, no toad prince of Germany you most certainly do not love me. Not in that sense anyway."

"What sense would that be? You really have the legal speak down to a science don't you?" He was still laughing as he started the car and eased into traffic. In a few minutes, he was easing into another parking space. "I thought you would prefer the central old city area rather than a new mall. You have malls back home. Besides the must-have postcards, we should get something for your friend Gina as well. Hell, I should buy her a damn diamond necklace as a thank you."

He slipped his arm around her waist, guiding her down the sidewalk. The first small shop they entered sold small ceramic figurines plus a supply of candies, chips, and a display of postcards. Rebecca chose one of the Palace and another showing people drinking beer in front of the Chinese Tower. As an afterthought, she decided on three of each. "One for the boss and one for my parents. The other one is for me. Gina got pictures, so she doesn't need a postcard saying I'm having a great time, wish you were here."

The older lady behind the counter overheard her. "Are you from the States?" she asked Rebecca.

"Yes. New York City."

"I'd like to go there someday. What brings you to Munich?"

"Visiting my friend for a week." Rebecca nodded in Page's direction.

Page stepped up to the counter and paid for the cards. As they left the shop he pulled her close. "So, I'm your friend, am I?"

"I'd like to think so."

"And since you're a girl, I guess that makes you my girlfriend then. Tiny step away from fiancée. We can work with that."

Rebecca groaned and rolled her eyes. "You, toad prince are a piece of work."

"I suppose I could put a ring on your finger."

"I still won't sleep with you."

"I don't remember asking you to, Rebecca. That would be your call."

"Yes, you did mention that yesterday." She lifted the small bag, determined to silence the thoughts creeping around in the back of her head. Things she should not be thinking about. Things he didn't need to know she was thinking about at any cost. "My shopping is done, so we can continue by looking at all the goodies you think I should shop for."

"Good. First things first. Why do you only wear a watch to work? Don't you like jewelry? I thought all women liked jewelry. I thought the word 'diamonds' was what the 'D' in DNA stood for"

"I need one at work because I can't look at my phone in a courtroom. It's not professional. I keep the watch at work because it might get damaged if I wear it all the time. What if I got in the shower with it on? Or put my hand in dishwater?"

"Is it a Rolex or something?" he asked.

"No, it's an off-brand, but it's pretty. It's gold with a fake diamond in it. I mostly worry about the stone coming loose."

"Then, I'm going to buy you a watch. One that will wear well will look professional and you can keep it on, or you can wear your old one other places." He guided her around the corner and down a side street, into a small jewelry store.

The man behind the counter was looking at a necklace with his jeweler's loop and glanced up when the door opened. He was well dressed with grey hair and a well-trimmed grey beard. "Ah, Lord Harlow. It's been a long time. My granddaughter tells me you're heading out on tour soon."

"In a few months, yes. Weston, I'd like you to meet Rebecca. Becca, this dear man is Weston Von Hand. The best jeweler I ever met."

"Nice to meet you, Rebecca. What is it you're looking for today?"

Page slipped his arm around her waist and smiled at the man. "She needs a watch. A really nice one. One that will go well professionally yet she can wear it anywhere.

"I have several you might like." He motioned toward a table and chair group off to one side. Rebecca and Page sat down while he retrieved a case from another display. "I just got these in this past week. Two Movado, three Cartier, and a Rolex."

Rebecca glanced over at Page. "A Rolex? Have you gone off the deep end?"

"It's a good watch. I own several." He picked up the watch and handed it to her. "Eighteen karat gold band, small, understated diamonds, and precise timepiece."

"I can't wear a Rolex."

"Why not?"

"Way out of my league. I'm a legal researcher Page, not one of the firm's partners."

"What does that have to do with what kind of watch you have? Given to you as a gift. Is there some sort of company policy against it?"

"No, but –"

"How about the Movado then? A slim band with fewer diamonds. A lot less expensive."

Rebecca slipped the watch on her wrist. "It still looks pricey."

"Price isn't the issue here, Becca. Do you like it?"

"What's not to like? It has diamonds. What woman doesn't like diamonds?"

"Fine. That was easy. Now, we need to get something for Gina. How about a gold chain necklace? Maybe a small stone?"

They stood up and walked over to the glass cases. Rebecca studied the display of necklaces. One caught her eye immediately. "The one with the quarter moon and a little star. She would love that."

Weston removed the necklace from the case and placed it on a piece of black velvet. A small diamond was at the lower tip of the moon, in between the points of the star. Page nodded. "Do you want to take it to her or should we have it sent UPS?"

"I'll take it to her. Just to watch her eyes light up when she sees it, knowing it's from you. I'll bet she never takes it off."

Weston put the necklace in a gift box. "Will you be wearing the watch Miss Rebecca or shall I wrap it?"

Rebecca held her wrist up and studied the watch. The diamonds sparkled as she moved. "It's exquisite. I'm speechless."

"Care to pick out an engagement ring while we're here?" Page asked with a grin.

"Ah, no."

Weston looked at Page and retrieved a tray of diamond rings. "I'm guessing a size six?"

"No," Rebecca said. "No rings."

"Why not?" Page asked.

"Because…"

"Not a real reason. Because of what?"

"Because we aren't engaged. We aren't getting engaged. So no rings."

"Fine. No rings. Not now." Page winked at Weston who returned the rings to their case.

They left the shop, Rebecca admiring her new watch as they walked. "You know you shouldn't have, Page. The watch I own was serviceable."

"A beautiful woman deserves beautiful things. Jewelry, handbags, clothes, shoes. And my gifts to you are not going to be up for debate. So, where next?"

"I'd like to see Hard Rock."

"Good. I could use a drink. It's not far." They walked in silence, Page's arm around her waist as he guided her through the crowd of people.

The club wasn't crowded, and they took a table in a corner, away from the bar where most of the people were. He ordered Crown Royal on the rocks and Rebecca ordered a beer.

During the evening, several people stopped by the table to say hello, ask about the tour and the CD, and wish him well. As one woman approached, Page sighed and muttered a quiet 'Well shit," but immediately hid his dislike behind his smile. Rebecca studied the woman. Tall, brunette, slender, well dressed. When Page grasped Rebecca's hand under the table, she looked over at him.

"Page, are you going to introduce me to your date?"

"No."

"Well then," the woman turned to Rebecca. "Allow me to introduce myself. Brenda Franks. A journalist for 'What's going on.' We try to keep on top of the music scene. And you are apparently the contest winner."

"Obviously," Rebecca said calmly. "We were having a discussion, so if you don't mind?"

Page couldn't hide the grin. Brenda wasn't used to rejection. However, she would spin this entirely out of context, given an opening. "Yes, this is the contest winner. If you'd like a run-down of our day so far, take notes. We went horseback riding. Had lunch. Went to visit Nymphenburg, then went to the English Gardens, had a snack, went to both major museums, walked around downtown, and ended up here. We were getting ready to head back to the castle where Rebecca would go to her room, and I would go to my studio to complete a song. Next question?"

"Do you plan to stay at the castle for the entire visit?" The question was directed at Rebecca, who glanced at Page.

When he nodded, Rebecca leaned on the table, meeting the woman's gaze and not backing down. "Actually, no. We are going to be visiting all the tourist spots. An opera and the Louvre plus Monte Carlo, perhaps Venice. This is my first trip to Europe and Page promises to be a great tour guide."

"I see. Let me take a photo of the two of you."

Page sighed. "Fine."

"Could you at least look like you're enjoying each other's company? Good grief Page, you look pissed off."

Rebecca arched a brow. "How would you like someone to come to your table uninvited and start asking questions?"

Brenda shrugged. "Price of stardom. He's our 'local boy who made good' success story. His fans love him."

"His fans are welcome. You aren't a fan. However, take your pictures." Rebecca leaned against Page's chest and looked up at him. He cupped her chin in his hand while Brenda took her photos.

When Brenda lowered her camera, she smiled at Rebecca. "So tell me, woman to woman, how would you rate him on a scale of one to ten?"

Page leaned across the table and gripped Brenda's wrist. "That is a line you do not cross. Not this time."

"Ohhh, did I touch a nerve? When did you ever object to the press announcing your exploits?"

Page released her wrist. "When I finally met a woman I sincerely care about as a person instead of just a romp. I will not have Becca dragged through the mud for your ratings, Brenda. Don't push me on this. You may state that Miss Morrison is having a wonderful time and we plan on visiting as much of Europe as we can in the ten days we have. You may mention that her interest is in art galleries and opera mostly, so those are at the top of our to-do list. Fair enough?"

"So, after the contest ends, and the tour begins, will you two keep in touch?"

For the first time, Page smiled. "We will absolutely keep in touch. She won't be able to beat me off with a club. Rebecca is beyond a doubt the woman of my dreams. And yes, Brenda, that is a quote."

"Okay then. Thank you both for the interview and photos." She scooped up her camera and handbag and returned to the bar across the room.

Rebecca looked at Page and chuckled. "Woman of your dreams? Wow. She didn't see that one coming, did she?"

He squeezed her hand and then raised it to his lips. "Facts are facts, Becca. It's the way I feel."

"Why?"

"Why? Do you need to ask? You're different. You're real. You're honest. Ethical. You have morals, goals, and beliefs. You have plans. You're intelligent and independent." He took a deep breath and continued. "Becca, you make me want to be a better man. Someone you could date, or have a relationship with. Someone you could love."

She gazed into his eyes in total silence. What could she say? That he had already affected her. Made her question all she had been taught. Made her want what she shouldn't. Did she dare admit to him she was fighting the desire to ask him to show her how to love, to react? No that would never do. What about her white wedding? She inhaled slowly. At her present rate, she would die an old maid. No marriage. "I'll see you in New York, won't I?" she asked. It was a much safer answer.

"Without a doubt. Let's get out of here before I haul you into my arms and Brenda gets better photos for her magazine."

"You say that like it's a bad thing," she whispered.

"Wouldn't be for me, but your reputation would take a hit. Lots of suggestions, rumors, and speculation. Trust me. Her paper is the German version of the sleaze tabloids at the supermarket counters."

She followed him from the club back onto the sidewalks, back toward the car. He opened the car door and watched as she slid in, her dress exposing smooth bare legs. He leaned in and boldly captured her mouth, pressing her against the leather headrest. Instead of the light kiss he expected, she molded against him, her arms circling his waist. When she moved slightly, her skirt rode higher, but instead of adjusting it, she turned toward him as he leaned further inside the car. When he stopped to catch his breath, she ran her fingers across his chest and up into his hair, urging his mouth back to her own. Her breathing came in gasps, a soft moan slipping out as the kiss lingered. Finally, he pulled away, a startled look on his face. Closing her door, he walked around the car and slid behind the wheel. When he turned to speak, she pressed a finger against his lips. "Shhh, let me savor the moment, Page."

Page started the car and eased into light traffic. What in the hell just happened? He had kissed her off and on during the day, but this kiss rattled him to his toes. And it was mostly her doing. He glanced over and even though her eyes were closed, he knew she was watching him. What was going through that mind of hers, he wondered. By the time he pulled into the driveway and put the car in park, she had dozed off. When he cut the engine, she opened her eyes and offered him a smile. He came around and opened her car door retrieving the small bag from the floor. Standing close enough he could smell her light cologne, he knew better than to touch her. Not a kiss, not even hand-holding. Whatever had happened in town was not a promise of things to come. She was pure, and she would stay that way. "We should go in, Becca," he suggested.

"It's a beautiful night Page. I thought we could walk in the garden." She boldly reached for his hand. When he nodded, she smiled up at him. "Are you angry about something?"

"No, why should I be angry?"

"Did I seem like a tease? I mean when I kissed you back. I'm not at all experienced in that."

"No Becca, you didn't seem like a tease. But I don't want to take advantage of your lack of experience."

"Then I have somewhat of a dilemma, Page." They arrived in the garden and sat on a bench facing the roses. "I am not experienced, and you don't want to take advantage of said lack of experience. So, tell me, Page Harlow, how do I ever become experienced if no one wants to be first? Someone has to be first don't they?"

"First at what?"

"Okay, let's say I return to New York. Let's say, for argument's sake I find someone, and he proposes. What happens then? Other than listening to Gina rave about her exploits, I do not have a clue what to expect."

"So, are you saying you want me to be a Guinea pig for your experiment? Have you lost your fucking mind? You want me to screw you just so you know what to expect on your wedding night?"

"You don't have to be so vulgar about it!" She inhaled sharply, surprised that his refusal stung slightly.

"No, no, and hell, fucking no! Kisses are one thing. Touching is one thing. But I will not, under any damn circumstances be the one to take your virginity. I thought we had that discussion yesterday!"

"We did. Shall I quote you? You said… and I quote… 'I vow to you that unless you specifically request it, I won't even attempt to seduce you.' End quote. So what would happen if I ask you to seduce me?"

"Rebecca, sweet Rebecca. In my opinion, for what it's worth; I believe you are overwhelmed by everything that's happening to you and around you. And possibly a part of you is attracted to me, physically and sexually. I know I am attracted to you. I know I want you in the worst way. But honey, if I took your virginity, trust me, you would hate me for it and hate yourself for allowing it. So as much as it kills me, I am refusing. There are other ways to satisfy you besides taking you physically. We can work our way through those, bit by bit. You will have a pretty good idea of what to expect on your wedding night. That's the best I can offer. Unless you agree to be my wife. In which case I will make your wedding night one to be worth the wait. But, you have to love me the way I love you and right now you don't. I would marry you tomorrow. Hell, we could wake up a judge tonight. Now, I want you to go to bed and think about that for a while. And know this, Rebecca Morrison. I love you. I know it seems unbelievable and maybe a bit crazy, but there you have it."

"I can't marry you, Page, for a lot of reasons. I barely know you. I live in New York, you live in Europe. I have a career, and so do you, and they are on opposite ends of the spectrum. I mean, I haven't known you for two whole days yet. Marriage is forever. At least it would be for me." She sighed and looked away. "Why are we having this lame conversation anyway?"

"You started it, Rebecca, so you tell me. In approximately eight days, you will be headed back to New York. To your career. Your home. Your friends. And so help me, you will be returning the same way you left. A virgin. Period. End of discussion. Unless you decide you love me and agree to become my wife." He pulled her to her feet and led her into the house and up the stairs. "Goodnight, Becca. Get some sleep."

She stood in the hallway, outside her bedroom door and wondered why she was crying. He had respected her ethics. Shouldn't she be happy? She offered herself to him, which was a first and he turned her down, which was also probably a first. Entering her room, Rebecca undressed and sobbed herself to sleep.

Chapter Sixteen

Page was up at dawn, riding Thunder across the fields to the lake. Last night had been sleepless, his tormented mind on the woman at the end of the hall. The one woman in the world he couldn't touch and the only one in the world he wanted more than anything. She had a valid point. Someone had to be first. Someone was always first at everything. The thought of her giving herself to anyone else bothered him for a multitude of reasons. What if the guy was cruel and rough? What if he hurt her; or caused her physical pain? Still, she wanted to be a virgin on her wedding night. But why? Because that was what she had been raised to believe was moral. It wasn't because she was frigid, or because she found sex distasteful. It was because that was what had been beaten into her head her entire life. Maybe he should be her first. At least he would be gentle and loving. He shook his head. Why in the hell was he even having this argument with himself? After his rejection last night, she was probably mortified. He sighed and turned Thunder back toward the castle just as the rain started. By the time he arrived at the stable, he was soaked to the skin. Good thing there was a cozy room attached so he could shower and change.

Rebecca had spent half the night staring at the ceiling, her hands nervously caressing the satin sheets. What the hell had she been thinking? Even as wild as Page was no man wanted to be used and discarded. Oh sure, that was what happened on tour. One-night stands. He'd told her himself, that he wasn't even a person to his bed partners, just an object.

Hadn't she done precisely that? *Gee Page, we both know you aren't the type I would ever in a million years marry or even have a relationship with, but could you at least go ahead and take my virginity so it won't be an issue whenever I do find someone suitable?* No wonder he exploded. How did he really feel about her? Oh man, she had probably ruined the entire vacation. Just as the sun was coming up, she climbed out of bed and went to the window. She watched as Page streaked across the field on his black stallion. Was he still angry? The horse was at full gallop, Page leaning forward in the saddle. *Probably angry.* But then, maybe not. With a long sigh of exasperation, she headed for the massive bathtub for a long soak and deep thoughts. Serious thoughts. Even as a child, she did her best thinking in a bubble bath. *How could he love her and want to marry her after just a couple of days? A more important question was how did she feel about him? There were feelings. Never before had she felt like she did around a man.*

An hour later Rebecca was dressed in the black mini skirt Gina had talked her into and a soft scoop-neck white blouse that accented her cleavage. She would just let nature do what nature did with a little help. She studied herself in the mirror and decided her mother would have a screaming fit about the outfit and therefore was perfect for the day. A second glance stopped her cold. This was the most insane harebrained scheme she had ever thought of. It wouldn't work. He would refuse her attention out of spite if for no other reason. With a sigh, she changed from the mini skirt into a longer one and headed down the stairs, out the back toward the stables. A search of the stalls confirmed Thunder was not there, so Page was still out. She went into the cottage area and curled up to wait on the sofa when the rain came. Within moments, it had turned into a torrential downpour.

Page entered the stable, removed Thunder's saddle, and quickly ran a towel over the stallion's coat and mane before peeling off his soaked jeans and shirt. As he shoved the room door open he stopped, inches from Rebecca, who had been coming out. His hair was dripping across his bare chest, and her eyes followed the wet droplets before returning slowly to his face.

"Page…" Anything else she had wanted to say stuck in her throat.

"I would almost believe you ordered the rain." His blue eyes drilled into her green ones, unblinking.

"There were things I wanted to apologize for saying to you last night."

"Which things?"

"Ah, well…" She stepped back enough to allow him to close the door.

"Which… things… Rebecca?" He advanced toward her, intending to back her into a corner. He didn't anticipate her standing her ground until he was touching her shoulders. When her fingers eased his hair away from his shoulders, he inhaled sharply. Clamping his hand around her wrist, he stopped her. "Becca. Do not play with fire. I told you I will not ruin you and I meant it, but you should not tempt me to a breaking point."

"Even if I ask?"

"We covered this last night." He blew out an exasperated breath. He was not having this type of conversation while he stood here dripping wet and stark naked, was he? "Jeeze, Becca, let me at least get dressed. I cannot have this type of conversation with you while I'm nude."

She took a deep breath, decided she had officially lost her mind, and stepped forward, boldly pressing against him. "I am here to tell you all men are not created equal," she whispered in his ear, standing on her tiptoes.

Page silently cursed himself for ever letting himself get into this situation in the first place. "You don't know what you're doing to me. Don't let me, Becca."

"Let me ask you something Page. If I wasn't untouched, or if you didn't know I was untouched, would we still be talking about this?"

"No. But I do know, and I won't do this to you."

"I was under the impression women were expected to change their minds a lot."

"Not about this. Damnit!"

"Fine! Get dressed. I'll be in the house!" She turned and walked toward the door.

Page grabbed her arm. "It's raining."

"I noticed. I won't melt." She sighed and lowered her head. "I'm sorry, Page. I don't know what is happening to me and I don't even know how to begin to form an explanation. I don't mean to make you angry, and it seems as if I do anyway."

"You don't make me angry. You make me insane. Stark raving lunatic crazy. Now, why don't you sit down and let me put some damn clothes on?" He released his hold on her arm and motioned toward the sofa.

Rebecca nodded silently, and he left the room, closing the door behind him. A few minutes later he came back, wearing black sweatpants and a white tank top, his hair towel-dried and tied in a blue bandanna. Without saying a word, he dropped onto the sofa beside her and pulled her into a tender embrace, his fingertips trailing up and down her arm. When she turned slightly to gaze up at him, he lowered his mouth, trailing soft kisses across her face, down her throat, and across her exposed shoulder. Her breath escaped in a soft sigh as she arched against him, her hands kneading his back. The only other sound was the rain pounding against the window panes. "I love how you make me feel," she finally whispered. "I never in a million years thought I would want to be..." His mouth covered hers, silencing her words. As he urged her back against the soft pillows, she moved, so they were both stretched out, side by side. His hands slid beneath the blouse, exploring her body while never releasing her mouth. Her own hands were beneath his shirt, gripping his shoulders. He wondered when she would call a halt to his exploring hands and mouth.

"I should have let you go back to the house," he whispered, laying his head on her chest.

"I'm just fine where I am. I'm dry and quite contented, thank you."

"I had planned on us driving to Venice and doing some sightseeing."

"Plans are flexible, and it's not safe to drive in the rain."

"This isn't exactly safe either, you know."

"Maybe not but I can't seem to care at the moment."

"You should care, Rebecca."

"Page, I'm twenty-seven. I think that's over the age of consent, don't you?"

"Not necessarily in your case."

"I'm guessing I'm not the first virgin you've encountered."

"I was fourteen. She was fourteen. I don't think I've encountered one since. Until now."

"Are you saying none of your groupies were virgins? You were never anybody's first encounter?"

"That sums it up, yes," he said softly. "They're sort of like unicorns."

"So rather than be my first lover, you would let me return to New York and allow somebody else to have me? What if they hurt me or something?"

"I would allow you to take your newfound emotions, use your God-given common sense, and start dating nice eligible men who would make you a good husband. Of course, that's my second choice."

"Your first choice would be …"

"You agree to become Lady Harlow, I'll make this my final tour, and we will live happily ever after."

"Page, you have no idea how oddly nice that sounds, but at this point in our relationship, I would have to decline your proposal." She kissed his throat softly, "That's legal speak for you are a raving lunatic."

"Yes, I believe I am." He curled her into his arms and held her in silence while the rain pounded outside. Within minutes both of them drifted off to sleep.

Chapter Seventeen

Rebecca opened her eyes slowly, aware of Page's body pressed against her. Her heart pounded as she went over their conversation in her mind, her emotions running the gamut from horrified to steamy lust and she was helpless to stop them. For the first time in her life, she questioned everything she had ever been taught. Right from wrong used to be black and white with no shades of grey and no questions asked. She had accepted what her mother told her as gospel fact. On the opposite end of the spectrum were Gina's views on life and relationships. Gina had no intention of settling down for another ten years, and she had a new boyfriend every month or so. Yet she was always upbeat and happy at work, the model of efficiency. A breakup never depressed her. Rebecca couldn't remember Gina ever being sad or upset. Rebecca's mother would have considered Gina a slut in no uncertain terms. How many times had Rebecca been admonished as a child not to associate with particular girls at school because they were 'loose' or 'immoral'?

"Penny for those thoughts," Page whispered.

"I was thinking back over my life. Not getting into that conversation with you. Much too depressing."

"Your mother meant well, Becca."

Rebecca shrugged. "I know she did."

He stood up and pulled her to her feet. "It's stopped raining. I suppose we should head for the house while we can before Anna comes hunting me with a switch."

His grin took her breath away. If there was a more handsome sensual man on the planet, Rebecca had never noticed. "I think there should be a statue of you made in ivory or gold. 'World's sexiest male' written at the bottom."

"I like the way you think," he said with a wink. He went into the stable and picked up his wet clothes, tossed them over a metal rod, and scooped food out for each of his horses. Rebecca followed him, rubbing her hand across Jenny, who seemed to enjoy the attention. "She likes you. See, even my horses know a keeper when they see one."

Rebecca chuckled, "She likes being the center of attention. Just like her owner."

"Ouch, that hurt me to the quick."

They were laughing when they entered the back of the castle. Page stopped in his tracks when he spotted the woman sitting on the living room sofa. Rebecca jerked her head up, recognition forming in an instant. *Tall, drop-dead gorgeous blonde. Brains of a gnat.*

"Sasha, I would say nice to see you, but you know I won't because it isn't. What do you want?"

The woman stood up gracefully, a wicked smirk on her lips. "Oh, did I interrupt something?"

"What… do… you… want?" he repeated.

"I was going to drop Eric off for a few days, but I can see you're too busy to be bothered with your child." When Page didn't comment, she continued, "I have a photo shoot in Paris and Darcie needs some time off to visit her aunt."

The look Sasha was giving Page was one Rebecca was all too familiar with. If Page refused, Sasha could use it against him in court in the future, denying visitation at her whim. It was the oldest trick in the books in custody cases. With Page's reputation, it might hold up. Rebecca squared her shoulders, offered up her best courtroom posture, and smiled. "Sasha, Page would never be too busy for his son. Obviously, you would be too busy with your photo shoot and all those publicity parties to adequately care for your own child. Our plans are flexible, and I'd love to spend time with Eric."

Sasha looked as if someone had pulled the rug out from under her and Page glanced from one woman to the other. Sasha finally found her composure and said, "And who are you anyway?"

"Rebecca Morrison. I'm with the New York Law Firm of Ferris, Jarrett, Morgan, and Hadley."

Anna appeared at the doorway, having heard the exchange between the two. "Oh, Miss Weeks, I see you've met the future Lady Harlow. She's such a charming young lady, don't you think? I'll go prepare Eric's room."

Page caught the wink Anna gave him and wanted to hug the woman. If it had come from his lips, Sasha would have laughed in his face, but there was no questioning the statement coming from Anna. Rebecca decided not to object. Instead, she moved closer to Page, who eased his arm around her waist. Sasha opened her mouth to comment, then closed it. Finally, she looked at Rebecca and Page and shrugged. "I'll get back to you on the exact time. Darcie might change her mind and not go visit her aunt. Or the shoot may be postponed. Page, do you remember what my schedule was like? So, is there a date set for the two of you?"

Rebecca went with the flow, beginning to enjoy the charade, watching Sasha's composure fade. "Well, there's a logistics problem. I would need to give ample notice and lease my house. Plus there's the tour in the works. You must remember how hectic that can be, don't you? So, to answer your question, a date hasn't been set. I have met with the jeweler in Munich. Nice man. Beautiful rings, I must say. You must remember how difficult it is to choose the right stone. We've made plans to do some sightseeing but nothing that can't be changed for the joy of Page and I spending quality time with Eric. So, please let us know when to expect him as soon as you know your plans. Is that suitable, Miss Weeks?"

Sasha was unable to answer so she just nodded her agreement and picked up her handbag from the sofa. Finally, she said, "I'll let you know," and without another word, headed for the front door.

Page leaned down and kissed Rebecca. "You are truly a piece of work, Lady Harlow. What would happen if she tried to check with your law firm? She's that type of sneaky."

"She would be told that Ms. Morrison is presently in Europe." Rebecca crossed the room to stand by the window.

"That should make her sick to her stomach for a few days. See, both before and after Sasha I was not thinking regarding a long-term relationship. On the first and second tours, I had a huge ego and strutted my stuff on stage and off. Women from sixteen to sixty were offering up sex and more sex. It was surreal to the point I just went with the flow. When I met Sasha, I just fell and fell hard. We were inseparable from day one. I put a ring on her finger and stopped participating in the wild parties. She went with me on a part of the tour, and when I found out she was pregnant I was beside myself. Tommy agreed I should curb my schedule. I began seriously planning for the day we got married and started our family. Slowly, I noticed Sasha was becoming more and more distant. Quiet. Chilly. Unresponsive. I finally suggested we set a date and figure out where we were going to live. She informed me she had been to an attorney and all she expected of me was reasonable child support. It went downhill, and for a while, we only spoke through our attorneys. In the end, I signed over a house, and a car and agreed to generous support, plus medical coverage for Eric. Eventually, I got my shit together and returned to the road. I stopped thinking about any long-term relationship. Until now. Until you."

"Don't think of me as long-term Page. I have too much emotional baggage to deal with. Plus I love my career, I have my own home, and it's all on the other side of the world. Long-distance relationships seldom work. You have a nine-month tour, and you need to be the Page Harlow your fans expect."

"Will you at least consider the insane possibility that after the tour, you could come back to me?"

She stepped into his embrace, and they stood in silence. There was a part of her that wanted to say yes, but her sensible part denied the possibility. "People don't make long-term commitments, at first sight, Page. Hell, last week I didn't even know you existed."

"Well, last week I didn't know you existed, except in my dreams. You've always been the woman in my dreams. You could ask Tommy. He can vouch for me on that. Look, I'm not going to keep bringing it up because I don't want you to feel pressured or uncomfortable. This is your vacation, and I still plan on making it one you will always remember. But Becca, you can't make me change how I feel about you either."

"This is all still so new to me. I'm still struggling with emotions I never knew I could feel. I want what I know I shouldn't. Well the ice maiden part of me knows I shouldn't anyway. But I love how I feel around you. How you make me react. I need time to absorb all the newness."

"Well, I'm glad we had this chat," he said with a grin. "It's progressing at least. Now, since Sasha believes we are indeed engaged, I know she will cover all bases. This means, my sweet, we really do need to visit Weston and put a ring on your finger. I'm guessing Sasha will drop by to shop and mention it to him, so we need to be one step ahead."

"Did you put Anna up to making the comment she did? I thought that I would stroke out. Then I realized it was a good plan. Sasha can't go to the judge and complain about your having your fiancée here without putting her own position in jeopardy."

"Let me run up and put on some decent clothes, and we'll go into town."

"You're seriously going to buy me a ring?"

"Yep. I seriously am." He kissed her on the forehead and darted up the stairs, while Rebecca dropped onto the sofa.

Anna came in carrying two cups of coffee and sat down in the chair across from Rebecca. "I apologize if I put you on the spot, but I cannot stand that woman because of the way she used Page and then discarded him like trash."

Rebecca chuckled and sipped the coffee. "I only met her for ten minutes, and I can't stand her. I don't like it when people use others for their personal selfish gain. Besides, she's using Eric as leverage, and that won't be good for the child."

"I want you to know, that Page cares a good deal for you, Rebecca. He and I had a long chat over cake the other night. He's always been hoping the right woman would come into his life. He believes it's you."

"How do you feel about that Anna?"

"To be honest, it would make me happy. The question is, how do you feel?"

"I don't know. I was raised so strict, hand-holding was barely tolerated. I never gave any thought to a serious relationship. Never have the time or the inclination to look for Mr. Right."

"I was just like you. I didn't date much, and when my friend wanted to set me up with a blind date, I almost didn't agree. We've been married for over forty years, Hans and I. You don't go looking for love, it comes looking for you. Usually when you least expect it. Now, that's all I have to say on the subject, Rebecca." The woman winked at her, "Make sure it's a lovely ring, you choose."

Page entered the room, dressed in stonewashed jeans and a blue shirt. This hair had been dried and fell like gold silk across his shoulders. "If the two of you are finished talking about me behind my back…"

"Nothing we wouldn't say to your face, Toad Prince," Rebecca teased.

Anna stood up and carried the cups past him toward the kitchen.

Chapter Eighteen

In town, Page parked close to the jewelry shop and walked around to open Rebecca's door. She shoved a strand of hair out of his eyes, smoothing it back through her fingers. He curled his arm around her shoulder, pulling her into an embrace, releasing her just enough to enable her to walk on her own to the doorway.

Weston looked up from his paperwork. "Twice in one week? What can I help you with today, Lord Harlow?"

"Diamonds, Weston. For the future Lady Harlow. The third finger left hand."

"Oh, I am so thrilled to hear the news. Congratulations to you both. Here, let's have a look."

While he unlocked a small safe, Page led Rebecca to the sitting area. Weston produced three trays of solitaires, all different. Page glanced over at her, and she shrugged. "Help me out here Page. I've never so much as thought about going shopping for an engagement ring."

"Which one do you like best?"

"All of them, I'm afraid."

"Ok. What shape would be your favorite? Marquis, Pear, or Round?"

Rebecca looked at the jeweler. "What would you recommend?"

"A single marquis stone in a platinum setting, surrounded by several smaller pear-shaped diamonds. I have one of those in the back safe. Keep looking at these, and I'll be right back."

Rebecca picked up a simple solitaire and slipped it on her finger. "I never even dreamed of trying one of these on. Well, maybe when I was ten and saw Cinderella. Then my mother made certain to tell me all the horror stories about marriage and well, that ended that."

Weston returned with the most beautiful ring Rebecca could have ever imagined. She replaced the solitaire in its case and allowed Page to slip the new ring on her finger. Page watched her face light up as she stared at the ring in awe. "Do you like it?"

"Of course I like it. What's not to like? It's absolutely beautiful."

"Weston, do you also have the wedding band or would you recommend plain platinum?"

"The band is here. Along with the one for you. Lady Harlow's has fourteen small stones, and yours has fourteen as well, but smaller."

"Done."

"Excellent choice," Weston said, replacing the trays in the small safe. "Shall I just bill your card?"

"Yes, that would work great."

"Have you set a date for the big event?"

"Probably after the tour. Unless I can convince her to marry me before she returns to New York. However, we all know the legal paperwork involved in marrying someone from another country."

They walked out into the bright sunlight, and Rebecca gasped as the light seemed to turn the diamond into streaks of fire. She looked up at him as they walked. "That went well, I thought. This isn't a real diamond, is it? I mean you're just doing this because of Sasha. Aren't you?"

Page stopped and stared at her. "Weston doesn't sell fakes. So, yes, Rebecca it is a genuine diamond. That is real platinum, and Sasha has nothing to do with the way I feel about you. You still don't get it, do you?" "It's hard to believe that within the span of a few days, you have fallen in love with a total stranger to the point of proposing marriage. I can't wrap my head around the concept."

"I don't know how to convince you I'm serious, Becca." He started walking again, and they turned into Hard Rock, where they chose the same table from yesterday. They were served by the same girl. After their drinks arrived, Page leaned on the table with his elbows, sipping his bourbon, his eyes never leaving her face. "Okay, listen carefully. I told you I wouldn't continue to badger you because I didn't want to make you uncomfortable, so let me say what I need to say and we won't harp on it. Fair enough?"

"Fair enough," she agreed.

"I told you I have always wanted a woman who would be the one for me. In my mind, I wanted a woman who would be loving and kind. One who was intelligent, one who liked the same things I did. I'm talking about opera and art and classical music. I dreamed of having a family, a wife who loved me for me, not because of my status or reputation. When Tommy was talking about this contest he thought up, I told him I wanted a woman who liked opera and played chess. A woman like the one he has. His wife adores him. When they're together, you can feel the love that surrounds them. He told me women like that didn't listen to the noise I called music and sure as hell wouldn't enter a stupid contest to spend ten days with me. And yet, here you are. The woman I have prayed for my entire life. Sitting here, sharing a drink, going to art galleries and an opera. All I've ever wanted, Rebecca. I know it sounds crazy, but there you have it. I didn't believe in love at first sight until now. Until you."

"Page… I don't even know where to begin to address all that. I will say that I have never felt this way around anyone in my entire life. It's overwhelming. I don't know what I feel. I can't describe it. No one ever prepared me for my reaction to you. So, keeping in line with being totally honest, let me say at this stage of our relationship I won't rule it out."

Page seemed to exhale a sigh of relief. "Is that a maybe?"

"Maybe it's a maybe," she grinned.

He sipped his drink and frowned. "Don't look now, but here comes our favorite reporter," he said softly.

Rebecca glanced up as Brenda Franks stopped at the table. "Might as well have a seat, Brenda. More questions?"

"No, actually not. I just stopped by to say hello. I'm sorry if I came on a bit strong yesterday. Page is usually so open about his lifestyle."

"Well, let me set the record straight then. My secretary entered my name in the contest without my knowledge. I had no clue who Page Harlow was. Most men I meet are the suit and tie type, or they're judges. I come from a rigorous religious background. I am not married, and I am too busy with my job to go out much. I own my own home and pay my own bills. That being said, I am delighted I agreed to come."

Page arched a brow. The comments were all facts but entirely unexpected. He decided to sit back and be quiet. Brenda had retrieved her notebook and was scribbling notes when the flash of Rebecca's diamond caught her attention. "Is that an engagement ring? Did Page give you an engagement ring? Page?"

He nodded. "Yes, Brenda, it is an engagement ring, and yes I did give it to her."

"Are you going on tour with him, Rebecca?"

"No, I have a career to return to."

"So marriage vows before or after the tour?"

Rebecca smiled. "Not before a nine-month tour. That would be insane. He needs to focus on his music and his fans."

"Is this up for publication? Page?"

"Well Brenda, facts are facts, aren't they? Just make sure there are no hidden innuendoes in the reporting. Now go away," he added with a grin. Turning to Rebecca after Brenda was out of sight he said, "I hope you're ready for full-blown press wherever we go. Her column is widely circulated here in Germany, and that tidbit will probably be picked up by other magazines. Maybe you should give Gina a heads up in case someone calls there for you."

"And say what exactly? Hey Gee, remember when you said opposites attract? Well, you were right. Page asked me to marry him. First off, she would think I was joking. She would probably laugh in my ear."

"Well, I'm keeping to my part of the promise, not to harass you about it. Let's order some food." He got the attention of their server and ordered burgers and fries for them both.

After their lunch, they drove back to the castle where Anna was happy to see the beautiful ring on Rebecca's finger.

Page looked down at Rebecca, and his heart ached. It was crazy to even hope that she would ever honestly feel about him the way he felt about her. She was convinced the announcement of their engagement was strictly for show although he was as serious as he had ever been. His mother had explained to him about love at first sight when she spoke about meeting his father. He didn't believe it was possible. With Sasha, it hadn't been exactly love at first sight. More like lust. They had been good together. They looked good in photos, she had been passionate, and he was happy to oblige. It morphed into what he believed was love, at least on his part and he thought she felt the same. He was wrong in thinking the baby would make everything perfect for them. Was he wrong this time? *Was this the real thing?* When she boarded the jet to return to her life in New York, would she file away his memory, their times together? Would she even keep the ring? If she did, would she keep it in a drawer somewhere? He smiled inwardly as she continued talking to Anna. It would be a bit difficult for her to claim nothing happened now that Brenda Franks had it all on record. Brenda would make sure the engagement was a headline feature of the next issue. He leaned over and kissed Rebecca on the cheek. "I'll be in the studio or the fitness center." Without waiting for an answer, he walked away, not looking back.

After Page left, Anna arched a brow. "So, now what? You have the ring. Sasha believes it's a sure thing and Page seems happier than he has in a very long time. How do you feel?"

Rebecca heaved a long sigh and walked into the kitchen where she pulled out a chair. Anna joined her. "I don't know what to think.

How to feel. I honestly don't know. I have never had a real boyfriend in my entire life, and I'm twenty-seven. I was beginning to think I was emotionally void of feelings. Those types of feelings, anyway. Men would openly make comments about me, and it always made me feel dirty. My mother was a good teacher about the horrors I would have to submit to after marriage. I was a good student. Even in college. I went on a date once, to a party and when the guy started groping, I literally threw up in his lap." Rebecca laughed at the memory. "He was the star quarterback, so I was immediately labeled a 'seriously maladjusted crazy bitch.'" She fingered the ring. "Yet, around Page, I want to just throw myself at his feet. I have even offered myself, and he refused. He said I arrived a virgin and would leave a virgin. Although the first day I was here he sort of gave me the 'unless you beg' line. At the time I laughed. Anna, I have gone through so many dramatic emotional changes since I got here. I honestly don't know how I feel."

"Well, child, no one said you had to get married tomorrow. You have a career, and he has a tour. For what my advice is worth, wear the ring, accept that he cared enough to buy it for you and I know for a fact he adores you. See if somewhere in your heart or mind you could envision life after the tour. He doesn't tour because he needs the money. He tours because he loves the music and the attention. He could always cut back the touring, and work with other bands, and other singers. Just relax, enjoy your time here, savor the experience, and keep an open mind."

"Great advice. Thanks, Anna." Rebecca hugged the woman, who returned the embrace. "I think I'll go raid Page's library while he's in the studio.

Chapter Nineteen

It was dark when Page came out of his studio. He had pounded on the drums and toyed with the keyboard and some new lyrics. Then he beat up his weight bag, ran a mile on the treadmill, took a shower, and changed into what he referred to as his 'rock-star look' of skin-tight leather pants and an open leather vest over bare skin. Fringed suede moccasins completed the look. Well, Rebecca might as well know what to expect when or if she saw him on the road, he thought with a grin.

He found her in the library, asleep on the sofa, a book on the floor next to her. Her skirt rode high on her hips, exposing smooth thighs and a peep of white lace. Did virgins wear white lace underwear, he wondered fleetingly? Crossing the room silently, he picked up the book and almost dropped it. He had expected Poe or Shakespeare, Thor, Baldacci, or a John Grisham legal thriller, but not the secrets of Kama Sutra. An empty glass sat nearby on the end table, a small amount of bourbon at the very bottom. Dropping to his knees next to the sofa, he leaned over and pressed his mouth softly against hers. She tasted of whiskey and smelled like vanilla. She opened her eyes when he played the tip of his tongue at the corner of her lips. Instead of pulling away, she pressed against his mouth, her lips parting in invitation. "I see you've been reading naughty books," he teased.

"Mmm, oh very enlightening. Are those positions even humanly possible?"

He grinned at her and stood up, taking her empty glass to the bar, pouring her a refill and making one for himself, then returned to the sofa. She moved slightly, giving him room to sit but didn't bother to adjust her skirt. "Most of them are possible," he said handing her the glass. "Did you find any particular one you were curious about?"

"Several. It was an eye-opening education."

"I'll just bet it was," he chuckled, eyeing her over the rim of his glass. His free hand explored her exposed leg, starting at her ankle, wondering how long before she called a halt to his touch. He hesitated when he reached the inside of her knee. Instead of the protest he expected, she covered his hand with her own. He took a deep breath, debating his next move. Must have been one hell of a conversation between her and Anna. First the book, the booze, now this.

Rebecca felt her body react to his fingertips. She could do this. She would do this. Her hand moved from his, to do some exploring of her own. When she brushed across his bare chest, she felt him inhale so as boldly as possible, she ran a finger down to the waist of his pants. And stopped.

He exhaled and downed his drink in one swallow, then deliberately pressed her back onto the sofa. His leather-clad muscular thigh moved easily between hers, and his one hand boldly slid beneath the skirt. Between hungry kisses, he asked roughly, "What do you want from me, Rebecca?"

"I haven't got a clue, Page. All I know is my mother lied."

He closed his eyes. He prided himself on his control and regardless of the press releases he had never taken any woman against her will. The problem here was, he wondered, could he stop if she didn't stop him? *He had to.* Unless she agreed to marry him, which was not a bet he would wager, he would not defile her. But nothing was wrong with driving her to the edge of insanity. A smile crossed his lips. He eased the lace over her hips, and her skirt rode higher. The blouse ended up on the floor along with the lace, next to the book. He turned his attention to her silk bra, baring both breasts to explore their smoothness. Still, no protest came from her. He moved his thigh more possessively between hers, leather meeting flesh. He felt her arch against him, and he closed his mouth around a nipple, his hand exploring its mate. Her breathing was ragged, and he could feel her heart pounding against his palm. "Let yourself go, Becca. Don't think; just react."

Rebecca was wild with a desire she never knew existed. Her body arched, moving against the leather. Could anything feel better? The more he pressed, the more she trembled until she felt her entire body convulse. "Page…"

He knew the second her release hit her and his mouth pressed hard against hers, his tongue plundering while she gasped in surprise at what just happened. Slowly, he released her mouth and relaxed his own body to stretch out next to her, his fingers drawing playful circles up and down her thigh.

"Page, what the hell just happened?" She reached for her discarded drink and noticed her hand was trembling and her breath was still coming in short gasps.

"Well sweetheart, I do believe you just had your very first orgasm."

"But that's impossible. You didn't… we didn't…"

"I said I wouldn't take your virginity, Becca. I never said I couldn't give you pleasure."

"But I thought…"

He leaned over and whispered in her ear. "Your mother didn't tell you this was possible. Probably because this usually leads to that." He sat up and grinned at her. "You should probably put your blouse back on in case Anna comes in to announce dinner. The panties are optional."

She sighed, adjusted her bra, and slipped the blouse over her head. "You know, I wouldn't have stopped you."

"I know. Trust me, Becca, I wanted to, but I honor my word."

"A part of me is grateful one of us had sense, but another part of me is wanting to find out what all the hype is about." She cast him a mischievous grin and finished her drink.

"Remember, tomorrow night is the opera. I was thinking about heading out early, but not too early." He needed to steer the topic away from her desires before he lost all his resolve.

Rebecca leaned over and picked up her lace panties, looked at them, and started laughing. Page stared at her open-mouthed, hoping there would be an explanation, or else she had just lost it entirely. Finally, she stopped, hiccupped, and said, "I'm sorry. Something just struck me as funny." She laughed again. "When Gina was helping me shop for clothes for this trip, she informed me I had to buy new underwear. I informed her I didn't need to because nobody would ever see my underwear… especially not the Toad Prince of Germany. As you can see, I lost that argument about not needing new stuff plus here I am, thrilled to be showing off my new stuff to you."

"I really do want to thank this girl in person," Page chuckled.

"Now, I have a small request."

"Name it. I'm yours to command."

"I want to have a personal concert. You're already dressed for it. Just one song. In your studio." When he cocked his head, she teased, "I want to see what my fiancé does for a living."

"Can't possibly refuse when you put it like that, now can I?" He led her to the studio and pulled up a chair for her, played around with the lighting and sound equipment then picked up a wireless microphone. "This short performance is dedicated to the future Lady Harlow," he said testing out the sound system. Then he pressed play on the CD to add the band and went through the first five songs on the new CD.

Rebecca watched, totally mesmerized by his voice and his movements. In the tight leather, nothing was left to her imagination, and she finally understood what Gina saw in his moves. Bare-chested, after discarding the vest, his muscular chest glistened, and his well-toned arms were the result of daily disciplined exercise. Her mind flashed back in time to the men she had known and dated in high school and the two or three in college. None of them ever caused her to feel what she was feeling watching Page pace back and forth. She was breathing hard, holding her breath with the beat. When the songs stopped, he put the microphone down and came to stand in front of her. As her eyes traveled slowly from his moccasins upward to his blue eyes, she bit her bottom lip and stood up. "Now I understand what Gina sees. Why her fantasy was to spend ten days with you. Why she said, women eight to eighty wanted to be with you. I thought she was crazy." She ran her palm across his sweat-dampened chest and stepped into his arms. "She wasn't crazy at all." Boldly she guided his head down her mouth brushing across his.

Page held her against him, exploring her mouth and easing his hands beneath her blouse, massaging her back. "Becca… sweet Becca. Was it different than what you expected?"

"This entire trip so far has been different than what I expected. I didn't expect to meet a man who liked the same things I did and had morals and ethics. A man with honor."

"Then I guess we were both surprised. I was prepared for the typical legal type. Thick glasses, hair either pulled back or cut short. Boring as dry toast."

Rebecca pressed her head against his chest, content to stand in his gentle embrace. "So, now what do we do about all this?"

"For now, nothing. Maybe go see if there is anything to eat. Have a drink. Play the piano. We need to get our sleep for the trip to Vienna tomorrow. It's a little over four hours of driving time. I thought we could see the sights, hit up a museum, and have an early dinner."

"Are you avoiding the elephant in the room?"

"Damn right," he said with a grin. "What elephant?"

"Fine. Feed me, you toad." The spell was broken and their easy comradery returned as they headed for the door.

After raiding the kitchen and fixing sandwiches, they sat on the piano bench sipping their drinks and sharing a bag of chips. Page fingered the keys lightly, and Rebecca couldn't stop remembering those same fingers exploring her skin earlier. A chill ran up her spine as it occurred to her how close she came to begging for him to continue. Well, there were still a few days left, she thought, a smile breaking the surface of her attempt at remaining serious. As he played softly, she knew she needed to be one hundred percent sure of her decision if she made love to him even once. She needed to know for a fact it was what she wanted, more than she wanted her white wedding. Sitting this close to him, she couldn't think of anything else, except that if she didn't make a decision she would never have another chance. Page Harlow was one of a kind. Wasn't that what she wanted? Who better than Page, to give herself to?

"Do I want to know what you're thinking?" he asked.

"Do you? Really want to know? When Gina asked me what type of man I was waiting for, I told her I was waiting for Mr. Right. She said Mr. Right was made up by someone's mom to keep them in line and I should settle for Mr. So-so. She was wrong. There is a Mr. Right."

"Really?"

"Yes, really. You are Mr. Right. You're a gentleman, you're honorable, ethical, and intelligent and you have the body of a Norse God. What could be more perfect? You like chess, opera, classical music, and art."

"Answer me one question, Rebecca. Would you be embarrassed to introduce me to your parents as the man in your life?"

"No, I wouldn't be embarrassed. Not saying they would like it, but I'm on the age of legal consent, and I am done pleasing my parents or worrying about whether or not they approve of my friends."

He leaned over and kissed her tenderly. "And on that note, we need to get some sleep. That means in separate rooms."

Chapter Twenty

Rebecca was up early, surprised that she wasn't tired from bouts of tossing and turning most of the night. The thought of having an intimate night with Page didn't go away, no matter how much her stricter side argued the point. Her emotions were torn in half, and she could only wonder which would win. How would she feel later? That was her primary concern. When she got back to New York, would she look at life differently, having given up what she fought her entire high school and college years to keep? Did it even matter in today's world anymore? Gone were the days of shame at not having a pure white wedding. She glanced at the beautiful diamond on her finger and a tear threatened to escape the corner of her eye. What if he was serious? How could he be? If she refused to entertain the possibility, would she be losing out on true love?

She showered and dressed in the grey soft cotton slacks and a V-neck sleeveless top the color of green grass then pulled the gown out of the closet and draped it over a chair, her faux pearls and shoes in a separate bag.

Anna met her in the kitchen with a plate of eggs and sausage along with toast and a large cup of coffee. "Page took the car into town to have everything checked before your drive to Vienna. He said to tell you he should be back within the hour."

Rebecca sat at the small kitchen table and ate her breakfast. "Anna, I am going to be so spoiled when I get home. I'm not used to being waited on."

"It's my pleasure to see to your comfort while you're here. You are a charming woman, and it makes me glad to see Page laugh again."

"He's been a terrific host. So much a gentleman too, which was a pleasant surprise considering all that I read about him in my research."

"I want him to be happy, but a part of me hates it when he goes on tour. I don't see him for almost a year, and when he comes home, he usually doesn't leave his room for two or three days unless he goes across the estate on Thunder. I know he enjoys being on the road and loves the spotlight, but at some point, even the best of bands stop touring."

Rebecca sighed and sipped her coffee. "I don't know anything about his life on the road, but I'm sure it would have to take a toll on anyone. On the other hand, I can't see him giving it up any time soon. I watched him practice yesterday, and he seems to be in another world when he has a microphone and an audience. Even if it was only an audience of one person." She smiled, remembering the way he moved to the music seemingly lost in the moment.

"So, do you like the ring? It looks perfect on your finger. As if it was specially made for you." Anna changed the subject because she didn't want to tell Rebecca that she would be the one reason Page would quit the road. Page would stay home if Rebecca agreed to marry him. Anna could see how Page looked at Rebecca when they were together. It was the same look he used to have for Sasha Weeks. *No, this was a more intense look.*

Rebecca lifted her hand and studied the diamonds. "What's not to like? It's as exceptional as Page himself. Lord, don't tell him I said that. He's got an ego the size of a small planet as it is."

Anna laughed. "That he does. I take it you are enjoying yourself so far?"

"Oh, very much so. Doing things and seeing things I never thought I would experience. Two art galleries, the palace, now a real opera. I am utterly ecstatic." She hesitated, nervously fingering the ring. The older woman seemed like a great source of advice as well as a person she could confide in. "Anna," she said after a short silence, "I'm afraid I have a dilemma. I could use your wise advice." When the woman refilled both their cups and sat down with a nod, Rebecca tried to figure out where to start. "I am afraid I am going to become involved with Page before the end of this stay. One part of me says it's a terrible idea, but the other part says it would be the best thing to happen to me in my lifetime. I am not naïve enough to believe Page is serious about the marriage talk and I can't envision traveling with a band for all those months as his wife. I know all this was done to shock Sasha. I'm okay with that because the woman needs a good butt-kicking anyway. I'm sure Page can return the ring to the jewelers after I leave. Meanwhile, what should I do about the attraction between us?"

Anna was quiet for a few minutes as she studied Rebecca over the rim of her coffee cup. How best to answer? "Well, first I can tell you Page doesn't do or say anything he doesn't want to. If he bought you that beautiful ring and declared it to be an engagement ring, then you can trust he means it. I cannot and will not tell you whether you should give it back. I can say he doesn't expect you to give it back. I'm not sure how long a proper engagement would be under the circumstances Rebecca, but I will suggest you consider the prospect of being Lady Harlow, especially if you do give yourself to him. I will also say that he does indeed love you. I know that's difficult for you to understand given that you've known him for less than a week. I know Page inside and out. Make no mistake Rebecca, the man loves you with his very being. And we both know how hard-headed and stubborn he can be. That being said; if you and he became romantically involved, he would not rest until he has made you his wife." Anna stopped and sipped her coffee, waiting for Rebecca's answer.

"So, in the end, it becomes my decision as to whether or not I agree to become his wife. Do I hear you correctly? How can he love me after only three days? I didn't think the 'love at first sight' actually existed outside of fairy tales."

"Well, at least consider it as one of your options. Yes, love, at first sight, is genuine. The moment I met my Hans, I knew he would be my husband. I just knew it. And understand when I say he was a blind date I didn't want to go on in the first place."

Rebecca slowly sipped her coffee in silence. They both looked up as the front door opened and Page entered the hall. Dressed in jeans and a tank top, his feet clad in a pair of shoes with a sports logo on them, he could easily pass for the man next door. The thought caused her to smile slightly. *If the man next door looked like a god right out of a mythology book.*

He looked from one to the other and grinned. "Have you two been talking about me behind my back?"

Rebecca shrugged. "Why would you think such a thing? We might have been exchanging recipes or gardening tips."

"Okay, right. Are you ready?" Page asked Rebecca.

"My gown is on a chair along with shoes and jewelry, so pretty much. I assume we are returning here after the opera, right?"

"Yes. Then we can get Greg to fly us to Monte Carlo if you still want. I'll have a car waiting so we can spend more time exploring and less time getting there."

"Let me go get my gown, and I'm ready." Rebecca hurried toward the stairs, leaving Page to take her place at the table.

Anna poured a cup of coffee for Page, then sat down across from him, her brown eyes boring into his blue ones. "Page Harlow, you be very careful with Rebecca. She's having an emotional crisis concerning her attraction to you. It's none of my business what two consenting adults do but take care of her. On the other hand, if she truly does desire you like I think she does, who better to be her first?"

Page was silent as he sipped the hot liquid. Finally, he heaved a long sigh. "I'm a bit conflicted on the subject myself Anna. She needs to be positive it's what she wants. I have no way to second guess that decision. And once that line is crossed, there is no going back."

As Rebecca returned, Anna placed all three cups in the sink. "You two have fun. Take lots of pictures."

Page took Rebecca's packed gown and the small case and led her outside into the sunlight. "Since we're getting an early start, we have enough time to drive through Salzburg if you'd like. See a few sights, have a bite to eat, and then drive on the Vienna."

"Sounds like a great idea," Rebecca agreed as they pulled out of the driveway.

"It's only 85 miles to Salzburg. Maybe you'd like to hook up with a tour guide, and we can let them point out all the stuff to see. Then if you want to take a longer look, we can go back on our own. From Salzburg to Vienna is about 185 miles but most of it is the autobahn. Figure about two and a half hours. The opera starts at seven. We were fortunate because, for the most part, they just perform concerts. Mozart and Strauss mainly with some Beethoven tossed in. However, every once in a while they perform a real opera."

"Page you have no idea how much this means to me. Since I was a little girl, I have always wanted to attend a real opera. I had money set aside for a vacation to Europe, but Dad had a mild stroke, so I took a leave of absence and went home for three months. That almost wiped out my savings."

"It means a lot to me too Becca. I was set against the contest, but Tommy went ahead with it anyway. I was hoping the winner would be a guy so we could just bar-hop, go to all the clubs, and pick up women. My thought was I didn't want to be stuck with a female fan who was not one of my own choosing. All sorts of scenarios ran amuck in my mind. Instead, I got you. I sure wasn't prepared to be turned inside out, but here we are. I know it sounds lame. Love at first sight. Especially from someone with my reputation but there you have it."

"It does present a unique set of problems, doesn't it?"

"Well, we could go ahead and say the 'I do's' and get that out of the way. Then, of course, we would have to figure out how to handle the next nine months. I know you have a career and a home and you wouldn't just throw it all away to live out of a suitcase. Sadly, the tour is already set and scheduled, so I can't just cancel it. I think your term to Sasha was 'logistics.'"

"I suppose the 'I do's' could wait," Rebecca said. "I've waited twenty-seven years. A little longer won't matter." She studied his profile as he maneuvered in and out of traffic. *Was she having this discussion?*

Was it even up for consideration? Her gaze returned to the ring on her finger, and she remembered Anna's words over breakfast. "I guess I just need some time to absorb all that's happening, Page. It's a little mind-blowing. I mean… this time last month I had no idea who you were. I had never heard of you. Then Gina tells me about this contest. I immediately informed her it was rigged. I figured your promotions team already had someone picked out. Gina was hoping I would win either second or third place. The stereo set-up or the movie rental for a year. I don't remember anything about engagement rings."

"I'm sure it's in there, maybe in four-point type in invisible ink. Why was Gina hoping you would win second or third place?"

"She claims my stereo came over on the Mayflower and I would happily give her the Page Harlow CDs and the DVD. The other one was that since I didn't date, I would at least be able to watch movies."

"I would assume you make enough money to have a decent stereo and TV, don't you?"

"I do, but neither of them is a priority. I would rather put my money where it will draw interest. Some stocks and small investments. I got a great deal on the house. My car is paid for."

"So let's see if I got this straight." He glanced over at her, then back at the road. "You own a house in New York, own your car, don't date, and don't go out, don't blow money on movies or upgrade your TV or stereo…"

"I warned you I was boring," she laughed.

"Well, I would like to think you knew deep down you were waiting for Mr. Right. You just didn't expect him to live in a castle on the other side of the planet."

"Makes perfect sense, Toad." She was laughing, trying to make light of the statement, but in reality, he was correct.

He grinned at her, "Of course it does. I'm a perfect Toad."

Chapter Twenty-one

They entered Salzburg a little over an hour later and Page maneuvered the Mercedes through light traffic. "Most of the places we want to see we won't be able to drive there. The streets are narrow, with some nice alleys and of course lots and lots of parks and gardens. Your choice. We can just wander around, occasionally getting lost, or we can walk to the tour stop and be tourists."

"Personally, I think it would be fun to just wander around. Face it, if I wanted a tour I could have booked a tour. You are a fountain of information, and I'm sure you've been here a time or two."

He parked the car in a city parking lot, opened her door, and ran a fingertip across her jaw. "Damn, you're beautiful. Your hair looks like wine on fire. Not burgundy but not flame red."

Rebecca pushed a strand of long blond hair from his face. "I could say the same about you. It takes my breath away. You … take my breath away." She felt at ease when he slipped his arm around her waist, wordlessly guiding her toward the narrow streets and old buildings. The intimate moment between them was gone. As she walked next to him, it occurred to her that she was becoming more comfortable with his touch. It seemed natural to be by his side with his arm possessively around her.

Page guided her through the narrow streets, pointing out the sights as they walked. "Odd thing is, you know Mozart wasn't famous until he died. I mean, here's this genius little kid who composed before he could write, performed for royalty at age six or so and nobody who knew him gave a damn. It sort of makes me sad."

They spent some time touring the house Mozart was born in, Rebecca trying to absorb all the sights and the history. They left the home and Page guided her across the bridge, walking slow enough for her to take in the sights and sounds. She stopped to take pictures every few feet. He took her into Mozart's second home, content to watch her as she looked at everything with the awe only a first-time visitor could have.

From there they walked hand in hand to the Mirabel Gardens. She took pictures of Page with the Castle in the background, laughing when he informed her that the registrar's office was inside and they could be married in short order. "Not today, Toad. Nope, no, nada."

"Bit of history then. The castle was built by an archbishop for his mistress and their many children."

"They did that a lot back then, didn't they? Wives, mistresses, kids, and more kids."

Page shrugged and offered her an innocent grin. "Well, beats sneaking around in hotels like a lot of men do today, I suppose."

"I can attest to that," she laughed as Page took her hand, nudging her in the direction of the bridge. "I wouldn't tolerate it. Why get married if you don't honor your vows?"

He stopped, turning to face her, cupping her chin in his palm. "That's why I've waited this long. When I thought Sasha and I were getting married, I stopped sleeping with anyone. And you should believe me, I won't be sleeping around on you either."

"Page, it's a nine-month tour."

"Well, there are some logistics…" he grinned, "but nothing a little pre-planning can't fix. You know, I won't be on stage seven nights a week for the entire nine months. We usually do two nights back to back and then two or three off. I have a jet. I have a pilot. Problem solved."

They were walking again, slowly, arm in arm. "So, let me see if I get this straight. The planet's biggest, hottest playboy plans to settle down with a legal researcher who lives and works in New York, and said playboy plans to commute to New York for sex. Toad you are a piece of work."

"In between all the commuting, I see a lot of cold showers in my future. And no, it's not just sex. If all I wanted were sex, I damn sure wouldn't need to get married now would I?"

They walked along in silence, but she eased her arm around his waist. Finally, she glanced up at him. "Page, it's a lot to absorb so give me some time okay?"

"I never claimed to be the patient type, but I understand where you're coming from. I'll try to be patient. I promise. Now, what do you think about stopping for coffee and pastry? Then I have one more sight for you to see before we head out to Vienna."

"Okay. I'd like to sit for a few minutes and rest. The pastry is going to spoil me you know."

"If we had more time there's so much to see. You could spend hours just exploring the back alleys. They all cut through from one street to the next, and all of them have little shops. Some open up into patio areas to just sit, or small cafes."

He led her into a small shop near their starting point. There were outdoor tables, and she took the seat he offered. A young girl came over to the table with a small pad. "Hi, Page. Haven't seen you around much. How's the album coming?"

"It's finished. The tour starts in three months. Marci, I'd like you to meet my fiancée, Rebecca. Becca, Marci's parents own this café. They make pastry to die for."

The girl's eyes widened as she looked at Rebecca. "Seriously? You're getting married? The sky is falling. She's so gorgeous." The girl ran her hands across her apron. "I'm sorry I didn't mean to talk as if you weren't sitting here listening. I mean, it's just such a shock. After what Sasha did and all. There's going to be a lot of broken-hearted women in the world, you know."

"I know," Rebecca said with a grin. "My own assistant back home will probably throw herself off a bridge."

"Let me get you our pastry and coffee. I'll be right back." The girl darted for the door.

A few moments later an older woman came to the table carrying a tray with two pastries and two mugs of coffee. "Page Harlow, is it true what Marci says? Somebody brave enough to make an honest man out of you?" The woman turned to Rebecca. "You look like you are capable of keeping him in line. A redhead. Did you get the temper? You might just need it."

Page grinned. "Abba, you're going to scare her off, and I'm trying to be well-behaved. Becca, meet Abba Barron, the owner, and Marci's mother. Abba, meet Rebecca Morrison, soon to be Lady Rebecca Harlow if I'm lucky."

"What about the tour?"

"Still going. I can't cancel a world tour."

Greta studied Rebecca for a minute. "You going to go live out of a suitcase for a year? Not much of a good way to start a married life if you ask me, which you didn't."

"No. I have a career in New York, so I'll be working while Page is working."

"Long distance marriage is not a good start either."

"We may wait until after to tour to make it official." Rebecca took a deep breath. *What was she saying? It sounded like a foreign concept, coming out of her mouth.*

"She's a sensible woman. I give my approval. Now eat." With that, the woman turned and walked back inside.

"Wow," Rebecca said, taking a small bite of what seemed to be a sort of cream-filled strudel. "Oh my God this is good. Why are you telling everyone you know we're getting married?"

His blue eyes met and held her green ones. "Because we are. At some point. Maybe not this week or even before the tour starts, but we most definitely are. I told you I'm not patient, and I know I said I would give you time to comprehend, but you have to admit, what we feel is more than just physical desire. Much more. If you choose to wait until after the tour, that's fine. But as a child, I was told never to give up on something if I truly wanted it. And this … marriage to you is what I want more than anything."

"It just boggles my mind. You could have any woman you wanted with the snap of your finger."

Page grinned, reached across the table and held his hand in front of her face, then snapped his finger. "Done."

"I walked right into that one didn't I?" she laughed. "This is some seriously good pastry. Where are we going from here?"

"To the fortress." He pointed to the huge fort sitting above the city. "The view is spectacular. Can't miss it."

Rebecca looked at the fortress looming over the city, sitting high on a hill. "You know, when I originally planned my trip here about two years ago, I never dreamed I'd get to see so much. Granted, I had planned on taking a full two-week vacation, but I only thought about being with a tour group and seeing a few specific sites in a few cities. I think it included London, Paris, Madrid, and Rome."

"That's about typical. For the most part, they're good tours to go on if you've never been to Europe and don't know anyone."

She finished the pastry and most of her coffee while Page went inside to pay the bill. When he returned, he took her hand in his, guiding her through the narrow streets, apparently knowing exactly where he was headed. They came to what reminded her of the ski lifts she had seen on the Discovery Channel. Page spoke to a person who gave them two tickets and opened the door of the car. Once inside, the door closed and began its ascent toward the fortress. When they arrived at the top, Page helped her from the car and walked toward the waist-high wall.

The view was breathtaking. All of Salzburg was visible from where they stood. Page pointed out the different landmarks, the Cathedral, and all the domes and rooftops. As they walked, she could see the mountains in the distance, covered in a blue haze. She took pictures from every angle. At one point, Page asked one of the workers to take photos of the two of them, which the man was most pleased to do. Page kept his arm possessively around Rebecca's shoulder, and she didn't object, resting her head on his chest. Her diamond glistened in the sunlight. "It would be great if we had time to do the whole tour of the inside, but as you can tell, it's a lot of ground to cover, and we should be thinking about heading to Vienna soon." Page said as Rebecca thumbed through all the photos she'd taken. When she put her phone away, they returned to the lift and descended back to ground level. Page took her hand and led her toward the car by a different route, pointing out still more historical sites as they walked.

As he opened her car door, Rebecca turned and looked into his eyes. "Page? Will you do something for me?"

"Of course. Name it."

"Kiss me. I want you to kiss me until I can't breathe. The way a woman is supposed to be kissed. Especially a woman who seems to find herself suddenly engaged."

He wrapped her in his embrace and lowered his mouth to her. While his hands caressed her back, he pressed her against the car, captured between the metal and his own body. It was a deep, hungry kiss, filled with apparent desire as he explored her mouth and urged her to investigate his in return. Her hands eased into his hair, and she clung to him, the intensity of her desire surprising her. Slowly, he released her mouth, brushing his lips across her cheek and down to her throat. When he pulled away, he guided her into the car, leaned down, and kissed her again. When he finally stood up, she was breathless and wide-eyed. He got into the driver's side and closed the door, looking over at her as he started the engine. "That is the way a woman should be kissed, Rebecca."

"My mother was so very wrong," she whispered, her fingertips touching her lips. "It makes me question what else she was wrong about. Or did she deliberately lie to me?"

Page eased the Mercedes back onto the road, heading toward the autobahn. "Not all women react the same, Rebecca. Maybe for whatever reason, your mother truly found it distasteful. It was a different time thirty years ago. Women were treated differently. Especially in small towns."

Rebecca stared out the window in silence for a few minutes. "Well, at least it's not inherited, thank God."

"Happy to hear," Page said with a laugh.

"She warned me that my wedding night would be painful and traumatic, but I would have to submit to my husband's wishes. She said that usually the entire act didn't last very long and when he was asleep, I could go soak in a hot bath. I remember thinking, what would be the point of it all, in the first place? And she still expects me to give up my home and career, come home, get married, and have babies."

"That is the most fucked up thing I've heard in a long time."

"Well, I can tell you I followed her wishes about never getting involved." Rebecca turned in the seat and looked at him. "Until now. Until you."

"That's progress, Becca. I will make you happy, I promise."

"Well, I suppose we can figure it all out as we go along. I mean, you do have commitments with the tour, and I have commitments to the law firm."

"And at some point, you'd have to break it to your parents. I'm sure that in itself would be an interesting discussion."

"So far this entire experience has been surreal. I mean, it's as if I'm a completely different person. No one in New York ever caused me to look twice. I turned down invites to go clubbing and dinner. Most of the time I was alone. Walking in the park on a nice Saturday, taking a drive into the country to a park, or a library. I've never attended a rock concert in my life. I think I owned a Bee Gees record. Liked Bowie a lot. The rest was just noise." She shrugged. "I usually listen to classical."

"We are a lot alike, you know," Page said, maneuvering through light traffic. "I like classical. I love a good game of chess. Like my alone time in between tours. Very split personality. I have my wicked and wild rock image, and then there's the other side of me that just wants peace and quiet and riding my estate on my horse."

They drove in silence as Rebecca looked out the window at the scenery flying by. She didn't even want to know how fast Page was driving. There were so many things going through her mind that she didn't trust herself to speak. Could it work between them? Wasn't it worth trying? How else would she ever know what it was like to belong to someone if she didn't allow herself the chance? He made her feel special. Loved. Awakened a part of her, she never knew existed, and she didn't want it to stop. Well, it wasn't a decision she had to make on the spur of the moment, at least. She would enjoy the rest of her vacation time with him. Whatever happened… happened. The thought caused her to smile.

Page slowed down and exited the autobahn. "We made good time. There's a couple of hours until the opera. I can show you the sights, or we can go have a nice dinner. Then we'll need to rent a room so we can change clothes. After the opera, we'll return to the room, change back into our traveling clothes, and drive home."

"Another first on my list of things I never thought I would do," she laughed.

"What?"

"Check into a hotel with a man."

"We need to avoid the press at all costs. Given my reputation, that would cause a bunch of rumors flying wild."

Rebecca chuckled and slowly shook her head. "Page, if we haven't started any rumors by now, I'm sure they're out there lurking. I've spent my entire life always concerned about what others thought or said about me. Had to be beyond reproach. Gina was the only one who knew the truth behind this vacation. Everyone else just knew I won a free trip to Europe. My mother forbade me to come. So frankly, Page, I don't give a rat's ass about rumors."

"Works for me. Let's go eat something. As a matter of fact, let's check in to the hotel, take our clothes to the room and eat at the restaurant. Then we can slip upstairs, change, go to the opera, return, change back into our normal clothes, and head out. The hotel I have in mind is about three minutes from the opera house, and they have parking."

Rebecca nodded in agreement as Page maneuvered through the streets of the city. What would the reaction be if she was photographed at a hotel with Page? Did it matter? Would anyone think less of her just by the pictures? Her parents would think the world was ending and that she was going to rot in hell, but she couldn't change that. And, she decided, she didn't care what they thought anymore.

Page pulled the car into the valet section, and a man stepped up to open her door. Page retrieved the luggage, handed off the keys to the man, and led her into the spacious lobby. She silently absorbed all the beauty around her as Page dealt with the lady behind the desk. He handed her a card, and she handed over two key cards. Another man appeared and took the luggage, disappearing into the elevator after a few words from Page, who then turned to Rebecca. "Three restaurants, two bars. I would assume you would prefer local food?"

She followed him into a dining area where they were led to a table and given menus. Page ordered for them both after giving her several entrees to choose from. A server brought a bottle of wine, opened it, and poured it after getting Page's approval.

During dinner, Rebecca managed not to nervously spill her wine or her food on either herself or the linen tablecloth as she took in her surroundings and gazed at Page who acted as if it was every day he dined in five-star restaurants. "So," she teased, "do you come here often?"

"Not often, but I've been here before. This is the best of the restaurants and a great hotel. And, it's close to the opera. Since it's not one of my usual haunts, I can usually eat and go to the opera without being stalked by photographers and or fans. There are times I like my privacy."

"It's indescribable. Of course, I don't get out much."

"I'm honored to be able to share new experiences with you. To show you my home and the sights."

They finished dinner, declined dessert and Page led her to the elevator. When they arrived at the door to their room, he gazed down at her, then clicked the card and the door opened. Rebecca gasped aloud when the saw the size of the room. "My whole house isn't this big," she said, exploring the bedroom, closets and sitting area. Her gown, in its carry case, was draped across the king-size bed. Next to it was Page's bag, which she assumed contained his change of clothes.

"We still have time to spare if you'd like to freshen up. You take the bathroom, and I'll change in here. We can walk to the Opera House and get settled into our seats."

"Okay. I just need to redo my hair and splash water on my face." She scooped up her gown and small carry case and stepped into the bathroom, closing the door behind her. Stripping off her clothes, she stood and critically studied herself in the large mirror. Slowly, she dressed in her new silk bikini cut undergarments with matching bra, said a whispered 'thank you' to Gina for insisting on new stuff from the skin out, and then stepped into the emerald gown and matching shoes. She added the necklace and earrings. The bracelet went on the arm opposite her diamond watch, and the ring went on her right hand. "I feel like Cinderella," she whispered to herself. A few well-placed bobby pins pulled her hair away from her face and ears. With a deep breath, she turned the doorknob and stepped back into the bedroom.

Page was standing in front of a door mirror, adjusting his bow tie. The diamonds from his Rolex glittered in the overhead light. His tux was a silver grey, and he had a darker silver cummerbund and tie.

"Wow," he said, eyeing her head to toe. "You are absolutely beautiful. Only one small problem."

"What?"

"The pearls need to go. Lose the pearls, please."

"But, they match the pearls on the gown," she said in a slight protest.

He walked over to the small table and opened his case. "I think these would match as well, don't you?" He held up a velvet box with a strand of pearls accented with small diamonds. There were earrings to match as well as a silver bracelet engraved with pearls and diamonds.

"How did you even know about the jewelry? When did you find time to get these? We've been together all the time…" Her voice trailed off as she allowed him to replace hers with the real ones.

"You told me on the phone when you bought the gown. Remember? When I dropped the car off for the checkup early this morning, I stopped by to see what Weston had."

"You can't keep spoiling me, Page."

"I most assuredly can. And I will. Case closed."

"Wow. Well then, I can't very well refuse, can I?"

"Let's go shock the locals, shall we?" He gave her a devilish grin and took her hand.

Chapter Twenty-two

They entered the opera house, and Rebecca froze for a moment, trying to take in everything at once. Page acknowledged several people, causing Rebecca to believe he came here more often than he let on. He spoke to the staff, and they were led to a private area, with only two seats. The view of the stage was perfect, a little to the left of their position. She turned to look at him. "These are not 'spur of the moment seats,' Page Harlow."

He offered her a slight grin. "Busted. I have a season pass. However, the opera was a spur of the moment. We were fortunate because as I said earlier, most of the time there are just musicals. Mostly Mozart, some Strauss, and a little Beethoven. I thought when you asked for an opera we would have to find one in Paris or go to Italy."

Soon, the lights dimmed, and everyone became quiet. Page lifted her hand to his lips and kissed her palm, then sat back relaxed. He spent most of the time watching her as she watched the stage. He had never wanted a woman as genuinely as he desired her. Not even Sasha. Rebecca was the type of woman who would be there for him when life was crazy. She would be faithful. Of course, there was still a chance she would change her mind and say no. She hadn't technically said yes yet. She was right about the logistics. Where would she want to live? Would she move to the castle full-time? That, of course, would be perfect, but he owned other homes. Would she decide to keep the house in New York? Truth be told, he hated New York. If she was insistent about living in the United States, he did own a condo in South Florida and a beach house in Southern California. If she wanted to work, he would support her desire to become an attorney. Maybe they could visit each of his homes and she could choose her favorite. She was leaning forward in her seat, hanging on every word and movement on the stage and he was enjoying the fact she was enjoying herself.

When it was over and the curtain closed, he tilted his head and smiled. "Well, was it all you'd hoped for?"

"Oh Page, you have no idea. A dream come true. Granted, I didn't understand a word they sang, but it was truly beautiful."

He wanted to tell her how much he loved her. It was as if they were meant to be together, but he refrained, saying, "I'm happy to make all of your dreams come true, Becca."

They sat while the lower area emptied, before leaving their seats. As they descended the stairway toward the lobby, he linked his arm through hers. She carefully lifted the hem of her skirt as she took each step. He stopped one of the staff, spoke rapidly in German, and then asked Rebecca for her phone. She handed it over and the young man took several steps downward and turned toward them. He took several photos, before handing the phone back to Rebecca and hurrying on his way. In the lobby, Page asked softly, "Coffee or something stronger? I for one would love a drink about now."

"I can agree to that."

They walked back to the hotel and chose a small table near the bar. Rebecca agreed to Glen Fiddich on the rocks and a piece of Danish strudel. When she took her first sip, she gasped and quickly set the glass down. Page studied her for a minute in silence. "Another first?" he teased.

"Actually yes. I very seldom drink and it's either wine or a beer now and then, or more recently a little bourbon and coke with you."

"Well then, I'll cut you off after one. Two at the most. It won't do for you to end up sick or hungover after such a perfect evening, now would it?"

"True. I'll just sip this one while you enjoy as many as you want. As long as you aren't too drunk to drive us home." She grinned at him over the rim of her glass. "Of course, then we would be forced to stay in the hotel wouldn't we?"

"Are you insinuating you would try to take advantage of me if I were tipsy?"

"It's a thought." She boldly winked at him.

"Woman… do not tempt me. When I make love to you, I plan on both of us being sober. You can count on that Becca."

"This time last week, that very thought would have had me screeching in real fright."

"Becca, you have a very fucked-up set of parents. I'm sure they'll make great in-laws, once they get over the shock of their innocent baby girl marrying a rock star whose reputation reads like a porn movie. I will promise you this. Nothing in our bedroom will ever be horrid, disgusting, or painful."

She looked into his blue eyes and smiled, "I believe that, Page. But as screwed up as my upbringing was, I'm not the least bit sorry I waited."

"Now that," he whispered, "sounds like progress."

Chapter Twenty-three

After their drinks, they took the elevator to their suite. Page closed the door, locked it, and stood, wondering if either of them would follow through with their obvious desires. Should he take what she willingly offered or not? If he did, would either of them regret the decision in the morning? That was his only real concern. If this was just the heat of the moment or the excitement of all that had happened tomorrow would bring devastating remorse. Maybe the answer was to fulfill her desire without taking her purity. That he knew he could do. He prided himself on his ability to hold back. Passion without the total act was not only possible, it brought with it the thrill of promise for the next time. He smiled inwardly and reached for her.

She stepped into his arms and melted against him. His mouth held hers as he eased his jacket off, tossing it over a nearby chair. The tie followed. The cummerbund fell to the floor. Gathering her nerve, Rebecca slowly released the buttons of his shirt, thrilled at the sound of his sharp intake of breath. As she savored the look of his bare chest, she bit her bottom lip. "I'm going to need some guidance here, Page. I have exhausted all my knowledge on the art of seduction."

He had to resist what they both wanted.

She turned, her eyes taking in all of him from head to toe, almost afraid to breathe. "Page… Part of me wants to. I'm not sure I can."

"Don't think about it, Becca. Everything will be just fine. Better than fine." For over an hour he touched, kissed, and caressed every inch of her, paying close attention to her gasps of surprise and desire. Her gown ended up in a discarded heap on the carpeting His own body reacted to the intimacy and he gently pressed against her, not surprised when she didn't completely return his attention. She would learn, in time, how to please him, but tonight was for her. His kisses were gentle, teasing, and then demanding, dominating and possessive.

"Page…" He lay next to her, gently caressing the small of her back and the curve of her hips as she faced him.

"Yes, Becca?"

"I thought…"

"I told you, there are many methods of pleasing you without taking your virginity, Rebecca. I don't have to possess you to give you pleasure."

"But what about your pleasure?"

"I'm perfectly content, Becca. I remember telling you, that sex for the sake of sex is a full-contact sport. Making love to give someone you love is entirely different. Although at some point, the two merge, and that, my lovely Lady Harlow is guaranteed to leave you speechless." He kissed her gently. "We'll get there. Not just yet, but we will get there. If that's what you truly want. It's a choice only you can make, Becca. There are no do-overs. You need to be sure."

Boldly, she pressed herself against him from shoulders to feet and kissed him possessively, taunting him with the tip of her tongue against his. "Nice that we seem to be making progress, my lord. It sort of saddens me that it's obvious my mother never experienced what I just did. How could she consider any of this as disgusting or painful? It boggles my mind. From what she led me to believe, it was over in a few minutes. He went to sleep and she took a bath."

"I don't have an answer for that one sweetheart. Maybe your dad doesn't know any different either. Back then, women didn't have sex before marriage and sometimes men didn't either. So, you have two people who haven't got a clue, with no instruction manual trying to do what they are expected to do. Imagine trying to cook a full course meal before you ever saw a kitchen stove."

The mere image of that caused her to burst out laughing. "Page Harlow, you really have a way with words."

"So, do you think you need a bath now?" he teased.

"I may never take a bath again. It would wash away all those kisses you left on me."

"So, should we stay the night here, or head for home?"

"I don't know. Either or…"

"Then, let's go home, get some sleep, and plot out the rest of our week. Besides, I'm not sure if Sasha was serious about dropping Eric off or if she just wanted to try to corner me. She knew about the contest, so she knew, regardless of who won I would be tied up. There were only two options and either would have fit her agenda."

"Two?" Rebecca got up and retrieved her outfit from where she'd left it in the bathroom.

"If a guy won, I would have been taking him out on the town, drinking, and carousing. If a girl won, we would be engaging in that full-contact sport, most likely. No one counted on option three. The woman of my dreams and deepest desires would win and I would fall in love within less than twenty-four hours."

"I'm still trying to wrap my mind around that. My only problem is the tour. It's nine months Page. It wouldn't be fair to you to deprive yourself of sex on the road for an entire nine months while I stayed in New York, working and acting like nothing was different. Is there some sort of solution? I mean short of me traipsing around the world with you?"

"We still have time to work on that but hear me well. I will not be having sex on the road. My playboy days are over. Whether we are married before, during, or after the tour makes no difference. You will be the only woman for me from now until the day we die. Unless you tell me you want nothing more to do with me ever."

Rebecca stood silently as he got dressed and gathered up his tux and her gown. What was there to say? She had a taste of passion and she wanted more. Much more. With a simple nod of her head, she could have it all. There was no way she could return to New York and pretend this was just an interlude, a blip on the radar of life. She took a deep breath and held his gaze, then softly said, "Page Harlow, I love you."

He turned and looked at her, then smiled. "Now that, my Lady Harlow, is real progress."

"Are you sure you don't want the one last wild bachelor tour before settling down? I mean, honestly, I would understand. After all, that's your superstar image."

Page stared at her, silent for a full minute. "Becca, my music should be my image, not my backstage antics. There are lots of singers who are happily married and faithful. It happens when you love someone so much that no one else can compare and all you can think of is the amount of time lost until you are with them again. Do you think you could handle me sleeping with a different groupie every night for nine months then deciding 'Okay, honey I'm done, I can get married now'?"

"Honestly? I would probably cry myself to sleep every night wondering if you might decide marriage to a straight-laced, uptight, inexperienced woman wasn't what you wanted."

"Then let's settle this once and for all. I want you and only you." He scooped up their belongings and led her to the car.

Chapter Twenty-four

Rebecca fell asleep on the drive home and Page carried her inside, up the stairs, and into her room. Instead of trying to undress her and disturb her much-needed rest, he just removed her shoes and covered her with the satin spread. She lay perfectly still until he left, closing the door softly behind him before she sat up and finished getting undressed. She was a little disappointed that he didn't stay with her or that he hadn't taken her to his room instead. He was definitely a man of his word. She had a lot of thinking to do in the next few days. Life-altering decisions to make. Who could have foreseen that someone who seemed so opposite was, in reality, more like her than anyone she had ever met? The way he had treated her at the hotel was still lingering in her mind. She hadn't been prepared for the sensual caresses. He could have easily completed the seduction. She wanted him to complete it, to take her completely, yet he refrained out of respect for her views and desire for her pure wedding. Even now, hours later, she tingled at the thought of him being her first. In a way, her mother has done her a favor, because she was now able to give her innocence to a man who treated her like a woman deserved to be treated. One who respected her enough he denied himself.

She wondered what her parents would say. Would they be happy for her if she married Page? Oh, no doubt they would be shocked by his profession and his reputation but that was their problem, not hers. What about her career? Her house? The thought caused her to smile. Her mother always said a wife's place was by her husband's side, no matter what. Even if the 'no matter what' led to living in a foreign country? Or out of a suitcase, in hotel rooms? She laughed softly. Now, that was pushing the envelope. There were still things she had to do in

New York and she would have the nine months during his tour to do them. It occurred to her that the thought of marriage was taking up more and more space in her head. *And in her heart.*

She fluffed her pillow and curled up, a smile on her lips as she drifted off to sleep.

At the other end of the hall, Page paced his room like a caged panther. What if, during the long tour she changed her mind? How many times had groupies whispered the expected 'I love you' when he was finished? What if she decided she wasn't ready to get married to anyone? What about the tour? Abstaining wasn't a problem on his end, but given his reputation, would she believe or trust him to do so? Was he being selfish to expect her to give him a definite answer after less than a week? Sure, he knew what he felt was real, but did she feel the same way? How would she even know? Just from the way she reacted to his touch, he knew she had never even been fondled sexually before. The memory made him smile. She was so innocent, so pure and untouched. He didn't want to let her go back to New York but short of hogtying her to a post, he couldn't force her to stay. Even if she did agree to marry him, she still had responsibilities. And on top of all that, he wasn't about to rush her to a judge for a quick wedding. She deserved a real wedding with all the bells and whistles. With bridesmaids, her parents, and her friends. The long white gown. The mega-reception. The huge cake. Would she consider getting married during a break in the tour? He'd have to check the calendar for a time with at least several off days in a row.

He undressed and climbed into his king-size bed, staring at the ceiling. So much had happened in such a short time. It had taken him several months of dating Sasha before he felt close enough to her to let his guard down. And she had used his trust to walk on his emotions. He swore after the legal papers were signed there would never be another woman who would cause him to feel anything again. He was wrong. He'd been looking in the wrong places all along. What if she hadn't won the contest? *Hell, she hadn't even known about the contest.* The thought caused him to chuckle. She had been blunt and straightforward in letting him know her position on sex before marriage. At first, he almost didn't believe her but there was an aura of innocence that surrounded her. When he kissed her in the hall in front of her room, he just knew, she wasn't faking it. She had been waiting for the right man, a man she would marry forever.

Hadn't he told Tommy he wanted a woman like Janet? One who could carry on an intelligent conversation, who enjoyed classical music and chess? He hadn't hoped for untouched and unspoiled but yet, here she was. Everything he could hope for and more.

Grinning like a mischievous child he reached for his cell phone.

Tommy Madison looked at the caller ID and groaned aloud. Problems already? Obviously, because otherwise, Page wouldn't be calling this late. He knew the first words out of Page's mouth would be 'get her a hotel', or something along those lines. "Yes, Page?" he said with a sigh as he answered, preparing himself for the worst.

"Are you sitting down Tom?" Page asked in the most serious tone he could muster.

"Yes, Page. I'm sitting down. Let me guess. You want her out of there and put in a room somewhere?"

"Not even close."

"Shit. Do we need to get a lawyer?"

"Nope. Care to try for three wrong questions?"

"Just give me the news. What happened and how can I fix it?"

"Okay. You aren't going to believe what has been going on since you dropped this woman in my life."

"Jesus Page, it's only been four fucking days. How can you screw something up in just four days? What happened?"

"I need you to do me a favor."

"Okay fine. Name it." Tommy was gripping his phone so hard he thought it might crack. His wife was looking at him with an 'I told you the contest was a bad idea' look.

Page laughed softly. "Tommy, calm down before you stroke out. I would like you to agree to be my best man at my wedding. Not sure of the exact date because there's a lot of logistics involved. Her career, her house, the tour… She lives in New York, I live… well shit, I live in a lot of places. I'm sure her parents are going to hate me on sight, but we can deal with that I suppose."

"Are you drunk?"

"Nope. I am very sober, thank you very much."

"Is this your idea of a prank to give me a damn heart attack?"

"Tommy, do you believe in love at first sight? Do you believe that somewhere in the world everyone has a perfect mate?"

"You cannot be serious."

"Oh, but I can be and I am. She is wearing a four-carat marquise diamond, surrounded by smaller pear-shaped diamonds in a platinum setting. Also, we told Brenda Franks we were engaged. Oh, and Sasha."

"Sasha? You told Sasha you were going to marry a woman you just met and she believed it?"

"Well, to be honest, we didn't tell her. Anna did. It was a moment for the history books, let me tell you. And then Rebecca proceeded to eat Sasha for lunch."

"And, because of this, you decided to go ahead and marry her? Have you lost your damn mind?"

"No, Tom. I decided to marry her because she is the woman I have searched for my entire life. I decided to marry her because I am in love with her. With that being said, this will be my last extended tour. Maybe not my last tour ever and not my last album, but shorter tours. Tommy, she's my 'Janet'."

"Page, you need to think this over for a while. Don't make the same mistake you made with Sasha. You almost didn't come back from the edge."

"I know. For the first time in my life, I am thinking clearly. Probably more so than ever before."

"Page, do you know how much work has gone into this tour? Into your image? How do you think your fans are going to react to your news? Have you got any idea what this will do to ticket sales?"

"Rock stars get married all the time Tom. And this may come as a fucking news flash to you but I don't give a shit about ticket sales or concert attendance. My fans can either accept it and be happy for me or they can shove it up their ass. Have a good night Tom. I'm going to sleep now."

"Is Rebecca listening to this conversation?"

"No, because she is asleep in her room at the other end of the hall. I know this may come as a surprise but I haven't touched her. Good night." Page hung up before Tommy had a chance to voice his total disbelief on that subject.

Chapter Twenty-five

Page was awake at sunrise, riding across the meadow on Thunder. His blonde hair was streaming in the breeze as he allowed the stallion to run full out. Before long, he was on the far side of the lake, looking back at the castle.

Rebecca woke up and took a long shower, her mind still replaying the night before. Would every night with him be this glorious? Oh, she knew there would be arguments and disagreements but wasn't this what she had saved herself for? Marriage to a man who turned her emotions inside out? A man whose smile could cause her to melt? She carefully chose a pair of rust-colored slacks and a brown off-the-shoulder blouse. Her smooth neck displayed the strand of pearls perfectly.

Anna was in the kitchen and did not look at all happy as she poured two cups of coffee. "Miss Rebecca, Tommy Madison is in the great room. He says he'd like a word with you. He arrived about thirty minutes ago."

"Where's Page?" Rebecca asked.

"He's out on the property with Thunder, as far as I know. Mr. Madison asked the same thing when he arrived and said that was better because he needed to speak with you in private." Anna turned and arched a brow, "I don't care for his tone, let me tell you."

"Page's manager to see me? Why?" She frowned as she took one of the coffee cups while Anna carried the other one and sat it on the end table near the older man. The tension in the room was off the charts as Anna all but glared at the man and walked away, closing the door hard as she left. Rebecca turned to the man who was staring at her. "Anna said you wanted a word with me?"

"I want you to go pack your belongings. I'll drive you to the airport and put you up in the hotel of your choice in Paris."

"I don't understand…"

"Understand this, Miss Morrison. The contest was a mistake but I will abide by the rules set forth and pay your expenses. Let me make myself clear. I want you out of Page Harlow's life as soon as possible. I have taken the liberty of reserving a suite for you at the most expensive hotel in Paris with a full expense account included."

"You want what? You? I still don't understand." Rebecca lowered herself into the chair, keeping both hands on the coffee cup.

Tommy took a sip of his coffee and turned to face the woman who was responsible for the future downfall of everything he had worked so hard to keep up. "According to the contest agreement, either you or Page can terminate the castle visit and you will be put up in the hotel of your choice. So I am requesting for you to terminate this visit and enjoy Paris free of charge. You're a very bad influence on his career."

Rebecca shifted in her chair, to look the man in the face. "How exactly am I a bad influence? From my understanding, this entire contest was your idea. What did you expect to happen? He and I are enjoying the sights. He's been a perfect host."

"He believes he's in love with you."

"And for some reason, you think that's a bad thing?" Rebecca sat straighter now, believing she knew where this was leading. "Mr. Madison, I can assume Page isn't the one asking me to leave. You, for whatever reason, see me as some type of threat. I'm perfectly content here, with Page showing me the sights and I would, therefore, decline your offer of a hotel in Paris. If Page wants me gone, then he can tell me himself. So far from the conversations we've had, I doubt that's the case."

Meanwhile, Anna had gone to the back door out of earshot and called Page.

"Anna, what's up?" Page said, his heart clenching at the thought something happened to Rebecca. Anna never called him while he was riding.

"You need to get your butt back here as fast as that black devil will run. Your manager is trying to get Rebecca to pack and leave. Other than that, I've not got a clue."

"Coming… stall him until I get there. ETA ten minutes." Page put the phone away, turned Thunder toward the house, and ran flat out. The faster they ran, the more furious he became. Instead of stopping at the stables, he dismounted at the back door where Anna was waiting.

"He's trying to bribe her into not seeing you again. Already has her a hotel in Paris booked."

"What's her response?" *Would she go? Not that it would matter. He would follow her wherever she went.*

"She was a bit confused at first. No idea what was going on or why he wanted her gone. He's not saying. But on a good note, she's not budged from her chair either. Oh, and she's giving him a third degree that would put a judge to shame. She has refused to go anywhere."

Page went to the side door of the room and stood silently with Anna, listening to the conversation.

Tommy had leaned into his briefcase and withdrew his checkbook. "Well then, let me sweeten the pot, Miss Morrison. I will cut you a check for one million dollars to never see or talk to Page Harlow again. You don't owe him an explanation as to why you changed your mind. Just take the money and go."

"That's a lot of money. You don't think Page would wonder why I just disappeared in the middle of the morning without saying goodbye or even giving him an excuse. A reason?"

"Look," Tommy was saying. "It's a million dollars. You can have whatever you want in life with a million dollars. That's enough for full tuition to Harvard Law. Isn't that what you want? To be a lawyer? Here, take the check and go pack. The hotel is booked. I'll drive you to the airport."

Rebecca leaned over and took the check. Page held his ground in the shadows. This would be the defining moment. She looked at the check as if she had never seen one before, then very calmly folded it into a small square and dropped it into Tommy's coffee. "Mr. Madison, take your million dollars and kiss my lily white ass. I am not for sale."

"If Page marries you it will ruin his career. You will be responsible for the failure of a multi-million dollar star."

"Is that what this is about? Page told you he wants to marry me?" Rebecca kept a straight face, hiding her surprise. She had assumed that even though Page had insisted he was serious, he was just immersed in the moment because she was a lot different than the women he was used to. This revelation, however, put it in a whole new perspective. If he had discussed it with Tommy, he was more serious than she realized.

"He called last night. I'm guessing he was drunk off his ass but then, that's Page. I'm thinking about his career."

"Are you thinking about his career or your pot of gold? Lots of musicians are married. If Page and I do get married, it will be because we make each other happy. I doubt his career will go into the gutter."

"Did you say 'if'?" Tommy leaned forward, a hopeful look on his face. *'If' was a lot better than 'when', wasn't it?*

"Newsflash. I haven't said yes. Second newsflash. I haven't said no, either."

"But you live on the other side of the world…"

"Do you read the Bible, Mr. Madison? Read the book of Ruth. A wife will go where her husband goes. If I marry Page and if… he wants me to live here, then so be it."

Page chose that moment to step into the room. His hair was windblown and tangled and he still wore his riding gloves. "Tommy, you're fired. Get out of our house."

"Page, think of the long term. Your career. The fans. You can't do this!"

"I can and I will. I'm a damn good musician. I'm a great songwriter. I can produce other bands. I can write for other bands. So, yes, Tom, I most certainly can do exactly this. The only one who can stop me is Rebecca, by saying no."

"Page…"

"Tommy you've bailed me out of jail more than once for beating the crap out of someone. Get out of our house before you are on the receiving end of an ass beating."

Tommy stood up and looked from Page to Rebecca. "Fine. I'm betting she says no. Then what?" Without another word, he picked up his briefcase and stormed out the front door. *The check floated in the cup of now-cold coffee.*

Page walked to the bar and poured bourbon into a glass, forcing himself to calm his rage. He picked up a silver dish and threw it against the wall. Rebecca crossed over to his side and handed him an empty glass. Silently he poured her a drink and took a deep breath. "What did you say to him last night to get him so pissed, Page?"

"I asked him to be my best man."

"Well, I think it would be safe to say he refused," she said, touching her glass to his. "I was wondering how my parents would take the news, but this puts a whole new perspective on that. The worse they will do is disown me."

"I would have thought he would be thrilled. I mean, yes, I'm still going on tour. Yes, I'd still be strutting across the stage dressed in leather that leaves nothing to anyone's imagination. Yes, there will be rumors and probably slander in the tabloids. I can't stop that part. It's what they expect. The difference won't be in the performance, it will be the after-party action. While my bandmates are free to run naked through the arena and do what they have always done, to the delight of those eager to participate, this man will be taking a shower and after the expected drinks and probably a few hugs, I will be taking my married self; or my engaged self; to my room."

"So, since you are now short a manager, who will you get?"

"I've had at least ten other offers. Tommy Madison isn't the only one in the world who can manage a band and a tour. Most of the work has been done. Arenas booked, people hired. Several companies could run with it. Hell, Ashley could do it. Now let's talk about a more pleasant subject. What do you want to do today?"

"Let's skip Monte Carlo and go to Paris. I've seen more of Europe than I had planned and the only real thing left I had on my wishlist was the Louvre."

"Okay. You go toss some things in your bag and I'll finish grooming Thunder, call Nat, my stable boy, and let Anna know. Then I'll call Greg to get the jet ready."

"Slow down, toad. I didn't necessarily mean right this very moment. For a while, I'd just like to hang out here. I'll go with you to groom Thunder, maybe we could just walk through the garden, play a game of chess, and then leave for Paris."

She followed him back out the side door, where Thunder stood in the shade munching on a small bush. Page picked up the reins, patted the horse, and walked slowly toward the stables. He put some food in the trough and then removed the saddle. Rebecca picked up the brush and hesitantly started stroking the large animal. Page fed the other three, speaking softly to them as he paid them some attention, before returning to Thunder. "I love this big guy," Page said. "He was a lot smaller when grand-dad was alive. He was the one I learned to ride first."

"Another first on my list. The only horses I ever saw were the police horses in New York. Well, when I was a child we did have a small farm, of sorts. I always tried to avoid things bigger than I was."

"Will you be happy Rebecca? I mean if you decide to marry me, will you be happy? I'll be good to you. No lies, no affairs, no one-night stands. Just you and me forever. I understand you haven't made a total commitment yet, but I hold out hope."

"If I do marry you I would be happy. It will take some getting used to, living in a foreign country, but I don't have very many close friends, so it isn't as if I'd be missing everybody. Maybe Gina. But she can come visit."

"Am I getting the impression you've given this some thought? There's hope?"

"I've thought about it slightly. Of course, I wasn't sure you were sincere. Maybe it was a change of pace and you were off guard. You have to admit, coming from someone with your reputation it did seem somewhat off the charts. So, even though I allowed myself to toy with the idea, I hadn't seriously considered it a plausible proposal. And before you say it, no I didn't believe you were using the hint of a wedding to have sex with me. As much as I hate to blow your ego that much more, I would have done that last night. But you dropped me, fully clothed onto my bed, and ran away."

"I had to. It isn't my nature to assault a woman in her sleep." He grinned at her as he took the brush from her hand and led her out of the stable toward the garden.

"Secret newsflash Toad. I wasn't asleep. I was enjoying your carrying me in your arms and laying me on the bed. I was waiting for you to start removing my clothes."

"Devious little woman," he teased.

She leaned against his chest, her arms circling his waist. "But I'm your devious little woman," she whispered.

They sat on the bench in silence, just embracing each other, his fingers playing up and down her arm. Page felt totally at peace for the first time in many years. She still hadn't said yes, but she was closer to a yes than a no, by the way she talked. "Would your parents really disown you? I thought they expected you to get married. Your horrid lot in life and all that."

"It's not the marriage part. It is the occupation of my husband part. Even though they have no idea who you are, they will have by the time the news tabloids hit. But you know what? I don't care anymore. I am not going to move back to the small town and marry the banker's son to make them happy that I'll be financially stable and secure."

"The banker's son?" Page laughed aloud. "How secure is that, for God's sake?"

"He's the vice president of the bank so he makes about two-hundred thousand a year. Enough for the house, car, two kids, and picket fence, I suppose. He's also a deacon at my parent's church, which matters a lot in their eyes."

"So, to be fair in comparison, I am not and have never been a deacon in any church. As for the rest, well, I can afford a house, a car, and a picket fence. I'll even buy you a puppy. You'll have to help do your part about the two kids."

"Well Toad, this ah… house is a nice starter house," she laughed, gesturing at the castle. I doubt we would need a picket fence and the Mercedes is classified as a car, so we're good to go on the comparison stuff aren't we?"

"You didn't ask about my finances."

"Because I don't give a damn about your finances."

"What woman doesn't care about the finances of the man she's almost agreed to marry? Isn't that somewhere in the fine print?"

"You know what I care about? Honesty. Ethics. Morals. I have waited twenty-seven years for a man to come along and sweep me off my feet. Not because he was rich or even close to rich, good-looking, or a toad. Never mind him being a good-looking toad. I was looking for a man who treated me like an equal, not an object or a maid. I am no longer looking for him, Page Harlow. I'm looking … at… him. So, if we have to be homeless under a bridge with your guitar and a tin cup I would make do."

"Well, trust me we won't be homeless. I am a very long way from ever being broke in this lifetime. There is one thing I will insist on." He hesitated before continuing. "It doesn't matter to me if we make love before or after the 'I do' part but you will wear a white gown. That, Lady Harlow, is not up for discussion."

"Maybe I'll want to wear black leather," she teased.

"You can wear leather on our wedding night if you want to," he whispered playfully.

"I can't even envision us having this discussion. This entire scenario is unbelievable."

Page lost his smile and looked down at her. "Are you telling me no?"

"I am sad to break this to you but you can't get rid of me that easily. If I planned on saying no, don't you think I would have taken that asshole's million-dollar bribe? I just said it was un-freaking-believable."

"Well, to be honest about all of this, I am terrified to death."

It was her turn to frown. "Page we aren't having a shotgun wedding. You aren't being forced or coerced into anything."

"I'm not afraid of the wedding. I want you as my wife more than I want anything in my life. I don't want to hurt you. Physically. I mean… well shit, this is a conversation I never had before so I don't even know where to start…" He stared at the flowers.

"Okay. How do you think you would hurt me physically?"

"I did tell you the only virgin I ever had was when I was fourteen. She was fourteen. I remember she said it hurt at first. I don't want to hurt you."

"Well, we won't know until we get to that point, now will we? But if last night was any precursor, I don't see an issue."

"You would think at my age, with the multitudes of experiences I've had since age fourteen, I wouldn't be this lame. You're right. It won't be an issue."

They looked up when the back door slammed. Anna came toward them, a smile on her face. "Are you two planning to sit out here all day or did I fix food to throw in the trash?"

"Lost track of time." Page stood up. "Discussing marital issues."

Anna looked from Page to Rebecca. "So you are gonna make an honest woman out of her?"

"She is an honest woman, Anna. I give you the future Lady Rebecca Harlow of Herrington."

Rebecca jerked her head up. "Of where? What?"

"Of Herrington. It's a quaint village estate in the northern part of England. I inherited it from my father along with the title of Lord Harlow. It's a wretched place weather-wise. People are nice though."

Anna stood there, hands on her hips. "If you're funning her just to justify doing whatever two consenting adults do in private, I'll tan your Viking hide."

"Anna, I believe you and I had this conversation. I told you I wanted to marry her. I told her I wanted to marry her. I told Tommy I wanted to marry her. We even told Brenda Franks the reporter. We would get married here, today except I believe it's fitting she has the white wedding she saved herself for. Besides, if I don't marry her, she'd end up with banker Bob."

Rebecca elbowed him in the ribs. "George. Banker George Rollins of Janberg, Indiana. Junior. His father is George Senior. I'll join a convent first."

Anna stood there, staring at both of them. "You just don't break her heart. Now come eat." With that she turned and walked away, leaving them to follow behind.

Rebecca broke into a fit of laughter and when she stopped. "So it's either Lady Harlow of Herrington or Mrs. George Rollins Junior. Wow, that's a really difficult decision. I might have to consult a guru or a crystal ball."

Page dragged her against his side and walked into the castle, to the dining room which was already set up with breakfast. "Where exactly is Janberg, Indiana anyway?"

Rebecca shrugged. "It's about in the middle. The closest city would be Indianapolis or Fort Wayne, depending. Population under three thousand, give or take."

"In other words, it's a dot in the middle of nowhere."

"That about sums it up. A very small, microscopic dot. One bank, one zip code. A couple of hotels, motels, and a few small restaurants. It's, uh, quaint. Frozen in time."

"So do you wish to be married in the church there? To me, not Banker George.?"

"No. I don't care if I ever see the town again, except maybe to visit my parents. If I'm not disowned. I mean they are my parents, warts and all. They did what they thought was right, even if I know now it was screwed up."

"So have you thought about how you plan to drop this piece of news in their lap?"

"Trying not to think about it. She forbid me to come. The men here are unscrupulous. They'll take advantage of me. Her words. So gee, you think maybe 'hi mom, I met this single playboy rock star and we're getting married' would work?" She grinned at him over the rim of her coffee cup. "Maybe I could try 'Mom, I'm taking your advice. I'm quitting my job and selling my house because I've decided to get married to a guy I just met, who lives in Germany'."

"Damn glad it's your call and not mine," he laughed. "Are you up for getting your ass handed to you at a game of chess?"

"I'm up to show you a few moves of my own on the board, hotshot. You're on."

After they finished the breakfast of eggs, ham, toast, and a side of waffles, Page led Rebecca back into the great room and set up the chess board. It was a beautiful work of art, the pieces all carved from ivory with gold trim. "It belonged to my grandfather. He's the one who taught me to play. I picked it up pretty fast and he finally complained I was winning too much. I still miss him a lot. Seems like only last week we sat here playing chess, drinking whiskey or scotch."

"Sounds like a wonderful man. I'm sure he's still watching you, proud of your success."

"It's a nice thought," he said softly.

It was an hour later when she finally winked at him, moved her final piece, and said "Checkmate, Toad. That was a brutal match though."

"I have been totally humiliated by a mere wisp of a girl. Oh, the horrors of it all," he teased.

"So, what's my prize for winning?" She leaned forward, leaning on the chess board, playfully batting her lashes at him.

"What would you like, little girl?" he teased back.

"A long romantic night in Paris. Tommy said he already reserved one in my name. Maybe we can use it and he can foot the bill? Seems like poetic justice."

"You have a very evil streak don't you?" Page laughed as he put the chessboard away.

"Never did until recently. Must have something to do with the company I'm keeping."

"Are you insinuating I am a bad influence on you? Me?" He gave her the most wide-eyed innocent look he could and she couldn't stop laughing.

"What time is it in New York?" she asked when she finally wiped her eyes. "Never mind." She removed her phone from her back pocket.

Gina answered on the second ring. "You better not be calling to ask me to pick you up at the airport," Gina said as a way of an answer.

"And if I were?"

"Of course, I would. But it hasn't been ten days yet. I cannot believe you of all people would cancel out of the Europe trip until it was over. What went wrong?"

"What went wrong?" Rebecca winked at Page. "Why would you think anything was wrong? When did you of all people become a pessimist?"

"Well, because after the pictures you text messaged me, I figure he probably made some sort of sexual move, and rather than making a scene, you're calling it quits. Plus, it's six o'clock in the morning."

"Is that what you think?"

"You aren't the type to make a scene. I know you too well. Look, this is all my fault. I'm sorry I was stupid and inconsiderate enough to enter your name in that damn contest. I'll do anything to make it up to you."

"Good, because I want you to agree to something."

"Okay."

"Not a word to anyone at the office, okay?"

"Okay." Gina sounded so subdued it was all Rebecca could do to keep from laughing.

"I want you to be the maid of honor at my wedding. Not sure about the exact date or location but I want you to be there when I officially become Lady Rebecca Harlow of…" she arched a brow and Page grinned. "Of Herrington. Lady Rebecca Harlow of Herrington. Somewhere in North England. Page says the weather is horrid but the people are nice so there you have it."

"Oh crap, Ree, you had me going for a minute. I thought I was wrong and he molested you or something."

"Well, he hasn't yet but it's still early and we're headed to Paris. Last night was the opera. I know you don't care for opera but you should see Page in a tux. So, just agree to be my maid of honor and we'll talk about it later when I get back."

Gina was laughing hard. "Okay, yeah, sure. Wedding. Right. You got it. Enjoy Paris."

"Planning on it." Rebecca hung up and looked up at Page. "I don't think she believes me."

Anna came in as Page and Rebecca were both laughing hard. "I could use a bit of humor," she said with a smile. It was good to see Page enjoy himself like this. She'd been worried he hadn't gotten over the damage Sasha caused.

"Here's the person who can make a final decision," Page announced.

Rebecca finally stopped laughing and nodded. "I totally agree. Should I marry Page before the tour, in the middle of the tour, or wait until after the tour?"

Anna looked at them both and realized this was an actual serious question. "Would depend on a lot I suppose. If it's to be a small wedding then any time would do. However, if you want a big wedding with all the frills, it takes time to plan I would think. The tour is nine months, so sometime between today and then should suffice. Next. Will it be here or in the US? Or both? You could have a quiet ceremony now and the big hoopla affair after. I have work to do and I believe you two have a flight to Paris. Figure it out. It's what engaged coupled do, you know." She shrugged her shoulders and then smiled. "Welcome to the family Lady Rebecca."

Chapter Twenty-six

Greg met them at the airport and carried Rebecca's piece of luggage on board while Page parked the car. "Tommy Madison has called me about four times. Said Page fired him because of you," Greg said with an amused smile. "Somehow I believe there would be more to the story than he makes out."

"Suffice to say, Tommy tried to bribe me to leave Page and it didn't go as planned."

"But it was his idea to hold the contest that brought you here. Has he lost his mind?"

Page entered the jet. "Has who lost his mind?"

"Madison. He said if I saw you to tell you to call him."

Page shrugged. "Okay, you saw me, you told me."

"Did you fire your manager this close to the tour?"

"Yep. He decided to take it upon himself to remove Rebecca from my life. Seems she's a bad influence on me. Offered her a one million dollar check."

Greg looked from Page to Rebecca and back. "He did what? Why? No, I mean why would he even think that?"

"I asked him to be the best man at our wedding. I thought that was the thing to do since he brought us together."

"Wedding? Your wedding? You're shitting me, right?" He looked over at Rebecca. "He's… not… shitting me … Well hell, congratulations are in order. I never in a million years expected that to happen but I think you made a good choice. For whatever my opinion is worth." He pulled Rebecca into a hug. "I didn't see this coming."

She smiled. "That makes two of us, Greg."

"Hey, I told you on the way here Page doesn't do what's expected, but this takes the cake on shockers."

"You also told me he was a lot different than his reputation. I'm happy to say you were a hundred percent right on that."

"Well, you two go sit, and let's get this bird in the air. Paris is calling."

Greg headed toward the cockpit and Page led Rebecca to the leather sofa, where he pulled her into his arms. "I'm glad Greg is happy for me at least," Page whispered as the jet lifted off the runway.

"I think Tommy will come around, Page. You should look at it from his perspective."

"Are you taking up for him?"

"No, not for what he did, but maybe he thought it was the right thing at the time. Maybe he was thinking that it wasn't something you thought through. Maybe he thought I would dump you like Sasha did. I'm not saying what he did was right especially the way he went about it, but you've been his friend a long time."

"Leave it to you to be level-headed and forgiving." He kissed her gently, "Later, maybe, I'll call him. See if he's come to his senses. I can tell you, my heart stopped when I saw you take that check from him. For that split second, I couldn't even breathe."

"I've never seen a check for a million dollars, and definitely not one made out to me. I actually thought about wadding it up into a tiny ball and eating the damn thing, but the coffee cup was right there," she grinned at him.

"Rebecca Harlow, you are a piece of work," he said laughing at the thought.

"I guess I have my moments, Toad." She ran her fingers through his hair. "It's like silk. Gold silk. I love the way it feels."

"After my mother died and I was put in the private school, the first thing they did was cut my hair. Military short. Suffice to say I didn't last long."

"You were expelled four times from four schools."

"I never did get along with a bunch of rules. Granddad was the only one who could manage me. I would do what he said without question. He told me if I wanted long hair, I needed to keep it clean and combed and if I didn't he would shave it off." My father decided it was easier on everybody if he allowed me to stay in Germany. Anna home-schooled me."

"But everything you went through has made you what you are today. A brilliant, driven musician."

"Well then, I could say the same about you, Becca. If your mother hadn't been so strict, you might be married to Banker George with those two kids, hating your life. Instead, you left home, but those beliefs kept you waiting for Mr. Right."

She pressed her lips against his throat, "Found him. I remember you told me on the phone you don't go looking for love. It sneaks up on you. God, you were right about that. I never even saw it coming."

He traced her jawline, caressing her with feather touches. His hands eased beneath the blouse, exploring her ribcage and the curve of her back. When she arched against him, he easily guided her back on the sofa. "Becca…" he whispered between kisses. "I can't believe you're going to be mine. Only mine."

"And I expect the same from you."

"You'll get it. I'll be faithful to you. I promise you that." There was nothing more spoken as he taunted her with light kisses and exploring caresses until they felt the jet bank and started descending. "I guess you should straighten your clothes," he sighed.

She chuckled and smoothed her blouse just as the jet touched the runway.

Chapter Twenty-seven

Rebecca stepped into the bright sunlight, Page holding her hand while Greg brought up the rear with the luggage. They decided to get a cab to the hotel and forgo the hassle of driving. Greg put the bags in the trunk of the taxi while Page talked to the driver in fluent French. The driver was smiling as Page handed him several bills, then opened the door for Rebecca. "Before we get settled in at the hotel, Rene has agreed to give us a quick drive through the city's high spots. Just so you can get a feel of the attractions to be seen."

They cruised the streets for about an hour, while Rene tried out his broken English, pointing out the most famous of landmarks as they went. Finally, they pulled up in front of the hotel and Rene opened her door first, taking her hand as she stepped from the cab. Page followed and Rene retrieved the luggage, handing it to the well-dressed porter who rushed over before they even came to a complete stop. Page took the card Rene handed him, more bills exchanged hands and Rene smiled at Rebecca. "It will be my most pleasure to be your guide while you visit our city." With that, he returned to his cab and eased back into traffic.

The hotel lobby was breathtaking and Rebecca tried hard not to stare open-mouthed like a tourist. Page gave off the air of someone who was used to being in places like this as routine travel. She stood to one side while he conversed with the young girl at the desk. Could she ever get used to exclusive hotels and galleries? Thinking back, she hadn't seen any research on his finances, but considering he owned a castle, a Mercedes, and a plane, it would be a safe bet he was well off. The diamond on her left hand was worth a small fortune and if his manager had offered her a million dollars as a bribe he was far from poor. The thought brought a smile to her face as she pictured her mother's reaction, considering her mother thought George Rollins was well-to-do.

Page finished his conversation with the girl who handed him two key cards and turned to catch Rebecca's smile. "Let's go freshen up and forage for food if you're hungry. Then it's off to the Louvre. Tomorrow we can take in more art and do some shopping."

"Page? Page Harlow?" A slender woman with long black hair boldly approached them.

"Hello, Penny. How's my favorite reporter doing these days?" He pulled her into an easy embrace, kissing her cheek.

"Just great. They haven't fired me so that's always a plus. On the downside, I'm not nominated for a Pulitzer either. Introduce me to your friend?"

"Absolutely. Rebecca, meet Penny Hammond, a freelance journalist. She actually tells the truth, with no innuendoes or smut. Penny, meet Rebecca Morrison, soon to be Lady Rebecca Harlow. If the stars align and the moon does its thing."

"Seriously? Page? I mean, you aren't joking?"

"No, Penny I am most assuredly not joking. My playboy days are over. I have found the woman of my dreams. We enjoy the same things when we're not in the spotlight. Classical music, chess. Heading to the Louvre later."

"Well," Penny took Rebecca's hand in a firm shake. "I guess congratulations are in order. When's the big event and am I getting an invitation?"

"We haven't set a date yet," Rebecca answered. "There are some logistics issues we need to work on. I have a house and job in New York and he has the tour."

"Meanwhile, here you are in Paris, the city of love and romance."

Page grinned. "And the Louvre. The Eiffel Tower, French food…"

"So, between the sightseeing, do you think you can find a minute or two for a quick interview?" Penny asked.

"I don't see why not. Do you know about the contest Tommy set up? The ten-day visit as my guest?"

"It's been covered and speculated for months. Are you saying Rebecca is the contest winner? And you proposed?"

"That covers it in a nutshell, Penny so yes, you may have the exclusive. How about lunch tomorrow? Say noonish. Meet us at the foot of the Eiffel Tower?"

"Got it. Thanks, Page. Congratulations Rebecca," she said and walked away with a bounce in her step.

Rebecca looked up at him. "I think you just totally made her day."

"Count on it. Tommy was supposed to decide on the reporter and magazine for the interview and we had pretty much decided on Paris or somewhere nearby for the sit-down, but I just made my own decision. She's the only reporter who has ever been invited to the castle because I like her style. Plus, every other magazine will pick it up exactly the way it was written or she won't sign off on it." He eased his arm around her waist and followed the bellboy who was carrying their luggage. The ride up the elevator was in silence, although Page made his presence known by caressing the curve of her back.

The young man stopped in front of a door at the end of the carpeted hallway and used his master key to unlock the door. Page motioned for Rebecca to go first, he followed and the bellboy followed, setting the two pieces of luggage on the stands, near the closet door. "Enjoy your stay, sir; ma'am," he said with a smile.

Page thanked him for the service, handing him a bill which caused the guy to do a double-take and his smile widened. Then he was gone, leaving Rebecca to explore the huge suite, the two king-sized beds, and a balcony with a spectacular view of Paris. There were fresh flowers and a bowl of fresh fruit on the small round table in the outer room. Page followed her onto the balcony. "Sorry I couldn't get the executive suite on such short notice," he said softly.

"You mean this isn't the biggest one?"

"Junior suite actually."

"Maybe you should curb some of your spending Page. It's not as if you have to wow me with the biggest and best. I mean the ring, the watch, the opera, that hotel, now this."

"Thought you weren't interested in my finances," he teased.

"I'm not. I just don't want you splurging unnecessarily."

"Honey, trust me when I tell you, this isn't splurging. Maybe we should give you a short course on my finances and properties. Plural. Cars, also plural. One jet."

"I think I'd rather remain clueless."

"Well, at some point you need to see the properties at least. There's the estate in Herrington. My childhood home is in Norway, which is where I would like to take you. There's a villa in Italy, a condo in Florida, and a beach house in Southern California. I have a small cabin in Switzerland where I go skiing, sometimes. I own a recording studio in Vancouver, Canada as well. I also have investments in several condominiums in about five countries, all leased and profitable. My grandfather taught me at an early age to make my money work for me so I could do what I enjoyed most. And right now, what I want to do is spend time spoiling my lovely bride-to-be. Hopefully, my bride-to-be."

"Pinch me. I need to know I'm not dreaming. That I won't wake up in my one bed, alone in New York," she whispered, stepping boldly into his arms.

"You do know we are tempting fate, don't you? You need to seriously give deep thought as to how far we go. It's getting difficult for me to control what I want. I thought I should be honest about that."

"Page, I've thought about very little else. Especially after last night in Vienna. You did things I didn't know could be done. My reaction…

If someone had told me that was even feasible I'd have laughed at them. All I could think about was what the entire act would be like. And, for the first time in my life, I want to find out. I have thought it through, Page." She urged his mouth to hers and whispered. "I want to find out before we leave Paris."

He exhaled and possessed her mouth with his own, gently at first, then urgently. "Then, you will find out. Later tonight maybe. We should go eat and then visit the Louvre. After that, we'll see where we go from there."

"Then feed me. I think I might need my strength."

He held her for a few moments, his hands exploring her arms and sliding down her hips, while his mouth searched out the pulse at the base of her throat. With a sigh, he finally released her and led her toward the door. "I know this sounds strange to you Becca, but believe it or not I'm really nervous about this."

"So you've told me. So am I but I want you to make love to me. Of course, I don't have a clue how I'll react so you might have to be very patient with me. One thing I will tell you. If I say 'no' please don't listen to me. If all my strict upraising comes to the surface, I need you to ignore it, even if I can't. Promise me."

"And that's part of what I'm worried about. When a woman says 'stop', I stop. If you say stop, we'll just try again later."

They stepped into the elevator and she kissed him quickly. "Well then, we'll have to both work through this, won't we?"

Chapter Twenty-eight

Outside the sun was bright, but there were rain clouds in the distance. Page took her hand and guided Rebecca through the other people walking around. It seemed obvious he had a destination in mind so she walked beside him, absorbing all the sights and sounds of Paris. The Eiffel Tower was visible in the distance but they weren't going there until tomorrow. Until they met up with the reporter. She hadn't missed the way the woman looked at Page as if he was dessert on her menu. The thought caused her to smile. Something she would need to get used to; women who had been in his life before now. That thought brought a chuckle, which caught Page's attention.

"Do I even dare ask what struck you as amusing?" he said, arching one brow.

"Nothing important," she answered with a shrug.

"Right…" He turned the corner and crossed the street, opening a door to a small restaurant. It was dim inside and he simply nodded at the tall, older man standing nearby. "A quick lunch for two, Paul," Page said, then added, "preferably the back table if it's available."

The man he referred to as Paul simply turned and walked away, Page and Rebecca following close behind. There were only a few other diners inside, but on one side of the room, Rebecca saw an opening to a sidewalk café that was completely crowded with people. They were both given menus by Paul, who nodded and returned to his place by the door. The table was indeed in the back of the room.

They had barely sat down when a younger man appeared carrying a small pad and pencil. "Lord Harlow, good to have you back."

"Thank you, Kyle. I'd like a cup of coffee." Page glanced at Rebecca and when she nodded he added, "Also coffee for Lady Rebecca as well."

"My pleasure," Kyle said and left as suddenly as he had appeared.

Page grinned at Rebecca and said, "Go ahead. You and I both know you're dying of curiosity."

"Come here often, Lord Harlow?" she asked, fighting to hide the grin.

"Not as often as I'd like. Been a bit busy with working long hours and double-checking legal crap. Then there was this insane contest my manager conned me into…" he laughed softly. "Best day of my life and I'm sure by now he's kicking himself for even dreaming it up."

"You and Tommy go back a lot of years Page. I'm sure he meant well."

"Maybe he did, but he went behind my back and that's hard to take."

"Look at it from his point of view. I come waltzing into your life and you see all the things you said you wanted in a normal relationship. Maybe he figured if I had taken the bribe, he would be doing you a bigger favor because I wouldn't break your heart later. However, he found out I wasn't in this for his money or yours. I think he underestimated both of us. Is it worth breaking up a friendship over?"

"Are you going to break my heart later?"

"Not unless I catch you in bed with someone after the wedding. Then I would break your ribs getting to your heart so I could rip that heart out and put it in a blender."

"That paints a scene of violence I didn't see in you," he chuckled as Kyle positioned their coffee cups and tableware in front of them. "Thank you, Kyle. I'm not sure what Rebecca wants to eat. Something quick since we'll be seeing the Louvre after we leave here."

"Perhaps a fruit plate and croissants?" Kyle suggested.

Rebecca nodded. "Sounds perfect."

Page winked at her. "I love a woman who's so agreeable. I'll take the same."

After Kyle took the order and left, Rebecca kicked him in the ankle. "Toad," she whispered with a laugh. "Now tell me, did you sleep with the reporter who's interviewing us tomorrow?"

Page set down his coffee cup and frowned. "That came out of left field. Why do you ask?"

"Because she looked at you as if you were an ice cream dessert and she was starving. It occurred to me it was something I needed to get used to."

"To answer the question, yes, I have. As for what you have to get used to, I can't begin to tell you how to handle that. I will vow to you that whoever she was is definitely in my past. No replays. I need you to believe that and I know it's going to be difficult. Especially with me on the road, given the way the tabloids seem to make things up if the truth doesn't sell papers. All I ask is that if you have any questions about anything, you come to me with it."

"Fair enough. One thing scares me."

"What?"

She waited until Kyle set the two fruit plates down to continue. "What if I'm not good enough?"

"Good enough in what way?"

"You said yourself you never…" she took a deep breath… "What if I don't know how?"

Page blinked. "My lovely lady, that's the best part. I get to be the one to teach you. A real plus is I don't have to measure up to a former boyfriend's standards."

"But I'm competing with a million others before me." She closed her eyes and shook her head. "I can't believe we're discussing this over lunch."

"First, let me say, over lunch is as good of a time as any to discuss this, and second, you are not competing with anyone." He took a bite of his croissant and looked at her while she bit into a strawberry. "A million? Do you really think I've had sex with a million women? Three hundred and sixty-five days a year times ten years is only three thousand, six hundred and fifty times. Math wasn't your best subject, was it?" He chuckled.

"That's still a lot of women who knew what they were doing and I'm sure some were amazing."

"You worry too much. Either that or you don't think I can be faithful."

"I work in a law office. The word unfaithful is used a lot."

Page placed his napkin down and leaned across the table. "If you think that little of me Rebecca I suggest you don't marry me. Because you cannot be worried sick every time I go to the corner store for bread and milk. If or when we say our vows, there will never be any other woman. I've said it, I've vowed it and I've given you my word. If that isn't enough, I can't think of anything else."

"I told you it might take some time, Page. I guess this is part of it. Trusting anyone comes hard. This is a serious mega amount of trust. And I just can't picture you going to the store for bread and milk. Is there even a corner store near the castle?"

"Do you love me?"

Rebecca blinked, looked from his face to the ring on her finger, and back to his face. "Yes." *Somewhere deep in her heart, she had accepted that there would be a future for them.*

"Good, because I love you with every fiber of my being. Now, finish your fruit so we can go stare at Whistler's mother. And the Mona Lisa. Oh yeah, and a bunch of old pictures of naked women and men as well."

"Pervert," she whispered with a grin. "So, should I ask Penny the reporter for tips?" She laughed as Page almost choked on a grape.

"You have a mean streak hidden don't you?" he teased as he motioned to Kyle for the check.

Kyle took the credit card from Page's hand and hurried away.

"It's difficult thinking of you as Lord Harlow. Sounds so regal for such a bad boy," she said, finishing off the last grape.

"Took me a while to get used to it. All of ten minutes I believe. After my mother died and I was stuck in the school in England, I was referred to as Mister Harlow, even at age 13. Grandfather called me Page or sometimes 'the brat'. When my father died, I was the only living heir so everything became mine. I didn't want to inherit a damn village, complete with a manor and estate but it's passed down. You'll be the first Lady Harlow for a good many years."

"That should set my mother on her ear, I imagine. She's all about the financial stability part of the marriage, so I'm pretty sure marrying a man who owns a castle and an English estate should count toward forgiving me for not being a total virgin bride and marrying the banker's son."

"Do you plan on telling her? About the virgin bride part? Please tell her you aren't marrying Banker Bob. It's none of their damn business. I would marry you here, today except for the miles of red tape involved. You aren't a German resident so that's out and yes, I checked. I'm out of ideas, other than for me to say 'no' tonight, and to be honest, I don't see that happening tonight. Do you?"

Kyle interrupted the conversation by returning Page's card, which Page signed, relieving Rebecca of having to answer the question.

Page took her hand and they left the restaurant and headed down the street. After a few blocks of turns and crossing streets, Rebecca found herself standing still, mouth open, looking at the huge modern pyramid in front of an enormous building. She felt a thrill at the sight and Page squeezed her hand as if he could sense her excitement.

"Oh my God, Page. I have dreamed of this for most of my life." With total abandon, she threw herself into his arms. His kiss was deep and possessive, then light and teasing as he pulled her closer to him.

"You know there are a lot of other museums in Paris, don't you? Plus, there's the arc and Notre Dame. And shopping. You cannot come to Paris and go home without shopping. It's an unwritten rule, you know."

"Shopping. Okay, later. Right now, I am trying not to pass out with pure joy or croak of a heart attack from the excitement."

"Any particular place you'd like to start? Favorite must-see painting?"

"Definitely the Mona Lisa. Venus De Milo. Other than that, whatever we see, we see. I'll be too stunned to think, much less choose anything."

"Well then, we'll start with those two and check out all the in-between stuff. Lots of sculptures. Egyptian designs. Paintings and more paintings." He guided her past the line of people to a separate entrance and handed the woman two cards.

The woman, a tall brunette smiled at them as she handed him back the cards. "Nice to see you again Page. I was hoping you'd make time for Paris before you headed out to conquer the world."

"Bethany, I'd like to introduce you to my fiancée, Rebecca. She has always dreamed of seeing the Louvre. She's an art lover."

"I saw the write-up from the German magazine." She turned to look at Rebecca, "Is it true you had no idea who he was?"

"Absolutely. My well-meaning assistant entered my name, hoping I would win the second or third prize."

"I'm actually glad. He needs someone who is grounded and not out chasing the musical legend. Of course, a lot of women might die of a broken heart, you know," Bethany said with a grin.

"Well, they can still look. They just can't touch."

"Good strategy. Enjoy the art. I need to get back to work."

Page gave her a quick hug, then she turned and walked away without looking back. Page wrapped his arm possessively around Rebecca's waist and guided her into the huge building. "So, besides the obvious, you have French paintings, Sculptures, Egyptian, Greek, Oriental, Italian, Dutch, and even Islamic art. Venus is on the ground floor, actually right down the hallway. Mona Lisa is on the second floor."

"Obviously not your first time here, so lead the way, my lord," she said with a smile. "Is it acceptable to take pictures?"

"Sure."

"If the magazine is out, may we get a copy? I'd like to take one to Gina."

"We can do that. It's probably in French and German. Might be able to locate one in English somewhere." He nodded as they turned the corner and stood to face the famous statue of Venus de Milo. Page felt her inhale, the same as he did on his first visit. Pulling her close, he slid his arms around her. "I reacted the same way you just did when I first saw her. I went home and tried my hand at art."

"Anything good come of that?" she asked, leaning against his chest.

"Yeah, I learned that art wasn't one of my talents. Frustrated me a little until my grandfather told me that the person who carved her probably couldn't carry a tune and we were all born with different talents. Besides, when I tried to chisel something out of a piece of rock I ended up with seven stitches. Cured me of that real quick, believe me."

"Yeah, you need all your body parts intact."

He brushed his face against her hair, fanning it through his fingers. She caught one of his hands and kissed the palm. "Let's go visit with Mona," he whispered.

To get from Venus to Mona required walking past a lot of beautiful paintings, which Page promised they could look at later if time permitted. Twists, turns and steps made Rebecca wish she had spent more time working out and less time working behind a desk. However, she was determined to keep up, although she knew Page was not walking at full stride or she'd have been left behind. His hand remained on either her waist or shoulder when possible or he was holding her hand. She saw the crowd of people before she saw the actual painting, but Page was easing them through the onlookers moving forward. There were framed paintings covering almost every part of the walls, but everyone's focus seemed to be on the one toward the end. Then she was standing in front of the most famous painting in the world. She blinked and took several pictures, then turned to gaze up at Page. "I thought it would be bigger. Brighter."

"Are you disappointed?"

"To be here? No. But I guess I was expecting more from all the hoopla surrounding it."

He smiled at her. "I had the same reaction when Grandfather brought me here. Now if you want big, bright and bold, there are other museums nearby. Monet's Waterlilies are huge, I enjoy Picasso's work and then there are Rodin's statues and carvings. You specifically said you wanted to visit the Louvre so here we are. There's no rush so we can just wander from room to room, site to site if you want. You should see the crown jewels."

They left the Mona Lisa behind and Page led the way through the maze of hallways and rooms, stopping occasionally to admire a piece of artwork. Rebecca tried to take in everything at once, always aware of his hand curled possessively in hers. He knew his way around the building, causing her to smile as she remembered him telling her on the phone he hadn't been here in several years. He was right when he said that it couldn't be seen in a full day. "Damn glad you know where you're going," she commented, breaking the silence as they walked.

He smiled at her, leaned down, and kissed the tip of her nose. "We could hide and stay here after they close."

"I imagine we wouldn't stay hidden for long, so sad to say, not hiding out in the Louvre with you."

The room containing the jewels was covered in gold and ornate paintings. Even the ceiling was covered in paintings. Rebecca stood in front of the crown jewels designed for kings and queens and glanced at the diamond on her finger. "I like mine better."

Page pulled her into a light, playful embrace, "I'm glad because I don't think those would be in the budget this year."

When they left the room, they went in a different direction, slowly taking time to look at statues and even more paintings. "I always prided myself on being up to date in the art world. I mean, I recognize the names, hard not to, but the paintings are so different than what I pictured."

"They all look big and bright in the brochures. Now you've seen them. They're still awesome. I mean, these paintings and statues survived wars and floods, Hitler and his bunch. The Mona Lisa was stolen once, and taken back to Italy because someone felt it belonged there. I'm not a real history buff but it's safe to say it was recovered undamaged." He brought her out of the main area into the open space where they took an escalator down to the lower level. "We actually have a Starbucks here. And a McDonalds."

Rebecca burst out laughing. "That's just beyond weird. Paintings upstairs older than my country and a Starbucks and Mickey Dees in the basement. And yes before you ask, I would love a latte right about now." She was still shaking her head as Page motioned toward a single table with two chairs. She sat while he went to the counter. She took several pictures of him as he ordered and texted them to Gina along with 'having a great time'. Page returned to the table with two cups and some napkins. He pointed to her phone and tilted his head slightly. "Sending texts to Gina," Rebecca said, reaching for a cup.

"I noticed you don't spend much time on the phone. Drives me nuts to be with someone who is constantly staring at the phone texting or talking."

"I don't have many people I care to talk to, outside of the office. At work, my phone stays on silent because nothing pisses off a judge more than a ringtone. The same goes for work conferences each morning. My boss isn't paying me to chat with someone. He's paying me to listen to him and his client and get all the motions written and filed."

"Is the pay good?"

"It's a little better than average for a law clerk. Promotions are steady and there's a nice Christmas bonus. I actually make more than George the banker's son, but then New York is more expensive than Indiana."

"A much bigger dot on the map. More money, higher prices. The lesson in economics."

"So, why do you own a place in Florida and one in California? Property taxes must take a chunk of change."

"It's convenient. I spend a good amount of time there when I'm on tour. Greg can fly me to either to rest in comfort and total privacy. After a month or two of non-stop running across the stages under high-wattage lighting, I just need to get away. Up early, oversee the stage setup, test runs, dealing with personnel and paperwork, then spending time at the before-concert meet and greets, radio or TV interviews, and on it goes. Then two hours of high-energy performance, followed by more party people, more interviews, in your face issues that come up. Then comes the after-party which goes on until the wee hours. Trust me, the house and condo on each coast pay for themselves with what I'm saving in shrink fees and medication. It's the main reason musicians burn out. Then they start taking drugs to give them an edge. Soon it becomes a habit. I have no desire to travel down that path."

"You have drug-related arrests in New York and New Jersey," Rebecca said sipping the hot latte.

"Yeah. I was in the room. The room was registered in my name. Therefore I went to jail along with the rest of the people in the room. Paid a lot of money and the charges against me were dropped. Was drug tested, came up with zip." He grinned at her. "I have a lot of sex-related arrests as well. Want to talk about them?"

"Any of them worth discussing? I did read the words statutory rape and sexual assault or sexual misconduct in the lists."

"And yet you came to visit anyway. Very brave little girl aren't you?"

"They never made a charge stick. To me, that means someone cried wolf or tried to justify what happened. After being around you for a few days, I can guess you didn't force anyone to do anything against her will. Case closed."

"Does it seem odd to you we are sitting in the Louvre, having coffee while discussing my arrest record?" he asked.

"The Louvre and coffee part does seem a bit odd, yes." Rebecca grinned at him.

Page laughed, dropping his head to the table. The two teenage girls sitting nearby with their mother turned for a better look and recognition was instantaneous. Rebecca braced herself for what was coming even though Page hadn't noticed them. First one of them got up, the other one close behind, heading toward him, napkin and pen in hand.

"Excuse us for interrupting. If you're Page Harlow, can we get you to sign our napkin?" It was the older one who spoke, as Page sat up and wiped at his eyes.

Page offered up his rock star smile. "Absolutely love to," he said, taking the offered pen.

"I never thought I would see you here. I mean in the art gallery," the youngest one said. "Told my mom it was you and she didn't think so either. Oh, I'm Terri with an 'I' and this is my sister Evie."

Page signed two napkins with a flourish. Rebecca smiled, happy to watch the way he reacted to his fans, no matter where he was. It said something about his humanity and love for people. "Would you two like a picture with him," she asked. "I'd be happy to take them for you."

Both of them gasped in surprise and Terri was the first to hand over her cell phone, then threw both arms around Page in a hug. Evie turned to her mother who was watching as close as any mother would, considering Page's bad boy reputation. Finally, she stood up and walked over, surprising both her daughters and Page. "Hello, Page. It's been a long time."

Page looked up into a face he hadn't seen in years but still remembered. "Cassie, how have you been? It has been a long time. My first tour if I recall. Jackson Mississippi. Shall I continue?" Both of the girls went still. Evie was perched on Page's lap, staring at her mother with a look of shock.

"Wow. Did I leave that good of an impression?" His answer was a surprise to her and she glanced from her daughters to Rebecca and back to Page. "So, do I get a picture taken? You know, for old times' sake?"

"Mom?" Terri said, her wide eyes going from Page to her mother and back. "I never knew you liked rock and roll."

Cassie seemed to relax a little. "I wasn't always an uptight parent, young lady. Why do you think I keep such a close eye on you two? Because men like him are always on the make. Every night's a party, every girl's a target."

"Cassie, let me introduce you to my future wife. Rebecca, meet Cass Thompson. Is it still Thompson? Tour number one. I actually wrote a song about her. It's on the second CD. So what brings you to Paris?"

Cassie sat down, her eyes going from Page to Rebecca. "Married? But the tour. I saw the interview. Conquering the world, making your Norse ancestors proud. How do you fit marriage into that?"

"I did the interview long before I met Rebecca. I hadn't planned on meeting a woman who turned my heart to putty and melted my soul. That kind of love isn't something I went looking for, Cassandra. I'm thirty." His tone had softened somewhat, to Rebecca's relief. It wouldn't have been good for them to argue in front of the woman's two clueless daughters. Must have been one hell of a party for Page to remember her after all this time.

Finally, Page stood up, moved a teen to each side of him, and put his hands on Cassie's shoulders. "This is one for the books," he joked as Rebecca willingly took several pictures before Page sat back down in his chair. "You're looking good Cass. I mean that. Your hair was longer back in the day. It looks good shorter."

Page watched as the three of them walked away. Only Terri glanced back and made a little wave with her hand. Page waved back and then turned to Rebecca. "I know you have a million questions," he said with a sigh.

"First tour? You have a hell of a memory or it was one unforgettable party."

"I was still catching my breath. I had a Superman ego and a bad-boy attitude. Never thought about the other person's feelings. I mean here I am, stepping out of the shower, half drunk, high on success, and here's this woman 'Hi, I'm Cassie and I want you.' So I'm like 'Well, hello honey, come over here'. Only afterward did she tell me she was married with two kids. Little kids at the time. Hubby thought she was at a movie with a girlfriend, who was in the next room with the drummer. I always remembered her because I swore not to have sex with someone else's woman. Pissed me off and I threw her out of my room naked. Tossed her clothes after her. The cops came. Her girlfriend was pissed off. My drummer was pissed off. I threw a half bottle of Jack Daniels into a television set and trashed the room. The hotel didn't press charges because we paid for the damage. Never did find out if her husband ever found out."

"I love you," she whispered.

"Warts and all, huh?"

"You're a toad. Of course warts and all. The fact that even then when you were enjoying your different-woman-every-night tour you still had the morals to not sleep with married women. In that line of work that says a lot. At least to me, it does." She reached across the table and curled his hand into hers. "I love you Page Harlow and yes, I would be honored to be your wife."

"Holy shit."

She laughed, "Not the exact reaction I expected, toad."

Chapter Twenty-nine

Page and Rebecca left the Louvre and walked through the park to the edge of the river, where they stood in silence wrapped in a tender embrace. Finally, she ran her fingertips across his cheek. "I never knew such contentment as I do right now. I know life will have its ups and downs but I'm ready to deal with whatever our life together throws our way. I do have one request. I would like you to make peace with Tommy. If it hadn't been for him I wouldn't have ever known you existed. Plus, it should prove to anyone that the way I feel for you is real and everlasting. Please, Page? He's been your friend for years."

Page kissed her forehead and pulled his phone from the pocket of his jeans.

Tommy answered on the first ring. "So, let me guess. She left you?"

"No, she's standing right here beside me. She just officially agreed to be my wife, Tommy. We're in Paris. Just left the Louvre. I ran into Penny earlier and she's meeting us at the foot of the Eiffel Tower at noon. Look, I'm not happy about the way you went behind my back with Becca, but she doesn't think you did it with evil intent. She believes you had my interest at heart. Did you?"

"Page, I thought I was doing the right thing. I know she's everything you said you wanted and I guess I figured she was just too damn good to be true. I swear I have never known any woman to turn down one million dollars."

"She's not interested in my money, Tom. For the first time in years, someone loves me for me. As she says, warts and all."

"What can I say? I was wrong about her. You know, I'm really glad I was wrong. And Page I'm happy for you."

"Tom, I don't think it will have a major effect on my career. Do you? She's not out to break up the band. I'll still be the same on stage, just different after all the meet-and-greet stuff. Look at it this way… you won't have to bail my ass out of jail as much."

"So, are you rehiring me?"

"If you want to be rehired, I guess I am. Tom, you're the one responsible for her even being here so damn it, I'd like you to be my best man. You, Greg, the guys. Her, Gina and her friends. It's going to be a wedding fitting of a Lord and Lady tying the knot. Major fucking production. I want you there. Hell, she wants you there."

"Janet just told me she wants to meet this wonder woman who can tame you. Are you staying in your usual hotel?"

"Yes. Look, why don't you and Janet meet us at the tower tomorrow? We'll do the interview with Penny and then have lunch. Go to the top for a champagne toast to my new bride."

"Fine. See you at noon."

Page hung up and pulled Rebecca into a deep embrace. "I thought I was in love with Sasha, but you take me to an entirely new level. We'll have a great life together. Now, I suppose the questions are all logistical. Where and when? How big? Your dress. I do know that's an important decision."

"I feel like I'm living in a fairy tale. Castle and all."

"Well then, you should dress the part. Maybe we can pick up a bride magazine on the way back to the hotel."

They walked along the river hand in hand, content with the silence between them. Her thoughts were running wild with all that needed to be done. This was the biggest step she had ever taken. Bigger than packing her small suitcase and getting on a Greyhound bus leaving Indiana in the dust, and stepping off the bus in New York at age nineteen. She hadn't told her parents she had applied to a small college in New York until she received the acceptance letter. Her mother forbade her to go, but her father had the final say and ended up driving her to the bus station. How would her dad react to his future son-in-law? Could he overlook Page's past? Her mother would throw a total fit. Then again, maybe not. All she was interested in were finances and grandchildren. She exhaled as that thought hit her. Babies.

Page was attuned to her slight change of mood as they strolled. When she caught her breath, he stopped in his tracks. "What is it?"

"Babies. I was wondering how my parents would react. Mom wants grandchildren."

Page smiled at her. "I do believe I'm capable of making that happen."

"I don't know anything about babies. I never even babysat as a teenager."

"Well, first we have to take one step at a time. When you do become pregnant then we will deal with learning about the care and maintenance of them. I'm sure anyone who can handle lawyers and judges daily can deal with a small infant. I wasn't sure I could handle it either, but I was right there when Eric was born. Set of lungs on that boy, from the first breath. I managed to figure out which end got diapered. Sasha was off work and I was between tours so I think I did okay. We managed to be civil enough to interview nannies and she ended up with Darcie." He shrugged and stared into space for a minute. "Then we went our separate ways. I got visitation so it isn't as bad as it was when I was a kid. I think I saw my father maybe four or five times until my mother fell ill. Then he came and stayed for a week. He returned for her burial and took me to England, deposited me at the school, and left. I was thirteen. Besides, if we live at the castle you have qualified backup."

"There is that. Thank God for Anna." Rebecca breathed a deep sigh of relief.

"If you look straight ahead of us, you'll see the art gallery where Monet's Water Lilies is on display. We've got enough time before it closes at six."

"Maybe we can come back here after the tour and spend some time just going from gallery to gallery. The Louvre overwhelmed me."

"How about this? I'll call Rene and he can drive us to the shopping district. We can window shop or serious shop. Then he can come back and drive us out to the arc at sunset."

She nodded. "Ok, that sounds like a great idea. You're the tour guide."

"You'll come to love Paris in short order. If you need some quiet time, Greg can fly you here for the day. You can shop, have lunch, shop, have dinner and fly back. Of course, there's also Rome. Monte Carlo and Nice."

"Quiet time? I've had years of quiet time, thank you all the same."

Page called Rene who promised to pick them up in a 'jiffy', causing Page to smile. When he disconnected the call he guided Rebecca to the corner of the park. "Rene is happy to practice his English. His new word of the day is 'jiffy'. A few minutes later, Rene pulled over and stopped in traffic, put his flashers on, and opened the door for Rebecca.

"Where do you want to go?" he asked cutting back into traffic.

"Montaigne Avenue. Somewhere near Chanel, Dior, or Prada. We're going shopping. I'll call you when we're done, and then we might go to the Arc de Triomphe."

Rene grinned at them in the rearview mirror. "Okie dokie."

Rebecca chuckled, which seemed to make him even happier. He maneuvered the small car in and out of traffic finally stopping in front of Boutique Prada, got out, and opened her door. He and Page conversed in rapid French and he nodded, then returned to the flow of traffic. "He's going to go have a bite to eat and wait for our call."

Rebecca nodded but her mind was spinning as she looked around the shops. "Shopping in Paris. A distant dream of mine."

"A distant dream?"

"I'm not a fashion person. I wear professional clothes that mix and match well."

"So, this will be another first for you. I love being able to give you new experiences. Opera, art, chess, Paris. I want you to enjoy all the best the world has to offer. It makes me happy."

The stores took her breath away as Page led her from one to another. She found a beautiful blue silk dress, shorter than she was used to, but it fit like it was made for her. When she returned from the dressing room, Page had already told the young associate they would take it. Next came a small handbag, handcrafted and expensive. Page decided she needed shoes, heels as well as flats. The heels were blue with gold trim and Page nodded as she tried her most sensual walk. The flats were made for comfort and fit like a glove. He helped her choose several silk scarves and a light off-white lace jacket for the evening. Several outfits were nixed with a pained expression on his face. By the time they were finished, they had packages from most of the top Paris designers. She learned he loved to shop, and loved seeing her emerge from the dressing room in something outlandish or exclusive. The last item he chose was a leather mini dress that zipped up the front. There was no doubt in her mind, that she would be wearing it for his eyes only because there was nowhere she would go in public in a skirt that short or that tight. On the way back to meet up with Rene, she found a shop that sold magazines and bought an edition of Brides Magazine. He picked up the tabloid with their picture on the front page, taken at Hard Rock. Page quickly scanned the interview and told her Brenda had done a fairly good job reporting the facts. The girl at the register looked from the paper to his face, over to Rebecca, and back to him and began speaking in French. Page was answering her and Rebecca stood by, flipping the pages of her magazine. Finally, after Page signed a blank sheet of paper and kissed the girl on the cheek, they left with their purchases.

Rebecca grinned up at him. "I keep forgetting not everyone speaks English and I'm in a foreign country."

"She offered to have my baby, but settled for an autograph instead," he said with a shake of his head.

Rebecca looked up to see if he was teasing. "All-righty then. Since you gave her the autograph, I guess she'll just have to find someone to give her the baby. That's my job."

"And we're going to work on that."

Chapter Thirty

They returned to the same spot Rene had dropped them off, just as he came around the corner. All of the purchases went into the trunk and they pulled back into traffic. Rene took them to the hotel, where Page handed the packages to the porter, with instructions to take them to the suite. He then got back into the cab and they were off again, heading to the Arc de Triomphe.

At the Arc, Page invited Rene to join them for the view at the top, which delighted the Frenchman. "I would be so happy to be with you and your beautiful woman, looking at all of Paris." The three of them took the elevator to the top and then climbed the steps from there. Rebecca took a deep breath. Rene was right, it was a view of all of Paris. The sun was setting and the lights were coming on. She stepped easily into Page's arms and they stood in silence, enjoying the beauty.

After the sun disappeared from the horizon, they returned to the cab and Rene dropped them back at the hotel. "What do you want to do about dinner?" he asked her as Rene drove away. "We can eat here, walk to one of the nearby restaurants, or order room service."

"Did you have a nearby restaurant in mind?"

"There are several within a few blocks. I've been to most of the good ones."

"You lead and I'll follow."

"Just remember when we get to New York, you'll have to show me the sights."

"I'll bet you've seen as many sights in New York as I have," she teased.

"It's not one of my favorite cities," he admitted as they walked casually down the sidewalk. "Except for Madison Square Gardens of course."

"Since I wasn't a social person, I didn't see a lot of it, even though I've lived there since I was nineteen."

"Yet you own a house there?"

"I lucked out on the house. It was an older one and was owned by an elderly couple with no children. He passed away and she didn't want to live there. I was just starting at the law firm and she was a client. Rather than deal with the taxes and paperwork to rent it or lease it, she offered it to me at an insanely low price, if I would do some legal work for her. My boss offered to help me with any of the real estate laws to transfer everything and he did her work pro bono because he said that was the nicest thing he had ever known anyone to do. She knew I would need at least one or two roommates to afford a decent apartment."

They walked several blocks and he stopped in front of a restaurant and opened the door for her. The lighting was low and candles flickered on each of the small tables. A slender woman in a black dress informed them it would be about fifteen minutes but they could wait at the bar if they wanted. Page led the way, choosing a space at the end, away from the entrance. He greeted the bartender in French, ordered two drinks, and turned to look at Rebecca with a smile. "Before you ask, yes, I come here a lot when I'm in Paris. Right after Sasha and I signed all the legal papers, I think I was here for a week from open to close. Finally, Greg came in and literally dragged me back to the castle."

"At some point in her life, Karma will bite her in the ass."

"She seems to bounce back from any breakup and I didn't bring you here to talk about my ex."

"Other than the ex, did anyone ever catch your eye while you were on tour?"

He tilted his head and frowned. "Not that I can remember. We all had fans who always came backstage, each time we toured. Fans have their favorite band member. Almost like being stalked at times. I got all sorts of love letters, cards, notes…"

Rebecca laughed. "I'm sure they won't stop because you're getting married."

They were interrupted by the woman in black, who led them to a corner table. Page glanced at the menu. "The specialty is fish. Salmon, I think."

"I like fish."

When the server, a young man in a long sleeve white dress shirt and black slacks arrived, Page ordered the fish for both of them, with a small salad and a vegetable mix. When they were alone again, Page reached across and took her hand, touching the diamond ring. "Do you have any thoughts about where we are having our wedding? You nixed your hometown, so that leaves New York or where-ever you want."

"I don't know. I mean, I never seriously considered getting married until today, so I don't even know the rules. Who to invite? I don't attend a church, so I wouldn't even know where to start looking. I would hope my mother would cooperate and want to help but I don't know how she will react. So, probably New York."

"You do know that after the interview tomorrow, your name will be a household word. Our photos will be on the front of a bunch of magazines. I'm willing to guess your mother will see them before you get back from this vacation. You might want to give her a heads-up. Then again, maybe not. No matter what, it will be a beautiful wedding. We need to discuss a time frame. The tour starts in three months."

"I know."

The server returned with their dinner and two more drinks. They began with the salad, lapsing into a comfortable silence. Page glanced around the room, relieved that no one seemed to notice either of them. Fame was wonderful but for now, he just wanted to be alone with Rebecca, without any interruptions. He watched as she tasted the fish and it pleased him to see her smile. When she looked up and arched a brow he smiled back at her. "I would suggest we have a champagne toast, but I don't think it would be a good idea to mix your bourbon with champagne. I would hate for your first evening in Paris to be remembered by how sick you became."

She chuckled. "That would put a crimp in my evening."

"Besides, we'll have a champagne toast tomorrow at the top of the Eiffel Tower."

"I've never tasted champagne."

"Another first," he said softly. It still amazed him at how innocent and pure she was. He was eager to return to their suite but he wasn't about to rush anything. He wanted this to be the best night of her life. "I can't believe you're going to be mine. I love you with all my being, Becca."

"I'm still getting used to the idea myself," she replied.

The server returned and Page handed him his credit card. When it was returned, Page signed the receipt and led Rebecca into the cool Paris evening, walking back toward the hotel. When the entrance was in sight, Rebecca stopped and stepped into his arms. Her lips brushed across his throat as she kneaded his shoulders with both hands. "Remember what I told you," she whispered. "Don't take 'no' for any reason."

"You'll be fine," he assured her and hoped it was true. She turned and walked with him across the brightly lit lobby, into the elevator and exhaled as the door closed.

Page closed the door to the suite and stood completely still, collecting his thoughts. All of their purchases had been placed on the table in the sitting area. *"Slow and easy,"* he told himself. "Want to look at our shopping spree goodies?" he asked.

Rebecca crossed over to the table and pulled out each item. She held up the blue silk dress and turned to face him. "Is this okay for the interview tomorrow?"

"Absolutely."

"Page? Is something troubling you?" She noticed he hadn't moved from the doorway, hadn't approached her, or touched her. That didn't seem a good start to her first seduction.

"Troubling? No. Well, not exactly. I'm just concerned."

"You weren't concerned last night." She took a step toward him. "I remember every touch. Every place you kissed me." Boldly, she pressed against him, her lips trailing across his throat. She relaxed when she felt his hands exploring the center of her back, sliding down to cup her rear, urging her closer.

Page lifted her in his arms and laid her down on top of the bedspread. Their clothes ended up in a heap on the carpeting and he leaned across her. "Becca…"

"Shhh…" she pressed a finger to his lips, surprised when he took it in his mouth. "Teach me."

The time for words or objections was gone. She arched upward, not sure what to expect, only that she needed more. Her entire body seemed to tremble as he taunted her, still not taking her. His kisses were long and passionate and she explored the smooth muscles of his arms and back, finally gripping his shoulders. As she was about to beg him to stop tormenting her, his entry was swift, filling her completely and he went totally still. "Don't move," he whispered as he nibbled an earlobe. "Let your body adapt to me first." His kisses turned gentle and tender, caressing her lips lightly. Slowly, he moved inside her and she felt as if she would pass out from the passion. Several times, he brought her to the brink of release and stopped, each time more intense than the last until she was clinging to him with a desire she had never thought existed. When he gave her an explosive release she didn't know was possible, he joined her.

Neither of them moved, drenched in perspiration, molded against each other. She glanced over at him and whispered, "Damn."

"Ditto," he murmured against her throat. "So, is this the part where I'm supposed to roll over and go to sleep so you can take your bath?" he teased, propping on one elbow.

"I can't move. I have no muscles and my nervous system derailed."

"I didn't hurt you?"

"I don't think so, no."

He massaged a breast, caressing the taut nipple. "I think you would have noticed."

"Is it always like this?"

"I would hope so."

"Too bad we have that interview. I think it would be nice to just stay right here and never move."

"We would need food at some point."

"Room service," she whispered and curled against him, her hands exploring his bare skin.

"You keep touching me like that there's going to be a repeat, woman."

"Is that even possible?"

"Possible and probable. I don't want to overdo it your first time though. You're going to be a little sore in the morning, I believe."

"Oh, the horrors of it all," she laughed.

"Maybe we could both fit in the bathtub? I'll wash your back." Without waiting for a reply, he eased out of bed and she heard the water turn on.

She eased from the bed and felt her body protest. The bedspread was a mess. When she entered the bathroom he was bending over the tub and she playfully kissed his lower back, causing him to jump. He retaliated by lifting her and lowering her into the steamy water. "Shit, Toad, are you trying to boil me alive?"

He adjusted the water temperature and stepped into the tub, kneeling in front of her. They took their time lathering each other, using their hands instead of the washcloths "Are you trying for a repeat, in a tub of water?" he teased.

"What a timesaver. Great idea." She tried to keep the conversation light so he wouldn't know just how eager she was for more.

Could it get any better, she wondered as he brought her to yet another release. In a tub, in a hotel, in Paris. "I didn't know this was possible," she sighed.

"Lots of things are possible Rebecca."

"We trashed the hotel's bedspread," she teased.

He grinned at her, "I'll just bet we did."

They dried each other off and returned to the bed, where he tossed the spread onto the floor. He pulled her against him, holding her gently. "I'm glad I waited for Mr. Right," she whispered. "Glad my mother terrified me with horror stories, glad Gina entered my name in the contest. I don't think life gets any better."

"Glad I was your first, even though I didn't plan on it. Now, snuggle in my arms, and let's try to get some sleep. We need our strength for tomorrow's interview."

Chapter Thirty-one

Rebecca opened her eyes to find Page gazing down at her. "I don't want to get up," she teased with a playful pout. "I was having a nice dream."

"About what?" He had been up for a while. His hair was combed and he was dressed in a pair of black slacks and a pale blue long-sleeve dress shirt, Rolex on his wrist.

"My white knight rescuing me, swooping me up on a black stallion."

"Make it a Lord and that's doable. Who were you being rescued from?"

"A very boring life. I have a feeling life with you won't be boring."

"Be careful what you wish for. We still have the logistics of the wedding, the tour, your career, where to live, and when to live where. However, right now we need to think about coffee and breakfast, the interview, and then figure out what's next."

She sat up and winced. "I feel like I was run over by a truck. Did you get the tag number?"

"Saw the driver," he teased. She shot him a glare and then chuckled. He watched as she stood up and strolled across the room to her small suitcase. "There's no visual damage," he quipped.

"I better not go home sporting bruises, Toad."

"Never bruised one before. I'm certainly not going to bruise my wife. The bathroom is all yours. No rush. I'll have them send up some coffee."

"That's not necessary Page. I'll be ready in fifteen minutes."

"Never known any woman who was ready for the day in less than an hour. Usually two."

"Brush my teeth, brush my hair, wash my face, and get dressed." She shrugged. "What the hell would take an hour?"

"Beats me." He crossed over to the chair and reached for the tabloid. "I'll just read the paper then, like a good dutiful husband."

She disappeared into the bathroom laughing as she closed the door behind her. A few minutes later she returned to the room and chose a white lace bra and matching panties, then slipped the dress over her head. Stepping into the blue heels she turned toward him. "I'm ready. Unless you think I should wear jewelry."

"Pearls don't match the dress," he commented. "You need a blue sapphire. We'll have to look into that later."

"As much as I hate to quote my mother… pearls match anything."

"I'm not arguing with my mother-in-law. I am not a stupid man." He stood up and helped her clasp the necklace and handed her the earrings.

They left the room, Rebecca conscious of the looks they received crossing the lobby to the restaurant. They were shown to a table and served coffee almost immediately. "Gina was right," she said while pretending to study the menu. "When we were clothes shopping, she told me I needed to look good because people noticed you no matter where you went."

"Tell Gina it's not me they're looking at today. It's you. You're the most beautiful woman in the room. I watched a guy almost walk into a wall in the lobby. Do you want a light breakfast or a full meal?"

"I usually don't eat breakfast. A bagel or muffin would be fine. We're having lunch at the Eiffel Tower, right?"

"Yes, we are." He called their server over and ordered in French, offered the girl a smile that could melt stone and she hurried away.

"Okay. Besides the interview and the tower, lunch, and champagne, what else should we do today?"

"I'm open to suggestions."

"I want to take you to Norway. I've never taken anyone to my home there before. Not even Sasha."

"I've heard it was beautiful."

"After the interview and lunch, we can call Greg. Meanwhile, I'm just going to sit here and stare at you because I am the luckiest man alive."

"I'm still walking around in a haze. I can't believe all that has happened. I keep waiting for the other shoe to drop."

"Just be happy and be yourself and all is right in the universe."

"After I return to New York, what do you plan on doing? For three months?"

"Work on some music, spend time on my horse. See if Sasha will let me have Eric for a week or so. How about you? By the time you get back, the interview will be all over. It won't last, but be prepared for reporters and being watched for a while."

"The firm won't be happy with any publicity."

"Well, you can always come back to me."

"I still have stuff to do. Things to take care of. What to do with the house? My car, my stuff. What to say to my parents. I'll deal with it when I get back." Breakfast was served and they both turned their attention to the Danish and coffee.

After Page signed the bill, they walked outside. The news that Page Harlow was in town was out. Rebecca took a step back as the group of teens waved the article, pictures, and posters in his direction. He turned to wink at her, wrapping his arm around her waist. "Welcome to my world," he said as someone handed him a Sharpie. Before he began signing, he handed Rebecca his phone and Rene's card. "Call Rene and tell him to pick us up in front of the hotel as soon as he can." She stepped back inside where the shrieks were less and made the call. Rene's cheerful 'okie dokie' made her laugh. She took out her phone and slipped back outside to take pictures of Page surrounded by a crowd of women of all ages, shapes, and sizes. Slowly, the crowd thinned until there was one girl left, off to the side. The girl was in a wheelchair, accompanied by her mother. The girl looked up at Page as Rene pulled up and she had tears in her eyes, holding a small poster of Page, taken on his fourth tour. Page turned and knelt next to her. "Hi."

She barely spoke above a whisper, "Could you sign this? I hate to be a bother. I know you're busy."

"Never too busy for you. What's your name, sweetheart?"

"Jerri Anne. But I go by Jerri."

He quickly wrote on the poster. "Got a phone? I think we should do a selfie."

The girl's mother produced a phone as Jerri smiled so big she looked like she just won the lottery. They took several candid pictures. When he handed it back to the mother, she looked up at him. "I was wrong about you. I told Jerri you would be too busy. We almost didn't come here but I didn't want to disappoint her. I thought she could get a glimpse of you when you came out. Then all these others showed up and I wanted to leave."

"Glad you didn't. I'm never too busy for my fans. When the day comes I can't take the time to sign a poster it's time for me to retire."

"You met her once before. It was about four years ago. She was ten."

Page frowned. "Refresh my memory."

"You and the band did a concert at the Children's Hospital. In Virginia. She had been involved in a hit-and-run. On her bike. It happened a week before your concert. We had tickets." The woman stopped and took a breath. "After you finished your impromptu concert, you went from patient to patient. You signed the cast on her leg. She made them cut around that part when they removed it."

"Did they catch whoever hit her?"

"Yes. He went to jail. Jerri can walk but we decided to use the chair for the trip here. She's still not ready to do this much walking."

Page nodded, "So, which concert are you coming to this tour?"

"Richmond. If it isn't sold out."

Page reached into his wallet and retrieved a card with P. Harlow in gold embossing on the front of it. On the back, he wrote VIP 2 and initialed it. "Come in through the back. My security guys will take great care of you both." He leaned down and kissed Jerri on the cheek and then did the same to her mother. "See you both there." He reached for Rebecca's hand and they got into the cab.

They rode in silence for a few minutes, then Rebecca said, "Yet another side of Harlow the rock star. A children's hospital? I'm impressed."

"See," he grinned, "I did think of more than sex and alcohol. At times."

"Any more surprises I need to know about?"

"Well, you didn't run screaming back into the hotel so I think I'll keep you. I suppose I should mention that the band sponsors three orphanages in South America and one in Russia. We do several benefit concerts on each tour for different charities. Most of them are in the realm of kids or the hungry. Lots of Veteran appearances as well. You know, I'm more than a pretty face," he teased.

"Yes, Toad, I believe you are. Although that is a very pretty face."

Rene approached the huge Paris landmark and pulled over. As they reached the tower, Page spotted Tommy having a drink with Penny. Penny looked from Page to Rebecca and smiled. "Did you really put a million-dollar check in his coffee cup?"

"Yes, I did. Glad he got the message."

Page looked at Tommy and finally nodded, "Tom, good to have you back." His gaze went to a woman standing by a display of interest to tourists and grinned. "Janet Madison." He reached for her and she slung her arms around him.

"Page Harlow, you need a keeper. Jesus, give a woman a damn heart attack." She turned and pulled Rebecca into a motherly embrace. "Did you tell my husband to kiss your lily-white ass?" She was laughing hard enough to bring tears. "He came home in a trauma. Serves him right for meddling but you can't tell men anything. I told him to let it be. If you weren't the one for Page, you two were adults. You'd figure it out."

Rebecca nodded. "Tommy was instrumental in making up my mind. See, I didn't think Page was really serious. I mean, not the till-death-do-us part serious. Until he stormed into the room and fired Tommy. That's when I knew he was serious and I knew I was as well."

Tommy looked at her, standing next to Page with Page possessively holding her hand. "I'm man enough to admit I was wrong and to apologize. Looking at the two of you right now, I say you two have something special. Page Harlow, I do believe you found your 'Janet'. Having said that, I think the minute that check hit my coffee cup I knew I was wrong about her feelings."

Penny stepped up and hugged Page. "I'm going to miss you, but I'm happy for you. Now can we do the interview? My cameraman gets paid by the hour."

Rebecca didn't realize until now the entire interview was to be recorded and played later, just like the one she watched the night in her home with Gina. Well, she was dressed to kill, diamonds, pearls, and silk. This would be viewed in New York. And in Indiana. She squeezed Page's hand and he helped adjust her small microphone.

The entire process was laid back and relaxed as if they were all sitting at a table having a conversation. Rebecca told her side, not knowing who he was, her friend Gina entered her name. Page told his side of not being thrilled about it but then being shocked that she had no idea who he was. They discussed the art museums, the opera, and the chess match. They ended with him announcing it had been love at first sight and they planned to be married soon, somewhere in the States, honeymooning at one of his two properties during a break in the tour.

Penny turned off the recorder and the cameraman took several still photos of them. Then after the cameraman packed up his gear and walked away, they went to the restaurant overlooking Paris. After they ordered their food, Penny continued asking questions for her written article. Most of the questions were to Rebecca about her background, her childhood, and her career in New York. Penny seemed genuinely surprised to discover Rebecca didn't have a steady boyfriend, didn't socialize, and considered herself boring. Rebecca grinned, "I was waiting for Mr. Right. I just didn't know he would live halfway around the world. It doesn't matter. I found him and we'll be happy anywhere." She stated her plans to return to her job long enough to train a replacement and deal with her home and personal belongings.

After Penny put away her notebook and her recorder, she kissed Page on the cheek. "Thank you both for the career boost and congratulations."

Rebecca asked, "When will the interview be aired? I'm debating on whether or not I should give my parents a heads-up. Finding out in the news that their only daughter got engaged to a man she just met isn't going to be well received in Indiana."

"If there isn't much to edit, and Page knows I don't edit a lot then I'm guessing no later than forty-eight hours. Possibly on the air tomorrow. By the way, you look awesome. I love your hair color and that dress is to die for."

"The hair color I was born with and Page picked out the dress. And the jewelry. And the watch. And the heels."

Penny laughed and stood up. "Welcome to his world," she quipped, then headed toward the doorway.

Page looked at Rebecca and Tommy. "It's time to go to the top and have a champagne toast to my bride." He spoke to the waiter, paid the check, and led them to the elevator.

At the top, all of Paris was visible. Rebecca slipped her arm around his waist. "Every time I think it can't get any better, it does." She took a few photos with her phone, and then Janet offered to take some of her and Page toasting each other. Page wrapped his arm around hers and they sipped from each other's glass. Then Page dropped to one knee and took her hand in his.

"Okay, this is the official version. Rebecca Morrison, will you marry me?"

"Yes," Rebecca answered as Janet caught it on Rebecca's cell phone video.

"Something you can send to Gina," Page chuckled. "Since she didn't believe us when you called."

Rebecca laughed and taking the phone she winked at Janet. "I think that's a great idea, don't you? Gina was the one who entered my name behind my back. I took one look at the magazine and said 'Oh hell no' but you see how that turned out." She typed a few words, attached the video, and hit the send key. A moment later, the phone rang.

"Was that a real proposal?" Gina demanded.

"You were the one who said opposites attract. It's all your fault, you know." Rebecca handed Page the phone.

"Hi, Gina. This is Page. I've heard your name a lot and just wanted to say thanks for bringing me together with the woman of my dreams. Becca might need your help when she gets back. Make damn sure she has a long white gown and you gals figure out all the logistics, okay?"

"How about giving me some time to absorb all this news, will you? Give me a damn heart attack." Page laughed, handed Rebecca her phone, and walked away with Tommy. Janet stood sipping the drink, gazing out over the city. When the call finally ended, Janet suggested that Paris had some lovely bridal salons. Page and Tommy returned from their discussion and they all returned to the ground level of the tower.

"So what are your plans from here?" Tommy asked.

"Norway. Flying into Bergen, probably, and taking the train to the house. Then either back here or off to Monte Carlo. We're sort of winging it. No plans, no schedules."

"Janet and I are going to do a little shopping this afternoon then drive back to Munich. Call me later on in the week okay?"

"Okay."

"Again, I'm sorry I was such an ass. I'm really happy things are going well for both of you." Tommy shook Page's hand and hugged Rebecca, then he walked away, holding Janet's hand.

Page walked with Rebecca toward the river. "I love this city. The art, the lights, the river. I almost bought a house here a few years back but the owners changed their minds about moving."

"How many houses does a person need?" she asked, stopping to look up at him. When he smiled, her mouth went dry and she felt her heartbeat increase. Was she really going to have him for her own forever?

He shrugged. "It's been convenient with my profession so far. The castle is, of course, my main residence, but it's nice to be able to put my head down on my pillow no matter what part of the world I'm in. Even at my investment properties, I have at least one empty unit reserved if I show up. Had a villa in Spain, but Sasha got that in the settlement." He waved away the memory.

"I guess Darcie didn't take her week off," Rebecca chuckled.

"I've never known Darcie to go too far from Eric." He pulled her into his arms. "Let's walk across the garden area back toward the hotel. If you get tired, or those heels start to hurt, we can call Rene."

"Actually the heels are comfortable. Which is somewhat of a surprise since they're higher than anything I own. I was thinking about my parent's reaction to the announcement."

"You aren't getting cold feet are you?" he teased.

"No. I've spent my entire life trying to please them and you know what? Nothing I ever did was good enough. You'd think they would want me to have a career I enjoyed, to be able to buy a home at the age of twenty-three. But no, they wanted me to walk away from all of it and return to remain under their watchful eye. I'm thinking of maybe taking the first free weekend after I get back and just showing up on their doorstep. Tell them face to face. I just want them to be happy for me. And I want them to accept you as the man I love. If they don't there's nothing I can do about that."

"Well, it is going to be somewhat of a shock. My guess is, that even if they don't accept it right away, you just wait until you give them their first grandchild. Let's find a secluded spot so I can call Greg. I do want to take you home with me." They found a bench near a beautiful display of flowers. Page called Greg, and then he called Rene to pick them up in about twenty minutes on the corner where there was a small local bar.

Entering the bar, they found a seat and Page ordered each of them a drink. He paid for the drinks when they were served, explaining that they were waiting on their ride back to the hotel. "Greg said it would be at least an hour or two. He's having some routine maintenance done because he thought we would be here two or three days." Page tilted her chin, lifting her face, gazing into her emerald eyes. "We'll fly into Bergen and take the train over to Voss, then a bus to my hometown and walk from there to the house. It's been several years since I've been there, so no telling what condition it's in." He shrugged, sipping his drink. "I just couldn't bring myself to sell it."

"It's your childhood home Page. Where you were happy. No reason to sell it. It means a lot that you would take me there."

"You're my wife. It's your house too. Well, it will be after the papers are signed and sealed. Which brings me back to the ceremony. While you and Gina or you and your mother are making those decisions, remember cost is not to be considered. I'm dead serious about that, Rebecca. You deserve the fairy tale wedding and I want to make sure you have it. Promise me, no checking dollar amounts."

"I'd marry you in a phone booth."

"Settle for someplace bigger than a phone booth and smaller than Madison Square Gardens." He looked toward the street. "Rene's here."

Chapter Thirty-two

At the hotel, Page sat silently watching as she tried to figure out how to fit all of her new purchases into the small case she brought from the castle. Finally, in frustration, she sat on the edge of the bed and looked up at him. "No matter how I try, it won't fit. I need a bigger case or I can just carry out a bunch of packages I guess."

"Why don't we stay here for a few more hours? Later we can run out and get a bigger case. Maybe enjoy dinner." He moved toward her, standing, his hands on her shoulders. "We don't need to rush. Norway will still be there," he whispered, leaning over to capture her mouth with his. Her arms circled his waist, moving upward, urging him toward her. "When we were in the elevator of the Eiffel Tower, when we were sitting at the table, when we were sipping champagne, all I could think of was peeling that silk away from your perfect body."

With a smile, she stood up, pressing against him. "What's stopping you?"

He lowered the zipper and the dress slid off her shoulders, pooling on the carpeting at her feet. She stepped free of the material and her heels. Page sat on the mattress and pulled her close, his lips playing across her flat stomach while he guided the lace over her hips. He eased her onto the coverlet, trailing light kisses from her hip to her ankle and back up the inside of her thigh. She fumbled frantically with his shirt buttons, then his belt, whimpering with frustration when she was unable to remove his clothing. He teased her with a grin then stood up and painstakingly inched his clothes off, watching her eyes go wide and then narrow with desire. "Do you see something you want?" he whispered playfully.

"Yessssss…" she hissed, need obvious in her voice.

Unlike the first time, this time she knew what to expect as he eased into her. His kisses were tender and playful, and he urged her to follow his lead. This time, she moved against him, joining the rhythm, her hands exploring his back, her teeth nipping his throat as he coaxed her onward.

They lay in each other's arms, touching from shoulders to feet while she caught her breath and her heartbeat returned to normal. Her fingers stroked his hair. "Is it always this good?"

"It should be. I would hope so anyway. When we get home to the castle we can leaf through the Kama Sutra guide if you want to experiment. I'll do my best to help your tutoring." He kissed her long and deep before whispering, "We haven't begun to scratch the surface, Becca."

"Makes me wonder if my mother has a clue what she's missing. I mean who the hell would want to leave your arms and go take a hot bath, for crying out loud? Either that or my dad needs serious help in the 'how to' department."

"Not touching that discussion. No way.

"I don't want to move," she moaned softly.

"Sadly, we must. Let's take a quick shower and go find you some decent luggage. Then we'll pack and head out."

She sighed dramatically but followed him into the shower, where he taunted her by exploring all of her with soap-filled hands. The water was cold when they finally stepped onto the bath mat.

They dried each other off and took turns with the blow drier. Finally, she chose a pair of charcoal gray slacks and a red soft cotton top. The wardrobe was topped off with a pair of suede ankle boots. Page dressed in a pair of stone-washed gray jeans and a tight white body-hugging shirt. Rebecca's mouth went dry just looking at him. "Yeah, they need to make a statue of you in bronze."

He laughed as they left the room, heading back into the streets of Paris. She could tell he had a destination in mind from the way he crossed streets without hesitating to look at street signs. A few minutes later, she found herself looking at Louis Vuitton luggage the same blue color as the handbag he purchased for her yesterday. He examined the wheels, the handle, and the inside, declared it suitable, and then arched a brow. "Is this one okay? A smaller one goes with it so you'll have a matched set and I think you can spot it in baggage claim easy enough."

"Is it okay? Of course, it's okay. For God's sake Page it's a Louis Vuitton. What wouldn't be okay? You really have to stop spending this much money on me."

He took a deep breath and lowered his voice. "I want you to have things that will last. I don't have a problem shopping at Walmart but not for important items. A piece of luggage needs to be made to last." He turned his smile to the young girl standing nearby. "Sold. We'll just take them as is, no need to bag or box it." He pulled the handle in place, signed the receipt, and escorted Rebecca back into the streets of Paris. The sun was setting as they returned to the hotel. His phone rang and while she began placing all her items in the new case, he answered the call. "No Greg we didn't get lost. We had to make a slight detour. Go eat and we'll be there in about an hour or so."

He put the phone back in his pocket and sat on the bed, watching her fold everything with care. "Rebecca, hear me well because I'm not having this discussion repeatedly with you. I love you. You're going to be my wife. I am disgustingly rich and I enjoy buying you things. You might as well accept it and stop looking at price tags. I remember as a child, going to the store watching my mother checking for sales, putting things back for herself, and getting me something instead. After a while, I knew it was because she only had a specific amount of money and had to make it last. Even though my father sent her a monthly allowance, she was still frugal. I decided then if I were ever wealthy I would buy those I love whatever they wanted, price be damned. So, with that being said, please stop objecting to my spending habits."

Rebecca closed the two cases. "It might take a little adjustment on my part. I'm not living in poverty but I watch my spending. I look for sales and bargains. I guess in that sense I do take after my parents. We never had much. Don't get me wrong, we didn't do without. We had a house and a car, Dad always worked and we went to church every Sunday. I don't ever remember hearing my parents fight about money."

"Ready?" he asked as she stood up and picked up the purse. He took his piece of carry-on and her new piece while she pulled the smaller one down to the lobby. They left her old one in the room. He handed the key to the man behind the desk and then guided Rebecca toward the restaurant. "Food, then flight. I hate flying on an empty stomach and lunch was hours ago."

She whispered in his ear as he was holding her chair, "Plus there was that unexpected exercise we had."

He shot her a quick grin. "You have a mean streak. Just remember, my plane comes with a comfortable sofa and oversized chair."

After a nice dinner, he called Rene who showed up 'in a jiffy' and headed to the airport.

Greg was sitting on the steps talking to Penny, who sat close to him. The sight caused Page to grin at Rebecca as Rene removed the luggage from the trunk. Greg and Penny both walked over to the cab. Penny looked at the luggage and nodded. "Blue Louis Vuitton. Nice. I guess you're wondering why I'm here?"

Page shrugged. "I'm sure you have a reason," he said cutting a glance at Greg.

Penny smiled knowingly, "I wanted to get a final photo of you and Rebecca boarding the plane. Greg tells me you're taking her to visit your childhood home. He also said no one has ever been there with you before. I thought it would make a grand finale to the written interview."

"Okay by me. Becca?"

"Sure. Seems like a good idea."

Page nodded and then turned to Greg. "You two have something going on between you?"

"If I said yes, would you mind?" Greg asked.

"No. I'm practically a married man. You're single as all hell. I was just wondering if you wanted her to keep you warm under the Northern Lights while Becca and I are off for a day or two. You can take her sightseeing in Bergen and surrounding areas. I'm sure you can pick her up a spare outfit or two."

Penny looked from Page to Greg and back. "You're inviting me along?"

"No. Greg can invite you along. I no longer invite women anywhere, remember?"

Greg grinned from ear to ear. "Seriously? Penny, do you want to hang out in the cold north?"

"As much as I'd like to, I need to hit my deadline for this. I'd love to see you when you get back though. Really."

Page shrugged, "Well then, take your pictures, and let's get this thing airborne." He leaned over and kissed her cheek, then slid his arm around Rebecca's waist and headed for the steps without looking back. At the top, he turned while she stood with Greg beside her and waved. Rebecca waved, as Penny took several shots before turning toward her car.

Greg entered the cabin and glared at Page. "You knew she would refuse didn't you?"

"Not totally sure. Stranger things have happened. A piece of advice. Don't ever get involved with a reporter. Look her up when you're in town, have fun, and exit stage left."

"Is that it or you just don't want to see one of yours with someone else?"

"Dude, I'll give you my black book if you want it. Start with the ones with stars by their names and work your way through. There's at least one or two in every city I've ever been to so that should keep you occupied for a year or two. Hell, I'll give you Sasha's number if you want her. Penny is a great woman and if she was in it for you and not to fish for information she would be parking her car, not driving away. Besides, don't you have a sweet little girl in Bergen?"

Greg heaved an exasperated sigh. "Yeah, but it's been two years. She could be married with twins by now."

Page clapped his friend on the shoulder. "In that case, you get to find a new cuddle bunny. Can we go now? Pretty please?"

"Anybody ever accuse you of being an asshole?" Greg shot back as he entered the cockpit, laughing as he closed the door.

They were in the air in fifteen minutes and Page dropped onto the sofa next to Rebecca, after fixing them both a drink. "Weren't you a bit hard on Greg?" she asked.

"Better now than later. Penny would have used him to get tidbits on us. Only six months ago she told me there would never be anyone who could replace me, blah blah blah. Didn't take her twenty-four hours to latch onto my best friend."

"Maybe she did need to meet a deadline."

"She has a laptop. She could have met her deadline before we landed in Norway. Greg can call her when we get back. When I am not going to be in her line of sight. I've dealt with this shit for many years, Becca, and I know the signs. Backstage, women have a first choice and a second choice. I'm not available, they beeline for the drummer or the guitarist. Hell, sometimes it's the opposite. 'Hey Page, you're not Matt but can we…' so not much surprises me. If she had jumped at the chance to come along, then I would have figured she was sincere about Greg."

"I never realized what a sheltered life I've been living. That women just want to…" she trailed off, sipping her drink. "Of course, I can understand any woman who has a heartbeat wanting you. Just looking at you raises my blood pressure. Gina did try to warn me, bless her little heart."

"Not at first."

Rebecca chuckled. "Yeah you did, but I didn't act like it. I tried to concentrate on those roses instead of watching this human version of a Norse god walking toward me. They don't make men like you in New York."

"I'm sure they do, it's just you never noticed one up close and personal. And I am very happy about that. I never knew I could be this happy before I met you. I mean that."

"When I return to New York, I need to go face my parents. Tell them I'm getting married and they should be happy for me."

"And if they aren't?"

"Their loss, Page. I have a wedding to plan and a million things to deal with. Their approval isn't high on my list anymore."

He pulled her into his arms and they sat in silence, gazing out the window into the night sky.

Both of them dozed off, waking up when they heard the landing gear lock into place. Page kissed her tenderly. "Honey, we're home," he whispered.

"Right. Home. Norway home. Castle home. Florida home. California home."

"You forgot England and Italy. Oh, and Switzerland."

"I don't envy your accountant."

"I have all my bills and receipts sent to her. She figures out the difference between corporate and personal, has meetings with Tommy and life goes on."

"She? Now, why doesn't that surprise me?"

"Yeah. *She* is in her mid-sixties, married to a doctor, also in his mid-sixties. Her office is in the same building as his clinic, outside of

Rome. She's a genius in international finance. Her oldest son is a real estate attorney with an office on the other side of hers. She is the one who cuts Sasha's checks and puts money in a trust for Eric. Her name is Mary Sampson, with a bunch of letters after it."

"That doesn't sound like an Italian name."

"Born in Virginia. Army brat. Her husband was a doctor in the US Army. When he retired, they settled in Rome. What can I say?"

"I have a lot to learn about my new husband, don't I?"

"Just know that I love you and you can have anything your heart desires. Anything else you can pick up as we go."

The plane slowed to a rolling stop and Greg clicked the speaker. "This is your captain speaking. We have arrived in one piece in beautiful Bergen, Norway. Please watch your step as you exit the aircraft and pretend you aren't freezing to death." He laughed and opened the cockpit door. "Page, you might want to grab both of you a coat from the cabinet."

Page opened a narrow door and pulled out two fur-lined jackets with hoods. "We can leave the luggage on the plane. Trust me, you won't need a silk dress where we're going. We can grab jeans and sweaters when the stores open and a jacket for you that fits. We won't be staying at the house because there are no lights and no heat. I don't trust the fireplace to build a fire for us. I brought you here to show you the scenery, which you won't find anywhere else."

Rebecca laughed as she put the coat on, her face and hands hidden from view. When Greg opened the door and lowered the stairs, she exhaled as the chilly air hit her in the face. "Remind me I do not want to visit here in the winter. Feels like New York. Although it isn't as bad as I thought it would be. I was expecting minus zero from the way Greg talked."

"Well, we are almost at the Arctic Circle," Page said with a shrug. "It's warmer in the daytime. Of course, daytime begins at three in the morning this time of year, give or take. Sunset is at about eleven at night."

"Well alrighty then. Nice if you have a lot to do in a day. Weird if you aren't used to it, I guess." Rebecca followed him into a small building and Greg stayed with the plane.

"We'll be catching a bus to the hotel. I could rent us a car, but there's no sense in it since we're taking the train in the morning. Trust me, driving these roads to the house will give you white knuckles and a heart attack. Besides, this way we get to see the waterfalls and the sights and I can look at you without running us off a high cliff on a hairpin turn."

She grinned up at him. "You're still in charge of the tour guide stuff, toad. Train sounds much safer and I can relax knowing I won't be plunging to my death on the way."

Chapter Thirty-three

The bus ride to the hotel was comfortable, less than half full. No one paid them any attention and they got off at the hotel. Page went to the desk, paid for a room, and led Rebecca to the elevator. "Our first 'first' together," he teased. "I never stayed at this hotel. It's new so it should have all the necessities. Heat, running water…" he grinned at her.

"This might surprise you, but I used to be a Girl Scout. And I managed to spend two whole weeks at a Church camp when I was thirteen. We stayed in tents and used sleeping bags."

"Was it fun?"

"At the time, I suppose it was. Except for the one night, Katie Foster put a garden snake in my pillowcase. If I had known any cuss words I'm sure I would have used them."

"And how did you pay her back? I'm guessing you did."

"Ants. Sugar. I sprinkled some sugar inside her sleeping bag and all around the tent before we went on a three-hour nature hike. We discovered that she knew quite a few cuss words." Rebecca laughed at the memory as Page opened the door to their suite.

"From the way you told Tommy off, I believe it's a safe bet to say your vocabulary expanded since then," he chuckled, closing the door behind them.

"New York will do that to you," she grinned.

He pulled her into his arms and she came easily, her hands easing under his jacket and shirt. He peeled away her jacket, tossing it on a

"

nearby chair, followed by his own. "At least we didn't come here in December. God, I remember those winters. Of course, Germany is cold too. Usually, in the winter, I try to visit Italy, Florida or California."

"I never cared for snow. I take the city transport in New York rather than drive to the office. Indiana was worse. Open country, digging your way out of the driveway every morning."

"Well, that's one thing you'll never have to worry about. We can do winter where ever we want to."

"It still seems so unreal. From me telling Gina I thought the contest was rigged and I wouldn't spend ten minutes with you; much less ten days to being here in your arms. I still want to pinch myself because I want to make sure it's not a dream."

"I know. I keep praying you don't change your mind. I don't think I could stand losing you."

They lapsed into a comfortable silence as his mouth began exploring the arch of her throat and curve of her shoulders. When he eased her onto the cool sheets, she moved against him eagerly. Even though there were no lights on in the suite, the glow from the midnight sun gave off a dim haze.

Chapter Thirty-four

Rebecca woke up momentarily disoriented. So this was what it was like to be part of the jet set? Jet lag was more like it. And happily in love as a bonus wasn't a bad way to live, she thought. The suite was quiet. As she sat up she saw the note on the bedside table. "Stepped out for a few minutes. Be right back in time for breakfast. Love, Toad" She laughed as she read it, then wondered where he went this early. Hopefully, she would have time for a shower before he got back. If he came back while she was in the shower they would probably miss out on breakfast. That thought caused her to laugh again as she headed for the bathroom. As the hot water cascaded over her, she gave serious thought as to how best to approach her parents. She did want their approval and their blessing but if it wasn't going to happen, she would live with their decision. Page was probably right about a grandchild changing their mind. Her hand subconsciously went to her stomach. She could very well return to New York pregnant. Working in a law firm she was all too familiar with the fact that even a one night stand could lead to an expensive paternity suit. She'd done the paperwork for a woman and DNA proved the man she was suing was, in fact, the father. He had fought it to the bitter end and in doing so, pissed off the judge, ended up in contempt of court and lost. At the time she wondered what would cause a woman to have sex with such a man in the first place. In Page's favor, he wanted his child. She turned off the water and stepped out onto the thick bath mat, wrapping in a large towel. She should have at least brought a change of clothes from her luggage, although the outfit she'd worn yesterday certainly wasn't dirty. She dried off and walked back into the bedroom to find him sitting in the chair reading a magazine. On the bed was her luggage. She grinned at him. "So, you've taken up mind reading I see."

"Have I?"

"I was just thinking I should have at least brought a change of underwear, if not a different outfit and here it is. My Norse god is a mind reader. Lucky me."

"It occurred to me about five this morning that you would probably like to have a change of clothes, so I hopped the bus back to the airport, got your luggage, and returned. Have you been up long?" He grinned, "Nice that I graduated from Toad to Norse god in your eyes."

"No. I figured I'd get a quick shower while you were gone because otherwise, we might miss breakfast. And that would be the Norse god of toads if you don't mind."

"If you don't put some clothes on we might still miss breakfast," he teased.

She opened her case to discover a pair of new jeans and an emerald green knitted sweater. Dropping the towel, she eased into clean lingerie, watching him pretend to read the magazine he was holding. "What are you reading and where did this outfit come from?" she asked as she dressed in the new outfit.

"Clothes fairies. They seem to be everywhere. I guess they thought you needed to be warm and comfortable playing in the Norwegian dirt."

"These fairies have very good taste and oddly enough know my exact size," she grinned playing along. She didn't even want to know how much the sweater alone cost. He was holding up the magazine so she could see the cover. It was the bridal magazine from Paris. "Are you going to help pick my gown?" she asked.

"I'm pretty sure you won't need my help in that department. That's what Gina can help with. Or your mother." He shrugged and closed the issue, laying it on the table. "There are some beautiful gowns in there though."

Rebecca glanced at the flowing lace gown on the cover. "Gina would dress me in a satin or leather mini dress and mother would dress me in an old maid's gown. God help me."

He placed his hands gently on her shoulders and looked into her eyes. "Rebecca Morrison Harlow, hear me well. It's your wedding and your gown so do not let anyone make you wear anything that you don't love. I want you to choose a gown to die for, one you will be gloriously thrilled wearing."

"Page. I could get married to you in jeans and a tee shirt. The gown isn't important. The place isn't important. The guest list isn't important. The only thing important is that you and I love each other for the rest of our lives. All the rest is window dressing."

His mouth turned into a frown. "It's important to me, Rebecca."

"What? A wedding version of the production size of the casting for Ten Commandments? Why?"

"Did you stop dreaming about the perfect white wedding when you grew up? You can't tell me you didn't think of it as a child. I'm sure your mother has brought it up over the years."

"Don't bring my mother into this. Her idea of her only daughter's perfect wedding would be me walking down the aisle of our local church marrying the banker's son, the reception in the social hall and her sitting with a smug look on her face. Oh, it would be very important to mother to make sure the dress accents my very flat stomach to prove to all the good church people I didn't have to get married."

"If there was a point there somewhere I missed it. Are you planning to enlighten me about the last sentence?"

She sighed and crossed over to sit on the edge of the bed. "Page. We haven't taken any precautions. I've never needed birth control. What if… what if I'm already…" she stared at a spot on the wall and waited.

"What if you're already pregnant? Is that what you're worried about?"

"I'm not worried. I mean, not really about that. No. That's not it."

"Well, we aren't leaving this room until you tell me what the hell 'it' is."

"You have a nine-month tour, Page. If we, I mean, if I'm pregnant then I'll have the baby before the wedding."

"If on the slight chance you are pregnant then I believe that the wedding needs to be moved up. Especially if your mother will be making an issue about your flat tummy. I will not have anyone believing I married you because you're having my baby."

"In the course of your career, hasn't anyone ever accused you of being a father? I mean besides Sasha."

He dropped back into the chair and stared at her in silence for so long, she wondered if he was refusing to answer. "Becca, there are only three women I have ever had sex with that I didn't use every precaution in the book. Three. One was the very first time. I told you about her. I was fourteen, she was fourteen. The second was Sasha because I thought I would be spending the rest of my life with her. That was before she got pregnant with Eric so yes that was quite the event. And you are the third. If you wish I can start using precautions so if you aren't already, you won't get that way. Or…" he held his finger up as an exclamation point, "we can just go ahead and get married before the tour starts. By now the entire free world knows we are engaged. If your mother hasn't heard the news, I'm sure the town gossips will fill her in, so you need to have a date in mind anyway."

"So, I go back to New York and just pick a date out of thin air?"

"Or pick a date, then go back to New York. Either option works for me. This should not be all that complex, Rebecca. Unless you've decided not to marry me, in which case please let me know now. That way I can have a little time to update my will before I die of a broken heart."

She started laughing so hard tears were starting to form. "I'm worried about the date, the gown, the place, mother's reaction and the gazillion things involved with the ceremony and you think I'm going to back out?" She crossed over and stood in front of him then boldly devoured his lower lip before kneeling on his lap, her knees against his hips. "Baby or no baby, Lord Harlow, you're stuck with me."

"Back at ya, my lady. Can we go eat now because if you keep taunting me we will most definitely miss the breakfast buffet?"

She slowly slid away from his lap before standing over him, her head touching his. "Feed me then, you toad," she whispered and wondered when she had gotten so bold.

The restaurant was almost empty as they chose from the ample selections and took their seat at a table by a window. He explained again that they would be catching the train to the next town, catching a bus from there to the fjord. Instead of getting on the boat to tour the waterways, they would walk the short distance to the house, or what was left of it. Then they would return and depending on the time they could either tour the waterway or return by bus, then train to the hotel.

Taking a small bite of the egg she nodded. "I'm really looking forward to seeing your home. Where you grew up. If the house is in decent shape, do you think you'd consider ever living here? Not permanently, but maybe for a month or so every so often?"

Page dabbed a smidge of egg from the corner of her mouth and smiled. "I've not given it much thought, to be honest. Let's see what shape it's in first, then we can make that decision together. As you pointed out, I already have a lot of houses."

An older couple close to them spoke to each other and Page turned and answered them in their own language. Rebecca followed them with her eyes, not knowing what was being said but knowing the woman was referring to her in the conversations. She heard Page mention her by name and she offered up a friendly smile. The couple was getting up to leave and the woman waved her finger at Page, nodded toward Rebecca and walked away. After they were out of sight and out of hearing range, Rebecca arched a brow, "Do I get a translation or are you going to keep me in the dark?"

"Oh that. Mr. and Mrs. Narvon, celebrating their fiftieth wedding anniversary today. She said we reminded her of them when they were newlyweds. I told her we were getting married in New York next month, but we were celebrating our early honeymoon because we were both on vacation. She told me to treat you like a porcelain angel because that's what you reminded her of. I promised to do my best. She also suggested if I wanted to have a serious profession to sufficiently support my beautiful wife, I should consider getting a haircut. Her husband called her out on that. Said she's always been bossy. I told him I owned my own company and you would murder me in my sleep if I cut my hair."

"And how right you are. I love your hair. What language was that?"

"Portuguese."

"Well, that wasn't in my research on you. I knew you spoke French, German, Spanish, Italian and Norwegian but no others."

"Those are the ones I'm fluent in. I'm not able to read several others although I can get by in a conversation."

"You're just full of surprises aren't you?"

"I'll do my best to keep you entertained," he said with a laugh. "Come along ladylove, we have a train to catch." He took her hand in his and they stepped outside. The air was clear with a definite scent of salt water all around them, a slight breeze noticeable.

"I thought it would be colder for some reason."

He shook his head and guided her down the street. "It's not bad during the day in the summer. Winter here is a lot different unless you like snow and ice. Good ski country. I prefer something closer to the equator. It's only a few blocks to the rail station if you don't mind walking."

"I don't mind walking. It's a beautiful country, from what I've seen so far."

"Just wait until we get into the mountain area. Now that… is beautiful country. From there you can literally see for miles and miles." He motioned toward the mountains visible in the distance. "I grew up wanting to be a Viking with my own warship so I could conquer the entire world. I thought everybody lived on the water. England was a wake-up call from hell. Not that the country is bad. It's not. I like London and some of the towns. The countryside is great. Private boy's school was not something I was ready for. I remember the first time the headmaster called me Mister Harlow, I turned to see if my father was in the room."

They reached the train station and Page paid for their trip to Voss, a small town to the Northeast of them. Rebecca took the coffee he handed her while they waited for the next arrival. Glancing at the clock she was surprised to discover it was still early morning. Must be the fact that the official sunrise was about three or four in the morning. "You do realize it's going to take me days to readjust to New York, don't you?" she asked with a smile. "I don't know how you do this for months on end."

"The tour is different. We start at point 'a' and work our way across the country then back, before moving on to a different country. There is time between to readjust our body clocks, so to speak. The hard part is the long hours and lack of Anna's decent food." The train came to a stop and they boarded, choosing a seat not far from the Narvon couple who also boarded the train. "Our new friends are here," he whispered to Rebecca. "I'm looking forward to being able to celebrate our fiftieth wedding anniversary together."

"I'll be seventy-seven," she laughed.

"You'll be a beautiful seventy-seven. Our children can tell our grandchildren how we met and how you swept me off my feet, making me leave my playboy ways in the dust."

"Eric will have a sibling. I'm sure Sasha will just love that," Rebecca said with a playful grin.

"Sasha will make nice, believe me. With a stable lifestyle, she knows I could easily get custody if she pushed me. I wouldn't take Eric away from her, but at least I'll have decent visitation."

"What if he doesn't like his new stepmother?" Rebecca visibly winced. "Shit. I'm going to be a wicked stepmother. Somehow that thought never crossed my mind but yep, there it is."

"Hush, woman. Eric will adore you. He has my DNA after all."

"From the photo, he looks like you too."

"Viking blood is strong. I look like my mother. My father had brown hair and hazel, almost grey eyes. He had a habit of looking through a person instead of looking at them. Used to piss me off. A lot about him pissed me off. His title was all important. People were secondary. When I inherited the title the villagers were surprised at how different I was. They were prepared to dislike me because of my heritage and the fact he cheated on his wife yet even after her death refused to marry my mother. I don't know what they expected, but I do know I wasn't it." He shrugged. "I wasn't even old enough to legally drink and I admitted right off I didn't know a damn thing about leading an entire estate. I helped with some financial needs, built a second school, and updated a few things. Now let's enjoy the scenery as it flies by, shall we?" He embraced her and began pointing out different sights as the train headed away from Bergen.

When they came to a stop in the small town of Voss, Rebecca sat still, trying to absorb all the beauty that she had seen. "I think I can see why you wouldn't want to leave here as a child. Page, this place is beautiful beyond words."

He kissed her forehead and led her toward the busses that were parked nearby. "Voss is a tourist town. Winter ski resort. Lot's to do. If you want, we can return after the tour. Go skydiving or parasailing, maybe?"

"Not this girl. I will keep both feet on the ground, thank you all the same."

Page laughed and spoke to the bus driver standing near the open doorway. He paid their fare and guided Rebecca onboard. "I explained that we weren't going to be going on the cruise, but we paid for round trip so he will look for us when we're ready to return here." Page stopped to wave at Mrs. Narvon who was walking with her husband."

"Cruise? As in cruise ship?"

Page nodded. "It's deep water here, Becca. We can stay another day if you want and take the cruise down the fjord, then take the railway from there back to Bergen."

"But our clothes are at the hotel in Bergen."

"Well, we can return to Bergen tonight then cruise tomorrow if you want. It's up to you. I'm flexible as far as time goes. We're still going to get back to the castle before you have to leave for New York. Since Norway was a spur-of-the-moment, we could fly from here to Monte Carlo if you wanted. Or we can save Monte Carlo until after the tour."

"Time is going by too fast. I wish I didn't have to go back…" she looked past him toward the mountain.

"As far as I'm concerned, you don't have to go back."

"I do. I need to be responsible, Page. Go back and be professional about resigning. Offer to train my replacement. I plan to suggest Gina take the position if she wants it. I need to face my parents. Even if they have been alerted by gossips or the news, they need to hear it from me. But for now, I'm going to ignore the looming deadline and enjoy being with you." She snuggled against his chest and gazed out the window, toward the distant mountains. The bus took on several more passengers and then pulled out onto the roadway.

They made decent time, considering the narrow roads and the death-defying hairpin curves and finally pulled into a very small town. Several other couples got off and shortly the bus pulled back out, heading to the next town where most passengers would catch the ship to cruise down the fjord. He pointed toward the waterway, then took Rebecca's hand in his. "Ready to hike?"

"Hike or mountain climb?"

"Hike," he laughed. "At the end of this street, there is a dirt path and then we're in the heart of nature."

She nodded and walked beside him and soon they were making their way through a gathering of trees and bushes, small houses painted in bright colors breaking up the otherwise all natural greenery. He led her from one path to a different one, higher than the town they'd just left. Rushing water could be heard off to her left and she gasped when she caught a glimpse of it rushing by. Page squeezed her hand to reassure her they weren't going to fall into the river and then stopped. In front of them was a house in need of a new coat of paint. It had been yellow at some point. The door was a dark green, with a small porch. Page stepped onto the porch and turned the doorknob, pushing inward. He exhaled and she put her hand on his shoulder as he took in the old furniture. A sofa and chair near an old fireplace made up the living room. The kitchen had a wooden table with two chairs and a corner bench. There was a candle in the middle of the table, nestled in a wreath of green. Everything was covered in a layer of dust. Page walked silently into the first bedroom. "This was my room." He pointed to the window which had a beautiful view of the water rushing by. There was a single bed, a small chest of drawers and an empty closet. An old photo in a metal frame sat on top of the nightstand. Rebecca picked it up and looked at the woman in the picture and then up at Page. "My mother," he said softly.

"It belongs at the castle, Page." She handed it to him. "Maybe you could have it professionally touched up, for your office. Or a portrait for the great room."

"Okay. I forgot it was even here." He crossed the hall to a second bedroom, a bit larger but furnished the same. "Mother's room." Looking around, he frowned. "I believe it's time for me to end this chapter of my life and put it on the market. Maybe someone around here needs a house."

"Well, it doesn't seem to be in bad shape. Nothing some soap and water wouldn't fix along with a few gallons of paint."

They left the house and walked out back to the edge of the water. "Nice backyard. I played out here for hours. I'd climb that tree and pretend to look out over the land, watching for enemy ships. From the top of the tree, you can actually see the fjord. This is just a runoff stream." He eased his arm around her shoulder and said, "Let's walk back to town and grab lunch. We'll be there when the bus returns. If the real estate office hasn't moved, I'll stick my head in the door. Unless you want to keep it."

"Page, only you can make that decision. Unless you plan to make it a Northern getaway spot, I don't see any reason to keep it. Well, except for the fact you grew up in that house and you cherish your childhood memories to a point you don't want to give them up. It's quite the dilemma, but only you can make the final decision."

With a sigh, he guided her back along the path toward the small town. When they reached the main road, he smiled and nodded to himself. "I remember there was a community charity of sorts. When I was about ten, I went there with my mother because everyone was helping one of the elderly ladies. It seems a large branch fell across her house and everybody in the town was chipping in to help with the cost and replacement of her roof. I wonder if it's still operating."

Rebecca wasn't sure what this had to do with whether or not he should sell the house, but it intrigued her to watch him work a problem out in his mind. She followed as he turned down a side street, stopped and then entered a building with a bright blue door. A woman in her mid-fifties looked up from a corner desk. She asked a question in what Rebecca assumed was Norwegian. Page answered her, motioned toward Rebecca and switched to English. "I told her you were my fiancée and you didn't speak the language and asked if we could converse in English. Meet Mrs. Marta Denning."

"How may I help you today?" the woman asked coming around the desk to shake both of their hands.

"My mother and I lived here. I was born here and only left when she died. My father took me to England to school there."

"You're Page Harlow. I remember your mother. Gretchen Frommer, wasn't it?"

"Yes."

"You've become somewhat of an international celebrity, from what I have heard. How can I help you?" she repeated.

"I want to give you my house. You; being the organization. It's a small two bedroom on the river, north of here. I haven't been back here more than three times since I left and it's just sitting there vacant. It could use some paint and a good dusting. It's sparsely furnished."

"Just like that? Don't you want to sell it? Rent it perhaps? Not that I am about to turn down a gift of that type, mind you."

"I don't need to sell or rent it. I already own multiple properties in several countries. If you chose to, you could sell it and use the money to benefit those in need."

"Believe it or not, your decision couldn't have come at a better time. There is a young couple who just lost their home in a kitchen fire. They have an infant son and the three of them barely made it out. They're staying at the boarding house down the street. We've been helping them with the rent, but there aren't many houses available in their price range since she stays home with the child."

"Then we can consider it theirs. Problem solved."

"Why don't I call and tell them you're stopping by? You can give them directions. I can get the address of the house, so I'll help them with the legal paperwork."

"We'll be heading back to Germany in the morning or mid-day tomorrow, but you can fax me anything I need to sign." He wrote down his address and phone numbers and she wrote down the name of the couple at the boarding house. "We can go there now. We're catching the bus back to Voss and the train back to Bergen in a while."

"You have a couple of hours before the bus arrives. I don't know how to begin to say thank you. Words aren't enough."

"My mother told me once that there was a reason for everything in life. I mean, what were the chances that I would decide to bring my future wife here to see a house, decide to close the book on that chapter of my life and at the same time remember this organization from the one good deed I helped with twenty years ago? Only to discover there is someone who seriously needs a place to call home?" They shook hands again and Page guided Rebecca back outside.

"You are an amazing person, Page. You do know that don't you?" She stretched up and kissed his cheek. "I think you are about to make a couple very happy."

They walked down the street until they came to the boarding house on the corner. The young couple stood in the small room that served as a lobby, the infant sleeping in a stroller. The man had a concerned look on his face as Page approached. "I'm James. My wife Gwyneth and our son Brian. Tooley. James Tooley. Mrs. Denning called and said a man was giving us a house. I don't understand."

"Nothing to understand James. I own a house here. I live in Germany and this is the third time I've seen this house since I left at the age of thirteen, when my mother died. I remembered the community charity from when I was ten and helped raise funding and volunteers for a woman's roof. I stopped in with the thought of letting them have the house and was told you were in need of a house due to a fire in yours. So, I am giving you my house. It needs dusting and some cleaning and wouldn't hurt to paint it when you get time. It's sparsely furnished. Sofa, chair, two bedroom sets, table, kitchen stuff. There may even be plates and things in a cabinet. I didn't look." Page shrugged.

"What do you expect in return?" James asked, still skeptical.

"I expect you and your family to be happy there. Because you will own it free and clear, you will have one less thing to worry about. You'll need to have the lights turned on. Mrs. Denning is going to do all the legal paperwork and fax it to me to sign. My fiancée and I are returning to Germany tomorrow. I never had a key because we never locked our doors when I was growing up. There's a nice sized backyard but you might want to put a fence up on the side by the river, to keep Brian from learning to swim the hard way."

"It's on the river?"

"Yes. Here are the directions and the address. Consider it yours."

Gwyneth spoke up for the first time. "I know this is going to sound crazy, but when I was eighteen I used to have a poster of you in my room. You're Page Harlow aren't you?"

"Yes, I am. What happened to the poster?"

"My younger sister got it when I met James."

"Wait," James said, "You're the musician? God, I hated seeing that poster on her wall. Imagine my surprise when I found out she gave it to Fran!" He turned to Rebecca, "I still can't believe it. Does he do things like this often?"

"He does, he just doesn't talk about it." Rebecca guessed that was a good enough answer since he was active in charity work on tour.

Page invited them to have lunch at the small restaurant next door, and for the next hour they ate and got better acquainted. Toward the end of the meal, he excused himself and hurried down the street to the small bank, where he got a thousand dollars converted into Norwegian money, in a variety of NOK denominations and put in an envelope, then returned to the restaurant. As he paid the check he turned to James, "I understand how difficult it is raising a child and having to make do during a disaster, so I'm happy fate stepped in like it did. What were the chances of me even coming to Norway, deciding to do something with my house, stopping by the charity after not being there for twenty years and all this at the same time you and your family are dealing with needing a home? With that being said, the house is going to need to be cleaned and painted, plus you'll probably want some newer furniture. A baby's room for instance. So, I want you to take this to help out at least until you get back on your feet." He handed James the envelope.

James looked at it and glanced at his wife. "Normally, I'd refuse because I'm very self-sufficient and a hard worker. I make a decent living. However, this isn't a normal situation so I am grateful for the help. Thank you."

"Sometime in the future, you'll be in a position to pay it forward. Just talking to you for the past hour, I can tell that's the type of man you are." He shook James' hand and kissed Gwyneth on the cheek. "We have a bus to catch to Voss, so I'll wish you well. Brian seems to be having himself a good sleep through all of this." Page winked at Rebecca and added, "Hopefully when we have one he will be as quiet."

Rebecca rolled her eyes and grinned at Gwyneth. "What do men know? Right?"

"Brian is sleeping now so he can keep us up at two in the morning," she laughed.

James and Gwyneth walked as far as the bus terminal, before saying their goodbyes and heading back toward the side street to the charity office. Only after the bus pulled away did James open the envelope, his shock at the amount of money obvious. He handed it to his wife who inhaled sharply with surprise.

As Rebecca leaned against Page's chest on the bus, she gazed up at him. "Have I mentioned lately how much I really love you?"

"I'll never get tired of hearing it," he whispered.

Chapter Thirty-five

They arrived at the train station in Bergen and Page pulled her into his arms. "There's one more thing for you to see before we return to the hotel."

"What?"

"It's a surprise," he whispered playfully.

"You've already proven you are just full of surprises. From the first time I saw you in the stable up to today with you giving total strangers a house, the surprises just keep coming."

"It might drive you crazy after a while. Let me know if it does. You'll discover my mind works at warp speed and even though I am dealing with one issue or project, ten more are spinning through my brain. I guess I've always been that way. When I was in second grade the teacher thought I had a learning disability because she couldn't keep me focused on the lesson at hand. However, I aced every test so she admitted she had no idea how my mind worked." He shrugged. They had arrived at what appeared to be another rail car. Page paid their fare and they took a seat.

Rebecca realized they were going upward and she tried to see what was above them he wanted to show her. The car stopped and he escorted her to the side of the overlook. The entire town was below them, the sea shimmering in the evening sun. Immediately, she took a series of pictures, including Page in most as the wind blew his hair away from his face. Several selfies of the two of them followed before they returned to the rail car and back down the mountain.

At the hotel, they went straight to the room and Rebecca picked up the bridal magazine and sat on the small sofa, Page dropping down beside her. "I like the one on the cover," he said. They leafed through each page, dog-earing the pages they both liked.

When her phone rang she saw Gina's number show up. "You have reached the number for the future Lady Harlow, how may I direct your call?" Rebecca teased.

"You have officially lost your mind. When you get back here I'm going to shove you in front of a subway train. I just saw your live interview at the Eiffel Tower."

"Couldn't have been too live because I'm now in Norway. So, did I look okay?"

"Did you look… okay? Okay? Seriously? I know clothes and that damn dress cost more than I make in a year. And when did you start wearing four-inch spike heels?"

"You were the one who told me I had to look good with him because people always noticed him where ever he went. Don't be so shocked I actually can dress up for an occasion. Which reminds me, I need you to help me shop for a bridal gown."

"Yeah, about that… your mother called wanting to know when you would be returning. I can tell you, she's a little more than just pissed. If she hadn't been your mother I would have hung up."

"Typical reaction. I planned on taking next weekend to have a face off. It won't be the easiest thing to do, I guess."

"Better you than me. She said she heard about the interview because it was on the local news. Seems someone recognized you as the local person who moved to New York."

"Shit. Maybe it would be safer to just call her. I really don't want to get into a screaming match with my own mother but on the phone, I can hang up and hope she comes to her senses."

"I can tell you she doesn't believe you are getting married, much less to Page. She sure didn't have anything good to say about him either."

"Well, thanks for the heads up anyway."

"So how's Norway? Any other single guys who look like him in the area?"

"I don't know. I haven't bothered to look at other guys."

"Wow, what a surprise," Gina said laughing. "One thing is for sure. You never do anything half-assed. What about the tour? Are you going?"

"Probably not. I mean off and on maybe, but not the whole tour. I'd be insane. I'm going to offer to stay and train a replacement if the boss wants me to. Do you want me to suggest you take it?"

"What? Take your job?"

"You already do half the work. You're familiar with the firm, the judges, and the system. Why not?"

"Well yeah, but I won't get my hopes up."

"So anything else earth shattering I need to know about?"

"Well I was going to tell you I got a new guy in my life but that's not earth-shattering, considering my track record."

"At least you are out enjoying life. If it hadn't been for you I'd still be there, with my head in a legal volume, wasting away alone."

"Well, hey, I need to get off the phone. Good luck with your mother."

Rebecca hung up and turned to Page. "What can she do except scream at me into the phone?" She took a deep breath and tapped in the number. "Hi, mom."

"Rebecca Janay Morrison, what have you done? Do you have any idea how it makes your father and I look to discover you're cavorting all over Europe in the company of a man who –"

"That's enough!" Rebecca snapped. "I called to tell you I am getting married to a wonderful man. I'm in love and I had hoped you would be happy for me."

"In love? What do you know about being in love? You barely know this… this creature."

"I know how I feel."

"You're making a big mistake. I warned you not to go to Europe. I warned you about those men but would you listen? Oh no. Well, little miss smart stuff, I hope you can live with yourself."

"This coming from a woman who claimed I should quit my job and settle down, be a wife and mother? That was what you wanted, wasn't it? Well, that's what I'm doing."

"I didn't say marry a damn foreigner. How do you even communicate? You're in Paris. And he's some slick talking pretty boy who probably lied to you. He probably has a wife stashed somewhere. I thought we raised you better."

"No wife stashed anywhere. I've met his ex. I've met his housekeeper. I've met his entertainment manager and his wife. I've been to a real opera in Vienna, toured Salzburg, toured the Louvre, had lunch at the Eiffel Tower and now we're in Norway."

"Norway? Why are you in Norway?"

"Because he was raised here. Until his mother died, then he went to England. Then Germany."

"Sounds like a vagabond. What about that all-important job? That house you were so proud of? Are you going to throw all that away too? For some penniless musician? That's what I was told about the so-called interview. That he was in a rock band of all things."

"I called to see if you would want to help me with my wedding plans. I need a gown and a place and a cake and invitations."

"No. I'll not be a part of this foolishness, Rebecca Janay. This is a mistake and I will not be a part of it. When you come to your senses, you'll see, I was right. Don't drag your pitiful used up self home with a baby for me to take care of either."

"Well mom, I'm sorry you feel that way because I wanted to share my happiest most important day with you. I suppose I can get my boss to walk me down the aisle."

"Your boss is in New York."

"My wedding will be in New York. Page has a house in Florida and one in California."

"Oh, sure he does. You are so gullible. I'm betting he doesn't have a pot to piss in."

"I'm hanging up now, mom. You have my number if you change your mind. Otherwise, I'm sure you can keep up with the wedding on the news because God knows, the media will be all over your daughter becoming an English Lady." Rebecca hung up and buried her face in Page's shoulder and sobbed.

Page sat in silence, holding her in his arms, yearning to make everything go away, for her life to go back to normal, yet knowing he was not going to give her up just to please her fanatic self-centered parents. Finally, her sobs turned to soft whimpers and she heaved a resigned sigh. He laid his head against hers. "I'm sorry Becca. I wish I could make this right somehow. I can't help but feel responsible…"

Her head jerked up and her green eyes narrowed. "Don't. You aren't responsible because my mother is a clueless selfish moron. You are everything I could want, everything I ever dared to hope existed. You make me happy. And dammit, we have a wedding to plan."

"Do you think your father feels the same way? Can't he have a say so? I'm far from an expert of fathers, mind you, but I always thought there was a bond between them and their baby girls."

Rebecca tried to laugh and hiccupped instead, wiping away her tears. "But you defiled his baby girl. He might not take that too kindly."

"Guilty as charged," he said, pressing his lips tenderly against her forehead. "You defied me in return, you know."

She turned to face him, positioning herself on his lap, kneeling so she was leaning above him. "Yes, I do believe I did. And I plan to do so again." In a single motion, she dragged the sweater over her head, dropping it to the carpet. Her bra followed. Page needed no further urging as he began covering both exposed breasts with slow kisses and attentive caresses. Her own hands were busy with his sweater and she fumbled with the snap of his jeans as he made quick work opening hers. "I'll get better at this with practice," she teased. He guided her to stand up long enough to drag the jeans to her knees and then, shifted his hips to do the same with his own. With a gentle tug, he urged her back onto his lap, no material between them. She kicked off her boots and tried to rid herself of her remaining jeans, frustration obvious in her expression. The look of pure desire in his eyes stopped her from her efforts and her mouth found his lips. His fingers traced the curve of her back, her hips and across her stomach. "Page…" was all she could manage between ragged breaths and hungry kisses. How was this even possible? Could anything feel better? By now she knew what to expect, the reaction of her body merging with his. She took a deep breath, felt the shattering result of his possession and arched back, enhancing the moment, then collapsed against him. "Holy shit, Page. Damn. Oh damn."

"Normally this would be referred to as makeup sex. You know, after you burn my toast, or get mad at me for whatever reason you could find to be mad. I love that you initiated it this time."

She remained still, leaning against his shoulder. "So, my mother thinks you're a vagabond taking advantage of me. That is so clueless. You can't take advantage of me. I was on top."

"No complaints from me on what position you choose. We can get very creative."

"Can I ask you something? It's a question I've had for years and I finally have someone who can give me an honest answer."

"Ask."

"Why do men enjoy porn so much?"

"Wow. That wasn't a question I expected."

"No, in New York, at the firm I found in a lot of marital complaints, it was because men watched porn and women found it disgusting. Well, except Gina who thinks it's a 'hoot' in her words."

"I take it, you've never seen any? Never mind. Crazy question. Some men watch it because it's better than real life and there is no risk. They aren't actually cheating on their wives because it's a movie. You'd be surprised how many couples watch it as a way to get themselves excited."

"Would I find it educational?" she asked with a playful grin.

"We might discover a new position. They can get pretty creative. No real plot to the movie. No real conversation. Some can be downright funny."

"Seriously?"

"We can watch some at the castle if you want. They're available to rent online."

"In the quest for continuing educational research?"

"Oh, absolutely." He was laughing. "Woman, you are a perfect work of art. How did I get so damn lucky?"

"Back at ya, my Lord," she whispered between light kisses.

"I'm sorry about your mother's reaction," he said, holding her in his arms.

"Page, there is nothing I have ever done in my entire life that pleased her. The terrifying part was how hard I tried. If she chooses to believe what she does about you, I can't change it by arguing. Maybe she'll come around, maybe not. Gina is quite capable of helping. Now, let's work on a date for this event shall we?"

"You know, I could fly back to New York with you. Or fly in a week later."

"And Gina would be falling all over herself."

"So, let's get a good night's sleep and return to the castle in the morning. I'll let Greg know. We will have more access on my office computer for venues. You'll need enough time to pick the gown and make all the other arrangements. We can look at invitations and such, get some ideas."

"Sound like a great idea. I'd really like to talk to my father, just to get his take but his view is probably already poisoned. I'll just mail them an invitation and who knows, maybe they'll show up on a whim. Or, someone will actually give my mother the facts about your international fame."

Page lifted her into his arms and carried her to the bed, where he casually stretched out beside her. "Well, the first thing we need to decide is how many people are being invited? I have my entire cast and crew, plus the band. Even though I'll make sure Mary and Doctor Sampson get an invitation, they won't travel to the states for the wedding. Penny will. Brenda might. They can both write it off as a business expense. I'm guessing if my list is one hundred people, less than half will come. How about your side?"

"My co-workers, the nice couple from the corner store, a couple of friends from the library. Twenty-five max."

"So, should we aim for a Saturday or Sunday, since most of your friends are working during the week?"

"That would be best," she murmured, distracted by his exploring fingertips as they roamed across her stomach, circled her breasts, and slipped between her thighs.

"Here's a thought, for what it's worth. After the official wedding there, maybe later we could renew our vows here, perhaps in Munich so people like Anna and Hans, Mary, and her family could attend."

"Makes sense," she nodded.

"Guess I should go ahead and call Greg before I get sidetracked," he whispered, taunting her with his touch.

Chapter Thirty-six

Anna was thrilled to see them emerge from the Mercedes, noticing how happy they both seemed. Hans came to retrieve Rebecca's luggage and Page said softly, "Put it in the master suite, please," causing Hans to smile and nod his approval.

Once inside, Anna handed them both a cup of her steaming coffee. "I saw the interview from Paris. Looks like you have an official wedding to plan now."

Rebecca hugged the woman, "Before the tour, most likely in New York. I need to turn in my resignation, train my replacement, figure out what to do with the house. Then we're going to have a second ceremony over here, so you and Hans can come, along with Page's other friends who can't make it stateside."

"Oh, that's such a wonderful thing to do." Anna beamed at the words. "You know, we could have it here, in the garden. Of course, there's the Palace or any one of many beautiful locations to choose from. I'm excited just thinking about the possibilities."

"Good, because I'm going to need your help. I have this bridal book I'd love for you to look through. Page and I can't decide on my gown. Gina would put me in white leather mini-dress with spike heel boots if she could. We've narrowed it down to about ten or twelve. If I can get it down to five or six, I can look at them in New York next week."

"I'd be honored to offer my opinion. First, though, you need to take some downtime. A short nap, after a hot bubble bath. I'll start a nice lunch and later we'll look at the book. I'm betting the two of you have been going non-stop since you left here. Now shoo."

Page announced he was going to go check on Thunder and the stable boy, then he'd be in the studio for about an hour. The sultry look he gave her conveyed the desire he felt. If he followed her for a nap, neither of them would be sleeping. Rebecca nodded, smiled at him and turned toward the stairway.

She passed the door of the room she'd been in and continued to the end of the hall, opening the door to Page's bedroom. It was neat and orderly, a white fur carpet covering the black highly polished marble flooring. The king-sized bed was covered with a black comforter and black silk sheets and pillow shams. The furniture was all deep cherry wood. A shelf held several Rolexes and a matching tray had rings and gold chains. Definitely a man's bedroom, she thought with a smile. She undressed and slid between the sheets, aware of the woodsy scent of his cologne lingering on the pillow. Closing her eyes, she was asleep in moments.

Page talked to his stable boy, letting him know he'd be leaving for the states soon but would be back before the tour. Nat was a good kid, seventeen, studying to become a vet and loved the opportunity of staying at the castle with the horses. Anna made sure he got three meals a day and his clothes were washed. Plus Page paid him exceptionally well to be there doing what he loved to do, which was care for the animals.

"I heard you're getting married," Nat said with a grin.

"I am indeed. Hard to imagine it, but she's so perfect. It really was love at first sight. She was willing to learn to ride, which was a big plus. We've been to Vienna, Paris, Norway. She returns to the states in a few days with a laundry list of things to be done. Dress, cake, invitations. The thought of it gives me a migraine. We haven't even set a date." Page laughed. "Your time's coming, little brother. I can't believe I'm so nervous. Me. I can get in front of ten thousand screaming fans and not break a sweat."

"So, where is she?"

"I think she's taking a well-deserved nap. We ran our asses off. Now, I'm going to go work out and soak in the sauna or write another song. I'll let you know when I get ready to head out again." Page turned back to the castle, heading for the studio.

In the studio, Page turned his concentration to the tour details. He touched base with his other friends and band members, plus talked to Ashley for a long time. Everyone seemed genuinely surprised but happy for his future marriage. After soaking in the Jacuzzi and sweating in the sauna, he took a shower and dressed in a pair of running shorts and matching sky blue tank top, pulling his damp hair back with a blue scarf. His thoughts wandered to the woman asleep in his bed. At least he hoped she was in his bed and not in the guest room. That thought made him smile. Never in his life had he imagined finding a woman who enjoyed the exact same things he did and who was so pure and moral. She knew the value of a dollar and was loyal, honest and ethical. Add to that, she was brilliant, could hold an intelligent conversation… God how he'd missed that in his life. On the plus side, she was ravishing and had an easy-going sense of humor. He walked toward the elevator, wondering what if anything they would ever argue about. Her ten days were coming to an end and she'd be heading back to a different life than she'd left. Reporters would be on her doorstep, on her phone. She'd have to get used to living in a fishbowl until the novelty wore off. That thought brought him to the realization he'd have to do something about his future in-laws. No one would be permitted to cause the love of his life to cry the way her mother had. Mrs. Morrison would discover her future son-in-law was far from being a vagabond. Times like this was when he would use his title and his wealth like a gold plated hammer. He thought of the movie 'Dirty Dancing' and whispered to himself, 'Nobody puts Becca in a corner'. The thought caused him to smile as he stepped into the great room.

Anna was in the kitchen, taking a cake out of the oven. Page retrieved a beer from the refrigerator and sat at the table. "Is she still asleep?" he asked.

"Haven't heard a peep, so I'm guessing she probably is. What are you going to do with yourself while she's in New York planning the wedding?"

"For your ears only? I plan on visiting my future in-laws. Her mother was vicious on the phone and made her cry to a breaking point. Obviously, the woman believes me to be a worthless, impoverished, lying piece of crap and I intend to prove her wrong. It hurt that I was helpless to stop the hurt. All I could do was sit and hold her while she cried."

"That's what you're supposed to do. Hold her so she knows she's loved. It'll work out. Parents think they always know what's best."

"It wasn't that. It was that they decided they were disgraced by her being here. It's not like I'm shipping her home discarded and pregnant for cripes sake."

"Just don't get in a fistfight with the banker's son," Anna teased, handing him the spatula. "Make yourself useful and frost the cake while I tend to the rest of dinner." She pushed the bowl of chocolate frosting toward him and turned back to the stove.

Rebecca stood silently in the kitchen doorway, watching Page concentrate on scooping frosting on a cake at the kitchen table. She slipped her phone from the pocket of her red slacks and snapped a picture, causing him to turn, grinning at her.

"Anna's teaching me husband skills."

"Good, because I can't cook. Well, I can, but it's been easier for me to order takeout for one. There's a little deli near the office so I just pick up sandwich stuff. Potato salad." She offered up a smile. "I can enroll in a cooking class, I suppose. Or, just hang out and lean over Anna's shoulder."

Anna chuckled. "You can fix anything and everything in a Romertopf. Meat, potatoes, vegetables. Shove it in the oven and walk away for an hour. Dinner will be ready in about thirty minutes. Both of you go find something to do."

"Game of chess?" Page asked, putting the spatula in the empty bowl.

"Sure, why not?" she said cheerfully. "I'll happily kick your butt again."

Anna smiled as they both headed for the great room. Rebecca was the best thing to ever happen to Page. She was down to earth, easy going and would be loyal and honest. Page would be able to work on his music, ride the horses and she would be by his side every step. She was grounded and Page needed that in his insane career.

Anna interrupted their game for early dinner, then they were back at it, silent in serious competition mode. Finally, Rebecca leaned across the board, grinned at him and whispered "checkmate", then laughed at his expression.

"No, you did not just – no, I've been beaten by a mere slip of a girl twice."

"Well, I can give you a consolation prize. You put up a good fight but I was the chess champ in college. In this sport, I have an unfair advantage. Now, in the area of your favorite contact sport, I really need some coaching," she teased.

"I love your train of thought." He carefully put the chess board away and retrieved the book of Kama Sutra, grinning mischievously at her.

"I thought we might watch a movie first." The look she gave him was smoldering and it had the desired effect.

"Upstairs or downstairs?" he asked, pulling her into his arms, and making the decision for her by guiding her to the elevator.

Page settled her on the oversized sofa, then pulled up a list of X-rated movies on his phone, choosing one he'd seen before. He didn't want to immerse her in the pornographic film this early in her viewing. The one he chose was actually acted out in an empty courtroom which caused him to grin at her as he sent his choice to the sixty-inch screen on the wall. Amazed, she watched the entire movie, acutely aware of his hands removing her clothes as the movie progressed. He was right, the acting was terrible, and the plot was non-existent. Finally, she turned her attention from the screen to the man who gave her so much pleasure. The movie ended, but neither of them noticed as they lay together on the sofa, content in each other's arms.

He groaned when she ran her finger up the center of his back. "So, how was the movie?" he whispered.

"We should have a movie night at least once a month. I found it … entertaining and educational. However, I think I prefer the real deal, thanks."

"So, you weren't shocked to the core?" he teased.

"Before this trip, I would have been horrified. Page Harlow, you have been a very bad influence on me and I am so glad of that." She turned on her side and looked up at him, a chuckle slipping past her lips.

He narrowed his blue eyes, "Share the humor, woman?"

"Glad I'll be resigning from the firm. First, I don't think I could enter a courtroom without blushing after watching this and secondly, if some woman told me she was divorcing her husband because he watched 'filth' I would probably laugh in her face. Not a good career move."

"Probably not," he admitted.

"So what's on the rest of our to-do list?" she asked, mischievously running her fingertips across his chest and downward.

"If I had my 'druthers' it would be to keep you naked and in my room, for the next two days. Or naked down here in the playroom. Or in the cottage. Or by the lake. But we have a lifetime to enjoy each other so what would you like to do tomorrow, Becca?"

"Two days? That's all that's left?" She looked stunned as she realized her time to leave was rapidly approaching. "I know I have to go. It's the responsible thing to do. I don't want to."

"I don't want you to go either, but I know it won't be for long. Maybe we should spend tomorrow here and then both go to Paris. That way, we can spend every second together until you board the flight home. We still need to decide on a date, place and pick invitations.

Maybe you'd like to look at some gowns in Paris. Just a thought." He shrugged his broad shoulders. "Right now, let's soak for a few minutes," he said with a wink.

"Pervert," she shot back as he scooped her into his arms and walked to the hot tub.

Much later, they slept curled together in the massive master bedroom, her back against his chest, covered only in the smooth silk sheet.

Chapter Thirty-seven

When Rebecca opened her eyes, sunlight streamed through the narrow windows. What time was it? Where was Page? A glance confirmed he wasn't in the room or in the master bath. She sat up slowly and looked at her luggage sitting in the far corner on a low table, still unpacked from their travels. She opened the case, chose a pair of rust slacks and matching polo, slipped into sneakers and after washing her face, running a brush through her hair, she brushed her teeth, then headed for the stairs with the bridal book in hand.

Anna was in the kitchen, sitting at the table polishing a silver goblet. Four were already gleaming and one was still old and tarnished. The woman looked up from her task and smiled. "Coffee's fresh, but my hands aren't. There's a mug on the first shelf."

Rebecca poured her coffee and refilled Anna's mug, laying the bridal book on the side of the table. "Page wants me to shop for a gown in Paris. I don't know –"

Anna set the finished goblet aside and picked up the last one. "Something's bothering you. I can tell. You can talk freely to me Rebecca."

"I feel like this entire week has rushed by in a daze. I've just nodded and gone along with whatever was happening. It isn't like me to be so pliant. This time last month I didn't know who Page Harlow was and now it's like a different person inhabits my mind. I went from a timid legal researcher who stayed buried in her career to becoming the future wife of a playboy musician. Zero to sixty and I feel out of control. I'm not used to feeling out of control. Plus, he insists on some wedding extravaganza and I don't have a clue. I've never even been to a wedding, not since I was in college, and then I only attended. I'm going to screw something up."

Anna set the final goblet with the others, got up and silently washed her hands. Finally, she returned to the table. "Do you love him, Rebecca?"

"With all my heart, yes."

"Then the rest doesn't matter. Let's have a look at that book. Show me the gowns and then we'll make a list of the things you will need to deal with."

Rebecca breathed a sigh of relief. Anna had a calming effect on her and the woman would be great with advice. They narrowed it down to five gowns. Anna produced a pad and pencil from the drawer and they worked at finding a count for the number of people Rebecca planned to invite plus a list of bridesmaids. They listed the reception on another sheet, cake, and trimmings. Anna wrote 'indoor/outdoor' on a sheet so Rebecca could list the chapels or gardens, and then visit all of them to make her choice. After an hour they had filled up several pages of ideas and thoughts. Rebecca finished her coffee and dropped her head to the table. "I will be a crazy person before I get to the 'I do' part," she groaned.

"You could use a wedding planner, you know," Page said from the doorway. "Maybe that would be the way to go. I thought women wanted to plan their own ceremonies but if you feel overwhelmed, some people are paid to plan weddings. I'm sure you could find a few in a city the size of New York." He shrugged. "Just a thought. Anyway, I was downtown this morning and ran into Brenda so I gave her an update on the wedding in New York before the tour. Had a meeting with Tommy at Hard Rock, which is where I ran into Brenda, in case you were wondering."

"Page, I don't expect us to be joined at the hip twenty-four seven."

"I know. You'll be in New York, dealing with a lot of planning and I thought you might like a hand, besides Gina. So I mentioned it to Ashley. She lives in DC when we aren't touring. I thought she was going to crawl through the phone in her eagerness to help. No pressure, but she's there if you need her."

"Ashley? Your personal assistant?"

"Yep. I thought if she can organize the nine-month madness we call a rock tour she might come in handy."

"And it never occurred to you to ask me first before volunteering her services?"

Page stood straighter and his mouth went into a firm line. "Obviously it didn't and I didn't volunteer her services as such. We were actually discussing the tour and the pre-planning of the second leg which would be into Vancouver and through the west coast. I said it was too bad she didn't live closer to New York so she could meet you. She wants to meet you, by the way. Somehow in the conversation, I made mention of all the arrangements you would be dealing with and she volunteered to come to the city. On her dime, I might add. She said to give you her phone number and if you called she would hop the next flight or drive up."

Rebecca took a deep breath. "Okay. Anna and I made a list, but I do like your idea of consulting a wedding planner. Besides, Ashley has the tour to deal with."

Page shrugged and turned away. "I'll be in the studio. I need to fine-tune a guitar riff I don't like." He hit the button for the elevator harder than he meant to and the doors closed behind him.

Rebecca looked at Anna. "Is he pissed off?"

"He's touchy when it comes to Ashley Tinkers. She's the sister he never had. Tommy had to replace a bass player once in the middle of the tour because the guy tried to corner Ashley and Page broke his arm in three places. I've met Ashley. You'd like her. She's all bubbly and cheerful, nothing phases her. She will be able to relax after he's married because she won't be getting two a.m. phone calls." At the look on Rebecca's face, Anna added, "She's the one who always had to pick him up from jail, or a bar, or clear out his hallway of groupies."

"Should I go apologize?" Rebecca glanced toward the elevator.

"No. Hold your ground. I know he thought he was helping but he needs to learn a marriage is a partnership so the two of you will have to learn to discuss things. He's used to being in charge. You're used to making your own decisions. You'll have disagreements. Every couple does. Just remember why you're a couple in the first place. Besides, if he goes to the studio, the elevator locks down until he opens it."

"So, you're saying nobody can get down there? What if he trips and falls or slips in that hot tub?"

"He never has. Oh, I worry too, sometimes. After he broke up with Sasha I forced him to remove the lockdown mode because he stayed drunk for long periods and I worried the same would happen. After the beginning of his comeback tour, he reinstalled it because he was recording and he needed total concentration."

"So if he and I spat, I just have to wait until he resurfaces?"

Anna shrugged. "That's the short of it, yes. I'd consider finding something to do until he simmers down. He's got a temper, but so does every man in the world that I know of. They act all manly and beat their chest, then go pout like children. One wonders how they ever made it out of the Stone Age."

When Page came back upstairs, Anna was teaching Rebecca how to knead dough for bread. He slipped up behind her and started to kiss her earlobe but at the last minute, she turned and rubbed her floured hand across his cheek. His eyes widened and he looked momentarily stunned. Rebecca started to laugh but he recovered fast enough to wipe his hand across the dough and cover her entire face in flour causing her to shriek in surprise.

Anna shook her head in obvious amusement before running both of them out of the kitchen. "Go kiss and makeup. Go. I'll finish this up."

Page chased her into the other room and she stopped suddenly, causing him to run past her, but he spun around and circled her waist, dropping her onto the sofa and pinning her there. "You're so cute," he said, nuzzling her flour-covered face against his.

"We're getting flour all over the furniture," she said between giggles.

"Maybe we should go take a bath and clean up," he teased.

"Are we going to have makeup sex?" she asked, nibbling on his earlobe.

"Did we fight?"

"I shouldn't have been snotty about Ashley."

"Ashley means well. She'd be happy to help. She's excited for me. Let's not talk about Ashley while we're talking about having make-up sex, okay?" While he was talking, he released the snap on her bra and raised her shirt. "Damn you're beautiful," he whispered.

"You are pretty nice to look at yourself, Toad."

"Upstairs bath or downstairs hot tub?" he asked.

"Both have their appeal. Upstairs is close to the bed and downstairs the tub is bigger. You choose. Oh my God, why am I even able to know these things, much less suggest them?"

Anna chuckled from the kitchen as Page walked by with Rebecca in a fireman's carry over his shoulder and into the elevator. It was wonderful to see him happy again. She put the bread on the table and went to see about her own husband.

Chapter Thirty-eight

Rebecca woke up in the middle of the night and watched Page as he slept peacefully. Her emotions were off the Richter scale where he was concerned. How was it even possible to feel this much love in such a short time? How long did it take to plan a wedding the way he wanted her to plan it? And the dress. Never in her life had she believed she would be walking down the aisle in a full-length white gown. The only thing missing would be her father on her arm and her mother beaming with pride from the front seat. Well, some things wouldn't change and the way her parents believed was one of those things. She wasn't going to force them to be nice. Either they would or they wouldn't.

"Doesn't look like a happy bride face," Page whispered.

"I thought you were asleep. I was thinking about my parents. Page, why can't they be happy for me?"

"Because they think you're marrying a worthless vagabond musician, I suppose. Maybe they had their hearts set on being in-laws to a banker? I wish I knew sweetheart. I wish I could make it right. Give them time. It had to be somewhat of a shock to their system, you know. Little do they know, I could probably buy you the damn bank for a wedding gift. Might have to sell the Mercedes…"

"Don't you dare sell the Mercedes, Toad." She turned on her stomach and gazed over at him. "I'm going to miss you the minute I'm airborne."

"I'll let you know my plans. I can deal with New York for a while, to be close to you. I'm almost finished with all I can do with the tour plans. Tom and Ashley have it handled. No reason I can't stay at the Plaza in Times Square. I usually do when I'm in town."

"Odd the way life works. How many times over the past seven years have you been in New York and I had no idea who you were?"

"Four times. Who knew I would end up married to an American?"

"Oh? You have a problem with my country, Toad?" she teased.

"Well I am half English and you folks did kick our royal ass in the beginning."

"Who would have thought I'd end up married to a foreigner?"

"Certainly not your mother," he chuckled. "Once she meets me, she'll love me. Most women do, you know. I'm very lovable."

Rebecca grinned at him, "Maybe you're right. You're hard not to love. I think I loved you from the minute we met in the stable. The air just ignited, like an electrical shock wave. I tried to fight it. I did. I couldn't."

He pulled her against his chest and ran his fingers through her hair. "I know. Let's get a couple of hours of sleep if you want to return to Paris."

"I don't want to return to Paris. I want to stay right here. You can go with me when I leave from here to the airport, can't you?"

"I can do that." He kissed the top of her head, "Now, let's get some sleep."

"Do you think the wedding can be in six weeks or so?" she asked. "Is that enough time to plan?"

"Don't know why not. Oh, I almost forgot, I have a surprise for you. Remind me when I wake up, okay?" He grinned when she gasped in exasperation.

"Toad," she muttered as he closed his eyes.

Chapter Thirty-nine

Morning brought rain and thunder, the gray skies matching her mood as she began folding her clothes to place in the luggage. She opted to wear a pair of emerald green slacks and a sky-blue silk shirt from Paris. The contrast was stunning, even though she never paid attention to fashion. Gina could help her with that education. The thought made her smile. Page came in and kissed the back of her neck then pulled her into an embrace. "I don't want you to go," he murmured, his face pressed against her hair.

"I don't want to go either, but it's the responsible thing to do."

"I know. I won't be too far behind. I'll let you know when I arrive. Now, I want to give you this." He handed her a Visa card with her name on it. "I had it expressed overnight, to make sure you had it. I don't want you to deal with making a damn budget for our wedding, so this is for wedding stuff and whatever else you want."

"Page, I don't need your credit card. I have a job and money in the bank."

"I want you to use this. Let's not have a money fight before the wedding. Just use the card if you feel like it. Know it's there if you find a gown you love in the five thousand dollar range, or pay a wedding planner, or to take Gina to dinner. Definitely take Gina to dinner."

"Okay," she said, putting the card in her handbag.

"Also, brace yourself for the relentless assault of reporters who will probably be stalking the airport. My advice is to give a quick interview and be done with it."

"And say what?"

"Whatever you feel like. That you found love. That you are looking forward to becoming my wife. The usual questions. If they ask you crap you feel is personal, and they will, just tell them that the subject is off-limits. Don't be nervous. When you've had enough of their incessant questions, then tell them to kiss your lily-white ass and walk off." He grinned at her.

"Toad."

"I love you, Rebecca Harlow," he whispered, lowering his mouth to hers. She returned each kiss until they both stood there breathless, silently gazing at each other. Finally, he reluctantly released her and reached for her luggage. "I'll put these in the car while you say goodbye to Anna."

They walked down the stairs together. Anna was in the kitchen with coffee in a to-go cup. The two women hugged, finally letting go. "I'll miss you, Anna. You take care of my toad prince for me," Rebecca said, trying to remain cheerful. "I'll be back soon,"

"I hope so. I'd like to think you'll call this home."

"I already think of it that way. I promise I'll be back before you know it and we can work on the local wedding."

"It's going to be splendid," Anna said, handing Rebecca the coffee. "Now go, before the rain gets worse. Don't want you flying in nasty weather."

The drive to the airfield was quiet, except for the rain, which had lightened to a slight drizzle. Page held her hand the entire drive, his thumb making circles in her palm. Just his smallest act seemed to take her breath away.

Greg was waiting, the steps to the plane extended and covered by an overhead canopy. Page pulled next to the covering on the passenger side, then came around and opened her door. "I'll be right behind you with your bag," he whispered as he popped the trunk, retrieving her luggage. Greg took one piece and escorted Rebecca on board, while Page parked the car at the side of the building, returning at a sprint. By the time the canopy was removed and the door was closed, the rain had stopped.

They spent the flight time between Munich and Paris curled together on the sofa, enjoying the quiet closeness. Rebecca emitted a soft sob when the plane landed at the private side of the Paris airport. She swallowed hard and turned in his embrace to gaze up at him. "I don't know how I'll function without you for two weeks," she whispered.

He kissed her softly, "You functioned for twenty-seven years without me. It's only two weeks."

"It was different before. I never knew you existed. That's changed because now I know."

"Well, it's your decision whether or not to board the jet, sweetheart. Nothing would please me more than for us to return to the castle."

"That is so tempting."

They left the jet and got a taxi to the main airport hub, where Rebecca would catch the flight back to New York.

Page waited until she was airborne before he turned away. Several people approached him for autographs and even though he was cheerful to his fans, his mind was on the woman he had just watched leave on the plane. When she returned to her normal life, would she begin to have second thoughts? What if her bosses offered her what she had always wanted; a scholarship to Harvard? Now he needed to get a ticket to fly to Indianapolis. A hotel would be a must, as well as a rental car. He grinned again as he wondered what Mrs. Morrison would think of him after the meeting. She might still dislike him, but she would know he could care for Rebecca financially. "A lot better than Banker Bob," he said softly to himself.

At the castle, after eating the food Anna prepared, he called his accountant in Italy. When she answered he said, "Mary, this is Page. How's everything in Rome?"

"We're all well on this end. A little birdie informed me you got engaged to an American in the legal profession."

"Right on target. The wedding will be in New York and followed later by one in Germany, which I'd love for you to attend."

"I'd love to meet the woman who has finally put a leash on you," Mary laughed. "Saw her on the interview. Beautiful woman. Classy. Genuine. What other reason is there for this call?"

"I'm going to have a face-off with my future in-laws. They seem to believe their daughter is marrying a penniless vagabond and I intend to show them just what I'm worth."

"Why does it matter what they think? Once they see you, there should be no doubt you are far from penniless."

Page took a deep breath, "Because they made her cry. Her mother is a piece of work, Mary. All about security instead of happiness. Love seems to be a foreign concept to the woman. She wants Rebecca to marry the banker's son to have a stable life financially."

Mary laughed into the phone. "When is this meeting to take place?"

"Sometime in the next two weeks, after which I'll be in New York, looking over Rebecca's shoulder."

"I'll have all the paperwork overnighted to you, then. Everything down to the last nickel will be signed and stamped. I'll list all your properties and corporate holdings on a ledger along with the income generated with leases. No reason to take faxed copies. The originals on my letterhead are so much more official if you're going after the shock effect."

"You know me well," Page laughed. "Thank you, Mary." He hung up and went to the studio, where he finished the song he was writing just for his new bride. Satisfied with it, he did a complete workout followed by the hot tub. His eyes fell on the sofa and a smile touched his lips as he remembered holding her while they watched her first X-rated movie. Her reaction had surprised him. She was full of surprises, his woman. Closing his eyes, he could almost see her stretched out on the sofa. She had the greenest eyes and that hair… the color of a deep red wine. Would their babies have her looks or his, he wondered. With nothing left to do, he dried off and got dressed, returning to the great room, where he pulled a book of poetry off the shelf and dropped on the sofa. When he spotted a smudge of flour on the material, he laughed. Yeah, she was full of surprises. Hours later Anna shook him from his sleep in time for dinner.

"When do you plan on doing battle with the new in-laws?" Anna asked him as she handed him his plate.

"Within the next two weeks. Getting copies of my net worth from Sampson Investments and catching a flight out of Paris. Hoping to be able to make the trip unnoticed. Renting a car in Indianapolis, plus booking a hotel there. I hope that after all is said and done they will at least show up at the wedding. Rebecca would rather her father walk her down the aisle than her boss. From what I can tell, he doesn't stand up to his wife much." Page shrugged and took a bite of the cabbage and ham. "When Rebecca moves in here I plan to give you a raise. Don't let me forget."

"You pay me well enough Page and the woman is a joy to be around. Raise isn't necessary." She smiled at him as he ate. "Just seeing you happy is enough for me. I'm going to go feed Hans."

"While I'm gone you and Hans might be able to get in a vacation, you know."

"We aren't much for going off except for taking some day trips. That would be nice."

He watched her as she returned to the kitchen and called after her, "I'm capable of putting my plate in the dishwasher. Enjoy the night with your husband."

Anna turned and smiled at him before she left the kitchen, heading toward her own living quarters.

After he finished dinner, he set the dishwasher, then headed into his office to deal with any leftover last minute details concerning the tour.

Rebecca slept most of the way from Paris to New York, her dreams consisting of walking down the aisle, on the arm of her father while her mother cried happily from the seat. When she woke from that particular scenario, she requested a bourbon and coke from the flight attendant.

When the young woman brought the drink, she leaned closer and asked: "Are you the woman about to marry Page Harlow?"

Rebecca took a sip of the drink and nodded, holding up the ring for the attendant to see. "Yes, I am." With a grin, she added, "I guess I'd better get used to that question, huh?"

"Are you going on the tour?"

"Not all of it. I need to work training my replacement and figure out what to do with my house. Plus there's the wedding itself to plan. I'll be bald and crazy by the time it's over and the 'I do's' are said.

The woman was called away by another passenger, but she glanced back and gave a thumbs up sign. Rebecca sipped her drink and wondered if Gina remembered she was supposed to pick her up. Staring out at the clouds below the plane, she suddenly sat up and grinned to herself. "Perfect. If Page can give away a house, so can I." Gina was renting an apartment outside of town, commuting to work and still paying high rent. Her roommates were in and out, sometimes not paying their fair share. Plus, Gina said the couple upstairs always complained about the music, or that Gina was in the wrong parking spot. How many times had she said if rent wasn't so high she would move closer and live alone? Even though Rebecca's house was small, it was laid out well. It was an odd plot of land between two buildings so there was no space and no windows on the sides. Rebecca had added track lighting to make it brighter and a mural of Central Park covered one wall, making it appear bigger than it was. Something to think about. Should this be something she consulted Page about? He'd already made it clear he didn't care for New York, so it wasn't as if they were going to reside there. Still, something such as property should be a mutual agreement. She found her cell phone and punched in the numbers. When he answered, her breath caught and she felt her heartbeat quicken. "Hi," she whispered.

"Hi, back at ya," Page said with a chuckle.

"I have something I need to run by you."

"Shoot," he answered.

"I'm thinking about offering Gina my house. She's not happy in her apartment, the rent's high and sometimes her roomies don't pay their fair share. Since someone practically gave it to me and since I will be living in Germany, or somewhere…"

Page smiled. "It's your house, Becca. I think it's a wonderful idea, personally, but ultimately it's your decision."

"Well, after the 'I do's' it would be your house as well."

"I have zero desire to own a house in New York City. So, by all means, if you think Gina would like the house, then gift her with the house."

"Okay, I will. Providing she wants it."

"I miss you," he whispered.

"Miss you too, Toad."

"I'll see you in about two weeks or so."

"Good, because I'm going to be lonely without you."

"Be safe, Becca. I love you."

"Love you too, Toad. We're getting ready to land. Bye." She disconnected the call and finished her drink as the 'fasten seat belt' sign came on.

Chapter Forty

Gina was waiting for her when she arrived, holding a bunch of balloons. Behind Gina stood several people with microphones. Rebecca took a deep breath and shifted her handbag on her shoulder, lifted her chin and grinned at Gina.

"Hey!" Gina said, handing the balloons to Rebecca, then glancing over her shoulder. "I couldn't find a spot to hide out away from them."

"Something I need to get used to, I suppose." She turned toward the reporters and offered a smile, then began to answer their questions. Finally, she held her hand up. "I believe I've covered everything you need for your articles, so if you'll excuse me, it's been a very long flight.

"One more question," a woman asked quickly. "How do your parents feel about the news?"

Rebecca took a deep breath. "They would prefer I marry the banker's son. They've never heard of Page Harlow, so obviously they aren't jumping up and down with joy. Yet. I'm hoping they change their mind if they meet him." She turned and followed Gina through the airport where they caught a shuttle to Gina's car, after picking up the pieces of luggage.

At Rebecca's house, Gina helped her unpack, commenting on every new piece of clothing. Rebecca put water in the Keurig and programmed a cup of coffee. "There's probably wine and sodas in the fridge," she added, dropping onto the sofa. "So, what's been going on at work?"

Gina opened a Coke and sat in the overstuffed chair. "Same as when you left. Boss said he was going to try to get you to stay."

"Are we opening a branch in Munich?" Rebecca laughed. "I might help out until you get trained completely, but I won't be residing in New York so it's a temporary fix. Which brings me to an important question. Do you like this house?"

"I've always liked this house. Granted, you have no windows on either side but the window in front is nice and you have a ton of privacy."

"Do you want the house?"

Gina blinked. "This house?"

"Yes. This house. You don't like your apartment, your rent is high, and you have no privacy. I will be moving sometime after the wedding, so why would I want to hang onto a house in New York?"

"I can't afford this house."

"I don't remember asking if you could afford it. I asked you if you wanted it."

"I'm not following…"

"If you want the house, I'm going to give you the house. We can have everything transferred after the wedding." Rebecca shrugged. "If it hadn't been for you, I wouldn't know who Page was, I wouldn't have met him and fallen so much in love I can't breathe. He owns more houses now than anyone I know, and he doesn't care for New York City. I don't want to be someone's landlady either. Not even yours."

"Yes. I love this house."

"Great. Done. Now, I'm going to need your help with this damn wedding. Page wants an extravagant affair and I don't even know where to start. Anna and I made a list…"

It was several hours later when they finished a long list of places to look at, available dates, cake designers and bridal shops nearby. Gina hugged her and reminded Rebecca to lock the door after she left.

Chapter Forty-one

Page checked into a small hotel under the corporate name of Madison Ltd, hoping to remain off the media radar. How would Rebecca react when she discovered his visit to her parents? He dressed in his blue Armani suit and white tailor-made dress shirt, fastened the gold and diamond cufflinks, slipped the Presidential Rolex on his wrist, picked up the briefcase and went downstairs to the desk. "Has my rental car arrived?" he inquired from behind his expensive sunglasses.

The woman looked up, smiled and said, "Yes sir. It's the silver Mercedes out front." She handed him the keys. He glanced at the woman's name tag and returned the smile. "Thank you, Evelyn. Now, if you were me, where would you stop for breakfast?"

"IHOP or Denny's. Turn left at the light, head for the interstate. Can't miss the signs."

"Thank you. See you when I return."

Evelyn smiled at him. "My shift ends at noon, so probably not."

Page grinned, "Probably not, then." He went out and tossed the briefcase on the passenger seat and checked the mirrors, adjusted the seat and eased into traffic, whispering a thank you to Tommy and Ashley who had taken care of all the small details. He didn't want to show up at the Morrison house driving a compact rental, but he wasn't expecting a Mercedes. He followed Evelyn's directions, eased into Denny's where he had a peaceful breakfast, signed the check 'T. Madison Ltd' and returned to the interstate. His GPS guided him to Janberg in a little under two hours. Farmland. He cruised through the town and said, "yep, a very small dot on the map" to himself. A smile crossed his lips as he passed Janberg Bank which looked older than

Jessie James. One small strip mall held the post office, general store and a small restaurant called JoAnne's. Two churches stood across from each other. His GPS told him his destination was two hundred feet on the right. He again sent up a thank you to Ashley who had managed to provide the Morrison's home address.

It was a white house and had the cookie cutter look that was popular during the housing boom. A small white picket fence edged the sidewalk. He sat in the car and gathered his thoughts. Finally, he reached for his briefcase, adjusted his shades and released the clip holding his hair back, allowing it to fall over his shoulders. He walked up the walkway and touched the doorbell.

An older version of Rebecca answered the door and looked him up and down before saying, "Whatever you're selling, we aren't buying."

Page removed the glasses, his blue eyes meeting her amber ones. "Not selling anything, Mrs. Morrison."

"Then who are you and what do you want?"

"Lord Page Harlow. I'm your future son-in-law."

"I don't have time for jokes, whoever you are."

"I can see where Rebecca gets her feistiness," Page said slowly. "I can assure you I don't joke about my upcoming wedding to your daughter."

An older man came to the door. "Who the hell did you say you were?"

"Lord Page Harlow of Herrington. It's a small estate in England. North of London."

"You don't sound English," the man said. "What's this about my daughter?"

"I live in Germany, most of the time. I'm going to marry Rebecca. Your wife knows that."

"What's in the briefcase?" Mr. Morrison asked.

"Proof."

"Of what? I'm sorry, I'm not following you."

"Since Mrs. Morrison referred to me as a penniless vagabond, I thought you'd be more interested in my financial bottom line than in how much I love your daughter. I had my investment accountant list all my assets for your viewing." Page's tone was low and clipped. How the hell did these two manage to raise a woman as loving as Rebecca? "Obviously Mrs. Morrison isn't concerned with her daughter's happiness, only that the chosen husband be financially secure. Does that about cover it?"

Mr. Morrison glanced at his wife. "Rebecca called?"

"Not recently. Said she was in Europe going to marry some musician. She's throwing her life away and I called her on it. I don't believe she knows the meaning of the term 'love'."

Page shifted his stance, "Well, she certainly didn't learn it from you, I can tell you that much." It was taking a lot of willpower to remain calm.

Mr. Morrison unlatched the screen and opened it offering Page his hand. "I'm Ed Morrison. I think you should come in and have a seat. Obviously, I'm in the dark, here, so maybe you can bring me up to speed."

"Page Harlow," Page said, shaking the man's hand. "I'd be happy to bring you up to speed since your wife seems bent on not wanting her daughter to get married."

Ed motioned to the living room. "Let's have a seat, Mr. Harlow."

"Page." They went into the living area and Page sat his briefcase on the coffee table, making sure the diamonds on his watch and cufflinks caught the light. "I came because I believe Rebecca would like to have her parents attend her wedding. She's presently shopping for a wedding gown in New York. I have an upcoming tour that will last nine months, covering most of the States and into Canada. The honeymoon will be either at my home in South Florida or my home in Southern California. My main residence is a castle close to Munich. I know you have questions, especially about my financial stability so, here." He released the snaps of the briefcase and handed Mrs. Morrison the gold embossed folder from Mary Sampson. "Latest bank statements for five separate accounts, property listings, both residential and commercial. Amount of income received from rental properties in seven countries. Vehicles, plural. I believe it's up to date as of two weeks ago."

Mr. Morrison looked from Page to his wife. "I'm still not understanding why you felt it necessary…"

Page cut him off. "Because I held Rebecca while she sobbed after her mother launched a vicious attack over the phone. Rebecca held out hope that you would be happy for her but all she got was that you were worried about her being married to a penniless vagabond. Personally, I'd think her happiness should mean more than how big my bank account is but for some people I guess money is all important."

The older man looked back at his wife. "Is this true? Why am I just finding out my daughter is getting married?"

"Because Rebecca is not thinking clearly. He's a rock musician for God sake!"

"What the hell does his vocation have to do with anything?"

"They always end up broke."

Page arched a brow and tilted his head as if staring at a modern painting he couldn't figure out. "Only the stupid ones," he said as a reply. "I wasn't that stupid on my first tour. I invest, obtain, sell and reinvest. I believe my net worth as of two weeks ago is somewhere in the range of under a billion. That's with a 'B'."

Rebecca's father shifted in his chair, "I don't care if you dig ditches and work minimum wage. Do you love my daughter, Page?"

"With all my heart."

"That's more important than how much you make." Ed looked at his wife, his mouth set. "Janay, did it occur to you our daughter is an adult and her choice is not ours to make?"

"I knew you'd take her side. If you hadn't allowed her to go to New York, she'd still be here where she belongs, settled down the way women are meant to be. So instead she went to some fancy school, works for a fancy firm and now she's run off to Europe where she's decided to marry some rock musician and traipse around the world, doing God knows what! I know what's best for my daughter. She needs someone who is stable, who will work and come home each night and make sure she has a roof over her head."

Page bit back the retort at the edge of his tongue and said softly, "Here is the bottom line. Your daughter and I are getting married in New York before my tour kicks off. She will most certainly not be traipsing the world as you put it. She may stay in New York or return to my castle in Munich. If she doesn't wish to stay in Munich, she can choose any one of my other homes. Two in the United States, one in Italy, one in Switzerland, an entire village in England, or any one of my condos located in five different countries. Her choice. Most mothers would be content knowing their daughter will be loved and cared for. What is it you want, Mrs. Morrison? If not your daughter's happiness, then what? If money is all you worry about I have that covered."

The woman stared at her hands in silence, long enough Page wondered if she was going to respond. Slowly, she met Page's gaze. "I wanted her to come home and stay close by, marry someone in the community and buy a house nearby. So I could be there for her. My mother was never there for me and I wanted a different outcome for her. Yet, here you are, telling me she's getting married to you and will be living who knows where. What kind of a life is that?"

Page smiled. "I love her. We really aren't that far, considering the speed of air travel. It isn't as if you'll never see her again. That is if you want to see her."

For lack of anything else to do with her nervous hands, she thumbed through the stack of paperwork, carefully turning each piece of paper. "You really own all this?"

"Yes, I really do."

"A real castle? Who lives in a castle, for God's sake? Why would you?"

"A real castle. I inherited it from my grandfather. Complete with my housekeeper, Anna, and her husband Hans. Horses, lake, mountain. Mercedes. The house in Italy comes complete with a guest cottage and a Lamborghini. Both properties in the States are gated with pools and hot tubs. The English estate is the size of this town complete with a village. I just gave away my childhood home in Norway to a couple whose house burned down. There's a smaller house in Switzerland as well."

"Why are you in such an almighty rush to get her to the altar? Worried she's come to her senses and call it off? Do you need a green card? Is that it? You'll marry her so you can become an American citizen?"

"I don't need to marry her. I want to marry her. I'm an English Lord so I certainly don't have any desire to become an American citizen. Do you think your daughter can't make her own decisions? She's one of the most intelligent women I know."

"When is this wedding?" she asked quietly.

"Beats me. I'm sure she'll let me know. I'm leaving here, going to New York. Not that she's not capable of planning a wedding on her own but she has a hard time learning how to spend my money. I'll be staying at The Plaza if I can get a room on short notice. Summer in New York City is somewhat busy."

"She's probably too mad to talk to me."

"She's not mad. She was hurt. Now me, I was mad. Nobody will make Becca cry. No one. Not even you." Page turned to his future father-in-law. "She had hoped you would walk her down the aisle. She'll settle for her boss if you won't."

"Of course I will. I will damn well be a part of my daughter's wedding." He glared at his wife. "If you hadn't shown up, I might not have even known she was married. Makes me wonder what else I don't know about."

"I take care of the house, Ed. All you ever did was work, come home, eat dinner and go to sleep. Why would you want to be bothered by day to day issues?"

"I wouldn't call my daughter's engagement a day to day issue, Janay."

"I was just concerned she hadn't thought it through. Maybe because she was in Europe she was caught up in the moment. Hell, I don't know. I just didn't want her to make a big mistake."

"Well, I plan to walk my daughter down the aisle. It would be nice if you decided to treat her like an adult and be there for her."

"Good. I'm glad we had this little chat." He offered his mother-in-law one of his earth-shattering media smiles. "I'm sure she'll be happy to hear from you."

"I'm curious," Janay said, "We aren't exactly in the middle of point 'a' going to point 'b'. What made you decide to stop here? How did you even find us?"

"I flew from Paris to Detroit and into Indianapolis. My management team is good at finding the addresses of people I need to talk to. So, I hopped a jet, rented a car and here I am."

"Why? I mean, isn't that a lot of time and money?"

"I wanted you to get an up close and personal look at me. Face to face. I'm not passing through your life. I take this till death do us part thing seriously and it helps if my in-laws don't hate me." He flashed the smile again.

"What did Rebecca say when you told her you were coming here?"

"I didn't tell her." He shrugged.

"Why not?"

"Because I didn't want her to object, or tell me it didn't matter or directly tell me not to come. I came on my own. If this meeting went south, I might have mentioned it in passing. Maybe next year. You know… 'by the way honey, your parents are jerks' sort of comment…" He shoved a strand of hair from his face and shrugged.

Janay laughed. "Jerks, huh?"

"Well, you did make her cry. Sort of a pissy reaction to a wedding announcement. And, you called me a foreigner, which was rude, even though it was technically correct."

"Well, you speak English at least."

Page laughed. "I also speak German, French, Spanish, Italian and Norwegian fluently plus I can hold my own in Portuguese, Chinese, Japanese and Dutch. That being said, your daughter kicked my butt in chess. Twice."

Janay nodded, "I neglected to ask if you wanted something to drink. Not very sociable of me. We have coffee, tea, and coke."

"A coke would be great. Minus any rat poison, please."

Janay disappeared into another room. Ed looked Page up and down. "I didn't even know Rebecca left the country, much less got engaged. How long have you been engaged?"

"Under a month. It was literally love at first sight. I mean that. Like I'd been hit with a two by four."

"You've been engaged under a month? How long have you known her?"

"Under a month. Well, we talked on the phone for about a week before we actually met in person. Then, after I proposed, well after I mentioned I thought about it, my manager tried to bribe her into stepping out of my life. She dropped a million dollar check into his coffee cup. I fired him on the spot. Two days later I rehired him only after Becca suggested it. She's amazing, but then you know that. Life is strange, you know?"

"I know. So, you're really a rock musician? A big name I haven't heard of?"

"Lead singer and songwriter of Harlow's Black Angels. Five tours worldwide, lots of broken hearts. One ex with one child, my son Eric.

He's six. Sasha got the villa in Spain, twenty thousand a month in support plus my red Ferrari. I miss that car."

Ed laughed. "I think we're going to get along. You're straightforward."

"I find it's easier to just cut through any bullshit. If you or your wife had an issue with me, then I'd accept it and not mention this visit. I find it saves time to know where I stand."

Janay returned with a can of coke, a glass of ice and a tray of cookies. "Homemade, chocolate chip." She sat the tray down. "I don't know if Rebecca ever learned to cook. She never cared for it when she was growing up. As a matter of fact, she didn't like any part of the housewife routine."

"Anna was teaching her how to make bread at the castle. Anna does all the cooking and cleaning. Anywhere else, we can eat out."

"So, how old is Anna?"

Page chuckled. "In her sixties. I would never ask a woman her age. She and Hans have their own attached quarters on the side of the castle. I have a cottage for my stable boy, Nat who cares for my horses when I'm gone. It's not a huge castle as far as German castles go but it's six stories tall, about 40 rooms. Studio and fitness center on the lower level, kitchen, dining room, den, office, main room on the first floor, eight bedrooms on the second floor, all furnished. Eight more on the next level, not all furnished and the rest is dust bunnies."

Ed glanced out the window and smiled. "I like the car."

"Tommy rented it for me, through the business. I told him to find me something nice and not a compact Toyota."

"I didn't know they even rented Mercedes."

Page shrugged. "You can get anything if you're willing to pay the asking price."

"Rebecca wasn't raised with money. I mean, we weren't broke and we always had food and shelter, but she was never interested in expensive clothes." Janay said softly.

"She mentioned that. I wasn't either, although my father saw to it my mother and I had what was necessary. When my mother died he dropped me in a private boy's school in Britain. At sixteen I went to live with my grandfather in Germany. He was English but married a German woman. It's all interesting reading on the web. Try to ignore my petty arrest records. Part and parcel of being a single hell-raising rock star. The image was everything. Past tense. I am about to be a happily married rock star. As for her not being interested in expensive clothes, I had a hell of a time getting her to shop in Paris without looking at price tags. I gave her a credit card for her wedding expenses, but I'm thinking I should be hovering nearby to remind her she's going to be an extremely wealthy woman and she should start thinking like one. I don't remember ever having anyone complain their watch had too many diamonds until Rebecca. She flat refused to even look at the Ladies Rolex."

Janay stopped, holding her coke in one hand and looked at Page. "Oh dear. You actually tried to buy her a Rolex?"

Page nodded. "She finally settled for a Movado with smaller diamonds. I thought all women loved to go shopping. Not Rebecca. Although, she finally got the hang of it. We talked about looking at bridal gowns in Paris, but she wanted her friend to go with her. I'm guessing it's a girl thing and I'm smart enough not to get in the middle."

"How do you feel about children, Page?" Janay asked.

"I have one. Would be great in a year or so to add a brother or sister. Ultimately that's a decision Rebecca and I will make. I've already determined this will be my last extended tour. My manager wasn't too keen on that decision but he'll live with it."

"What is Rebecca supposed to do while you're on tour?"

"Whatever she wants. She can stay in New York at the firm to train her replacement. She could go back to Germany and be around Anna. She could go on a vacation to anywhere on the planet." Page shrugged. "She could go on the tour if she wants to. The three of you could take an extended cruise somewhere."

"Most couples get married and settle down and start housekeeping," Janay said.

"Safe to say, we aren't most couples. Don't get me wrong. If Becca wants to buy a new house and furnish it herself, we can do that although she's already commented that we have more houses now than necessary. She's concerned with property taxes since I can't homestead the ones here in the States."

Janay handed Page the folder. "You know, this wasn't necessary. I know I took the engagement announcement badly. It was just so unexpected. Rebecca was always so level-headed and then she moved to the city. There's nothing wrong with a mother wanting her only child to live close by."

"There is a point when she's no longer a child. And I don't think she much cares for the idea of marrying the banker's son." Page offered her his brightest grin. "Plus, you get to come to visit us if you want to, wherever we happen to be. When was the last time you two visited your daughter? She's been in the city for over eight years."

"You're right, of course. I probably should have. The last time I saw her was the time she came home when Ed had heart surgery. She stayed for three months. I was hoping she would realize this was where she belonged but she left as soon as her leave was up at work. Wasn't as if she couldn't find a job here."

"She grew up. She went to college. She settled into a career, which she loves. She owns a house in New York. You should be proud of her accomplishments. I've met women her age who don't have one thing going for them and they think the world owes them just for being alive. I've never in all my years of playboy single road trips met anyone like Rebecca."

"She's probably never met anyone like you either, I suppose."

Page chuckled. "Probably not."

"You mentioned you had an ex. Does she know you're getting remarried?"

Page decided not to correct the assumption he had married Sasha so he shrugged. "She knows. She and Becca sort of butted heads once. Becca came out on top and Sasha left looking defeated for the first time ever. I always found it easier to just give Sasha whatever she wanted and not fight over petty stuff. Eric has a trust fund set in place for his future so I don't worry about Sasha running through his college fund." He glanced at his watch. "I suppose I need to head back to the hotel in Indianapolis and get out of your hair."

Janay stood up when he did and Ed followed. "I was wrong. I'm woman enough to admit when I'm wrong and I was very wrong about you. I've watched you when you mention her name. You always smile. I never really believed in love at first sight, but that's the only explanation for it. Tell Rebecca I'd really love to be at the wedding."

"I think you should tell her," Page said as he turned to leave.

They walked him out to the car and stood at the edge of the walkway when he pulled away from the curb.

Chapter Forty-two

Rebecca spent a long time behind closed doors with her boss after her return. She agreed to stay on as a consultant until the time came to relocate to Germany at the end of the tour. Her hours would be flexible as she trained Gina to take over. When she left the office, Gina met her at her own office doorway. "Well?"

"My desk is now your desk. It will be made official by the end of next work week. I'm going to be looking over your shoulder for a while since Page will be invading the world. I'll officially be a consultant after you're trained. Now, let's go to dinner. Page is buying."

"I take it we aren't going to McDonald's then," Gina teased.

"I'm thinking steak."

"Well, we're both well-dressed so we don't have to run home and change. The upside of working in a law office. Of course, only one of us is wearing clothes from Paris."

"Don't be mean," Rebecca laughed, picking up her handbag.

The steaks were perfect, as was the atmosphere as Rebecca and Gina made a list of things to be done over the weekend. They broke things down into time frames so the day wouldn't be spent on just one project. Rebecca decided to window shop for the five gowns she had chosen in Germany. Then they would spend a maximum of two hours looking at several venues. She decided not to waste time looking into churches since most required you be a member. Dessert arrived when Rebecca's cell phone rang. She glanced at it and sighed. "It's my mother," she said, resigned not to argue with the woman. "Hello, mom."

"Rebecca? I'm not very good at apologizing but I called to say I'm sorry for the things I said about your fiancé."

"What?"

"I was very wrong about him. And you. I never believed in love at first sight but it seems that's what you have. Your father and I would really like to be a part of your wedding celebration. I know it's going to be in New York, so if you'll let us know, we can fly in. Maybe we can come a few days early and you can show me your house."

"What brought about the sudden change of heart?" Rebecca stared at the phone. Her mother had never in her life apologized for anything. Ever.

"Well, he came to visit. He made me see how wrong I was. He's a charming young man, your Page Harlow."

"Wait. What? Page was in Indiana? Why?"

"Well, he was a bit angry when he arrived. Brought all his financial statements. Said he wanted to prove you would be well cared for because he thought I was more interested in that than I was the fact he loved you. He really does love you."

"Well, yes he does, but he shouldn't have interfered in a misunderstanding between you and me. That really wasn't his call. I can't believe he didn't mention it. I've talked to him several times and he never said he was going to visit you. How can he think that it's okay to keep secrets?"

"Oh dear. I assumed he called you right after he left here. I think he's heading to New York. I hope I didn't spoil his surprise. But when I asked him to tell you I would love to be part of your wedding he said I should tell you myself. "

"I just think it would have been nice if he would have mentioned he was going."

"Well sweetheart, men don't think the same as we women do. Maybe he thought you wouldn't mind and he could straighten out the misunderstanding first."

"Still, he should have asked me. You're my parent."

"Well, I'll be his mother-in-law, dear. Now tell me what I can do to help."

"I've got it handled, I think. Narrowed it down to five gowns. I'll be looking at venues tomorrow. Look, I'm at dinner with Gina and I can't eat and talk at the same time. Can I call you later?"

"Of course honey. Not too late, though. Your father goes to bed early you know."

"Well, if not tonight I'll call tomorrow evening." She narrowed her eyes at Gina and added, "Bye mom."

Rebecca laid the phone on the white linen tablecloth and took a deep breath. "I'm going to kill him with my bare hands."

"Who?"

"Page fucking Harlow. He took it upon himself to have a face-off with my parents. He actually showed up at their house in Indiana with all his financial statements. What the hell was he thinking?"

"Well, it must have ended okay if she called."

"God only knows what he said to them. Is he going to meddle in my life every day? Doesn't he think I can handle my own mother?"

Gina frowned. "You can't handle your own mother. Remember, I'm the one she was screaming at on the phone. I don't know how he managed to even talk to her."

"It not his place to talk to her. It's mine. Oh, I am so pissed." She took a bite of her Chocolate cake.

Gina sighed. "Look, normally I would keep my opinion to myself but this time I'm telling you if Page went to visit your mother he had a damn good reason and obviously he straightened out her original dislike of him. You should be happy. Isn't that what you wanted? Your parents to be a part of your wedding?"

Rebecca motioned for the check and handed the server the card Page gave her. "He doesn't even think I can pay for my own gown, Gina. It's like he's got to have his say in everything."

Gina shrugged. "Well, it's his wedding too. Shouldn't you both be involved? As for the gown, the ones you are looking at are in the thousands of dollars range. Let him pay for the dress. He can afford it and you can save your money to buy stuff later."

"That's what I just said. If he was going to visit my parents, why didn't he tell me? We could have gone together."

"Rebecca. Page did what most men would do. He saw a problem and fixed it. You had already tried to talk to your mother and it didn't end well, did it?"

"I'm your friend. Why are you taking up for him?"

"Because you are my friend. And this time, you're wrong to be mad at Page for fixing a problem that needed to be fixed."

"He could have at least called me."

"He probably will. Maybe he's on a plane, or in a car. When was he in Indiana?"

"I don't know. Mom didn't say."

"You do realize if he just left there, he's probably on his way here, don't you? It wouldn't make any sense for him to return to Germany just to turn around and come back. You did say he was coming here, didn't you? He probably figured he could just as easily mention it when he saw you as he could by calling you and have you get the wrong idea; which you just did."

"Damn it, Gina, I just feel like I'm being manipulated around him. He always gets his way. It's as if he has to have the last word. I would have called my mother again."

"And I can tell you, you would have had the same result as before. Whatever the hell Page wanted to prove to her was successful so why are you so pissed?"

"Because – "

"Yeah, that's a great reason. Did you hit your damn head somewhere? This is Page Harlow we're talking about. And he loves you. He didn't want your wedding less than perfect and that meant making nice with his mother-in-law. So what? He went to Indiana. Your mother now adores him so you can have peace in the family."

"It still should have been mentioned. I've spoken to him multiple times. You can't tell me it was spur of the moment. Not if he took all his financials." As mad as Rebecca was, a laugh broke through. "I'll bet mom almost stroked out."

Gina sipped her drink and chuckled. "I imagine there are a lot of zeros on the bottom line."

"A lot, along with a couple of commas before the decimal point. Still, he should have mentioned it to me. He can't think it is okay to go behind my back and do important stuff."

"Well, I suggest you sit down and have a heart to heart talk with him about the way you feel. Now, what time are we going shopping?"

"I don't know. Not real early. My body clock still hasn't gotten regulated from German time. I'll call you when I wake up. Probably around ten." Rebecca picked up her handbag and they left the restaurant.

Chapter Forty-three

Rebecca fixed herself a bourbon and coke and sat down at her dining room table, with her laptop. She looked up several different venues and made some notes on each about the size and price. Most important was the availability within the three-month time frame. Since most of the guests on her side would be her co-workers, she jotted a note to ask about his list. His band, Tommy, Ashley, the crew and who knew how many that was? Her father would need a tux. She could buy her mother a dress. What the hell had Page said to the woman? Even though Gina was right, it still irritated her that he'd kept it a secret. Why would he do that? She sipped her drink and frowned. Because he figured she might tell him not to go and then he would be stuck. If he went anyway, she would have been really pissed and if he didn't go, her parents would have remained hostile. So, by not asking, he avoided a confrontation. The thought caused her to laugh out loud. "I'm marrying a dominating toad," she declared, returning to her research. With a sigh, she reached for the phone.

"Hi mom, I'm home. Do you have time to talk?"

"Certainly, Rebecca. How are things in New York?"

"Fine, so far. Page hasn't called, but Gina thinks he might be on his way here and he figures what would be the point. Are all men so hard-headed?"

Her mother laughed. "Yep. In one way or another, they are. You have two choices. Live with it or try to change it."

"What about compromise? I'm sitting here looking at different venues for the wedding and realize I haven't got a clue. Up until last week, marriage was the last thing on my mind, much less on my agenda.

He wants something akin to the casting for the Ten Commandments and I don't even know where to begin. My list is under fifty people but I'm not sure about his. We are going to plan a second ceremony in Germany for those who can't make it stateside. He suggested I could think of hiring a wedding planner or calling his personal assistant, who volunteered to help. She lives in DC so not far."

"He has a personal assistant who's female? How does that work?"

"Like a sister. She's an employee and from what I was told he's very protective of her. I'm thinking if she can put together a world tour, she could help with a wedding."

"Well, it wouldn't hurt to have a second opinion. I don't know anything about big weddings or anything about New York. The bigger the event, the more bridesmaids and groomsmen you'll want. No less than three each, plus a maid of honor and best man."

"See, this is why I wanted to just go to a justice of the peace or a judge, say I do and be done with it. Page won't hear of it. He says I waited my whole life, saving myself for my wedding and it will be a wedding to remember. The man is so pig-headed at times."

There was silence on the other end of the phone for a long time before her mother asked, "Are you saying you saved yourself physically all this time? I tried not to think of you being in a big town like New York, not that way. Wait, that didn't come out right at all. Oh dear. I guess I assumed that by twenty-seven you would have had a few relationships."

"Well, according to you, having an intimate relationship was worse than a root canal without Novocain."

Her mother chuckled, "Well, sometimes the outcome is the same. In today's society, it seems men like to change partners like they change socks. I have to admit I was a concerned parent. I could only hope for the best."

"You didn't want me to leave Janberg. You wanted to keep me there. I guess I knew there was more in the world than a farm town in Indiana. It didn't occur to me, I would discover the man I would marry on the other side of the world." She hesitated. "I almost refused to go, but I really wanted to see Europe and who better to show me the sights than a native? I figured I would announce that I planned on saving myself for my wedding and he would ship me off to the nearest Hilton. Happy to say, Page and I are more alike than I realized. He likes opera, classical music, has a library to die for, has a wicked sense of humor and loves art museums."

"You sound happy, Rebecca and that's the best any mother can ask for. Plus, I have never seen a more handsome man than your Page Harlow. Have you discussed having a family? I still hold out hope of having a grandchild or two, you know."

"We talked about it, yes. He has a nine-month tour and we'll be apart a lot of that time but I can safely say there will be one or two in our future. Plus, he has a six-year-old so I'll be a wicked stepmother." She laughed. "So technically, that makes you a grandmother to a six-year-old already. Poof. Instant grandchild."

Her mother laughed. "He mentioned you butted heads with his ex-wife and you won."

Rebecca didn't correct the statement. "Sasha is used to having a hold on him through visitation. She deserved a smackdown and I gave her the legal attitude I learned working for a bunch of attorneys."

"So, when is Page arriving? Do you have the refrigerator stocked? Men get grumpy without breakfast. Or at least coffee."

"Mom, he isn't staying at my house. He isn't sleeping over at my house. I'm guessing he will rent the suite at a hotel."

"Seems to be a waste of money, since you two will be together anyway."

Rebecca stared at the phone, not quite believing her mother was advocating she allow Page to stay with her. "That's one thing he does really well, is spending money. I still need to make an appearance at my job, until I get Gina trained. Then I'll be a consultant while Page is on tour."

"Wouldn't you rather be with your husband, than be alone in New York?"

"It's not practical, mom. Page is in a band. Each night is a different city, a different hotel."

"He's very good looking. Aren't you worried about different women?"

"No, I'm not. If he wanted different women he wouldn't need to get married to one. Trust is an important part of us. I have to trust him or I'll worry myself sick. We already had this discussion when we first discussed marriage. I actually asked him the same thing."

"Well, he didn't think to mention he was flying to Indiana, now did he?"

"No, but he never said he wouldn't either."

"Well, I can only hope you're right."

Rebecca wanted to say 'so do I' but she wouldn't give in to any doubt. "I'm sure we'll have our share of misunderstandings. I don't think being unfaithful will be one of them. He's used to getting his own way and I'm used to being alone but we'll work through all that."

"Well, your father just informed me it was past bedtime. By the way, Page and your father got along great, and your dad is excited to walk his baby girl down the aisle."

"Kiss dad for me. We'll talk again soon."

Rebecca hung up to discover she had two missed calls from a New York number. A glance at the clock made her decision not to return them until morning. As she undressed for bed, she stood studying herself in the full-length mirror. Well, she didn't have 'harlot' written on her in red, the way her mother had always insinuated when she was growing up. What exactly had caught Page's attention? There were a lot of women in the world prettier than she was. Just look at his ex. What about the ones he would meet during the tour? She frowned. Could he just drop his playboy ways cold turkey? Would there be others? Would she find out? Then what? What about a prenup? He hadn't mentioned one but no one with his money would get married without one, would they? Trust. A marriage had to be built on mutual trust. Could she trust him? Did she? She heaved a long sigh and slipped between the sheets, asleep the minute her head hit the pillow.

Chapter Forty-four

Rebecca woke up and dressed in a pair of her Paris slacks and silk shirt, both an emerald green. She fixed a cup of coffee and called Gina who said she'd be there in about an hour. While she waited, she went back over her notes and looked at the ads for the five gowns. Remembering the missed calls from last night she listened to her voice mail. It was Page, calling from the Plaza. He left his room number and asked her to call when she checked her messages. Well, at least he remembered she didn't live on her phone so he wouldn't be surprised because she hadn't called last night. Instead of immediately calling him, she toasted a bagel and covered it with cream cheese and returned to her notes about venues to look at. Maybe she would ask for his help on that part. He knew more about venues and what to ask than she did and this was no time for her to be stubborn about needing his wisdom. The thought caused her to smile. She dialed the number he left and it ring a dozen times before she hung up. Maybe he was at breakfast.

Gina arrived and when Rebecca answered the door, she pointed behind her where Page stood. "I found this homeless guy on the sidewalk. Can we keep him?"

Rebecca laughed. "I don't think my fiancé would want me keeping a man as a pet although he is kinda cute and my fiancé did promise me a puppy."

Page made a face at her. "Do I look like a puppy? No, don't answer that."

"I just tried to call your room," Rebecca said as he closed the door behind him and followed Gina into the kitchen. "I have coffee, cokes, and bourbon. I know it's too early for bourbon by our time, but probably not in Germany, so your choice."

"Coffee is fine," he said and moved toward the Keurig on the counter. Gina handed him a cup and a coffee pod then retrieved a coke from the fridge and dropped into a kitchen chair, picking up the notes.

Rebecca waited until Page sat down, then refilled her own coffee cup. "Okay, three of the bridal gowns are in one shop, so I'm thinking that should be the first stop."

Page sat his cup down and looked at her. "I met your parents."

"I know. Mom called me."

"Are you mad? I mean, maybe I should have mentioned it but I didn't want you to get your hopes up. In case it went south. Also, I didn't want you to tell me not to go, because I had already made up my mind to tackle this head-on."

"I was mad yesterday, but I had both Gina and my mother take up for you. I was told it's a 'guy' thing. Obviously, whatever you did or said worked because she called to apologize and trust me, she has never apologized to me in my entire life."

"I told you she would love me if she met me. And she's now convinced I can take better care of you financially than Banker Bob." He grinned at her over his coffee cup. "Of course, I showed up in an Armani suit, with a Presidential Rolex, diamond cufflinks, driving a rental Mercedes, so that got her attention."

"Not to mention your financial report," Rebecca chuckled.

"There was that," he laughed. "So what's on your day planner?"

"Buying a wedding dress and getting your opinion on venues."

"Okay. I might have a suggestion on that. If you think it sucks, that's fine. On the second album, I did a video, here in New York, in a wedding chapel. If I remember, it's big enough for about three hundred people. I forgot about it until last night and only remembered because coming into the city from the airport, I passed places I remembered. Maybe it's still there. Maybe not."

Gina nodded. "Worth a look, I think."

"Do we even know three hundred people?"

"It doesn't need to be packed, but I'm guessing between one hundred to two hundred people there," he answered.

"All but a few will be on your side of the aisle," Rebecca chuckled. "Mom said the bigger the wedding the more bridesmaids I need so, uh, I'm thinking the smaller the better."

Page sipped his coffee as he looked over the list she made. "No churches on the list?"

"I'm not a member of any. Figured they would be the last resort if all else fails."

"Okay." He finished off the coffee and rinsed out his cup, placing it in the drainer.

Oh my God," Gina teased, "The man is housebroken."

"I've been known to be able to separate whites from darks and do laundry," he quipped back at her.

Rebecca picked up her handbag and her notes and the trio headed out when the Uber arrived.

The bridal shop was filled with mannequins wearing gowns, bringing a gasp to Rebecca's lips. She immediately spotted one of her choices and the reality of her being able to walk down the aisle in something so exquisite made her light-headed. A well-dressed woman in her early to mid-twenties came over, looked from Rebecca to Page and back to Rebecca. "I'm Mindy. And you are obviously Rebecca Morrison, soon to be Mrs. Page Harlow."

Page laughed. Gina giggled softly and Rebecca nodded, never taking her eyes off the gown. "I want that one," Rebecca said.

Page tilted his head, "Don't you want to look at others?"

"No need. I'd just come back to this one. Out of my five choices, this was the one I was always coming back to anyway."

Page shrugged. "I think this is the time for me to go sit down, while you and Gina do whatever it is to do to find your size." He smiled at Mindy. "She wears a perfect size seven."

Mindy went into the back and returned with the gown on its hanger and escorted them to the fitting area. Rebecca stepped into the gown and Gina zipped it up. "Needs to be about an inch shorter in the front," Mindy stated, "We can have that taken care of. Can't have you falling on your face now can we?" She removed a veil from a shelf. "This is the one in the catalog, but you can choose any you'd like."

With the veil positioned, Rebecca handed Gina her phone. "Take a picture. I want to send it to my mom." After Gina took several pictures, Rebecca called her mother. "Hey, I'm texting you a picture of the gown I chose. Call me right back." Before her mom could answer, Rebecca hung up and sent the photo. A minute later the phone rang.

"Oh sweetheart, that must cost a fortune."

"Probably, but isn't it the most beautiful gown you've ever seen?"

"Well yes but…"

"Good," Rebecca cut off the protest. "Now, what color do you think for my bridesmaids? What about your dress?"

"I'm sure I can find something suitable, Rebecca."

"We can shop when you get here, then. I'm thinking blue or peach for the rest of the group."

"Both will be pretty."

"Okay, since Gina is my maid of honor I'll let her figure it out. I gotta run. Page is out front, but knowing him, he's out front shopping. Bye." She hung up and looked from Mindy to Gina as she slipped out of the gown. "Gina gets to choose a color and gown for herself. Page is on his own." The dress was returned to the hanger with the instructions for tailoring and the three of them went to a different area for gowns in a variety of colors. Page wandered over and slipped his arm around Rebecca's waist, making comments about each dress Gina looked at until they had narrowed it down to a full-length peach and a powder blue.

They finally chose the blue after Page told her that it was a better color for her complexion. "Besides," he added, "if one of the other women you choose for a bridesmaid has red hair or really pale skin the peach will look like crap on them."

"This coming from a man who wears red leather on stage," Gina shot back.

Page batted his eyes playfully at her, "I'll have you know I looked damn good in red leather. Of course, I look damn good in anything."

"No ego left in your family," Gina quipped back at him. "Fine. Blue it is."

Mindy took a deep breath. "I have to say, this has been an honor to be the one to help with your wedding. And the fastest decision making I have ever witnessed."

"I started with five and three were here so this was our first stop. If I had tried on all five, I would be overwhelmed so I went with my favorite first. Now it's on to choose a place and time."

Mindy grinned, "You've got this. When you decide on the time, date, and location, we have a good line of wedding invitations I can help you with."

"Awesome idea. I'll see you soon, then." Rebecca said as they headed toward the register to pay for the outfits.

"The gown will be ready by next weekend."

"Well then, I'll see you next Saturday."

They exited the shop and walked toward a nearby restaurant where they enjoyed sandwiches and fries. Page called Ashley and wrote down an address on a napkin, then hung up with "love you. See you soon, brat." Whatever Ashley said caused him to laugh. He returned the phone to the table. "I now have the address of the wedding chapel. I told you the woman was organized. We could never run the tour without her."

"Sounds like it," Gina said slowly. "So, who is Ashley again?"

"My personal assistant. She keeps track of my life. A human computer with a sense of humor. Tells me where to be and when to be there."

"I see."

Page turned toward her, a frown on his face. "Maybe you don't. I pay Ashley a damn good salary to be my secretary slash assistant. She has a genius IQ and photographic memory. She is on call when I am on the road and awake. She deals with hotels, security, venues, issues that come up and handles the press. She's an employee and close enough to me to be considered my sister. She is irreplaceable and I would hurt anyone who hurt her in any way. As a matter of fact, I have done just that."

"No romantic interest?" Gina asked.

"Not even a smidgen." He grinned at her. "I have you and Tommy to thank for my only romantic interest. By the way, I was told you were hoping for the entire CD collection and DVD. I think I can make that happen."

He paid the check and they left the restaurant and walked toward a nearby taxi stand. Page handed the driver the address and they got into the vehicle.

The chapel was just as he remembered it. Designed to appear like the inside of a cathedral, it had high ceilings and gold inlays. The carpeting was deep and wine-colored and the pews were padded and looked expensive with their gold armrests. Chandeliers were putting off light which seemed to reflect off the mirrored windows. The three of them stopped just inside the doors to study the entire effect. Gina whispered, "Holy shit," while Page walked toward the altar.

A moment later, a man stepped out of a side door. He looked at Page and then toward where Rebecca and Gina stood. "Somehow, I had hoped to see you again," he said grasping Page's hand. "Heard about your upcoming wedding and I almost called your manager."

"Father John, you should have known when they said New York, I'd remember this place. I almost didn't, until I arrived yesterday and the streets on the way to the hotel looked familiar. Let me introduce you to my lady."

Introductions were made and they went into Father John's office. The man turned to Rebecca. "You have no idea how many prayers I have said, hoping this young man would finally find his true love. It took long enough to give me gray hairs. Now, let's talk weddings."

An hour later, Rebecca had three available Saturday dates. They still needed a reception area, a caterer, and flowers. Father John had provided her with several contacts for the food and flowers. They agreed to get Ashley to use her contacts to find a location for the reception. Ashley informed them she would get right on it and have several from which to choose.

Chapter Forty-five

After spending the night in Page's arms, Rebecca sighed as she opened her eyes to the sunlight streaming through the hotel window. She sat up to find him sitting in the chair fully dressed, reading the paper. A tray sat on the small table, with a bottle of orange juice, glasses, cups, bagels, and coffee. She narrowed her green eyes at him as he slowly laid the paper aside. "Do you always get up at the crack of dawn?" she muttered.

"Always. It's Sunday. What's there to do in the city on Sunday?"

"Not much."

"Good. I took the liberty of making an appointment for you at the hotel spa."

"What? Why?"

"Because you deserve to be pampered. And before you protest, if I had mentioned it you would have said no, so this way you can't." He shrugged. "Well, I suppose you could, but it would hurt my feelings. I'm very sensitive, you know."

"Toad."

"I'm a thoughtful toad, though. After your masage and whatever else they deem necessary to pamper you, I'm going to make myself scarce. I thought it would be nice for you to have a girl's day out."

"What girls?"

"Well, I did ask the spa to hold an extra spot for Gina if you think she might want a treatment and Ashley will be arriving this afternoon. You have all those wedding details and I'll be in the way, so I thought

I would go look at Madison Square Gardens. I have some numbers to run and I'll be on the phone with Tommy for a while."

Rebecca sat up and Page poured her a glass of juice, which she gratefully drank. He poured the coffee and she moved from the bed to the chair. There was a single rose in a bud vase on the table. "I have to be the luckiest woman on the planet," she whispered, touching the rose petals.

"That's because you're marrying an extremely lucky man. Now, eat your breakfast like a good girl." He grinned at her and reached for the TV remote, scrolling to the financial news.

Rebecca finished her bagel and coffee, then headed to the huge master bath, where she discovered all the items she could need, still in packages. Toothbrush, hairbrush, mouthwash, lotion. She turned toward the doorway, "I don't remember these here last night," she said.

Page laughed. "I don't think you were looking for them. If I remember, your attention was elsewhere."

A warm tingle surged through her as she remembered the erotic, yet tender touching that ended in a spectacular release. It seemed that each time with him was better than the last as he taught her to return his exploring caresses. Turning on the shower spray, she stepped beneath the steam and inhaled, a smile on her lips.

When she returned to the bedroom, the breakfast tray was gone and Page was on the phone with someone, taking notes as he listened. She walked into the sitting area and called Gina, inviting her to a spa day at the hotel, and gave her the room number. Glancing around the room, Rebecca found herself wondering what the going rate was for a suite here at the hotel. It was bigger than her entire house. Page appeared in the doorway, crossed the room, and dropped onto the sofa next to her. "Do you always reserve the biggest room in a hotel?" she asked.

"It depends. I don't like cramped areas. Trust me, this isn't the biggest in this hotel. Normally I opt for a suite on the road because I usually have to deal with the press, producers, management, and do business meetings so it's easier than having to reserve a conference room. We usually reserve the entire floor for security reasons as well. Ashley handles all that."

"Ashley. How long has she been your personal assistant?"

"Since the first tour. She was on a six-month probation to see if she could run things and if she needed an assistant. Tommy thought we would need three people to handle the job. All the dates, the publicity, knowing when I was supposed to be where, and making sure transportation was on time."

"And all this time as close as you two work together, you've never…?"

"No, I've never…" he laughed, "so, you don't have to worry about Ashley."

"I wasn't worried. I was just curious how, with your playboy reputation, you didn't at least sample someone who was always there."

"Several reasons. Mainly because she was always there. She has seen me at my very worst, my very drunkest, my very sickest, my angriest and she's seen me so tired I couldn't keep my eyes open. Sex would have destroyed all that and she was more important than just a bed warmer. Plus, it would have been somewhat uncomfortable after, don't you think? The next night, different city, different bed warmer? And she has her own reasons so it was very mutual. A great arrangement for both of us."

"I called Gina who will be here when she stops hyperventilating. I swear, sometimes she acts like a thirteen-year-old. And, it's mostly your fault, you know."

Page playfully batted his eyes. "Mine? What did I do?"

"You breathe. You're her idol as if you didn't know."

"She'll survive. I hope."

"I'm sure. At some point, I need to go back to my house. Tomorrow is a work day and I have a routine for getting ready and being on time."

"So, you're saying you aren't staying here tonight?"

"You can stay at the house, you know."

"And do what, while you're at work? Believe me, I'll have plenty to do and I work better being here. If I'm out, the desk takes messages for me. So, we can all hang together today and I'll have you home whenever you think you need to be there. Fair enough?"

Rebecca nodded. "So, what's on the planner for today?"

"I told you. Girls' day out. By the time you get done at the spa, Ashley should be here. The three of you can go over whatever you need to go over for the wedding. Me? I plan on making myself invisible."

"It's your wedding too. Don't you want a say in any of it?"

Page shrugged. "Not really. We have the place. I helped with that. I helped decide on the color for your bridesmaid's dresses. You don't need me for a reception location, flowers, and cakes."

Rebecca heaved a sigh and shrugged. "It's just I've never planned so much as a tea party."

He leaned over and lightly kissed her forehead. "Three women, planning a wedding. I'm sure it will be fun."

Gina arrived, dressed in jeans and a pullover. "Wasn't sure what the plans were so I opted for New York normal."

"You look great," Page said with a smile. "Your spa appointment is at noon. Ashley's will be here around two thirty. She'll come here and then the three of you are on your own."

Gina glanced from Page to Rebecca and back. "Ashley?"

Rebecca shrugged. "His assistant. She's going to help with the reservations and whatever else we need help with. Come on. Let's go get spoiled and pampered."

On the way down to the spa, Gina turned to Rebecca. "Tell me about this Ashley person again."

"Don't know much. She's his personal assistant and has been since tour one. He's very protective of her. She lives in DC."

"And not a girlfriend?"

"He says no."

"And you believe that?"

Rebecca stepped off the elevator and turned to face her best friend. "It's about trust. I have to believe him. Otherwise, what's the point in all this?"

"See my eyebrows? I'm officially raising my eyebrows here. Is there a woman on planet earth capable of being close to Page over a period of years who hasn't succumbed to his sex appeal? Just one?"

"I can't allow myself to answer that and please don't put thoughts in my head."

"You're going to come right out and grill her like a witness though, aren't you?"

Rebecca grinned. "Yep. Now shut up and let's enjoy spending some serious money."

"I've never been to a spa this pricy," Gina confessed.

"I've never been to any spa, but here were are," Rebecca answered, stepping through the doorway.

Chapter Forty-six

After extensive pampering for almost two hours, both of them dressed and returned to the elevator. Entering the suite, they heard voices. Rebecca took a deep breath as she rounded the corner into the bedroom. A young woman with a riot of brown curls sat cross-legged in the middle of the bed. Page was sitting at the table shuffling through a stack of paperwork. There was a laptop open on the pillow. The woman looked up and in one fluid motion slid off the bed and crossed the room, pulling Rebecca into a hug. "Oh, you are just gorgeous! Rebecca Harlow. The name so fits you. Page said you were beautiful, but he didn't say how beautiful. The interview didn't do you justice. Not at all. When we talked about the wedding, I could tell he was just so in love. That is just perfect for him. You… are perfect for him. I hope we can be friends." When the woman seemed to stop for a breath she turned toward Page. "I need all those contracts signed as soon as but make sure you read the fine print. I read it all but I know how you are so please read before signing."

Page glanced up. "Yes, dear. See what hell she puts me through? Did you enjoy the spa, sweetheart?" He crossed the room and pulled her into an embrace. "Well, Becca meet Ashley. Ash, this is obviously my bride and her best friend Gina."

Rebecca glanced up at Page and over to Ashley. "Hi. Thanks for volunteering to help. I'm hopeless when it comes to parties."

"I'm excited to be a part of it. Why don't we go to the restaurant, and toss some ideas around while we eat? I haven't had anything since early breakfast. Page has work to do before he can join us. Those contracts need his signature."

Page returned to the table and picked up the pen. "Ash, you play nice, you hear? No bullying."

She headed toward the doorway, glancing over her shoulder. "Wouldn't dream of it, sport. Come to find us when you're finished."

He muttered an 'okay' and returned to the paperwork as they left the room, heading to the restaurant.

Gina broke the silence. "Where are you staying?"

"Here. Not in a suite, but here in the hotel overnight and driving back to DC tomorrow. Why?"

"Call me curious." Gina forced a smile.

"When we're on tour I usually have the adjoining room to Page. That man can be a royal pain in the ass. I knew what I was getting into though and he's fun to be around." She shrugged and added, "Most of the time."

They entered the restaurant and Ashley requested a table for four somewhere quiet and out of the way. Rebecca noticed she was carrying her laptop. After they were seated and drinks were ordered, Ashley powered up the computer. "What colors are we going with? Page said you were going with Father John's chapel. Good choice. He said Gina was your maid of honor and she was wearing blue. What shade of blue?"

Gina frowned. "Medium."

"Okay, what's a good secondary color? Gold? Silver? Copper maybe? Pink roses? Yellow?"

"Peach," Rebecca said decisively. "I like peach. The guest room at the castle was decorated in peach and blue. My two new favorite colors."

"Great, we can work with peach and blue. Good combo. I'm pretty sure we can get peach roses and blue lace as a floral choice. How many bridesmaids?"

Rebecca took the drink that was served and they toasted the upcoming wedding before she answered, shaking her head. "Clueless. Gina?"

Gina shrugged. "What's normal?"

Ashley chewed on her bottom lip. "Let's opt for four. Page will probably have the band as his groomsmen and Tommy as his best man. Plus Greg."

Rebecca sighed. "This is why I suggested getting married in a phone booth."

Ashley pulled out a pair of glasses from her bag and typed on the laptop. "Okay. Four people plus one. Gina, you need to be in charge of the bridal shower and get a list for the invitations. Which leads to invitations. Again, anything favorite?" While she was talking she had pulled up a site of wedding invitations and they began scrolling through the choices.

They stopped long enough to place their order, then returned to the task at hand. They were finishing their steaks when Page joined them. He kissed Ashley on the forehead, Gina on her cheek and Rebecca on the lips. "Well, are we progressing?"

Ashley moved her glasses to the end of her nose and glanced at him. "Somewhat. At least I'm not dealing with someone who has every little detail of every little thing in her memory banks and if it is a millimeter off they throw a banshee fit. Speaking of Banshees, is Ms. Sasha being civil?"

"Very civil."

"Good. One less worry." Ashley turned to Rebecca. "You don't strike me as the type to put up with Sasha's bullshit."

Rebecca grinned. "I have red hair and I work for a bunch of pit bull attorneys. Which was your first clue?"

"The red hair. So, back to business. I can send this site to your email so you can peruse it at your leisure. Now, are we up for looking at reception venues? My recommendation would be one of the big hotels. We can start with this one and hit the top three or four. Then you decide bigger or smaller and we go from there. Fair?"

"If you were me, and this was your wedding, which would be your choice?"

"My wedding? To him?"

"Yes."

"I would throw myself from the top of a tall building first. Lucky him, it's not my wedding. We would kill each other before the 'I do' part."

"Yet you've been with him through his entire career."

"He's like a fungus. He just won't go away." Ashley cut her eyes at Page and back to Rebecca. "He's not my type anyway."

"I would find that impossible to believe," Gina commented. "I don't think there is a woman on the planet who would say no. Well, I would now, because he's marrying my best friend but before that…. Uh, I have a heartbeat."

Page sipped his drink. "So this is how you talk about me behind my back? I am sitting right here, you know."

Ashley arched a brow. "And when I get back upstairs you had better have signed every damn page, Page. Please tell me I won't be getting any more late-night calls from you on the road this time out. Praise the lord, you'll be a married man and the rest of the band is not my problem. Now, make yourself scarce so I can help with your wedding. Or, you can tag along, if you behave."

"I'll pass. I'm going to go check out the Garden."

"It's still there. I saw it on my way in. We'll need all the lights and sound equipment. Full pyro and smoke. Chill, Page, and know I've done my fucking job."

"You know how I am opening night."

"I know, but I've had this dance several times. That stage is the exact dimensions it was on your last tour. Focus on the present. Your wedding to one of the most beautiful women I have ever seen. A wedding that will make front-page news around the world."

Rebecca groaned. "Okay, now I'm nervous."

"Let's do this. Do we have a date set yet? That might determine the location availability."

Rebecca nodded, "Father John made a list of what he had available. I thought we could work on those dates." She handed over the list from the chapel.

"She even thinks like you do. Great. We have a place to start. Page are you coming or not?" Ashley signed the receipt and they all stood up. She put her glasses back in her case, glanced at the list from Rebecca, and closed the laptop. "I need to chat up the manager. Meet me in the lobby in fifteen minutes," she said and strolled out as if she owned the building.

After meeting with the Manager on Duty they were given a tour of the rooms available for the dates on the list. The man, who introduced himself as Daniel Devon, went over all the options and services. Rebecca could work with their on-staff design team to handle the menu, the cake, and even the flowers. Back in the office, they went over pricing, then Ashley told him they would be in touch by the end of the week. Page decided to return to his suite to make some calls and Ashley requested her car be brought around by the valet service.

It was a short drive to another hotel where they looked at more venues available on the required dates. Again, Rebecca was told their in-house team would be available to assist with all the details. By the end of the third hotel, Rebecca took a deep breath and said: "Stop."

Ashley reversed direction in mid-stride and headed toward the bar. "What?" she asked Rebecca.

"Do you have another speed other than full steam ahead? I have not thought this through. I don't know and I don't care which venue. I don't care about the menus, the seating, or the damn cake. I told Page I didn't want an extravagant wedding, but so far, that's all there is."

"I thought every woman had their wedding planned out to the teeniest detail. This is Page Harlow. Lord… Page Harlow if you choose. Do you think I will stand by while he gets married without all the hoopla he deserves? Rebecca, you need to get used to this. Do you know how many reporters will be lurking? Dozens."

Rebecca took the drink and downed it in one swallow. "Then you and Page plan it. Call me and tell me when to show up."

"No deal." Ashley tossed back her drink and ran her hands through her curls. "Look, let's do this by the numbers. Of the three, which one did you like most?"

The first one. Mr. Devon was nice. There was lots of room."

Ashley pulled a pen and a small notepad from her purse. "Okay. Would flowers be something in peach? Cake size will depend on the guest list but I'm guessing four or five tier, plus the topping. The menu is simple. Pick your favorite foods from the ones listed. Done. Next Saturday you can trot in and tell Mr. Devon you've decided on his venue. Any thoughts, Gina?"

"Black leather table covers and black and red roses. Play Goth music or something from Phantom of the Opera. Page could wear a black cape. Oh, wait. That would be my wedding. Hell if I know. I'm just in charge of a names list and a bridal shower. What the hell do you even buy someone who will have everything? A freekin' toaster?"

Ashley started laughing and Rebecca joined in. Soon all three were dabbing their eyes as the fit of giggles ran their course. "Look at us. We look like crazy ladies," Rebecca said finally. "I have an excuse. Pre-marital stress."

Gina giggled. "You know that is PMS. Well, this was fun."

Ashley nodded, "I think we got a lot accomplished today. So, it's down to the three dates the hotel can match up with Father John and we pick out invitations and it's just sit back and wait. Oh, make sure Mr. Devon gives you a good deal for any out-of-town guests. Gina, try to get the list done soon so we can get a rough number for pricing." She paid the tab and headed toward the valet. "Can you call us a taxi, please? I'll be back for my car. The last thing I need is a DUI in New York."

The three of them exited the cab in front of the hotel and caught the elevator to the suite. Page was dragged from his nap by Ashley, who bounced on the bed like a two-year-old, chanting "Wake up rock star, wake up wake up."

"Jeeze, Ash, are you crazy?"

"Crazy happy. Happy for you. Now, I'm going to take my happy happy self to my room and double-check the paperwork. Unless you missed a page, I'll see you later."

Page pointed to a key card on top of the stack of papers. "I got you the room next door."

"That was an unnecessary expense. I'm heading home in the morning. Unlike you, I actually need to get to my office and work. Unless you plan on canceling the second leg of the tour, which… call me crazy, but I don't see happening."

As Ashley scooped up the papers and key, Gina said, "I'll go with you. I think the lovebirds need to be alone."

"Great. Let me toss my overnight bag in the room and we can hit the bar if you want. I don't want to go there as a single. I hate being hit on."

"Who knows," Gina said, following her down the hallway to the next room, "you might meet your Mister Right. Or at least Mister second-best. Since Mister Right is getting married."

Ashley tossed her overnight bag on the bed, put the laptop on the chair, and shook her head with a grin. "You don't trust me around Page? You don't believe there is nothing between us?"

"Call me cynical. You're sexy, perky and smart, plus you're around him each night for months at a time…"

"I also have a significant other in DC who is just as sexy, perky and smart. Her name is Taylor. She's an entertainment attorney." Ashley wiggled her eyebrows at Gina. "I would have thought Page would have mentioned it to Rebecca. I'm taken. Maybe one of the reasons Page and I work so well together. He's like a big brother, except I'm older than he is. My next birthday is the big three-five."

Gina opened her mouth and then closed it. With a shrug, she finally said, "Okay then. Makes sense. Let's go bar-hopping."

Chapter Forty-seven

Monday morning, Gina brought in two cups of coffee. Rebecca was already at her desk. "What's Mister Right doing while you're at work?" Gina asked, sitting the coffee on the desk.

"He's flying to California, then to Vegas. He has a house in California. Did you head straight home?"

"No Ashley and I hit the bar. That woman is a hoot. I can see why she can deal with Page."

Rebecca sighed. "I know it shouldn't but it still bothers me. It's stupid to be jealous. I'm not really jealous. Still, it's like the elephant in the room. I don't know."

"You know, for a woman with a genius IQ, you just made zero sense. Ashley is gay. She thought Page told you."

"Gay? What? Really?"

"She's also in a relationship with a female attorney in DC. Who knew?"

"Seems Page could have mentioned it."

"Maybe he thought it wasn't his place. Maybe he thought you believed him when he promised to be faithful?" Gina sipped her coffee. "Now, don't I have some stuff to learn?"

"Yes. Yes, you do." Rebecca sipped her coffee while they worked on a new case together.

After work, they went to Rebecca's to retrieve her personal address contact lists. Gina read through it quickly. "Not even fifty people. You should call your mother. There might be some people she would like to send an invite to. Yes, I know they're in Indiana but it's the thought. Besides, they might buy you a toaster or a vacuum cleaner."

Rebecca nodded and picked up the phone. "Mom? Hey, Gina and I were putting the invitation list together. Is there anyone you can think of to invite? If so, I need names and addresses. Love you, bye." She hung up and shrugged. "Answering machine." Pulling up a calendar on the computer she stared at the three available Saturdays. "Should we just pick a date or what?"

"Go for the middle. That's six weeks out. Who will be your four bridesmaids?"

"I'll make a list tomorrow. All office people."

"What else?"

"Okay. Saturday is going to be crazy. I'm thinking reserve the hotel first. Date and time. Drop by the chapel to confirm the date with Father John. Then go get the gown and your dress. I need to open an account for the bridesmaids dresses and tell the girls where to go and who to see. Then we need to seriously look at invitations."

"Aren't the bridesmaids responsible for their own cost? Just asking."

"I don't know but I have the card Page gave me. Why not put it to use?"

"Okay, makes sense."

"Good." She typed her notes onto her laptop and printed two copies, handing Gina a copy as the phone rang. As she was reaching for the phone, Gina waved and let herself out the door, double-checking the lock as she went. Rebecca spent almost an hour on the phone with her mother, who offered suggestions on everything from bridal bouquets to rehearsal dinner suggestions. She offered to fly in on Friday night to help with the decisions on Saturday. "Only if you let me pay for your airfare, mom."

"Honey, we aren't broke, you know."

"I know, but it makes no sense for you to spend your hard-earned money when Page gave me a credit card to spend on wedding stuff, plus whatever else I wanted. I insist." While she was talking she pulled up the travel site. "Okay, I can get you a flight on Delta at noon on Friday, arriving at two seventeen. Nonstop into Kennedy. Return flight on Sunday at five and home by ten till eight."

"It will cost an arm and a leg on short notice."

"Mom, I haven't seen you in three years. I don't care what it costs. I'll have your tickets emailed to you. Tell dad he will have to fend for himself for three days. I'll pick you up at the airport. You have until then to get together any names and addresses for invitations."

"I'm so excited. I know I wasn't when you first told me, but he loves you so much. I could tell when he spoke your name; by the way he smiled."

"Another bright side is you and Dad will get to travel. He'll see to that. Especially if and when we have your grandchild. You'll get to see Germany. Or Italy. Or Switzerland. Or we could all vacation anywhere you want. Wherever we happen to be at the time I guess." While she talked, she was making the travel arrangements. "I'm sending you the flight information now. Make sure you print it out. For now, I'm heading to bed."

"Where's Page?"

"He left for California this morning. Details about the tour, I think. Ashley returned to DC to also work on the tour. She made it so easy to get stuff done. Of course, this is what she does for Page and she's really good at her job."

"Well, that's always helpful. When I married your father, I had three aunts to help out and they pretty much made all the decisions and I didn't have a say-so."

"That doesn't work with me. Wait until you see the chapel and the reception venue at the hotel." Rebecca hung up, powered off the computer and double checked the front door lock.

Lying in bed, she reviewed all that had transpired from the time Gina told her about the contest until now. Never in a million years would she have believed all that had happened in such a short time frame. She had always believed that when she finally met the man she would marry, she would know, by instinct. She was right. When she saw him in the stable, the electricity between them was there and even though she tried to fight it, her heart knew. The revelation about Ashley took the one small inkling of doubt away and as far as she was concerned, she was the luckiest woman alive. And her mother! What an about-face. Leave it to Page to be able to pull that off. And she would get to share all her plans with her mom this next weekend. The chapel, the reception hall at the hotel, the dress. She could get her mom the mother of the bride dress on Saturday. She'd need to discuss her dad's tux as well. There were still a million small details but it was coming together, thanks to Ashley.

When Rebecca dropped off the sleep, there was a smile on her face.

The week passed quickly. Rebecca chose her four bridesmaids, all of whom expressed their excitement at being part of such an important event. Page called her every night and they talked about everything and anything. He went from California to Vegas, then to Japan to check on his investment property. From there he returned to the castle, to finish some details about the tour. She told him her mother was coming into town for the weekend and all the details of the wedding should be nailed down by Monday. Each time she asked if he wanted any input at all and he said he thought she could handle it.

Friday Rebecca took the day off, giving Gina a list of cases to research. She was waiting in the airport lobby when her mother's plane was announced. Her mom walked with the group of people, looking around in complete amazement.

Her mother traveled light, with no luggage to claim besides her carry-on. After several hugs, Rebecca led the way to the parking area. "Are you hungry, mom? I thought we could have lunch and catch up. After that, we can go to the house. You'll like the house. It's small but since it was just me, it was all I needed."

"I am a little hungry. What are you going to do with the house after you get married?"

"I'm giving it to Gina."

"Giving? Free of charge? Who gives away a house?"

"Page gave away his childhood home in Norway. Gina is living in an apartment with room-mates who sometimes don't pay their fair share. She doesn't have a place to park half the time and her neighbors are complainers. Since she's the one who caused me to meet Page, I thought it was a nice thing to do. I don't want to try to sell it. When you see it, you'll understand, and for the same reason I don't want to rent it."

"How big is it?"

"One bedroom, one bath, kitchen and living space." Rebecca pulled up to the restaurant where she had taken Gina. "Let's eat. I haven't had anything since this morning when I had a bagel and coffee."

"I warned Page you didn't cook. He told me about Anna."

"She's going to teach me the basics so I can cook if we are at another house. It still boggles my mind."

"You know, when I yelled at you when you called to tell me the news, I obviously had never heard of him. I usually tend to jump to conclusions and I had been told by a neighbor, who had been told by her daughter that she'd seen you on the news with a long-haired musician. Then she said the interview was from Paris. I should have given you more credit. Somehow, in my eyes, you are still ten. Now tell me about the castle. My baby girl is actually going to live in a castle…" her voice trailed off as they entered the restaurant. "Oh lord, Rebecca, this looks expensive."

"Mom, it's not the most expensive in the city but I'm not taking you to McDonald's." A woman dressed in a black pantsuit and heels led them to a table. Rebecca's cell phone vibrated and she glanced at it as she sat down. "Page, call me back. Mom and I are just sitting down for lunch." She mouthed a thank you to the young girl and took the menus. "Wait. What? The same hotel? Okay. We can do that. Beats my twin bed, not that you would know how crappy my bed is. You know you're spoiling me. Love you too. Bye." She slipped the phone back into the pocket of her black slacks and picked up the menu. "Page got you a room at a hotel for the weekend. It's the hotel I've chosen for the reception so you can see all of it."

"Oh honey, he didn't have to do that. You have a sofa don't you?"

"Yes, I have a sofa, and a bedroom with a twin daybed, but he has great taste and I learned he loves spending money on people. It's a nice hotel." Saying the Plaza was a nice hotel was like saying the sun was a pretty star.

They ordered cokes to drink and steaks, with salads, potatoes and carrots and her mom caught her up on the happenings in Janberg. "I brought a list of addresses if you really want to send them invitations. You do have two aunts, an uncle, and some cousins. I doubt they would fly to New York though."

"Well, it's the thought that counts. I'm leaning toward three hundred invitations, to be safe. If we need more for Page's side, Ashley can handle that."

"Who's Ashley again?"

"She's Page's personal assistant. If it wasn't for her I'd be staring at the New York phone book trying to figure out where to even begin."

"Page has a female assistant?"

Rebecca chuckled as she waited for the server to deliver the food. "Yes, mom, Page has a female assistant, who has a significant other in Washington."

"Is she pretty?"

"Yes. She's also a ball of energy and knows what she's doing in the event planning department and no, she's not a girlfriend or ex-girlfriend."

"Okay. Tell me about Page. The castle. He's quite handsome. Takes good care of himself too. Dressed to the nines when he showed up. His watch looked pricy."

"His watch was probably his presidential Rolex, which runs well over thirty thousand. His suits are not off the rack and the man loves to shop. The slacks I have on are from Paris as well as this shirt. And you haven't gotten a good look at the ring yet." Rebecca lifted her left hand and held it out for her mother to see."

"Are those real? Must have set him back a small fortune. Don't you worry he'll overspend?"

"No, mom, I don't. As we speak, he's been to California, Vegas, Japan and back to the castle. He has investment properties in Japan. He has property damn near everywhere. Most important is he's kind and giving. He's sensitive and caring. And we are so much in love I need to pinch myself. I always thought I would know my true love when we met. I used to wonder why no one in New York ever caught my eye. Not other attorneys, not people at the courthouse. Never saw anyone I found attractive even at the art museums. But mother, the minute I saw him, it was like an electric shock. No other way to explain it. I fought it. I knew he had a bad boy reputation. And I let him know I was untouchable. Hands off. And he respected my wishes, which was really weird because I was prepared to have to have an altercation of some sort. Nope. And our feelings just exploded. He took me to art museums, to a palace, to an outdoor garden. We went to look at Mozart's place and then to a real opera in Austria. We went horseback riding on his property. I agreed to be his wife at the Louvre in Paris."

"I'm so happy for you honey," her mom said dabbing at her eyes with a napkin. "I thought love, at first sight, was only in the movies."

They finished dinner and Rebecca drove to the hotel. The room Page reserved was a smaller suite, still on the fancy side. Rebecca had to smile as her mother looked at everything. "My word, he didn't have to go to this expense."

"Try telling him that. Just try. I dare you." Rebecca responded. "Let's go see if Mr. Devon is in so I can let him know this is the place I chose. Then if you want to be a tourist for a few hours, we can go see stuff." They got back in the elevator and returned to the lobby. "Lord knows there's plenty of stuff to see."

Daniel Devon was thrilled to see her and happy to go over the three choices again, showing them off to her mother. They finally returned to his office and opted for a maximum of three hundred guests for the reception, which would work in two of the three choices. He agreed to discount a block of rooms for any out-of-town guests. Rebecca said she would return at noon on Saturday to go over menus and decorations because she wanted Gina to be a part of the choices as well. They settled on blue and peach for the colors. An hour later they were shaking hands, Mrs. Morrison telling him how impressed she was with the hotel and her room.

After leaving the hotel, Rebecca took her mother on a tour of the city, before taking her to her house. Inside, she offered her mom a coke and they made themselves comfortable in the small living room. "It's a nice house, Rebecca. I must say, you have done well for yourself. I know I was against you leaving Janberg at nineteen, but I wanted to keep you with me. Maybe when you have a daughter, you'll understand. That being said, I'm not sorry you rebelled and here we are."

"I may have a son. Then what?" Rebecca teased.

"Oh dear. If he looks like his father, you'll have your hands full. You were a darling child. Quiet, polite, obedient. Well, most of the time. Then you were all grown up and gone. I wish I had handled it better. Eight wasted years when I could have at least kept in touch more. Now you'll be overseas."

"We will still keep in touch. You're my mother. Nothing will change that. They have flights to Europe. You'll need to get passports for you and Dad. Soon. I'd like to have you at the German wedding."

They moved to the kitchen table and Rebecca showed her the site with invitations and they narrowed it down to two. One had a cathedral on the front. "So how do I word this?" Rebecca asked. "Mr. and Mrs. Morrison? Edward and Janay Morrison? Or just Rebecca Janay Morrison and Page Eric Harlow request the honor of your presence?"

"Honestly, I would just use your name and Page's since you are here and not getting married in your hometown. None of your friends know us. He isn't your high school sweetheart. Pick it out for the two of you. Does he have a preference?"

"No, he basically left me to my own choices with help from Gina and Ashley. I'll touch base with Ashley sometime tomorrow."

It was late when Rebecca called for a car to take her mother to the hotel. When the car arrived, she hugged her mom. "I'll see you tomorrow. I'll call you when I know what time. Won't be too early I promise."

As she looked around the small house she smiled. Yes, she had done well for herself. Well, she hadn't made it into law school and certainly not Harvard or the other big ones, but she was content with her life. Much more so since she met Page.

Chapter Forty-eight

Gina arrived while Rebecca was still on her first cup of coffee. "So where's your mother? Did she come?"

"Page put her up at the hotel. His idea. You know how he just makes a decision and acts on it. Got her a junior suite no less. At least now, she's no longer giving me grief. For once, she's acting like a real person."

"That's good to hear," Gina agreed, fixing herself a cup of coffee. "So what's on the day planner?"

Rebecca pulled up the invitation site and highlighted her favorite. "I like this one, I think."

"Yep. I totally agree."

"Since we were already at the hotel I talked to Mr. Devon, but I told him I wanted your input as well so we are going back today. It's between two of the three that we looked at, a maximum of three hundred for the reception. Plus there's the rehearsal dinner for ten to twenty. I think that's the night before. It's for the bridesmaids and groomsmen. Plus me, you, Page, Ashley, and my parents. Probably Tommy and his wife, Janet. And Greg. Anyway, I want your ideas."

"Go for finger food for the reception. Not a sit-down dinner for that many. Maybe a full spread but a long buffet table. Or two." Gina shrugged.

"Then we need to set the date and time with Father John. Then off to the bridal shop. Then lunch or dinner or drinks."

"Okay, let's do this."

Rebecca called her mother to let her know she was on the way. They agreed to meet in the restaurant, where they would have coffee before going to Mr. Devon's office.

At the hotel, Rebecca found her mother sipping coffee, and talking on the phone. The woman looked up and smiled. "Your father says hello."

"Hi back to him," Rebecca said quickly.

After introductions were made and coffee was consumed, they made their way to the manager's office. By the time all the decisions were made and Rebecca had talked to the consultants and chef and everything was agreed to and signed for Rebecca was nursing a slight headache. They left her car in the hotel parking and took a car service to the chapel, where she introduced her mother to Father John. Times were agreed on and arrangements were made, then it was off to the salon to meet up with Mindy. She had taken a piece out of Page's playbook asking the driver to remain on call for the entire day. When Rebecca stepped out of the dressing room in the gown, her mother burst into tears. Obviously, it was something Mindy was used to so tissues were readily available. "Mindy, my mother needs to look at dresses."

"Honey, I can buy one at home, I'm sure."

"I'm sure you could, but this is my wedding and Page's money, so shop or I'll call Page. Let's see you argue with him. Ha!"

Mindy laughed. "She's right you know. Besides, he's already called this week. Trust me, Mrs. Morrison, you do not wish to do battle with Lord Harlow."

"He called?" Rebecca asked.

"He's a stickler for details. He was checking on the progress of the gown plus giving us measurements for his groomsmen and best man. He told me to show you the different options for their suits and you were to pick the color. Oh, he also wanted to make sure your father would be coming in for a fitting."

"Okay, I guess that makes sense." She eased into a chair and pressed her fingers against her forehead, "I have a splitting headache and Page wants me to say what my dad has planned. How in the hell do I know? Page is the god of knowing all things so maybe he should ask him."

Gina arched a brow. " I'll go check on your mother's progress. You just sit for a minute. I'm all too familiar with migraines."

While Gina was gone, Rebecca returned to the dressing room and removed her gown, then went to find her mother and Gina. A dress had been chosen. Ankle length pale blue with a peach sash. "It's beautiful on you mom," Rebecca said.

"Oh honey, do you get headaches often?"

"I'll be fine. Just trying to do it all at once. Trying to get through the jitters. Now, show me the suit material, Mindy."

The men's area was filled with different tuxedos, some with tails and some more along the design of regular suits. She chose the regular tux in dark blue with peach shirts, complete with ruffles. Choices were made and her mother provided Mindy with her father's measurements. Mindy said they could do any last-minute alterations as needed when her father arrived. When Rebecca mentioned setting up an account for the bridesmaid's dresses, Mindy agreed it would be a nice gesture and they filled out the paperwork. With the gown, her mother's dress, and Gina's dress in dress bags, they returned to Rebecca's house.

"I'm starving," Rebecca announced. "Since my car is still at the hotel, we have two options. Hotel restaurant or pizza delivery."

They agreed on hotel restaurant food and headed out again, this time taking Gina's car which had been left at Rebecca's that morning. Rebecca still had a headache but not as bad. She ordered salmon and a salad for dinner. "No wonder you have a headache. Is that all you've eaten today?" her mother asked.

"Yes. Mom, I really don't eat much."

"That's not healthy dear."

"I've never eaten much. Usually, I have something for breakfast though and today it was just coffee. I'll make it up with dessert."

They polished off dessert and escorted her mother to her room. "Dear, you should go home and take something for that headache. Now is not the time to get sick."

"Good idea. I'm going to try for a full night's uninterrupted sleep. We'll do breakfast in the morning and I'll take you to the statue of liberty before you fly out."

"Sounds wonderful. Get some rest."

In the drive, waiting for their cars to be brought around, Rebecca looked at Gina and exhaled. "I'm going to the house for a drink. You're welcome to join me. We might as well order the invitations and I'll have everything checked off."

"Meet you there."

At the house, Rebecca fixed them both a bourbon and coke and they sat down at the laptop. A few minutes later, Rebecca lifted her glass. "Done. Is he going to be looking over my shoulder the rest of my life? Making decisions? Micromanaging?"

"If it bothers you, tell him."

"I'll drink to that." She sipped the drink and frowned. "Why is he micromanaging? Doesn't he think I'm capable?"

"Where would you be if it hadn't been for Ashley? Face facts. You have no issues in a court case but this is way, way, way out of your comfort zone."

"But still..." she trailed off, gazing into the glass in her hand.

"Deal with it or set him straight. Either or. No middle ground. With that sage advice, I bid you a goodnight. Have fun with your mom tomorrow and drive safe." Gina wiggled her eyebrows, polished off her drink, and scooped up her handbag. "See you on Monday, boss lady."

Rebecca double-checked the lock, got ready for bed, and was asleep in no time.

Chapter Forty-nine

Sunday morning Rebecca did feel better. She decided to skip the coffee and have a full breakfast with her mother. Then they would look at tourist brochures. Maybe the statue of liberty or the empire state building? Maybe just a stroll through part of Central Park? She called her mom to let her know she would be there in about thirty minutes, then stood in her closet and stared at all the designer clothes. She chose the pale blue dress from her Paris interview, the pearl necklace and earrings, and her blue heels and blue handbag. Her watch glittered on her wrist.

Her mother met her in the restaurant and smiled, "Beautiful dress."

"Page picked it out, along with the handbag and heels. And the watch. The pearls were a surprise gift on the night of the opera."

"Is he spoiling you or is he a control freak?" her mother asked.

Rebecca shrugged. "Probably a little of both. We both have some adjustments to make because we're both used to being in charge. I've got to get him to lighten up on the micro-managing and he's going to get me used to being spoiled. I can't believe he called the salon to check on my gown but it's the way it is. And if it's not him, it would be Ashley. I'll call her tonight and run down the list of what I've done so far in case I forgot something."

They stopped talking long enough to order breakfast. "Glad you're feeling better. At least you're eating."

"What would you like to see today, Mom?"

"I don't know. Where do you go on a Sunday in the city?"

"Central Park. We could go see Times Square, the Statue of Liberty, The Empire State Building or Grand Central Station. No way to see it all, even if we took two weeks." Rebecca laughed, "I should know because I tried when I first moved here. Finally, I had to limit myself to one new site each Saturday."

"What's your favorite?"

"The art museum. Of course, the Louvre spoiled me. The Mona Lisa up close is a lot smaller than I imagined but Venus was a lot bigger."

"So Page went along to the Louvre with you?"

"Page has a split personality. The public image is this sultry bad boy but he's not. He plays chess, owns horses, has season tickets to the opera and passes to the art galleries."

"Well, he has good taste in clothes. Yours and his. He said you turned down a Rolex."

"I'll probably end up with one anyway. My reasoning was it was too much for me to wear to work, although this one wasn't cheap. I don't think he knows how to shop on a budget. Guess I'll get used to it."

"Nothing wrong with having nice things and he can afford them. And you wear them well, so why not?" Breakfast was served and their coffee was refilled. "Rebecca, what will you do while he's on this tour? Have you decided?"

"Part of it, I'll still be here. I'll be a legal consultant for the firm and Gina was promoted to my position so I have to train her. If Page wants me to join him I will for a while but I don't think I could live on the road for long. That being said, I might go back to the castle. Anna is a wonderful person."

"You could come home for a while before you left the country. Maybe we could throw a small party for those who didn't get to attend the wedding."

"It's a thought. Would be nice to see some of my old friends again." She hated to admit she had no idea where any of her old friends were or what they were doing. When she moved away from Janberg, she never looked back. She paid for breakfast and they started out to tour the city. After stopping by the front desk and glancing at brochures, they decided to just walk into Central Park to the zoo.

After the leisurely tour of the beautifully landscaped zoo, they crossed over to the restaurant and ordered a light lunch.

It was three in the afternoon when they returned to the hotel to retrieve her mom's suitcase and head toward the airport. They still had time for a cup of coffee before the flight was called and Rebecca watched her mother get in the TSA line.

Back at her house, she took a hot bubble bath and slipped into her old terry cloth robe and fuzzy slippers. Sitting at the table with her notes and a drink, she called Ashley. For the next hour, they went over every small detail of the event. Rebecca agreed to email all her contacts to Ashley in the morning. They discussed the rehearsal dinner, all the times, and arrangements. One thing Rebecca forgot was the photographer, but Ashley said they could use the guy who did the photography and videos for the band unless Rebecca had someone in mind. Rebecca didn't. Ashley said she would get in touch with the florists the hotel was using and commission them to do the arrangements for the chapel as well, plus the bridal bouquet.

"Ashley, I couldn't have done this without you. I want you to know that. You are a lifesaver."

"Happy to help. Now, just make sure your bridesmaids don't drag their asses getting those dresses. I'll touch base with Mr. Devon and if there are any issues, I'll call you. Otherwise, you got this. How was your visit with your mother?"

"Better than expected."

"That's good. Okay, for the next six weeks, just relax. No worries. Got another call coming in so let me scoot. I'll be in town in the near future. Bye."

Rebecca stared at the phone, but Ashley had hung up already. "Relax. Yeah, sure. Right. As if." She dropped onto the sofa and flipped channels on the TV, settling on a documentary. When she woke up it was three in the morning and the TV was doing a segment on polar bears. With a sigh, she turned off the lights, the TV and checked the door.

Morning arrived with a crack of thunder, bringing her from a dead sleep to wide awake in an instant. A glance at her clock told her she was up five minutes before the alarm went off. She stretched and stared at the diamond on her finger. How long had it been since she hadn't had to be awake and dressed for work? What would it be like to not have anywhere to be? How long before she got bored to death without Page in the house? How many more tours after this one? She would never ask him to give up his career and she couldn't see herself as a tag along. Maybe she would find some sort of charity work as a legal assistant to the poor. She'd try to remember to run it past Page to see his reaction. She grinned as she got ready for work. Page. The man who cared for orphans, homeless and visited children's hospitals. Rock and roll's bad boy. A throwback to the eighties hair bands. In the days of rap and noise, he still strutted in leather and tight pants with long hair. And he was still on top. For how long was anybody's guess, though. What then? He already said he could write or produce other bands. Would he? She toasted a bagel and brewed a cup of coffee, sitting at her small table. Handwritten notes were everywhere. She gathered up the list of addresses her mother gave her, adding them to her own, scrawling a note to double check the ones from work. She needed to check with the four friends who would be her bridesmaids and see if maybe they could all meet on Saturday to decide on the final dresses. She wanted them to choose. Maybe of the four, two would rather have peach with blue instead of blue with peach. Other than that, Ashley was right. She could relax. Six weeks. It wasn't that long. Some women started a year in advance. She heaved a sigh, rinsed her cup and picked up her handbag and briefcase.

Page called every night during the week and they talked about every subject. Each night she marked off the day on her wall calendar as one day closer to the 'event'. Friday evening, Gina asked her to stay a few minutes to help her in the law library with a particularly difficult research project. Rebecca tried to tell her it could wait until

Monday because she knew how much Gina enjoyed her weekends, but Gina swore it would only take a minute for Rebecca to point her in the right direction. Rebecca sat down her handbag and briefcase and followed Gina to the room, where to her total surprise everyone who worked for the firm waited, wedding gifts wrapped and stacked on the side table. After the cake and drinks were consumed, Rebecca discovered Gina had decided that since the new bride did not need a toaster, iron, or dishes, all the gifts were for use in the bedroom, ranging from a flowing black silk gown and a sheer red risqué teddy to adult toys and DVDs. Gina laughed as each gift was opened and Rebecca blushed. The party broke up around eight and everyone agreed they'd had a great time and were certain these gifts would get more use than any household appliance. Gina helped Rebecca carry all the gifts to her car and followed her to the house.

"Gina, you are a piece of work. How did you manage that behind my back?"

"Elves and inner-office memos. We snuck everything in while you were in Mr. Harris' office. Bonnie stayed inside and locked the door, just in case you got the idea you needed something from there."

"You know I have a key to the law library."

"Yeah, but it would have at least given us time for plan B. Bonnie turned off the lights and ushered the rest of the office in through Jerry's office. By the time you got your key, from your desk, it would have been ready anyway. Oh, before I forget, we're all meeting up with Mindy at the salon at eleven tomorrow. I'll be by to pick you up at about ten-thirty if that's okay."

"It's great. This is the last detail. Ashley told me I should relax for the next few weeks."

"She's right. Other than occasionally double-checking progress, I think it's all covered."

"Quick question Gina. When is your lease up?"

"Five months."

"Okay. After the wedding, we'll get with Mr. Harris and have him help with the property transfer. I should be packing my personal stuff, what little I want to keep, and shipping it to the castle. Mom suggested I come home for a couple of weeks before I vanish from here to live in Germany so I might do that. I'll run all this by Page and get his thoughts. Maybe when you get vacation time you can come to visit."

"Visit? At the castle?"

"Sure. It will be fun. Munich has a Hard Rock Cafe and we can go to Paris for the day."

Gina nodded. "I'd like that. Never been to Europe. Actually, it's never been on my to-do list. But hey, I didn't know anybody there. Now I do." She gave Rebecca a quick hug. "See you in the morning."

"Drive safe."

Gina left and Rebecca carefully placed all the gifts in the bedroom closet, making a stack of cards so she would remember to send out thank you notes. She would pick some up tomorrow and fill them out on Sunday. When the phone rang, she grinned. She took the phone into her bedroom and talked to Page while she got ready for bed.

Chapter Fifty

Time seemed to fly by. Ashley came into town and they spent an entire day double checking every detail. The invitations had been sent along with an enclosed pre-stamped RSVP for the reception dinner. They walked the chapel, Ashley making notes as they looked at everything again. The four bridesmaids had all loved the peach color, more than the blue, so Gina would be the only one in a blue gown. Ashley made an appointment with the florist to discuss the flowers at the chapel to match the ones at the reception. Daniel Devon showed her pictures of three cake designs with the peach and blue theme. They ordered the menus, napkins, and wedding programs from the same site as the invitations.

Rebecca's boss took care of the application for the marriage license since Page was not an American citizen. As the days went by and the RSVPs began coming in, it was all Rebecca could do to not chew her nails. Her nerves were strung tight and she didn't feel like eating much. It wouldn't do for her to get sick on the most important day of her life, so she added more vitamins and protein and put herself on a schedule to include an hour lunch break.

Two weeks before the wedding Page arrived at her office at noon on Friday. He was introduced to the entire staff, most of whom at least was somewhat familiar with his music and reputation. He ordered several pizzas for everyone and lunch turned into an impromptu party. As it was winding down, he followed Rebecca and Gina back to their office. "Do you two have any previous plans for the weekend?"

Gina glanced at Rebecca, "I don't. Everything to do with the wedding in on schedule. Next weekend, Rebecca's parents are arriving

I think. Bridesmaids have their dresses. We still need to look at gifts for the wedding party but that should be able to be done any evening after work. You're in charge of the guy's stuff, except for Mr. Morrison's suit fitting. Why?"

"I was wondering if you two would like to hop a jet and see my other houses. One in Florida and one in California. I promise to have you back in time for work on Monday."

Gina shrugged. "I've never been away from New York and New Jersey so it would be different. Rebecca? What do you think?"

"I need to get accustomed to being on the move at a moment's notice so sure, why not? I need to pack a couple of clothes changes."

"Okay, why don't I pick you both up at Becca's at about seven?"

"What about tickets?" Gina asked.

"I have the plane and Greg is at the airport, so no tickets required." Page winked at her. "The perks of being a rock star, I guess."

Page arrived at seven sharp in a limo and the three of them were off to the private side of the airport. Greg came down the steps and swept Rebecca into an embrace, kissing her on both cheeks, causing her to laugh as he playfully kissed the tip of her nose. Page cleared his throat trying to hide the grin. "When you're done making out with my wife…"

"She's not your wife yet, sport," Greg teased.

"Close enough. Find your own girl."

Rebecca shook her head and turned to Gina, "See what I have to contend with? Greg, this is my best friend Gina DeMarco."

Greg turned his attention to the woman standing next to Rebecca. "Hi. I'm Greg the pilot."

"Nice to meet you Greg the Pilot." Gina grinned, then glanced at the plane. "So this is how the rich and famous travel, huh?"

"Um, yeah. Private and stylish. Let me get your bag," he said reaching for the case he knew wasn't Rebecca's. Page already had the handle of her blue Louis Vuitton. "Welcome aboard, Gina DeMarco."

Gina glanced at Rebecca, wiggled her eyebrows, and followed Greg up the steps into the jet. He placed her bag next to the bar and smiled. "Complete with a bar?" she asked. "What more could a woman want?"

"We can choose from bourbon, gin, vodka or scotch. There might even be a bottle of white wine. With a good Italian name like DeMarco, please don't tell me you don't drink," Greg teased.

"And please tell me with the title of 'pilot' you don't drink and fly. I'll have mine and yours, so you won't be tempted."

"Okay, and I'll make up for it when we land. Speaking of landing…" he turned to Page, "Where the hell are we going?"

"Florida. Don't get so drunk tonight that you can't fly this bird to California tomorrow." Page winked at Gina. "My pilot is a womanizer so watch yourself."

Gina looked at Greg and laughed. "I've been warned. Ree, did you warn him about me?"

"Nope. You and Greg play nice because it will be a long walk home if he crashes because he's not paying attention to the clouds."

Greg chuckled. "Page would murder me if I dented his baby. Haven't crashed one yet. Since you two lovebirds want privacy, I'm inviting Gina to join me in the cockpit."

Gina accepted the bourbon and coke Greg handed her, shrugged her shoulders at Rebecca, and followed Greg through the doorway.

Rebecca chuckled and stepped into Page's arms. "Greg might have met his match."

"Or Gina met hers," Page answered. "Now, update me on the progress of our wedding."

They relaxed on the sofa and once Rebecca was comfortable she looked up at him. "Ashley has been a Godsend. Every little detail has been checked and rechecked. Every possible contingency has been accounted for. My parents will be here next week. Dad will have his tux altered if necessary. I've received all the RSVP's so the reception staff has the final count. Ashley had the notice put in the paper and has requested a special roped off section for reporters. Janet called and said she and Tommy would be here a couple of days before. I did want to run a couple of things by you. After the wedding, when you hit the tour circuit, mom suggested I come to visit. She wants to have a party for all of my old friends who couldn't make it to New York. I told her it sounded like a good idea and I'd run it by you."

"Becca, you don't have to run anything by me you want to do. This isn't a master and slave relationship. It's a marriage. An equal partnership. Granted, if you decide to purchase a Lamborghini I'd like a heads up, but I'm not going to keep tabs on your every move."

"It might be fun. Some of these people I haven't seen in ten years. The other thing is how to fill my time while you're on tour. I know this won't be your final tour and I don't expect it to be so I was thinking I might like to do some sort of volunteer work in Germany. Helping people in some way. I haven't worked out any more than that thought yet."

"Okay. Let me know what you decide. We can turn a room at the castle into your office if you need one. You know you can come on the road if you wanted to."

"I probably will, but not for the whole tour. It would drive me nuts and then I would get cranky and bitchy. Next thing you know we'd be fighting about stupid shit."

"I cannot imagine you cranky or bitchy but it is nerve-racking if you're used to having a routine."

"So, tell me about the house in Florida," she said, abruptly changing the subject. Working at a law firm gave her deep knowledge about how the smallest argument could turn into a mudslinging divorce. She vowed never to become a statistic.

Page shrugged. "Five bedrooms, six full baths, three half baths, pool, Jacuzzi, beachfront. Lots of glass. Two stories." He grinned at her. "The master suite is decorated for a single rock star, so we'll need to rework it. That can be a project for you."

"Maybe I'll want to keep it the way it is. We can come here when we feel like getting crazy. I guess we'll see."

"It seems odd, looking back on it. When I bought the house, I decided to keep it as a private getaway when I wanted to be alone, although why I thought I needed something so big, I don't know. Then, it morphed into a party house for the third tour. Then it returned to being my private home again. I just never bothered to redecorate. Usually, I slept in one of the other bedrooms anyway."

"Well, people can't party their entire life."

"The house in California is a small three bedroom bungalow. Not even in an upscale neighborhood. Well, it is beachfront and secluded. I bought it on a whim."

"You have expensive whims, don't you?"

"I do indeed. At some point, we need to visit the estate in England and the villa in Italy."

The jet shifted and Page suggested they buckle up for landing. "There should be a car for us."

"Let me guess. Ashley's magic?"

"She's worth her weight in gold." Page nodded.

"Whatever you're paying her probably isn't enough."

"Probably not but I pay enough nobody can steal her away from me."

"That reminds me. My boss said if you would like, he would be happy to do our prenup. Unless you already have one for me to sign."

Page tilted his head and looked at her in silence while the jet landed and Greg taxied toward the hanger. "Rebecca, do I need a prenup?"

"I'm sure your legal staff and accountant would advise it, considering your net worth."

"Do. I. need. A. Pre. Nup?"

"It's not a matter of what you need. Its good business sense, isn't it?"

"Only if, in the back recesses of my mind I thought we would ever break up. I hadn't had that thought since you agreed to be my wife. Even if in the slim case it did happen, I would be fair. I was fair to Sasha. There is nothing else I need to add. I don't need a legal piece of paper for an issue I don't expect to ever occur."

"Always nice to know you love me so much. I keep waiting for someone to pinch me and I wake up alone in New York."

He playfully reached over and pinched her arm gently. "Nope. This isn't New York. We're in hot and sunny Florida and I promise you won't wake up alone."

Gina returned to the cabin carrying her empty glass. "Holy shit, what a view! I'll never be the same. Did you two behave?"

Rebecca chuckled. "We were discussing stuff. Mostly the wedding."

"And the fact I do not have a prenup to be signed and sealed."

Gina blinked. "Really? I thought that was standard form these days."

"I don't foresee a divorce in our future, so there's no reason for one, is there?"

Greg stepped through the doorway. "See, arrived in one piece." He opened the outer door and lowered the steps, offering Gina his hand. He had retrieved her piece of luggage on the way. Page and Rebecca stepped down and Page pointed to the private parking area. Greg walked ahead of them into the private lounge area and returned with a set of keys. "It's the red Challenger. I'll drive."

"Red. Well, that's low key, isn't it?" Page commented as Greg opened the trunk and deposited the luggage. "Okay. You drive."

"So what exactly are our plans, boss?" Greg asked as he started the car and pulled away from the airport.

"I thought to show Becca the house, spend the night and after a nice breakfast with a stop for shopping, you fly us to California. We can spend a few hours playing in the Pacific Ocean, then head back to New York so they can be at work Monday."

They pulled up to the gate at the house and Greg punched in the security code. As soon as they were clear, the gates swung back into place. "I see Ashley called ahead," Greg commented as they stopped in front of the brightly lit front driveway.

"What if we had refused to come?" Gina asked.

Greg laughed. "If on the rare chance that did happen, Ashley would have called, canceled the car rental, and told the housekeeper to turn the lights off when she was finished dusting."

They entered the foyer and Greg looked at Gina. "I'll put your luggage in the first bedroom at the top of the stairs. It has an ocean view. Really soothing at night."

"Okay, thanks," Gina said as she followed Page and Rebecca as they walked through the massive great room. Page opened the glass doors onto the patio area. The sound of the waves was the only noise to be heard. Lights shone from the pool and with a remote, Page ignited several tall torches next to the chaise loungers.

"Okay, the kitchen is probably stocked with munchies. Chips, nachos, cokes, coffee and the like. There's an outdoor bar here and an indoor bar on the other side of the kitchen. I for one would like a drink." He crossed over to the bar and retrieved glasses from a cabinet. There were cold cokes and ice in a cooler. When he finished making a round of drinks, he lifted his glass. "Here's to my wife and our eternal happiness."

Greg arched a brow toward Gina. "Almost makes it sound inviting."

Gina took a sip and chuckled. "About as inviting as a root canal for some people."

Rebecca nodded. "Just remember, I felt like that once, not so very long ago."

Gina narrowed her eyes. "Don't try to marry me off. I'm happy being single. You were never happy being single. You just didn't know it."

Page shook his head. "I am not saying a word. Not one."

"Wish I'd remembered to bring a swimsuit," Gina said, abruptly changing the subject.

"Up the stairs, third door, bedroom closet. There are suits in every size in there. I never found time to donate them from my party days. Feel free to help yourself."

Gina looked at Rebecca and Rebecca nodded. "You came along to enjoy yourself. You want to swim, then swim. I don't swim but you can."

"Third door. Got it. Greg? Please tell me you swim, because I don't want to be the only one in the water."

"I do. I have my own room here with a couple of swim trunks, so sure, why not?"

After they headed for the stairs, Page pulled Rebecca into his arms. "I have a really good movie collection," he whispered as his lips trailed across her throat.

Chapter Fifty-one

When Page and Rebecca entered the kitchen in the morning, Gina was sipping coffee. An empty cup sat close by. "Greg said he'd be back by ten-thirty. Went to the airport to get the plane prepped."

"Did you enjoy your swim?" Page asked while Rebecca poured coffee in two cups.

"Oh God yes. It was so great swimming at night. Clear sky. Had to be eighty degrees. Greg turned the torches off and we just sat in complete silence, watching the stars and listening to the waves. I am now officially spoiled."

"You sound relaxed," Rebecca commented, handing Page his coffee.

Thirty minutes later they were back in the car, Greg behind the wheel, cruising through the shopping area of Palm Beach. After an early lunch and stops for beach souvenirs, they headed back to the airport. Gina, Rebecca, and Page sat in the cabin while Greg did his preflight check and chatted with the service crew. When he entered the cabin, he flashed them a grin. "Wheels up in fifteen minutes. California in five hours but there's that three hour time zone issue, so we are leaving here at one and arriving at three but it will really be six."

Gina groaned, good-naturedly. "Oh hell no."

"Quite okay darlin'. You pick them up on the way home to New York when we would land at six but it will really be nine. Welcome to my world."

After they leveled out Gina took him a bottle of coke and joined him in the cockpit. Page arched a brow and Rebecca chuckled. Page fixed them each a drink and slipped his arms around her shoulder. She looked up at him. "Were you playing matchmaker with Greg and Gina?"

"Not really, but I thought they'd get along okay."

"Well, she didn't sleep in her own bed last night," Rebecca stated softly.

"Her choice. His choice. They're adults."

It was raining when they arrived in California although the sun was out and it was warm. Greg eased the jet as close to the building as possible, shut everything down and announced he was going to go see what kind of car Ashley stuck them with this time. In what seemed like less than thirty minutes he returned, driving a yellow Camaro convertible. Page shook his head and laughed. "Wondering what possessed her," he chuckled. "Let's go to the beach, shall we?" He got both pieces of luggage and followed them down the steps where Greg waited with the doors open as well as the trunk. Page, Rebecca, and Gina got into the car while Greg went back to finish securing the jet.

Soon, they were pulling away from the airfield, onto the highway. Page told them about the house as Greg drove. "Smaller than the Florida house. Three bedrooms, nice sized great room, full kitchen. Patio opens onto the beach. I don't have housekeeping here, so it might be a bit dusty. Last time I was here was midway through my last tour. I took a week off and did nothing except sleep and swim."

Gina nodded, "Something to be said for that. A week of doing nothing. It's not how I would spend a vacation though. Well, unless I was totally exhausted, which I'm sure you were."

"I was. I think I scared the shit out of Tommy because I literally fell off the earth. I turned the ringer off on my phone. Told the rest of the guys to meet up in L.A. in a week." Page laughed. "When I got to the club where we agreed to meet, Tommy was pacing back and forth like a crazy man. I had to vow never to do that again. I honestly was so tired I forgot to tell him and everybody else thought he knew I was taking a break."

Greg drove down a narrow street lined with palm trees and turned into a driveway. He got out, manually raised the garage door, and pulled the car inside, closing the door behind them. After removing the luggage from the trunk, he opened the door to the kitchen area. Page walked through, turning on the lights, the air conditioner, and all the ceiling fans. Greg checked the refrigerator and kitchen pantry. "We have ice, old cola, and out-of-date chips. Later, after we get settled in, I could go to the store, if you want me to."

"It's only four. Let's get settled in, catch our breath, and go to dinner. Maybe dancing. We can swing by the store on the way home. Also, need to pick Gina and Becca up some swimwear or shorts and shirts for the ocean."

Gina laughed. "The man loves to shop, doesn't he?"

"You have no idea," Rebecca answered as she stepped into his embrace.

"Hey," Greg teased, pretending to pout, "I love to shop."

"If I died and went to heaven, don't resuscitate me," Gina sighed.

They left the house and headed into town, deciding on a small out-of-the-way restaurant. Gina and Greg exchanged stories of childhood and teen years. Greg launched into tales of first meeting Page and the shock of the first tour.

As they were finishing dessert Gina looked at Page. "I'm glad I didn't win your contest."

"Oh?"

"If I had won, we would have spent the entire ten days in bed. You know it and I know it. I would have never gotten to know you as a person, much less to be a friend. The friendship is much better."

Page laughed. "True words. The same goes. I'm glad you didn't win. I'm really glad you were crazy enough to enter your best friend's name. You would have been another name in my book, with a star and a phone number. Much better this way."

Greg spoke up. "You going to burn the book?"

Page shrugged. "Unless you want it. I told you in Paris you could have it."

"Burn it. I don't need it." He glanced over toward Gina. "I do okay on my own, thanks."

"Time for some shopping," Page announced, handing the server his card.

Returning to the parking lot they discovered a young man sitting on the hood of the Camaro. "Which one you dudes own this pretty ca-mare-o?" he asked, flipping a butterfly knife in one hand.

Page grinned at him and stepped in front of the women. "Avis. Why?"

"Then you ain't gonna give me trouble over the keys, are you?"

Page took another step and tilted his head as if examining something. "Why? Is yell-ow your color, dude?"

The guy stood up, several feet in front of Page. "Sissy boy with long hair? You hinting I'm scared?"

Page leaned forward, almost within reach. "Nope. But you are stupid as all shit." Before Rebecca or Gina could take a breath, Page dropped the guy on the pavement and straddled his back, pressing the side of his face against the sun-baked cement. "For future reference. Never let someone get into your personal space. That's how you get totally fucked up and get your ass kicked."

Greg chuckled, glancing from Rebecca to Gina and over to Page. "I love watching him pull this shit," he said as he reached down and dragged the guy to a standing position. Leaning into the guy's face he spoke slowly. "Not smart to pull a knife on a fourth-degree black belt and try to steal his car."

"He broke my arm. I think he broke my arm!"

"Lucky you. I've seen him do much worse. Badass scrapper for a long hair sissy boy. Me, I'm more of a street fighter. You know, the type to gut you like a fish with your own knife and leave you flopping in the sun to die. He's a little neater." He marched the guy to a curb. "Sit." With a sigh, he called the police, relayed the incident and hung up. "Lucky us. There's a unit nearby. ETA five minutes."

When the guy looked like he wanted to try to run, Page wrapped his fingers into his shoulder. "Don't. Try. It. I was having an all-around nice peaceful day with my future wife and my friends and then you show up like a bad scene from a B movie. You got some sort of a death wish dude?"

"It was a nice ride."

"Yes. It is that. Not a Lamborghini, but okay for General Motors. Personally, I prefer the Corvette, but there are four of us."

Rebecca and Gina retreated to a bench in the shade. "Did you know he was a black belt?" Gina asked.

"No. I was told he beat up his bass player over Ashley. Now I see how."

Greg glanced over. "This is not an everyday occurrence in this neighborhood. Sorry for the inconvenience."

Rebecca shook her head. "Life won't be boring, that's for sure."

It took the police fifteen minutes to complete the paperwork, put the guy in the back of the patrol car, and drive away. Page ran his fingers through his hair and dusted his jeans off. With a shrug, he looked at Rebecca and grinned. "Shopping?"

"When my heart gets back to normal, sure. Any more surprises?"

Page leaned over and kissed her hand. "Would you have me share all my mysteries at once, my lady?"

Gina rolled her eyes and walked over to Greg. "Gut him like a fish and leave him flopping in the sun to die? Seriously?"

Greg shrugged. "It fit at the time. I wasn't always a sissy boy's pilot and driver. I had a life once."

"I can hardly wait for that tale," Gina said sliding into the front passenger seat when Greg opened the door for her.

After shopping, Greg pulled into a corner store, said "Be right back" and got out. They sat listening to the radio while they waited. When he returned he carried a case of cokes and two bags, all of which went into the trunk.

Back at the house, Greg and Gina put the snacks away and Page announced he wanted to order a pizza. When the pizza arrived, they all fixed a drink and went outside to enjoy the view of the sunset in their new swimwear. Rebecca had picked out a one piece in deep green, while Gina chose a black bikini.

"It seems odd to be sitting here at the pool, with the ocean so close," Gina commented as she eased into the water.

"You know you're supposed to wait a half hour after you eat before swimming," Rebecca said.

Gina shook her head. "I'm not swimming. I'm soaking. I'm not even dog paddling. See? I'm standing on the bottom. I've got to tell you, this is the height of luxury. Pizza, drinks, pool, shopping, and two hot looking dudes to hang with. What did we ever do before all this?"

Rebecca rolled her eyes and glanced at Page. "Now you've done it. How is she going to be content in New York after this?"

Greg spoke up. "Hey, I love New York. Wait until you see Paris, though."

"Makes me want to get my passport and plan a real vacation. I'll wait a while though. The bosses would have a cow if I started jetting around the world. I think they still hold a grudge because I'm partly to blame for Rebecca leaving."

Greg laughed, jumped into the water, and immediately tossed a handful of water in her face. She shrieked, returned the gesture and the chase was on while Page and Rebecca watched, shaking their heads. After an hour, Rebecca felt herself nodding off and told Page she was probably jet-lagged. They left Gina and Greg in the pool and headed inside. She fell asleep curled into Page's embrace, his breath caressing her neck.

Rebecca woke up alone in the dim light of dawn and lay there gazing out the window at the ocean. She still felt tired, as if she could spend the rest of the day in bed and still not catch up on her rest. How did Page do this for months on end? Coast to coast within forty-eight hours. Could she keep up, even on an occasional visit? She studied the diamond on her finger. Two more weeks and she would be married. The whole idea still seemed surreal to her. With a contented sigh, she slipped into a pair of shorts and a tee-shirt and headed out of the room to find her future husband.

She found him on the patio, coffee cup in hand, staring out at the water. He smiled down at her, pulling her into an easy embrace. "Want to walk on the beach?" he asked.

They took the sandy path to the edge of the water and Rebecca watched as a wave covered her feet. "It's peaceful, isn't it?"

He brushed his lips across her forehead. "Peaceful is a good thing. I try to absorb it whenever I get the chance. One of the reasons I have a house on each coast I suppose. It gave me a place I knew I could run to at a moment's notice. I believe that's one major reason I haven't burned out like a lot of musicians. Yes, my schedule is nine months of touring but the dates are never back to back unless there are less than a hundred miles between cities. At least once a month we schedule a three to five day off time."

"Is the tour totally in the US?" she asked as they walked.

"The first five months are. Then I take a two-week break before we start in Canada, which is two months. Then a month off before the European tour starts. Europe is three months but fewer shows per week. It's going to be crazy for us, you know."

"I know. However, while you are strutting across stages, I will be training Gina in the fine art of how not to piss off the court, which judges to go to for favors, and which private investigators are the better ones. Plus, there's the party mother wants to have. So, maybe I'll stay stateside until you finish this part of the tour. Then we can both go to Europe. It's an idea," she shrugged.

"And a damned good one. So, are you feeling better this morning? You were out like a light last night the minute your head hit the pillow."

"Jet-setting is going to take some getting used to. I'm still tired. I think tomorrow I'll go into the office long enough to get Gina started on an upcoming case and I might slip out and get some rest. It wouldn't do for me to catch the flu before my big day."

"I promise to love honor and ach-choo?" he teased.

"Right. And I don't think it would be good for me to sneeze on the cake either. But I needed this short break with you. I was overthinking every detail. I would wake up in the middle of the night wondering if I had forgotten something."

"It's going to be perfect, Becca. Do you know why it's going to be perfect? Because you, my love, are perfect."

They turned back toward the house, walking in silence hand in hand. Gina and Greg were sitting in the kitchen, each with a bowl of cereal and a banana. Gina pointed toward the coffee pot and Rebecca poured herself a cup.

Greg glanced up at Page. "So what's on the day planner?"

Page shrugged, "Being lazy. Becca is still jet-lagged and there's not much close to see without driving a distance. If you and Gina want to do something, feel free."

"What time did you want to fly back?"

"Not real late. They do have serious jobs to report to in the morning and you know from experience what that three-hour time change will do."

"Well, Gina and I thought about playing in the ocean. Not long though because we forgot the all-important sunblock. So, unless you think otherwise, maybe lunch in town and then head back? We can have dinner in New York, can't we?"

"Becca?"

"Sounds good," she said as she peeled a banana.

"Great. You two have fun and don't drown. Becca and I are going back to bed until she feels like getting up."

In the bedroom, Page closed the heavy drapes and lay down beside her still dressed. "Can I get you anything? Motrin? Coke? A hot bath?"

"Just you. I just want to be held until I feel better. I'm sure it's just stress, combined with doing way too much and then jetting cross-country. This lifestyle is going to take some getting used to."

Page pulled her into an embrace. "The good news is you don't have a fever. Now is not the time to get sick. You have a wedding to attend in two weeks."

She grinned up at him and chuckled, "Yeah, there is that. I can't believe it's only two weeks away. Everything has flown by. I'm hoping your touring flies by as fast. Then at least for a while, we can just be a happy couple in a castle."

"Or a happy couple in an Italian villa. Maybe a happy couple in Switzerland?"

"Don't remind me," she groaned.

"Six months from now it will be second nature to you."

"I doubt that. I'm not into living out of a suitcase."

Page eased his hand under her shorts, drawing designs with his fingers on her stomach. "We won't be living out of a suitcase. The trick is, that you keep clothes in each house. You keep personal items in each house. No need to pack. No suitcases required."

Rebecca curled against him, sighing softly, and closed her eyes.

Chapter Fifty-two

Monday morning Gina and Rebecca were both suffering from the shock of the time changes, but they had a trial to help prepare for and a lot of research to do. Gina sported a slight sunburn from losing track of time in the ocean. As usual, they lost total track of time while searching through legal books in the huge library. When Gina took a break to go to the vending machine, she returned and announced they were the only two left in the office because it was close to six. They carried three books to their office to pick up where they left off. As they turned off the lights, Rebecca suggested dinner, since they both skipped lunch.

They chose a new French restaurant because it was within walking distance of the office. "Did you have fun over the weekend?" Rebecca asked after they placed their order.

"I did. Seems odd to spend Saturday morning on the East Coast and Sunday morning on the West Coast. I don't know how Page and Greg can adjust to the time changes."

"They don't change overnight. From what I understand they schedule the tours from city to city working from east to west. He said they take breaks to keep from burning out."

"Do you plan on going along? It might be fun."

"I still don't feel comfortable with change. At least not this much change. I suppose if he has a three-day break somewhere, I could join him." She shrugged as she sipped her coffee. "Unless I decide to return to the castle. Makes no sense to fly from Germany to here just for two or three days."

"Might make sense to him. Just sayin'."

"Well, I am planning to spend some time in Indiana. Not sure how long. Mom wants to throw a party and invite people who couldn't travel to New York."

"Your mom's done a one-eighty turnaround." Gina laughed. "Of course, having Page Harlow for a son-in-law would have that effect, I suppose."

After dinner was over, they returned to their cars and went their separate ways. Rebecca locked her doors and ran a tub of hot bubbles. She still hadn't recovered from the time change. Either that or she was catching a damn virus, which was not what she needed. Maybe she would leave early and drop by her doctor's office to get an antibiotic or vitamin 'C'."

Sitting at her table she stared at the to-do list with all the check marks. Everything had been taken care of. Nothing to chance. The service would be from noon until about one thirty. They would then be driven to the hotel, where the reception was slated to be the most talked about event of the year. The list of reporters alone was mind-boggling. Television news crews would be there as well as all the supermarket magazines. The morning of the wedding, she had a hair and nail appointment as well as a full facial. Her dress would be in a side room at the chapel.

Easing into the bubble bath, she allowed herself to relax and tried to clear her mind. Being tired worried her. What if she ended up with washed-out skin and shadows under her eyes? Vitamins were at the top of her to-do list. Might as well go ahead and get a doctor's visit out of the way. That way, she reasoned, if she was catching something, they could cure it before the wedding. She'd turn Gina loose with the research files and slip out at lunchtime. No sense in getting Gina all concerned and it needed to be looked at before her parents arrived.

Tuesday, she chose a baby blue dress with matching heels and arrived at the office appearing to be in a terrific frame of mind. In truth, she had slept in spurts, waking up every three hours and she had wanted to call out. But Gina needed to start on the research so here she was.

After she pointed out what Gina needed to be looking for and how to locate the statutes, she said she needed to run some personal errands. Things to take care of before her parents arrived and she'd be back in a couple of hours. Before Gina could ask any questions, she calmly left the building.

Her doctor agreed to work her into her schedule so she sat down to wait, her mind racing with concern. The flu? Maybe. Ulcer? Not likely. Stress? Possibly.

When she was sitting with Dr. Kensey she explained what had been going on with her life, how she was suddenly having headaches and sleeplessness.

"Your wedding is in two weeks. I received the invitation. My daughter was overjoyed because Page Harlow is her favorite of the year." The doctor chuckled. "I think it's probably stress-related. A regular wedding takes a toll but marriage to a celebrity would get the best of anyone. We'll do some blood work to make sure it isn't anything else. I'll prescribe an antibiotic and something to combat the stress level."

"Okay, then. I'm going to try to maintain my sanity and get better."

"Well, congratulations. I'll see you at the wedding."

"Is Nancy coming?"

"As if I could keep her away. She's going to buy a new dress for the occasion."

"Bring her over to us at the reception. Page loves his fans."

"That will seriously make her day. Now, make sure you get enough rest, enough to eat, and keep your stress level as low as possible. It won't do for you to walk down the aisle with a headache."

Rebecca left the office with mixed emotions, stopped at the pharmacy, and filled the prescriptions. Placing the medications in the trunk, she returned to the office. Gina was in the library, making notes on her tablet, and didn't ask about her errands. The rest of the day passed without any issues and Gina slipped the files into a folder on her desk. Picking up her handbag, she turned to Rebecca. "Do you like Greg?"

"Greg?"

"Greg the pilot. You know, brown hair, smoky eyes, six feet or so tall. Hangs around with your hunky blond."

"Greg's a nice guy. Why?"

"Well, I like Greg. Maybe more than I should. Anyway, he called me today and he'd like to hang out when they get to town. Before the wedding."

"Okay."

"I'm a little nervous," Gina confessed.

"You? Nervous about hanging out with a guy? Since when?"

"I don't want to like him too much, in case he doesn't like me too much."

Rebecca tilted her head. "Can you repeat that in English?"

Gina heaved a dramatic sigh. "I don't want to feel serious. If I feel serious and he's just thinking of me as just another passing date… Ah hell, Ree… I do like the guy."

"And this is you asking me for advice on romance? Try asking him how he feels."

"I thought maybe you could ask Page his opinion. Page might have a clue about how he feels. You think?"

"I can do that. Not sure he would know."

"If Greg mentioned it to Page, that might mean he cares a little."

"It was only one weekend. One of many, many weekends in your busy life. Why do you feel different?"

Gina shrugged. "Most times, I never get a call afterward. I mean not a serious 'hi, how are you, did you get enough sleep' kind of call.

It was nice. Different. Would I consider seeing him again? We talked about favorites. Foods, movies, music. Like real people."

"Isn't that normal?"

"Not with the guys I've dated. We usually hooked up at a club, sometimes prearranged, sometimes not, hung out and then said, hey that was great, see you around. I don't remember any guy being interested in who my favorite actor was."

"Okay, I'll see if he's said anything to Page. See you in the morning."

Chapter Fifty-three

Page called that evening from Canada, where he was working with the rest of the band members on some not-yet-released music for the tour. He asked about her day and she shared Gina's concerns about a budding romance with Greg.

"He hasn't said much," Page said. "Although for Greg, that's not abnormal. He keeps his feelings to himself for the most part. He did say he enjoyed the time they spent together. He doesn't usually even say that. If he called, that's more than he usually does so who knows?"

"Will I see you before the day of the wedding?" she asked.

"Probably. I already wrote the songs we're working on so we're just fine-tuning the cords. Do you want to see me?"

"Silly question, Toad."

"Your parents are arriving on Friday. Do you need me to run interference?"

"No. I need you to keep me sane. Keep me from shoving mommy dearest in front of a subway train."

"I thought she'd come around. Do I have to take my bad self… to Indiana for a come to Jesus meeting?"

"No. I just worry that's all. Jitters. Nerves. Stress."

Page lowered his voice, "I have a cure for the stress part of your problem."

"Hmmm, now that's what I need to hear. I'm putting the phone on speaker because I'm getting ready for bed."

"Too bad I'm on the other side of the country."

"Ditto that, Toad." She slipped out of her clothing and studied her full reflection in the bedroom mirror.

"Did you eat?"

"Not this evening. I ate earlier. Picked up some vitamins. Wouldn't do for me to be sick on my wedding, now would it?"

"No, it would not. I expect our wedding night to be one for the books. Have I mentioned how much I love you, Becca?"

"I recall that being said, but it's been so long ago," she laughed.

"You can be such a tease."

"Says the toad."

It was over an hour before they ended the call and she lay in bed gazing at the bedroom ceiling. On occasion, she still wanted to pinch herself to assure her this was happening. That he loved her as much as he said. Would he succumb to temptation on the road? If he did, what would her reaction be? Her fingers wound around the corner of the sheet. Sanity would dictate she try to be understanding. The temptation would be strong, and he was only human. She fell asleep convinced it wouldn't end the love they felt. Might be a hiccup in the road but she loved him with her entire being.

The week flew by and suddenly it was Friday. Time to pick her parents up at the airport. Page had reserved a suite for them at the Plaza and insisted she treat her mother to a spa day as well as visiting the tourist hotspots. He said he would probably be there no later than Monday to spend time getting to know his future father-in-law.

The airport was crowded so Rebecca text-messaged her mother suggesting they meet in the coffee shop located near the arrival gate.

She spotted her dad first and waved. He waved back and headed toward the table, leaning down to kiss her cheek. "Your mom stopped by the restroom."

When her mom arrived they ordered coffee and cheesecake. "So, what's on the agenda, baby girl?" her dad asked. "Your mom said the hotel reservations were confirmed and we didn't need a rental car."

"Your room will be available by two, so by the time we finish our coffee, you get your luggage and I get my car from the lot. I thought we'd go there first, and get you settled in. If you want to rest for a while we can meet up later for dinner. Tomorrow, you need to go check out your tux, so Mindy can get any last-minute nips and tucks done. Then we can play tourist for a few days. Page will be here on Monday. Said he wants to spend some guy time together, while Mom and I have a day at the spa. Next Saturday I have a gazillion things to do before noon. My facial, hair, nails, dress, God I hope I don't forget anything."

Her mother patted her hand. "It'll be fine. We can make a list if you want."

"I have been informed I will be interviewing on Friday afternoon. The press is having a feeding frenzy. Some British reporter called for a phone interview."

"British?" her dad asked.

"Well, they wanted a statement from the future Lady Harlow of Herrington. Hell, who knew? I said I was thrilled to be accepted as part of their traditional heritage. Blah, blah etc etc." She took a bite of her cake. "I talked to Page about spending time in Jansburg. He's okay with it. He reminded me that marriage was an equal partnership and I didn't have to run my decisions past him. He did ask for a heads up if I decided to buy a Lamborghini." She laughed, shaking her head.

"My baby girl, all grown up. Getting married." Her mother dabbed at her eyes with a napkin. "Moving to a foreign country."

"You will love the castle. The property has hills and a lake. Horses. A huge library. The house in Florida has five bedrooms and six bathrooms.

A pool within view of the ocean. The house in California has three bedrooms and a pool. Haven't been to Italy, Switzerland, or England yet. Just thinking about it makes me tired."

They finished their coffee and cake, Rebecca paid the bill and they went toward the baggage area. While they were claiming their luggage, Rebecca went to get the car.

They arrived at the hotel and Rebecca smiled at the expression her parents had when they opened the door of their suite. In typical Page Harlow fashion, no regular room would do. Again she was reminded of just how special the man was when it came to the way he treated everyone around him. After her parents walked through each room, her dad stood in the middle of the entry room, shaking his head. "Do I even want to know what a night here costs?"

Rebecca chuckled. "Don't ask. Trust me, you don't need to know."

"You know, I always imagined I would walk you down the aisle in our small church. You in a pretty white gown, me in a nice suit, handing you over to some nice young man who would hopefully be able to keep a roof over your head. I never imagined this. Well, I thought when you got into the legal work, you might marry an attorney but…"

"I always figured I'd be single, maybe get a cat or two. I took one look at the picture Gina showed me and told her there would be no way in hell I would spend ten seconds with him and the contest was rigged. Wrong on all counts."

Chapter Fifty-four

Page arrived late Monday night, and left a text for Rebecca letting her know he was in town and checked into the hotel but thought she needed her rest so he was just texting. She saw the text at four am when she woke up to use the bathroom, smiled, and went back to sleep. He was just so unbelievably considerate. Her weekend had been spent showing her parents the sights. At the Statue of Liberty, a journalist recognized her and politely asked if she had a few minutes to talk. The woman bought them all a coffee and they chose a table in a small outdoor area. She asked the usual questions about how they met, what she thought of him, how he proposed, where they would live, and other general information. Rebecca was candid, posing with her parents; the Statue of Liberty in the background.

Tuesday, Rebecca got dressed and went into the office long enough to go over what Gina had worked on, made some suggestions then left for the hotel. As she entered the lobby, she spotted Page and her parents in the restaurant. Standing there watching them she felt so grateful the three of them seemed to be getting along. Maybe that was what was bothering her. Since they first spoke on the phone, she and Page had not had the first disagreement. Granted, there had been a misunderstanding about Ashley, and there was the irritating way he micromanaged everything. Still, overall, nothing serious. She squared her shoulders, took a deep breath, and crossed over to the table. She kissed her mom and dad on the cheek and Page on his lips before easing into the chair.

" I can't stay because I need to check back into the office at some point. The three of you are free to sightsee or whatever. Call me later, I love you." Rebecca stood up and Page pulled her back down in her chair. "What? I have a job still. I still… have a job."

"You said 'at some point'. You didn't say right this second and what is the worst they can do? Fire you? Sit. Eat. I know you didn't eat breakfast so order something and eat. We can decide what to do today." He kissed her cheek and added, "Or we can decide where I should take my in-laws and what we are all going to do when you get off work."

Rebecca took a sip of her coffee and smiled. "He can be such a bully at times."

"Only when you are pig-headed," he shot back with a grin.

The waitress returned to the table and Rebecca ordered a bagel with cream cheese and a side of bacon. When the girl left Rebecca arched a brow and said, "There. Happy now? I ordered breakfast."

After everyone finished their meal, it had been decided the three of them would visit the main tourist spots, starting with Broadway and Times Square and wing it. Page promised to have them all meet at Rebecca's after she finished work. Rebecca returned to the office with mixed feelings. Looking around the room it seemed insane that this part of her life was closing. Soon her career would be wife.

Gina snapped her fingers in front of Rebecca's face and laughed when Rebecca blinked. "I was asking if you wanted to review my research on the Moore versus Moore case."

"The mega-millionaire and spouse? Why can't people be civil? They can't get along so they want to make the other one suffer. People amaze me."

"Custody fight."

"I don't remember them having kids."

"Buffy is a pot-bellied pig."

Rebecca dropped her head to her desk dramatically. "Jeeze." She reached for the stack of paperwork and glanced over it. "What's your take?"

"Mrs. Moore is a socialite and parties a lot. Sometimes gone for entire weekends. I don't think that's a good environment for the aforementioned minor pig. Mr. Moore works in an office. He's the CEO so his hours are flexible. Besides, he has stated his desire to relocate to the country, upstate.

His parents owned a farm there. The pig would be able to be outside, playing in the dirt. I think Mrs. Moore just wants Buffy because he does."

"Randy Keene is our legal handling this? Tell him your thoughts. The dude gets the pig. A townhouse in Central Park as opposed to a farm upstate? It should be a no-brainer." She handed the papers back to Gina. "Page is spending the day with my parents. Hopefully, no blood will be spilled."

"How does he feel about that?"

"Calm and casual. Typical Page. Do you know we have never had a serious disagreement? I keep waiting. Wondering what will set him off, you know."

"Count your blessings. My parents fought all the time. About everything and anything. The weather, the car, the bills, politics, religion, the TV station. I was sad when he walked out but at least it was quiet in the house."

"I don't remember my parents fighting. At least not in front of me. I'm sure they did, but Dad was just so laid back. She would get upset and he would just retreat to the garage until she calmed down. Page locked himself in his basement studio. I can't even remember why. Anna said he has a lock on the elevator so no one can disturb him when he's recording but he uses it when he is upset. It needs to be removed. I'll put my foot down. He can install one of those signs that light up and say 'now recording' or something." She laughed. "It can read 'Leave me alone' or 'Go away' in red neon"

"So you must have had at least one misunderstanding if he locked himself in the basement."

"I suppose so, but nothing major. Something to be said for that, I guess."

They worked on several other legal briefs until Gina pointed out it was after five. Rebecca scooped up her handbag and they walked to the parking garage. Rebecca walked in her front door at a little past six and texted Page to let him know she was home.

Chapter Fifty-five

Saturday morning Rebecca got up and looked around her bedroom. The gown was draped across the chair along with a small cosmetic case and a bag with her shoes. Gina had stayed over and was in the kitchen with a coffee cup. Rebecca took a cup, got coffee, and sat down. "I am a nervous wreck."

"Everything has been handled. We need to get you to the salon by ten. Then we go to the chapel and you get dressed. Your mom and I will help with that. Then you glide down the aisle like a fairy princess and become Lady Harlow of wherever. A piece of cake. Then we all jump in cars and limos and go to the Plaza where we eat and party until we drop."

"Sounds easy enough."

Gina rinsed out the cups and scooped up her dress and overnight bag while Rebecca got the gown and accessories.

At the salon, she sat as still as she could while a friend of Gina's worked on her nails and Gina's hairstylist pulled her red curls into an elegant style, making sure the veil was going to fit. Gina took several pictures and texted one to Page, then dug into her handbag. "Page wanted me to get these to you today, before you got to the chapel, so here." She produced a small black leather case. It contained a pair of diamond stud earrings and a diamond necklace. A tennis bracelet sat off to the side. "The man has seriously great taste," Gina said as the stylist held the necklace up to Rebecca's neck.

"Here's hoping I don't get mugged."

"I'll carry them. Nobody would mug me. I look poor," Gina laughed. "Just don't let me forget them when you get dressed."

They left the salon and Gina drove them to the chapel, parking in the back lot. They entered through the side door and were immediately joined by Father John, Rebecca's mother, and Ashley. Rebecca looked around. "Where's Page?"

"He's still at the hotel with the guys. They're getting dressed there," Ashley said. "I told him if he was late I would kick his ass. Don't look out front. The place is already filling up and there are a lot of reporters on the back row. Come on, let's get you ready. Love your hair, by the way."

Father John led them into a dressing area and closed the door on his way out. Rebecca stood while her mother took the dress from the bag. Gina produced the jewels. Ashley fitted the veil onto her hair carefully clipping it in place. Once she was dressed, Ashley stepped out and returned with Father John who led them down a narrow hall to the back where the rest of the bridesmaids were. Rebecca's bouquet was full of peach and blue roses, surrounded by baby's breath and peach silk ribbons. Each of the bridesmaids had a single blue rose with a peach ribbon to match their gowns. Gina had two peach roses with a blue ribbon. Ashley took several pictures. "Do you want to talk to the press or wait for Page to arrive?" she asked.

"What do you think?"

"I hate reporters so I would avoid them until absolutely necessary."

"Right. Besides, Page is so much better at dealing with them."

"You can hold your own. I read the interview you did with your parents at the Statue of Liberty."

"She was easy to talk to. It didn't seem like an interview, I guess."

"Well these are eager and in a frenzy, so you might want to make them wait. Besides, that way you only need to answer the questions once."

The door opened and Greg stuck his head inside. "Mrs. Morrison, they are ready for you to take your seat." Greg was followed by Rebecca's dad, who seemed to be on the verge of tears. Ashley snapped a picture of Greg, Gina, Rebecca, and her dad, then winked at Rebecca and the four bridesmaids. "It's show-time." Music came through the chapel and Ashley squared her shoulders and opened the door. Rebecca squeezed her father's hand as each of her friends walked the aisle, following Ashley to the front. Gina was last and then Rebecca took her first step into the crowded room.

Page stood next to Greg and Tommy and he watched as she took each step toward him. When their eyes met, she offered him a nervous smile.

Finally, they stood facing each other and she realized Page's hands were shaking. So were hers. There was Father John, speaking softly to the people who came. Rebecca concentrated on repeating her vows with slow precision, holding Page's gaze the entire time. She heard Father John say, "I now pronounce you man and wife. You may kiss the bride," and she was scooped up into Page's embrace, his hands gently caressing her spine while his kiss took her breath away. When they parted, she looked down at the band on his finger and brought his hand to her lips. They turned and for the first time, she saw how full the chapel was. Reporters crowded the back, taking pictures as Father John stated, "May I present to you, Lord and Lady Harlow?"